nowledge. 知識工場
Knowledge is everything！

nowledge. 知識工場
Knowledge is everything！

偷吃步！

3招強效 口說訓練課

An English Class in Forming Your Chatting DNA

抵制學習僵化、英語制式化的第一本！

從現在起，我們用偷吃步講英文。

張翔 /著

使用說明
User's Guide

從不會說英文到開口和老外聊天，就是可以這麼簡單！

Point 1

囊括各大生活主題

包括節慶、日常、吃喝、娛樂、職場、校園、旅遊等各大主題，涵蓋所有日常生活最常遇到的情況，讓你在任何情境下都能用英文聊天。

Point 2

先聯想相關單字

先學一看到主題就先想到的「核心聯想」單字，並同時擴充「進階學習」單字。只要用聯想就能建立單字基本功，替流利的會話奠定扎實基礎。

Point 3

深度追蹤國外文化

補充各國文化、飲食、禮儀……等等新知，學英文的同時也能學習不同文化，讓看世界的角度更深、更廣，還能避免出國時誤觸禁忌。

4 Point

套句型就能組織句子

只要把單字套入句型，馬上就能
講出完整的句子，每一個句型底
下還補充了豐富的例句，教你怎
麼靈活運用。有了這些好用句
型，才能將單字連結成有邏
輯的完整英文句！

句型隨堂步 背單字，更說的秘訣這邊！

MP3 002

sb. can't wait to... 某人等不及要…。

★ I can't wait to go on a vacation!
我等不及要去度假啦！
★ She can't wait to show her **latest** design to her boss.
她等不及要展示她最新的設計給老闆看。
★ The little boy can't wait to **open up** his presents.
小男孩迫不及待地想打開他的禮物。
★ All the employees can't wait to **get off work**.
所有的員工都迫不及待要下班。
★ The **onlookers** can't wait to see what will happen next.
圍觀者們迫不及待想看接下來會發生什麼事。

latest
['letɪst]
形 最新的
open up
片 拆開
get off work
片 下班
onlooker
['on,luka]
名 觀眾

be heading to/for... 某人／某物正前往…。

★ Frank will be heading to Boston in three days.
法蘭克三天後將會前往波士頓。
★ The high school students are heading to class.

5 Point

開口必學萬用句

提供與單元主題相關的「開口必備句」，讓你用例句練習口
說。學完單字、句型，下一步就是練習、練習、再練習，
讓你熟悉語感、把會話句內化成自己的知識！

MP3 093

開口必備句 老朋友聊聊開懷，就靠這幾句！

I want to go to a night market and try some local snacks.
我想去逛夜市，嚐嚐一些道地的小吃。

Shi-Lin Night Market has some of the most famous food stands in Taiwan.
士林夜市裡有幾家台灣最知名的小吃攤。

Do you like the steamed spring roll at Ningxia night market?
你喜歡寧夏夜市裡賣的潤餅嗎？

My favorite food at this night market is tapioca milk tea.
在這個夜市裡，我最喜歡的是珍珠奶茶。

Many Japanese tourists especially love the pearl milk tea at this drink stand.
許多日本觀光客特別喜歡這個飲料攤賣的珍珠奶茶。

Have you tried chicken feet galantine before?
你吃過雞腳凍嗎？

I want to buy some pepper cakes for tomorrow's breakfast.
我想買一些胡椒餅當明天的早餐。

What is a double layer sausage?
什麼是大腸包小腸？

6 Point

聽聽老外怎麼說

隨書附贈英文朗讀 MP3，特邀
專業的外籍老師錄音，讓你可
以輕鬆跟讀，向道地美國人學
習說話時的抑揚頓挫以及正
統美式發音。

　　對於許多已經學了很久英文的學生來說，無法說出完整的英文句子常常是學生們最想克服的問題；而沒辦法說出完整句子的原因，通常都出在單字想不出來，或是無法將單字連接成有邏輯的句子。再來，學生們也因為缺少全英文的學習環境，所以缺乏練習英文的機會，也無法將自己所學到的應用到日常生活當中，更造成了許多人「會」英文，但不會「說」英文的現象。

　　至於學習英文的方法，很多學生經常會透過背下書中的句型或文法來學習，但死記硬背單字和文法之後，才發現不知道怎麼把學到的東西應用出來。所以，期望本書能幫助因為說不出英文、不知道如何將英文應用到生活之中而苦惱的學生們，以融會貫通的方式、有效率地學習，並成功擁有英語基本溝通能力。

　　本書將先教大家建立基本單字量，用主題來「聯想單字」的方式，讓讀者不必死背單字，自然而然就可以想到相關的單字；再來，每一單元都會提供兩大句型，只要套個單字進去，就能講出好幾句完整的英文句子，再運用每個句型底下的例句多加練習、自己嘗試造句，簡簡單單就能組織出有邏輯的英文句，不必再費心背一堆文法，卻不知道怎麼應用；最後，還有提供與單元主題相關的各種「開口必備句」，不論是想要走捷徑的你、還是想練習口說的你，都可以運用這邊的例句來練習並培養語感，將各種句子內化成自己的知識。

　　希望讀者能用以上的學習方式，只需要聯想相關單字、熟悉運用句型、再多多練習各種句子，順利增加英文會話能力的基本功。而其中收錄的單字和句型都非常實用，就算是英文零基礎的讀者，也可以運用以上方法，學習怎麼用簡單句子就和老外對話如流！

張翔

Part 01

一月歡慶新的一年

Part 02

二月生活進入軌道

Part 09

暑假結束九月收心

Part 10

十月好個出遊時節

Part 01

一月歡慶新的一年

January Highlights:
All About Fun

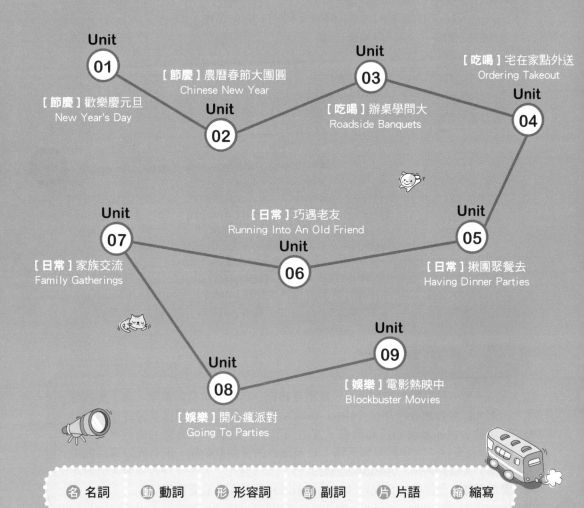

Unit 01
[節慶] 歡樂慶元旦
New Year's Day

[節慶] 農曆春節大團圓
Chinese New Year

Unit 02

Unit 03
[吃喝] 辦桌學問大
Roadside Banquets

[吃喝] 宅在家點外送
Ordering Takeout

Unit 04

Unit 07
[日常] 家族交流
Family Gatherings

[日常] 巧遇老友
Running Into An Old Friend

Unit 06

Unit 05
[日常] 揪團聚餐去
Having Dinner Parties

Unit 08
[娛樂] 開心瘋派對
Going To Parties

Unit 09
[娛樂] 電影熱映中
Blockbuster Movies

名 名詞　動 動詞　形 形容詞　副 副詞　片 片語　縮 縮寫

01 歡樂慶元旦
節慶
New Year's Day

 單字基本功 掌握關鍵字 = 開口第一步

 核心聯想 新年新希望 New Year's resolution

anticipation [æn͵tɪsəˋpeʃən] 名 期待；預期	**event** [ɪˋvɛnt] 名 事件；大事	**firework** [ˋfaɪr͵wɝk] 名 煙火	**wish** [wɪʃ] 名 願望 動 許願
applaud [əˋplɔd] 動 鼓掌；喝采	**worldwide** [ˋwɝld͵waɪd] 形 遍布全世界的 副 遍布全世界地	**whole new** 片 嶄新的	**reflect on** 片 反省

歡喜跨年 Celebrating New Year's Eve **進階學習**

desire [dɪˋzaɪr] 名 動 渴望	**enthusiasm** [ɪnˋθjuzɪ͵æzəm] 名 熱情	**enjoyment** [ɪnˋdʒɔɪmənt] 名 享受	**excitement** [ɪkˋsaɪtmənt] 名 興奮；刺激
amuse [əˋmjuz] 動 使歡樂	**cheerful** [ˋtʃɪrfəl] 形 愉快的	**delightful** [dɪˋlaɪtfəl] 形 令人欣喜的	**fond** [fɑnd] 形 喜歡的

 深度追蹤 *Knowing More*

　　一月一日是每年的第一天，象徵著嶄新一年的開始及新希望。為了慶祝這一天，世界各地從跨年夜（New Year's Eve）開始，便積極準備各種倒數計時活動，例如台灣的跨年晚會，常邀請歌手們獻唱；在英國的倫敦眼（The London Eye；大型觀景摩天輪）以及澳洲的雪梨歌劇院，則有光彩奪目的煙火秀；美國紐約市的時報廣場則會舉行「降球儀式」，是全球規模最大的新年慶祝活動。而世界各地在跨年夜的倒數計時後，都會高聲歡慶新年的到來！

套個單字，想說的都能表達！

sb. can't wait to... 某人等不及要…。

★ I can't wait to go on a vacation!
我等不及要去度假啦！

★ She can't wait to show her **latest** design to her boss.
她等不及要展示她最新的設計給老闆看。

★ The little boy can't wait to **open up** his presents.
小男孩迫不及待地想打開他的禮物。

★ All the employees can't wait to **get off work**.
所有的員工都迫不及待想要下班。

★ The **onlookers** can't wait to see what will happen next.
圍觀者們迫不及待想看接下來會發生什麼事。

> **latest**
> [`letɪst]
> 形 最新的
> **open up**
> 片 拆開
> **get off work**
> 片 下班
> **onlooker**
> [`ɑn,lukɚ]
> 名 觀眾

be heading to/for... 某人 / 某物正前往…。

★ Frank will be heading to Boston in three days.
法蘭克三天後將會前往波士頓。

★ The high school students are heading to class.
那群高中生們正要去上課。

★ The **tropical depression** is heading to Taiwan.
那個熱帶低氣壓正朝台灣的方向移動。

★ The **deceased**'s relatives are heading to the graveyard.
死者的親戚們正在前往墓地。

★ An **unmanned spaceship** is heading to the International Space Station.
一艘無人太空船正在前往國際太空站。

> **tropical**
> [`trɑpɪkl̩]
> 形 熱帶的
> **depression**
> [dɪ`prɛʃən]
> 名 (氣) 低氣壓
> **deceased**
> [dɪ`sist]
> 名 (正式) 死者
> **unmanned**
> [,ʌn`mænd]
> 形 無人駕駛的
> **spaceship**
> [`spes,ʃɪp]
> 名 太空船

開口必備句　和老外聊開懷，就靠這幾句！

New Year's Day falls on January 1 and marks the start of a new year.
元旦就在一月一日，標示著嶄新一年的開始。

New Year's Day is the beginning of a whole new year.
元旦是嶄新一年的開始。

The New Year is also a time to reflect on the past and to envision the future.
新年也是反省過去、展望未來的時刻。

The Taipei 101 fireworks kick off exciting celebrations for a whole new year.
台北一〇一的煙火開啟了熱鬧的新年慶祝活動。

There will be a great celebration in Central Park on New Year's Day.
元旦當天，在中央公園會有盛大的慶祝活動。

What is your New Year's resolution?
你的新年新希望是什麼呢？

What do you think is the best way to start a new year?
你覺得開啟新的一年最棒的方式是什麼呢？

Setting new life goals can be a good way to start the beginning of a new year.
想開啟新的一年，訂定新人生目標會是個好方法。

Mason and his band will welcome a whole new year with graceful music.
梅森和他的樂團要用優美的音樂迎接嶄新的一年。

Tradition has it that the first-footer to your place on New Year's Day can bring you good luck.
傳統上，新年的第一位拜訪者會為你帶來好運。

UNIT 02 節慶
農曆春節大團圓
Chinese New Year

單字基本功 掌握關鍵字 = 開口第一步

核心聯想 家族團聚 Family reunion

aunt [ænt] 名 阿姨；伯母	**gathering** [`gæðərɪŋ] 名 聚會	**grandchild** [`græn͵tʃaɪld] 名（外）孫子／女	**grandparent** [`grænd͵pɛrənt] 名（外）祖父母
uncle [`ʌŋkl̩] 名 叔叔；伯伯；舅舅	**reunite** [͵rijuˋnaɪt] 動（使）重聚	**Chinese New Year's Eve** 片 除夕夜	**reunion dinner** 片 團圓飯

 春節傳統 Traditions & customs
進階學習

custom [`kʌstəm] 名 習俗；習慣	**firecracker** [`faɪr͵krækɚ] 名 鞭炮	**couplet** [`kʌplɪt] 名 春聯	**traditional** [trəˋdɪʃənl̩] 形 傳統的
lion dance 片 舞獅	**paper cutout** 片 剪紙	**red envelope** 片 紅包	**sweep away the bad luck** 片 除舊

 深度追蹤 *Knowing More*

　　根據民間傳統，春節是指從十二月二十三日的祭灶（Kitchen God worshiping）那天起，一直到一月十五日的元宵節（Lantern Festival）為止的期間。春節期間要注意許多傳統習俗，像是年前要大掃除、貼春聯，初一拜年要送紅包，大年初二回娘家，初四拜財神……等等；而最重要的活動之一，就屬除夕夜的圍爐（reunion dinner）了，圍爐又稱年夜飯，在這天晚上，大家都會攜家帶眷回到老家，和許久未見的家族成員一起吃團圓飯。

句型偷吃步　套個單字，想說的都能表達！

...be one's favorite.　…是某人的最愛。

★ **Setting off** firecrackers is my favorite on Chinese New Year's Eve.
在除夕夜放鞭炮是我的最愛。

★ Green chicken curry is my favorite since it tastes really great.
綠咖哩雞是我的最愛，因為它真的很好吃。

★ Hanging out with my friends after work is my favorite.
我最喜歡下班後和朋友們聚會。

★ **Bamboo shoots** with mayonnaise is my favorite in summer.
我夏天最愛吃竹筍沙拉。

★ The balcony with **potted** plants is my favorite after the **redecoration**.
重新裝潢後，放滿盆栽的陽台是我最愛的地方。

> **set off**
> 片 點燃
> **bamboo shoot**
> 片 竹筍
> **pot**
> [pɑt]
> 動 將…栽入花盆
> **redecoration**
> [ri͵dɛkə`reʃən]
> 名 重新裝潢

...be essential for...　對…來說，…是必要的。

★ Having a reunion dinner is essential for us on Chinese New Year's Eve.
我們在除夕夜一定會一起吃年夜飯。

★ Free **media** is essential for **democracy**.
媒體自由對民主國家來說是必要的。

★ **Adequate** exercise is essential for modern people.
適量的運動對現代人來說是必要的。

★ **Your** signature is essential for the package **claim**.
你必須要簽名才能領取包裹。

★ A delivery date is essential for every **commercial transaction**.
每次貿易往來時，一定要訂定送貨日期。

> **democracy**
> [dɪ`mɑkrəsɪ]
> 名 民主國家；民主精神
> **adequate**
> [`ædəkwɪt]
> 形 適當的
> **claim**
> [klem]
> 名 認領；索取
> **commercial**
> [kə`mɝʃəl]
> 形 商業的
> **transaction**
> [træn`zækʃən]
> 名 交易

MP3 ▶ 006

開口必備句　和老外聊開懷，就靠這幾句！

Chinese New Year is one of the most important festivities in Chinese culture.
農曆新年是中華文化裡最重要的節慶之一。

According to Chinese mythology, Chinese New Year originated in a fight against a monster called Nian.
根據傳說，農曆新年起源於對抗年獸。

In tradition, the lion dance is used to scare away Nian.
舞龍舞獅是傳統上用來嚇跑年獸的方法。

There are twelve Chinese zodiac signs, with each of which represents a year.
中國生肖共有十二種，每一種各代表一年。

It is the year of the Snake this year.
今年是蛇年／小龍年。

People serve dumplings, which symbolize wealth, during Chinese New Year.
人們會在農曆新年吃象徵財富的餃子。

It is customary to leave some fish during the reunion dinner for good luck and wealth.
習俗上，團圓飯要留下一些魚肉，以祈求富貴好運（年年有餘）。

During the Chinese New Year, sweeping should not be done for fear that good fortune will be swept away.
因為人們害怕好運會被掃走，所以農曆新年期間不能掃地。

People will reopen their businesses and set off firecrackers to welcome the God of Wealth.
許多公司會重新開張，並放鞭炮以迎接財神。

Turnip cakes are one of the traditional snacks for good luck during Chinese New Year.
蘿蔔糕是農曆新年期間，象徵好運的傳統小吃之一。

UNIT 03 吃喝
辦桌學問大
Roadside Banquets

單字基本功 掌握關鍵字 = 開口第一步

核心聯想

海鮮滿桌 All kinds of seafood & dishes

broth	lobster	oyster	scallop
[brɔθ]	[`labstɚ]	[`ɔɪstɚ]	[`skaləp]
名 高湯	名 龍蝦	名 牡蠣	名 干貝

Buddha's Delight	ham hock	sea cucumber	shark fins
片 佛跳牆	片 蹄膀	片 海參	片 魚翅

辦桌文化 Taiwanese banquet
進階學習

arrangement	banquet	ceremony	hospitality
[ə`rendʒmənt]	[`bæŋkwɪt]	[`sɛrəˌmonɪ]	[ˌhaspɪ`tælətɪ]
名 布置;準備	名 宴會;宴請	名 儀式;禮節	名 好客;款待

street	taste	delicate	typical
[strit]	[test]	[`dɛləkət]	[`tɪpɪkḷ]
名 街道	名 味覺 動 嚐	形 精緻的	形 特有的

深度追蹤 Knowing More

　　在台灣，一有婚喪喜慶、廟會慶典……等活動，就一定會看到馬路邊搭起棚架、擺設大圓桌的「辦桌」文化。辦桌並不是只把佳餚搬上桌就好，其中也有很多學問，菜式和禮儀都會隨著不同主題而變化，甚至連碗筷、桌椅的陳設都有一定的規矩。例如滿月宴一定要使用全雞，來祝福孩子十全十美；生日宴要以壽桃做收尾，象徵福壽吉祥；新居宴通常會有白斬雞，取其「孵錢」與「起家」之意；婚宴則會以禮餅及甜湯收尾，象徵婚姻圓滿甜蜜。

MP3 ▶ 008

套個單字，想說的都能表達！

It takes time to...　…很花時間。

★ It takes time to prepare and cater for a Chinese New Year banquet.
準備及承辦農曆新年的辦桌很花時間。

★ It takes time to **replenish** food and water supply.
補足食物和水很花時間。

★ It takes time to **interpret** this strange **phenomenon**.
要說明這個奇怪的現象很花時間。

★ It takes time to recover from mental **trauma**.
從心理創傷走出來需要花些時間。

★ It takes time to **acquaint** yourself with a new occupation.
要讓自己熟悉新工作很花時間。

replenish
[rɪˋplɛnɪʃ]
動 補足

interpret
[ɪnˋtɝprɪt]
動 解釋

phenomenon
[fəˋnɑmə͵nɑn]
名 現象

trauma
[ˋtrɔmə]
名 精神創傷

acquaint
[əˋkwent]
動 使熟悉

sb. be careful about...　某人注重…。

★ The chef is careful about the taste of the dishes and **food safety**.
那位主廚很注重菜餚的味道和食品安全。

★ A clean person would be careful about personal **hygiene**.
一個愛乾淨的人會注重個人衛生。

★ A **faultfinder** is careful about every **detail**.
吹毛求疵的人很注重每個細節

★ Our president is careful about the new policy on **immigration**.
我們的總統很重視移民的新政策。

★ Idols are careful about their appearances.
偶像都很注重自己的外表。

food safety
片 食品安全

hygiene
[ˋhaɪdʒin]
名 衛生

faultfinder
[ˋfɔlt͵faɪndɚ]
名 吹毛求疵者

detail
[ˋditel]
名 細節；瑣事

immigration
[͵ɪməˋgreʃən]
名 移民（入境）

"Bun Dough" is a kind of Taiwanese-style banquet that is usually held outdoors.

「辦桌」是一種台灣式的宴會，通常會在室外舉辦。

"Bun Dough" means "to treat" in Taiwanese.

「辦桌」的台語意思是「請客」。

Holding a Bun Dough is considered a way to bring people closer to each other.

辦桌是一種拉近人際關係的方式 。

Bun Dough is a unique culture in Taiwan. Some scholars even wrote essays about it.

辦桌是一種特殊的台灣文化，有些學者甚至以它為題來撰寫論文。

Bun Dough demonstrates the hospitality of Taiwanese.

辦桌展現了台灣人的好客精神。

People can sit outdoors and enjoy a feast prepared by the catering staff.

人們可以坐在戶外，享受廚師們準備的大餐。

Buddha's Delight is a typical Bun Dough dish. It has scallops, sea cucumbers, ham hocks and chicken in it.

「佛跳牆」是辦桌常見的菜餚，裡面有干貝、海參、蹄膀和雞肉。

When there's something to celebrate, people hold a "Bun Dough" to treat relatives and friends.

每當有值得慶祝的事情時，人們就會「辦桌」來宴請親朋好友。

Bun Dough dishes may not be fine cuisine, but they are very delicious.

辦桌的菜餚或許不算精緻料理，但都非常美味。

Whenever you see people setting up canopies and putting down red tables, it must be a Bun Dough preparation.

如果你看到人們在架棚子和放紅桌子，那一定是在準備辦桌。

MP3 ▶ 010

UNIT **04** 吃喝

宅在家點外送
Ordering Takeout

單字基本功 掌握關鍵字＝開口第一步

核心聯想

接單外送 Food delivery

address [ə`drɛs] 名 地址 動 稱呼	**change** [tʃendʒ] 名 零錢 動 改變	**corner** [`kɔrnə] 名 轉角；角落	**delivery** [dɪ`lɪvərɪ] 名 遞送；交付
tip [tɪp] 名 小費 動 付小費	**arrive** [ə`raɪv] 動 抵達；到來	**extra** [`ɛkstrə] 形 額外的	**answer the door** 片 應門

就想宅在家 Staying at home

進階學習

homebody [`hom͵badɪ] 名 宅男／女	**carefree** [`kɛr͵fri] 形 無憂無慮的	**disposable** [dɪ`spozəbḷ] 形 一次性使用的	**lazy** [`lezɪ] 形 懶惰的
reclusive [rɪ`klusɪv] 形 隱遁的；孤寂的	**couch potato** 片 整天躺在沙發上看電視的人	**home delivery** 片 宅配	**slack off** 片 懈怠

深度追蹤 Knowing More

　　在美國叫外送，常常是叫披薩或是中餐的情況較多；值得注意的是，外送雖然通常會額外收運費（delivery fee），但仍需要給小費；一般小費標準介於10％～15％之間，但叫外送並不用給那麼多，只要付1或2元美金就好。另外，如果是在吃到飽餐廳（buffet）用餐的話，離開時可在桌上留下一人1到2美金，或是一桌5美金的小費給清潔員。而叫外送的方式除了打電話之外，最近更有手機應用程式，提供人們更快速、更方便的點單方式。

Now that..., ... 既然…，…。

★ Now that everyone is here, we had better order some more pizza and beverages.
既然大家都到了，我們最好再多叫一些披薩和飲料。

★ Now that you're back, we can move on to the next **subject**.
既然你回來了，我們就來討論下一個議題吧。

★ Now that the **crops** are **ripe**, they're busy **reaping** them in the field.
當農作物成熟了，他們便忙著在田裡收割。

★ Now that you feel a lot better, you can give me a hand.
既然你感覺好多了，就來幫我的忙吧。

★ Now that my father has retired, he can spend more time with us.
既然我爸爸現在已退休，就能多花一點時間陪我們了。

subject
[`sʌbdʒɪkt]
名 議題

crop
[krɑp]
名 農作物

ripe
[raɪp]
形 成熟的

reap
[rip]
動 收割

How do you like...? 你覺得…怎麼樣？

★ How do you like the dinner?
你覺得這頓晚餐如何？

★ How do you like your Christmas present?
你喜歡你的聖誕禮物嗎？

★ How do you like the romance movie **starring** Jennifer Lawrence?
你覺得珍妮佛·勞倫斯演的那部愛情片怎麼樣？

★ How do you like the **mannequin** in the **display window**?
你覺得櫥窗裡的模特兒怎麼樣？

★ How do you like the way we handled the problem?
你覺得我們處理得怎麼樣？

star
[stɑr]
動 主演

mannequin
[`mænəkɪn]
名 人體模型

display window
片 櫥窗

MP3 ▶ 012

開口必備句　和老外聊開懷，就靠這幾句！

This Thai restaurant has delivery service.
這間泰式餐廳提供外送服務。

Do you deliver after 8:00 p.m.?
你們晚上八點後可以外送嗎？

I would like to order a number three and a number ten.
我想點三號餐與十號餐。

Can I order a number seven and a number thirteen with extra garlic and red pepper?
我想點七號跟十三號餐，可以多加一點大蒜和辣椒嗎？

Can I have extra cheese on my pizza?
可以在我的披薩上面多加一些起司嗎？

Let me repeat your order. You ordered a fruit salad, a large hamburger and a corn soup.
讓我重複您的餐點：一份水果沙拉、一個加大漢堡，還有一杯玉米湯。

May I have your address, please?
麻煩告訴我您的地址。

My address is Apt. 4, No. 168, Central Street.
我的地址是中央街 168 號，第四室。

Your order will be there in twenty minutes.
您的餐點將在二十分鐘內送達。

The delivery person finally arrived after one hour.
外送人員終於在一個小時後送達。

Can you answer the door, please? It must be our pizza!
能不能請你去應門？一定是我們的披薩到了！

I asked the delivery boy to keep the change as a tip.
我讓外送小弟留下零錢，當作他的小費。

★UNIT★ 05 日常 揪團聚餐去
Having Dinner Parties

 單字基本功 掌握關鍵字＝開口第一步

 核心聯想 | 上餐館飽食 Eating out

diner [`daɪnə] 名 小餐館	**restaurant** [`rɛstərənt] 名 餐廳	**diverse** [daɪ`vɜs] 形 不同的；多種的	**be hungry for** 片 渴望…
eat out 片 外出吃飯	**grab a bite** 片 隨便吃吃	**hot pot** 片 火鍋	**lazy Susan** 片（餐桌中央的） 圓轉盤

人多好熱鬧 Hustle & bustle　進階學習

accord [ə`kɔrd] 名 一致；和諧	**coincidence** [ko`ɪnsɪdəns] 名 巧合；一致	**animate** [`ænə͵met] 動 使有活力	**amiable** [`emɪəbḷ] 形 友善的
collective [kə`lɛktɪv] 形 集體的	**together** [tə`gɛðə] 副 一起	**take a rain check** 片 改天再約	**make a toast** 片 舉杯致詞

深度追蹤 🔍　*Knowing More*

　　有機會參加美國「家庭式派對」的話，可以更深切感受到當地的文化及友誼！家庭式派對通常以家庭為單位參加，賓客也大多是認識的親友、協會組織成員、或是教會教友。一般來說，主辦者會提前決定好時間和地點，一或兩個星期前再用 e-mail 通知客人，讓賓客們可以提前安排時間。而當受邀到好友的家裡做客，參加人數又很多的時候，大家便會各自準備幾道菜或飲料前往，所以派對的菜餚經常是琳瑯滿目，能讓參與的賓客大飽口福。

MP3 ▶ 014

句型偷吃步　套個單字，想說的都能表達！

Do sb. prefer...or...? 某人喜歡…還是…？

- ★ Do you prefer rice or noodles?
  你喜歡飯還是麵？
- ★ Do you prefer **confections** or **savory** food?
  你喜歡甜食還是鹹食？
- ★ Do you prefer living in a city or in a **rural** area?
  你喜歡住在城市還是鄉下？
- ★ Does she prefer going to a movie by herself or with her friends?
  她喜歡自己去看電影還是跟朋友去看？
- ★ Does Henry prefer traveling alone or joining a tour group?
  亨利喜歡一個人旅遊，還是參加旅行團？

> **confection**
> [kən`fɛkʃən]
> 名 甜點；糕餅
> **savory**
> [`sevərɪ]
> 形 鹹的；美味的
> **rural**
> [`rʊrəl]
> 形 農村的

sb. be (not) interested in... 某人對…（沒）有興趣。

- ★ I would be interested in eating out at that local diner.
  我有興趣去那家在地餐館吃飯。
- ★ I'm interested in exploring new tourist spots rather than **historic** sites.
  我對新景點比較感興趣，對古蹟的興趣不高。
- ★ She has been interested in performing in front of people.
  她對在大眾面前表演一直都很有興趣。
- ★ Ava is really interested in music and intends to be a musician.
  艾娃對音樂很有興趣，也想成為音樂家。
- ★ The customer is interested in a couple of **items** in the **catalogue**.
  那名顧客對商品型錄裡的幾項產品很有興趣。

> **historic**
> [hɪs`tɔrɪk]
> 形 歷史性的
> **item**
> [`aɪtəm]
> 名 項目
> **catalogue**
> [`kætələg]
> 名 目錄

How about having lunch at Lucy's together?
一起去「露西小館」吃午餐好不好？

Some of my high school friends are going to have dinner together next Wednesday.
我的高中朋友們下週三晚上要聚餐。

Do you want to join us for dinner tonight?
你今晚要和我們一起吃晚餐嗎？

What do you want for lunch, hot pot or teppanyaki?
你午餐想吃什麼，火鍋還是鐵板燒？

My colleagues just had a pizza party in celebration of the highest sales ever.
我的同事們為了慶祝史上最高銷售業績，聚在一起大吃比薩。

Let's meet over dinner at seven.
我們七點晚餐見。

I'd like to have some onion rings as my appetizer.
開胃菜我想吃洋蔥圈。

Excuse me. May I have two more plates?
不好意思，我可以再要兩個盤子嗎？

Do you want some dessert or some beverages?
你想要來些甜點或飲料嗎？

Frank made a toast to the hostess of the dinner party tonight.
法蘭克向晚宴的女主人舉杯致意。

My family enjoys having Christmas dinner together and connecting with each other at the same time.
我的家人喜歡一起吃耶誕大餐，同時彼此交流。

Kelly held a wonderful dinner party at her house last week.
凱莉上禮拜在她家舉辦了一個很棒的晚餐聚會。

MP3 ▶ 016

★ UNIT 06 日常
巧遇老友
Running Into An Old Friend

單字基本功 掌握關鍵字 ＝ 開口第一步

核心聯想

連絡老朋友 Keeping in touch

contact
[`kɑntækt]
名 聯絡

greeting
[`gritɪŋ]
名 問候；招呼

text
[tɛkst]
名 文字 動 傳簡訊

cheerful
[`tʃɪrfəl]
形 興高采烈的

inward
[`ɪnwəd]
形 裡面的 副 內心裡

jolly
[`dʒɑlɪ]
形 愉快的

surprised
[sə`praɪzd]
形 感到驚喜的

hear from
片 收到…的消息

回憶往日的美好 The good old days **進階學習**

meantime
[`min ˏtaɪm]
名 副 同時

memory
[`mɛmərɪ]
名 記憶；紀念

segment
[`sɛgmənt]
名 部分 動 分割

sentiment
[`sɛntəmənt]
名 情緒；感傷

indulge
[ɪn`dʌldʒ]
動 沉迷；享受

recollect
[ˏrɛkə`lɛkt]
動 回憶；想起

priceless
[`praɪslɪs]
形 無價的

vague
[veg]
形 模糊的

深度追蹤 ♪ ♪ ♪ ♪ ♪ *Knowing More*

　　巧遇老友時，可別只是講句「How are you?」，你也可以用以下兩句好用的英文，來適度地表達內心的喜悅：「It's so nice to see you. 能遇見你真好。」以及「Look at you! You look great! 瞧瞧你！看起來真容光煥發！」；而在聊天敘舊時，若想要進一步聊聊共同朋友的近況，可以先詢問知不知道某人或某事，藉此拓展話題，例如「Did you hear about Mike's wedding ceremony? 你有聽說麥克要辦婚禮了嗎？」……等等不同的問題。

sb. may not remember... 某人也許不記得…了。

★ You may not remember me; we took the same **course** back in **college**.
你也許不記得我了，我們大學的時候修過同一門課。

★ You may not remember me; I'm Michael Lee from Anderson Corporation.
你也許不記得我了，我是安德森公司的李麥可。

★ She may not remember me; we met at Tina's party two years ago.
她也許不記得我了，兩年前我們在蒂娜的派對上見過。

course
[kors]
名 課程

college
[`kɑlɪdʒ]
名 大學

★ You may not remember my name; I was your neighbor.
你也許不記得我的名字，我曾是你的鄰居。

★ He may not remember Sophia, who was my **secretary** two years ago.
他應該不記得我兩年前的祕書——索菲亞。

secretary
[`sɛkrə͵tɛrɪ]
名 祕書

sb./sth. ...for sure. 某人 / 某事確定…。

★ A good diet is **beneficial** to health for sure.
可以肯定的是，良好的飲食有益健康。

★ Christmas and Easter are two main Christian festivals for sure.
聖誕節和復活節無疑是基督教的兩個主要節日。

★ I am not going to take this course for sure.
我很確定不會修這門課。

★ He is able to **recite** the whole poem from memory for sure.
他一定能背誦出整首詩。

beneficial
[͵bɛnə`fɪʃəl]
形 有益的

recite
[rɪ`saɪt]
動 背誦

★ There will be another **alternative** for sure.
肯定還會有另外的替代方案。

alternative
[ɔl`tɜnətɪv]
名 選擇；替代

MP3 ▶ 018

開口必備句　和老外聊開懷，就靠這幾句！

Have you ever attended a high school reunion?
你有參加過高中校友會嗎？

Tim made a short clip with his high school photos for the class reunion.
提姆為了高中同學會，用照片作成了一部小短片。

How have you been all these years?
你這些年過得如何？

I haven't seen you since the graduation ceremony.
自從畢業典禮後，我就沒見過你了。

It was such a delight meeting all my dear friends at the school reunion.
能在校友會遇到我所有的好朋友，真是令人開心。

Long time no see.
好久不見。

What's new with you?
有什麼新鮮事嗎？

Doesn't my name ring a bell?
你對我的名字有印象嗎？

I am sorry, but your name has escaped me.
我很抱歉，但是我對你的名字沒有印象。

You've changed a lot.
你變了好多。

I can hardly recognize you.
我都快認不出你了。

The best things in life come in threes, like friendships, dreams, and memories.
人生最棒的三件事就是友誼、夢想和回憶。

07 日常 家族交流
Family Gatherings

 單字基本功 ▸ 掌握關鍵字 = 開口第一步

 核心聯想 家族關係 Family relationships

influence [`ɪnfluəns] 名 動 影響	**relative** [`rɛlətɪv] 名 親戚	**close** [klos] 形 親近的；接近的	**intimate** [`ɪntəmɪt] 形 親密的
strict [strɪkt] 形 嚴格的	**be named after** 片 以⋯命名	**family member** 片 家族成員	**get along with** 片 與⋯和睦相處

繼承這一事 Inheriting & succession **進階學習**

consent [kən`sɛnt] 名 動 同意	**follower** [`fɑləwɚ] 名 跟隨者；屬下	**heir** [ɛr] 名 繼承人	**succession** [sək`sɛʃən] 名 繼承權；連續
express [ɪk`sprɛs] 動 表達；表示	**inherit** [ɪn`hɛrɪt] 動 繼承；得到	**trust** [trʌst] 動 信任；相信	**lead to** 片 導致；造成

深度追蹤 𝓚𝓷𝓸𝔀𝓲𝓷𝓰 𝓜𝓸𝓻𝓮

　　打工度假或留/遊學時，為了更快融入當地文化，常常會選擇寄宿家庭（homestay），但入住之後，可別以為能像影集裡面那般肆無忌憚，熱情的美國人在生活方面，還是有許多自己的原則，像是對隱私權的注重，所以不要擅自亂翻物品或是隨意踏入別人的房間，若對環境有任何好奇之處，記得要事先詢問，相信他們都很樂於替你介紹環境。除此之外，美國人經常會於週末來個小掃除，別忘了主動和寄宿的家人們一起動手清理房子喔！

MP3 ▶ 020

句型偷吃步　套個單字，想說的都能表達！

be much alike in...　在…方面很相似。

★ The twins are much alike in ideas and **temperament**.
這對雙胞胎的想法和性格都很像。

★ They are much alike in appearance and **emotional** responses.
他們的外貌和情緒反應都很相似。

★ Those girls are much alike in the styles of their clothes and hair.
那群女孩的衣服類型和髮型都很像。

★ All members are much alike in their beliefs and **striving** for success.
所有成員都為了成功而努力，抱持的信念也很相似。

★ These two countries are much alike in social and economic terms.
這兩國的社會和經濟情勢很相似。

> **temperament**
> [ˋtɛmprəmənt]
> 名 性情
> **emotional**
> [ɪˋmoʃənl]
> 形 感情上的
> **strive**
> [straɪv]
> 動 努力

sb. be proud of...　某人為…感到驕傲。

★ Her father is proud of her success in the **real estate** business.
她父親對她在房地產業的成就感到驕傲。

★ Andrew was proud of himself for completing so many difficult tasks.
安德魯對於自己完成了許多困難的工作而感到自豪。

★ The director is proud of the movie's **box-office** performance.
導演對這部電影的票房頗為自豪。

★ Those **volunteers** are proud of themselves for having passions in life.
義工們擁有對生命的熱情，也對這點感到自豪。

★ The inventor is proud of his invention which took out a **patent**.
那位發明家對取得專利權的那項發明感到自豪。

> **real estate**
> 片 房地產
> **box-office**
> [ˋbaks.ɑfɪs]
> 形 票房的
> **volunteer**
> [ˌvɑlənˋtɪr]
> 名 志願者
> **patent**
> [ˋpætṇt]
> 名 專利

 **開口必備句** 和老外聊開懷，就靠這幾句！

How many brothers and sisters do you have?
你有幾個兄弟姊妹？

Who are you named after?
你是以誰命名的？

Do you live with your grandparents?
你和祖父母一起住嗎？

In my opinion, family is much more important than friends.
在我看來，家人比朋友重要多了。

Our family always gathers together on Chinese New Year's Eve for reunion dinner.
我們家族總會在除夕夜團聚吃年夜飯。

My dad is going to take my mom to Maldives on vacation.
我爸要帶我媽去馬爾地夫度假。

Mr. and Mrs. Watson are my parents-in-law.
華生夫婦是我的岳父母。

My father was very strict when I was little.
小時候，我父親對我非常嚴格。

What do you think is the best thing about your father?
你認為令尊最棒的地方在哪裡？

Mr. Thompson is the breadwinner in the family.
湯普森先生肩負著家中生計。

Olivia doesn't know whether to tell her children that she is going to divorce their father or not.
奧莉維亞不知道是否要告訴孩子們，她打算和他們的爸爸離婚。

Even though no family is perfect, family members should always be considerate to each other.
縱然沒有家庭是完美的，家人間總該互相體諒。

MP3 ▶ 022

★ UNIT ★
08
娛樂
開心瘋派對
Going To Parties

單字基本功 掌握關鍵字 = 開口第一步

核心聯想 為派對做準備 Preparing for parties

barbershop [ˋbɑrbɚ͵ʃɑp] 名 理髮店	**costume** [ˋkɑstjum] 名 服裝；裝束	**lotion** [ˋloʃən] 名 乳液	**perfection** [pɚˋfɛkʃən] 名 完美
perfume [ˋpɝfjum] 名 香水	**polish** [ˋpɑlɪʃ] 名 動 擦亮	**facial** [ˋfeʃəl] 形 面部的	**graceful** [ˋgresfəl] 形 優雅的

 派對上所見所聞 At the parties 進階學習

charmer [ˋtʃɑrmɚ] 名 有魅力的人	**theme** [θim] 名 主題；題材	**fabulous** [ˋfæbjələs] 形 極好的	**all the rage** 片 正在流行的
costume party 片 變裝舞會	**enjoy oneself** 片 享受；喜愛	**finger food** 片 可用手拿取的小點心	**life of the party** 片 派對中的靈魂人物

深度追蹤 ♪♪♪♪♪ Knowing More

　　國外常見的幾種派對包括：公寓派對（flat party），通常會邀約熟人到自己家來參加派對；變裝派對（costume party），會有一個特定主題以及服裝規定（dress code），參加之前務必先問清楚服裝規定，才能更快地融入派對氣氛當中；喝到掛派對（pub-crawl），顧名思義就是一個晚上跑好幾個酒吧喝到掛，但是花的錢和喝下的酒量都不可小覷，半夜或凌晨在路上看到的「屍體」們，或許就是喝太多而無法自行回家的派對人呢。

套個單字，想說的都能表達！

sb. spend...on...　某人把…花在…上。

- ★ I prefer to spend money on **insurance** than parties.
  我比較贊成把錢花在買保險，而非開派對。

- ★ Engineers spend so much time on the new solutions.
  工程師們花費很多時間來發展新的解決方案。

- ★ Emma hates to spend time on a **bumpy** ride.
  艾瑪討厭把時間浪費在顛簸的交通行程。

- ★ Many women spend too much money on the cosmetics.
  許多女性在化妝品上花了太多錢。

- ★ Many hikers are willing to spend money on the **wireless apparatus**.
  許多登山客願意在無線電設備上花大錢。

insurance
[ɪnˈʃʊrəns]
名 保險
bumpy
[ˈbʌmpɪ]
形 顛簸的
wireless
[ˈwaɪrlɪs]
形 無線的
apparatus
[ˌæpəˈretəs]
名 設備

...offer a variety of...　…提供各式各樣的…。

- ★ That famous pub offers a variety of **alcoholic** drinks.
  那間有名的酒吧提供各式各樣的酒精飲料。

- ★ Our cafeteria offers a variety of traditional snacks.
  我們的食堂提供各式各樣的傳統小吃。

- ★ Local museums offer a variety of **exhibitions** every day.
  本地的博物館每天都有各種展覽。

- ★ Mail-order houses offer a variety of **electric appliances**.
  郵購公司提供各式各樣的家電。

- ★ Most magazines offer a variety of information to their subscribers.
  大多數雜誌提供各式各樣的資訊給訂閱者。

alcoholic
[ˌælkəˈhɔlɪk]
形 含酒精的
exhibition
[ˌɛksəˈbɪʃən]
名 展覽
electric
[ɪˈlɛktrɪk]
形 電的
appliance
[əˈplaɪəns]
名 設備

MP3 ▶ 024

知老外聊開懷，就靠這幾句！

What's the theme of this costume party?
這個變裝派對的主題是什麼？

Everyone in the class will get an invitation to Mindy's birthday party later.
班上所有人晚點都會收到敏蒂生日派對的邀請函。

At a fashion party, you can get updates on the latest fashion news.
在時尚派對裡，你可以得到最新的時尚訊息。

The party is being held in cooperation with Louis Vuitton and Hermes.
這個派對是與路易威登和愛馬仕合辦的。

The 100th guest to arrive will win a free Hermes handbag.
第一百名蒞臨者可免費獲得一個愛馬仕手提包。

The brand is scheduled to reveal its latest collection of handbags at the party next week.
這個品牌預計於下週的派對上發表最新的手提包系列。

Emily decided to throw a private house party to celebrate the 10th anniversary of her brand.
為了慶祝個人品牌十週年，艾蜜莉決定舉辦一場私人派對。

Wherever Matthew is, there is always fun.
有馬修的地方總是充滿歡樂。

I really enjoyed the music and the atmosphere at your party last week!
我很喜歡你上週派對的音樂和氣氛！

For the convenience of our guests, only finger food will be served at the party.
為了方便賓客，這場派對只供應小點心。

UNIT 09 娛樂

電影熱映中
Blockbuster Movies

單字基本功 ✏ 掌握關鍵字 ＝ 開口第一步

 核心聯想　各種電影分類 Movie categories

bromance
[`bromæns]
名 描述男性友誼的電影

comedy
[`kamədɪ]
名 喜劇

documentary
[ˌdakjə`mɛntərɪ]
名 記錄片

drama
[`dramə]
名 劇情片；戲劇

romance
[ro`mæns]
名 愛情片

Sci-Fi
[`saɪ`faɪ]
名 科幻電影

thriller
[`θrɪlə]
名 驚悚片

chick flick
片 文藝片（主要吸引女性觀眾的電影）

 拍攝電影 About filmmaking **進階學習**

cast
[kæst]
名 卡司（演員名單）

character
[`kærɪktə]
名 角色

director
[də`rɛktə]
名 導演

producer
[prə`djusə]
名 製片人；製造者

screenplay
[`skrin͵ple]
名 電影劇本

shot
[ʃat]
名 鏡頭；拍攝

chase scene
片 追逐戲

leading role
片 主角

 深度追蹤 🔍　　　Knowing More

　　除了到電影院觀賞熱門片之外，也有很多人上網尋找看電影的平台。其中最為人知的平台就是美國的「網飛 Netflix」，人們可以用郵寄方式租借DVD並使用網路平台觀看影片，還能看到許多獨特的原創電影，這些電影都是由網飛主導，與著名導演和演員一起製作出來的，而且只在網飛及限定戲院上映。但2017坎城影展卻宣布，明年所有入圍電影都必須要能在法國影院上映，造成許多導演和製作人發出抗議、紛紛呼籲政府調整規定。

MP3 ▶ 026

套個單字，想說的都能表達！

recommend...to sb. 推薦…給某人。

- ★ You should recommend this romance to Mandy.
  你應該向曼蒂推薦這部愛情片。

- ★ You have to recommend this **prototype** to the boss.
  你一定要跟老闆推薦這個原型。

- ★ The concierge recommended a famous **boutique** to those young ladies.
  門房推薦一間著名的流行女裝店給那幾位年輕女性。

- ★ I would recommend this tourist attraction to people who love **trails**.
  對於喜歡步道的人，我會推薦這個觀光勝地給他們。

- ★ The clerk should have recommended this special offer to those who **asked for** discounts.
  店員應推薦這個優惠方案給那些想要折扣的人才對。

> **prototype**
> [`protə,taɪp]
> 名 原型
>
> **boutique**
> [bu`tik]
> 名 時裝店；精品店
>
> **trail**
> [trel]
> 名 小徑；小道
>
> **ask for**
> 片 要求某事 / 物

sb. be happy with... 某人對…很滿意。

- ★ The actor is happy with his performance in that action movie.
  那部動作片的男演員很滿意他在片中的表現。

- ★ We are happy with the **itinerary** and the accommodation.
  我們對這次旅遊的路線規劃以及住宿都感到很滿意。

- ★ All the staff are happy with the new **canteen**.
  所有員工都對新食堂感到很滿意。

- ★ The interviewers were happy with your slide presentation.
  面試官對你的投影片介紹感到很滿意。

- ★ Most **stockholders** are happy with the **steady** growth.
  大部分股東對穩定的成長都感到很滿意。

> **itinerary**
> [aɪ`tɪnə,rɛrɪ]
> 名 路線；旅行計畫
>
> **canteen**
> [kæn`tin]
> 名 食堂
>
> **stockholder**
> [`stɑk,holdə]
> 名 股東
>
> **steady**
> [`stɛdɪ]
> 形 穩定的

開口必備句　和老外聊開懷，就靠這幾句！

What types of movie do you like the most?
你最喜歡哪種類型的電影？

Twilight, a romance between a vampire and an ordinary girl, is adapted from a popular novel.
《暮光之城》改編自著名小說，是關於吸血鬼與人類女孩的愛情故事。

Nicole Kidman gave a stunningly great performance in Moulin Rouge, in which she not only acts well, but also sings perfectly.
妮可・基嫚在《紅磨坊》裡演出精湛，不只演得好、也唱得好。

The Karate Kid features Jackie Chan as an Asian kung fu master.
成龍在《功夫小子》裡主演一位亞洲功夫師父。

Who is the director of Transformers?
《變形金剛》的導演是誰？

Do you know when the Justice League will be on in the theaters?
你知道《正義聯盟》何時上映嗎？

The making of movies has been brought up to a higher level thanks to computer graphics technology.
多虧電腦動畫科技，電影製作已臻更高境界。

The movie trailer successfully drew a large number of audiences into the theater.
這部電影的預告成功地吸引觀眾前往戲院觀賞。

Three Idiots was at the top of the list of highest grossing worldwide Bollywood movies since its release.
《三個傻瓜》從上映以來，就是票房成績亮眼的其中一部寶萊塢電影。

The box-office sales of this new movie are not as good as what the producers expected.
這部新電影的票房不如製片人所預期的高。

Part 02

二月生活進入軌道

February Highlights:
Getting On Track

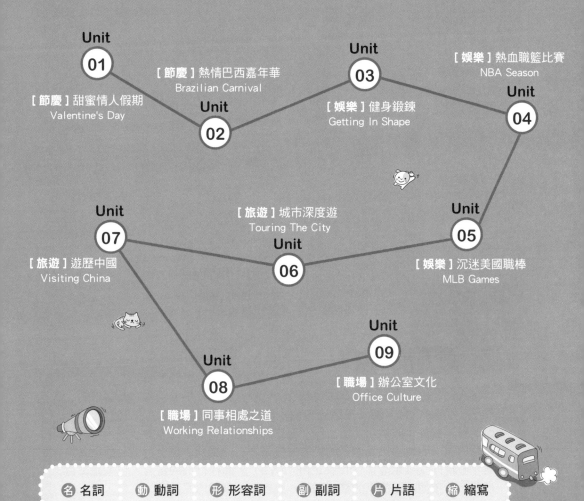

Unit 01
[節慶] 甜蜜情人假期
Valentine's Day

[節慶] 熱情巴西嘉年華
Brazilian Carnival
Unit 02

Unit 03
[娛樂] 健身鍛鍊
Getting In Shape

[娛樂] 熱血職籃比賽
NBA Season
Unit 04

Unit 07
[旅遊] 遊歷中國
Visiting China

[旅遊] 城市深度遊
Touring The City
Unit 06

Unit 05
[娛樂] 沉迷美國職棒
MLB Games

Unit 09
[職場] 辦公室文化
Office Culture

Unit 08
[職場] 同事相處之道
Working Relationships

名 名詞　　動 動詞　　形 形容詞　　副 副詞　　片 片語　　縮 縮寫

UNIT 01 節慶 甜蜜情人假期
Valentine's Day

 單字基本功 ▷ 掌握關鍵字 = 開口第一步

 核心聯想 ┃ 相遇的美好 Coming across the right one

encounter	fate	be destined to	break the ice
[ɪn`kaʊntɚ]	[fet]	片 注定要…	片 打破沉默
名 邂逅 動 遇見	名 命運		

get to know	have...in common	potted history	small talk
片 開始了解	片 在…有共同之處	片 個人背景簡介	片 閒聊

 甜滋滋雙人情 Sweet love 進階學習

bouquet	chocolate	kiss	lovebird
[bu`ke]	[`tʃɑkəlɪt]	[kɪs]	[`lʌv͵bɝd]
名 花束	名 巧克力	名 動 親吻	名 情侶

romantic	heart-shaped	candlelight dinner	fall in love
[ro`mæntɪk]	[`hɑrt͵ʃept]	片 燭光晚餐	片 墜入愛河
形 浪漫的	形 心形的		

 深度追蹤 🔍　　　Knowing More

　　情人節的由來之一，是在皈依基督教就會被判處死刑的時代，基督傳教士瓦倫丁（Valentine）為了掩護殉教者，自暴身分而被捕入獄，他為宗教潛心奉獻的行為感動了典獄長，還治療了典獄長失明的女兒，並與女孩墜入愛河，但當時的君王因為害怕瓦倫丁的能力，便下令將他處死；在上行刑台前，瓦倫丁寫了封信向女孩示愛（confess his love），而在行刑的當天，也就是二月十四日，女孩便在瓦倫丁的墓前種下一棵杏樹，來紀念瓦倫丁。

MP3 ▶ 029

sb. have a crush on... 某人喜歡上…。

★ I think the **chancellor** has a crush on you.
我覺得總理喜歡上你了。

★ The **journalist** has got a crush on the actress.
那名記者一直迷戀著那位女演員。

★ That **charming** gentleman has a crush on my good friend.
那位迷人的男士喜歡上我的好友。

★ He obviously has a crush on Lily, not her sister.
他很明顯喜歡上莉莉，而不是她妹妹。

★ The famous chemist had a crush on his neighbor when he was still a teenager.
那位有名的化學家年輕時喜歡上他的鄰居。

> **chancellor**
> [`tʃænsələ]
> 名 總理
>
> **journalist**
> [`dʒɜnəlɪst]
> 名 新聞記者
>
> **charming**
> [`tʃɑrmɪŋ]
> 形 迷人的

sb. can't help... 某人忍不住…。

★ I can't help falling in love with that **gorgeous** lady.
我情不自禁地愛上那位美麗的女士。

★ I can't help biting my **fingernails** when I am nervous.
當我緊張的時候，我會忍不住咬指甲。

★ Alan can't help laughing when he sees my funny face.
看到我滑稽的表情，艾倫忍不住捧腹大笑。

★ My sister can't help buying a lot of things when there's an annual sale.
一遇到週年慶，我妹就會忍不住買很多東西。

★ Mary can't help **exclaiming** in **delight** at the scene.
看到這情景，瑪莉忍不住高興大叫。

> **gorgeous**
> [`gɔrdʒəs]
> 形 非常漂亮的
>
> **fingernail**
> [`fɪŋɡə‚nel]
> 名 指甲
>
> **exclaim**
> [ɪks`klem]
> 動 呼喊
>
> **delight**
> [dɪ`laɪt]
> 名 愉快

開口必備句 和老外聊開懷，就靠這幾句！

Valentine's Day is a holiday celebrating love.
情人節是個慶祝愛情的節日。

Tom took his girlfriend to a nice French restaurant on Valentine's Day.
情人節當天，湯姆帶女友去吃一家不錯的法式餐廳。

Daniel always gets a lot of chocolate from his admirers on Valentine's Day.
情人節那天，丹尼爾總是會收到許多愛慕者送的巧克力。

The heart-shaped balloons fill the room with a romantic atmosphere.
心形的氣球讓房間充滿浪漫的氛圍。

The florist decorated his stall with hearts in various sizes on Valentine's Day.
這個花商在情人節當天用各種尺寸的心形來裝飾他的攤位。

How are you going to celebrate Valentine's Day?
你打算怎麼慶祝情人節呢？

On White Valentine's Day in Japan, boys will send girls white chocolate.
在日本，男孩會在白色情人節那天送女孩白巧克力。

Do you know the origin of Valentine's Day?
你知道情人節的由來嗎？

It is said that Cupid, the god of love, can compel people to fall in love.
據說愛神邱比特有讓人墜入愛河的力量。

A lot of lovebirds will spend Valentine's Day together and send each other love gifts.
許多情侶們會共度情人節，並互贈愛的小禮物。

MP3 ▶ 031

★UNIT★ 02 節慶 熱情巴西嘉年華
Brazilian Carnival

單字基本功 掌握關鍵字 = 開口第一步

核心聯想 前往嘉年華慶典 Going to the carnival

carnival [`kɑrnəvḷ] 名 嘉年華	**samba** [`sæmbə] 名 森巴舞	**incorporate** [ɪn`kɔrpə‚ret] 動 包含；加上	**annual** [`ænjuəl] 形 每年的；年度的
celebratory [`sɛləbre‚tɔrɪ] 形 值得慶祝的	**stream onto** 片 湧入	**participate in** 片 參加	**in the spotlight** 片 眾所矚目的

來看遊行花車囉 Glamorous parades **進階學習**

activity [æk`tɪvətɪ] 名 活動；活力	**characteristic** [‚kærəktə`rɪstɪk] 名 特色 形 獨特的	**excitement** [ɪk`saɪtmənt] 名 興奮；刺激	**freedom** [`fridəm] 名 自由
decorate [`dɛkə‚ret] 動 裝飾；修飾	**enjoy** [ɪn`dʒɔɪ] 動 享受；喜愛	**excite** [ɪk`saɪt] 動 刺激；引起	**sunny** [`sʌnɪ] 形 充滿陽光的

深度追蹤 Knowing More

　　每年的二月，在巴西的里約熱內盧（Rio de Janeiro）和薩爾瓦多（Salvodor）都會舉行盛大的巴西嘉年華（Brazilian Carnival），在這個為期五天的活動當中，不絕於耳的森巴舞曲充斥全城，人們大跳森巴舞，氣氛熱鬧非凡，故巴西嘉年華又稱為「狂歡節」。在每年的嘉年華會上，會有好幾百個森巴舞團齊聚一堂，他們會搭乘絢麗的造型花車（decorated float），身著色彩繽紛的服裝參加遊行、熱情地秀出舞技，與觀賞遊行的民眾一齊狂歡。

套個單字，想說的都能表達！

sb. have never...　　某人從來沒有…。

★ I have never heard of this custom in our country.
我從來沒聽過我們國家有這項習俗。

★ I have never seen such a pretty bride.
我從沒見過這麼美麗的新娘。

★ The food **critic** has never tried such delicious **roast** beef before.
那位美食評論家從沒吃過這麼美味的烤牛肉。

★ She has never fallen in love with anyone except him.
她從沒愛過他以外的任何人。

★ I have never met one who shares so many **common** interests with me.
我從沒遇過和我這麼興趣相投的人。

critic
[`krɪtɪk]
名 評論家
roast
[rost]
形 烘烤的
common
[`kɑmən]
形 共有的；普通的

...be best known for...　　…最出名的是…。

★ Brazilian Carnival is best known for **splendid** parades.
巴西嘉年華最為人所知的就是盛大的遊行活動。

★ That superstar was best known for his charming character and good **manners**.
那位巨星最出名的是個人魅力和良好的態度。

★ Ali Mountain is best known for its tea.
阿里山最出名的是它所出產的茶。

★ The summer **resort** is best known for its peaceful landscape.
那個避暑勝地最出名的是其寧靜的景色。

★ The TV commentator is best known for the **acridness** of his **satire**.
那名電視名嘴以他刻薄的諷刺聞名。

splendid
[`splɛndɪd]
形 華麗的
manner
[`mænə]
名 禮貌
resort
[rɪ`zɔrt]
名 度假勝地
acridness
[`ækrɪdnɪs]
名 刻薄
satire
[`sætaɪr]
名 諷刺

MP3 ▶ 033

和老外聊開懷，就靠這幾句！

The Brazilian Carnival is an annual celebration in Brazil before Easter.
巴西嘉年華會是巴西在復活節前舉辦的年度慶祝活動。

The Brazilian Carnival lasts from Friday to Tuesday.
巴西嘉年華會從週五持續到週二。

The Brazilian Carnival is one of the world's major tourism activities.
巴西嘉年華會是全球最主要的觀光活動之一。

Brazil is turned into a grand ball during the Brazilian Carnival.
巴西嘉年華會期間，整個巴西化成了一場盛大的舞會。

Millions of people gather and dance the night away with samba music.
數百萬人一同隨著森巴音樂舞動一整晚。

The Carnival manifests the abundance of different cultures in the area.
這場嘉年華會展現了該地區豐富的文化。

The masquerade party is the focus of the entire Brazilian Carnival.
化妝舞會是整場巴西嘉年華會的焦點。

Groups of people parade through streets playing music and dancing wildly.
人們會在街上遊行，邊演奏音樂邊瘋狂地跳舞。

There are samba schools for people interested in preparing for the coming carnival.
有意為即將來臨的嘉年華會做準備的人，可參加森巴舞學校。

A fat man is elected to represent the "king" of the carnival during the event.
節慶期間，一名身材福態的男子獲選為國王。

UNIT 03 娛樂
健身鍛鍊
Getting In Shape

單字基本功 掌握關鍵字 = 開口第一步

核心聯想 好好鍛鍊身體 Bulking up

bicep
[`baɪsɛp]
名 二頭肌
（常用複數形）

fitness
[`fɪtnɪs]
名 健康；合適

pace
[pes]
名 步速；速度

workout
[`wɜk,aʊt]
名 健身

regularly
[`rɛgjələlɪ]
副 規律地

build muscle
片 強化肌肉

get fit
片 保持體態

warm up
片 暖身

 健身房器材 Workout facilities **進階學習**

dumbbell
[`dʌm,bɛl]
名 啞鈴

stepper
[`stɛpɚ]
名 踏步機

treadmill
[`trɛd,mɪl]
名 跑步機

abdominal bench
片 腹部訓練椅

bench press
片 重量訓練機

military press
片 肩部推舉機

punching bag
片 沙包

stationary bike
片 健身腳踏車

 深度追蹤 Knowing More

　　美國的健身文化非常發達，除了學校有健身設備，市區也常設有許多品牌的連鎖健身房。但想要在健身房揮灑汗水、改變體態的同時，務必注意以下事項：(1) 穿運動裝：運動當然要著運動服裝，穿牛仔褲或拖鞋有可能會被拒絕進入。(2) 自備毛巾：大汗淋漓時，可以隨時擦汗，還能避免器材上沾滿汗水。(3) 事先詢問：若有人站在機械旁邊卻沒在使用，記得先問對方是否要用。(4) 保持安靜：大家都專注在自己的鍛鍊上，別因聊天而打擾他人了。

MP3 ▶ 035

套個單字，想說的都能表達！

sb. have to... 某人必須要…。

★ I have to work more on my abs and legs.
我必須要加強訓練我的腹部和腿。

★ Police officers have to **confront** danger **courageously**.
警員必須勇敢地面對危險。

★ The team has to complete the project within two months.
這個團隊必須在兩個月內完成企劃。

★ The couple has to invite all their relatives to the wedding.
那對情侶必須邀請他們所有的親戚來參加婚禮。

★ The worker has to support the family on his **meager** income.
那位工人必須用微薄的薪水來支撐家庭。

> **confront**
> [kən`frʌnt]
> 動 面對
>
> **courageously**
> [kə`redʒəslɪ]
> 副 勇敢地
>
> **meager**
> [`migɚ]
> 形 微薄的；不足的

...look..., especially... …看起來…，尤其是…。

★ The gym looks modern, especially the equipment.
那間健身房看起來很現代化，尤其是裡面的設備。

★ Instagram looks popular, especially as more people are using pictures to convey their thoughts.
Instagram 看來很受歡迎，尤其現在很多人都喜歡用圖片來傳達想法。

★ This costume looks cute, especially the **vest** and the hat.
這套服裝看起來很可愛，尤其是背心和帽子。

★ Victoria looks graceful, especially her dressing style.
維多利亞看起來很優雅，尤其是她的穿著打扮。

★ The boots look great, especially when **paired** with your **jeans**.
那雙靴子看起來很棒，尤其是搭配牛仔褲穿的時候。

> **vest**
> [vɛst]
> 名 背心
>
> **pair**
> [pɛr]
> 動 搭配
>
> **jeans**
> [dʒinz]
> 名 牛仔褲

 **開口必備句** 和老外聊開懷，就靠這幾句！

Going to the gym regularly is a good way to stay in shape.
定時上健身房是保持身材的好方法。

How can I get a membership for this gym?
我要如何成為健身房的會員？

How long have you been working out?
你健身多久了？

Ella does aerobics three times a week.
艾拉每週會做三次有氧運動。

I always warm up before working out.
我在健身前總是會先暖身。

The gym equipment should be shared by everyone working out in the gym.
健身房使用者應共同使用館內設備。

Every gym member should follow the gym regulations.
每位健身房會員都應遵守館內規定。

Lucas has been hogging the treadmill for two hours.
盧卡斯已霸佔跑步機兩個小時了。

Excuse me. Is anyone using this machine?
不好意思，請問這台機器有人使用嗎？

Who is your personal trainer?
誰是你的私人教練？

We have yoga classes from 7 p.m. to 9 p.m. every Wednesday and Friday.
每週三和週五晚間的七點到九點，我們都有瑜伽課程。

We have weights ranging from 2.5 lbs to 100 lbs. You'd better start with the 2.5 lb weights.
我們有從二點五磅到一百磅的舉重鐵餅，你最好從二點五磅開始。

MP3 ▶ 037

★ UNIT ★ 04 娛樂 熱血職籃比賽
NBA Season

 單字基本功 掌握關鍵字 = 開口第一步

 核心聯想 | 比賽必知術語 Basketball terms

overtime [`ovɚ,taɪm] 名 延長賽	**standings** [`stændɪŋz] 名 戰績	**wing** [wɪŋ] 名 底線區域	**first half** 片 上半場
free-throw line 片 罰球線	**home court** 片 主場	**road game** 片 客場比賽	**second half** 片 下半場

 得分方式 Basketball moves 進階學習

bank shot 片 擦板球	**double pump** 片 拉桿式投籃	**fade-away shot** 片 後仰式跳投	**free throw** 片 罰球
jump shot 片 跳投	**lay up** 片 帶球上籃	**three-point shot** 片 三分球	**slam dunk** 片 灌籃

 深度追蹤 ♪ *Knowing More*

　　美國的國家籃球協會（National Basketball Association / NBA）為北美地區的職業男籃組織，分成東區（Eastern Conference）和西區（Western Conference），分區底下由三個分組（division）組成，每個分組則有五支球隊，所以NBA是由三十支來自不同區域的球隊組成的。通常正式的賽季是從每年十一月的第一個星期二開始，每區隊伍在多達八十二場的例行賽結束之後，再由東區及西區的分區冠軍，來爭奪季後賽的總冠軍頭銜。

句型偷吃步　套個單字，想說的都能表達！

It's too bad that...　…真可惜。

★ It's too bad that your favorite team lost the game.
你最愛的隊伍輸了比賽，真的很可惜。

★ It's too bad that your **hypothesis** couldn't be proved in the **experiment**.
真遺憾你的假設沒有在實驗中被驗證。

★ It's too bad that they cannot send any **feedback** to this website.
真可惜他們無法把意見回饋到這個網站裡面。

★ It's too bad that my best friend can't attend my wedding.
真遺憾我最好的朋友無法參加我的婚禮。

★ It's too bad that all the wonderful things can only happen in my dreams.
真可惜這些好事只能出現在我的夢裡。

> **hypothesis**
> [haɪˋpɑθəsɪs]
> 名 假說；假設
> **experiment**
> [ɪkˋspɛrəmənt]
> 名 實驗
> **feedback**
> [ˋfid,bæk]
> 名 回饋

As a matter of fact, ...　事實上，…。

★ As a matter of fact, he didn't play well during the second **half**.
事實上，他下半場並沒有表現好。

★ As a matter of fact, it wasn't me who ate your pudding.
事實上，吃掉你布丁的人不是我。

★ As a matter of fact, the speaker knows nothing about **literature**.
事實上，那名講者對文學一竅不通。

★ As a matter of fact, the celebrity was in a most hopeless **quandary**.
事實上，那個名人陷入了無助的困境。

★ As a matter of fact, her **wild** ideas might be a good suggestion.
事實上，她異想天開的想法可能是個好建議。

> **half**
> [hæf]
> 名 （運動比賽的）半場
> **literature**
> [ˋlɪtərətʃə]
> 名 文學
> **quandary**
> [ˋkwɑndərɪ]
> 名 困境
> **wild**
> [waɪld]
> 形 荒唐的；古怪的

MP3 ▶ 039

開口必備句　和老外聊開懷，就靠這幾句！

Lebron James swept the floor last night.
雷霸龍昨天晚上橫掃全場。

Russell Westbrook shot a triple-double once again tonight.
「西河」衛斯特布魯克今晚再度達成大三元。

Who was the MVP of the game last night?
誰是昨天晚上的「最有價值球員」呢？

I feel that the Hornets are definitely going to win the championship this year.
我覺得黃蜂隊今年一定會贏得總冠軍。

It was such a pity that the Heat didn't win the championship.
熱火隊沒能贏得總冠軍，真的很可惜。

Who will be the new coach after Phil Jackson retires?
誰會在菲爾・傑克森退休後接任教練？

It was reported that Derrick Rose agreed to extend his contract with the Knicks.
據報導，德瑞克・羅斯同意和紐約尼克隊續約。

Though he sprained his toe in the previous game, Derrick Rose still sidelined the Knicks and won the game.
雖然腳趾在前一場比賽中扭傷，羅斯還是幫助紐約尼克隊贏得比賽。

Steve Novak just had his best game of the season.
史提夫・諾瓦克剛打了一場他本季最棒的比賽。

Jeff Green might miss the whole season due to his heart surgery.
傑夫・格林因為心臟的手術，恐怕得錯過整個球季。

The coach said regretfully that the guard will be out for two games because of his injuries in his lower back.
教練遺憾地表示，由於下背傷的問題，那名後衛必須缺席兩場比賽。

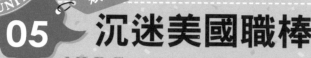

單字基本功 ▷ 掌握關鍵字 = 開口第一步

核心聯想

認識棒球場 Baseball fields

base [bes] 名 壘；基底	**diamond** [`daɪəmənd] 名 內場	**dug-out** [`dʌg͵aʊt] 名 球員席	**outfield** [`aʊt͵fild] 名 外場
batter's box 片 打擊員區	**foul line** 片 邊線	**home base** 片 本壘	**pitcher's mound** 片 投手丘

比賽實況 Enjoying the games 進階學習

steal [stil] 動 盜壘；偷竊	**base sliding** 片 滑壘	**double play** 片 雙殺	**run down** 片 夾殺
sacrifice hit 片 犧牲打	**tag out** 片 觸殺出局	**walk off hit** 片 再見安打	**wild pitch** 片 暴投

深度追蹤 *Knowing More*

　　美國職棒大聯盟（Major League Baseball / MLB）是目前世界上最高水準的職業棒球賽事，分成「國家聯盟」和「美國聯盟」兩個聯盟，共由三十支球隊組成。比賽先從每年四月初的一百六十二場例行賽開始，再由兩個聯盟底下的三支分區冠軍球隊進入「季後賽（postseason）」來爭奪總冠軍。此外，各聯盟戰績最佳的兩個球隊也會進行比賽，由贏的隊伍拿到「外卡（Wild Card）」名額，與分區冠軍隊進行「分區系列賽（Division Series）」。

MP3 ▶ 041

句型偷吃步　套個單字，想說的都能表達！

In spite of..., ...　儘管 / 不管…，…。

★ In spite of his low **ranking**, he still held on straight to the end.
儘管排名不佳，他仍然堅持到最後。

★ In spite of her age, Zoe is still very active and energetic.
儘管年紀大了，佐伊還是很活潑、很有活力。

★ In spite of our **opposition**, Joanna still insists on taking over the leadership.
不管我們的反對，瓊安娜仍然堅持接任領導位置。

★ In spite of my illness, I still went to work today.
儘管生病了，我今天還是有去上班。

★ In spite of the storm, the **warship** still held to its **course**.
儘管暴風雨來襲，軍艦仍然沒有改變航向。

ranking
[`ræŋkɪŋ]
名 排名
opposition
[ˏɑpə`zɪʃən]
名 反對
warship
[`wɔrˏʃɪp]
名 軍艦
course
[kors]
名 方向

Believe it or not, ...　信不信由你，…。

★ Believe it or not, the Yankees has **defeated** all the other teams in its division.
信不信由你，洋基隊已經打敗同一區域內所有的球隊了。

★ Believe it or not, my brother got full marks on the TOEFL.
信不信由你，我弟弟托福考了滿分。

★ Believe it or not, the **colonel rescinded** that soldier's penalty.
信不信由你，上校撤銷了對那名士兵的處分。

★ Believe it or not, I am going to **migrate** to Australia next month.
信不信由你，我下個月就要移民澳洲了。

★ Believe it or not, my grandparents have seen real mermaids.
信不信由你，我的祖父母看過真的美人魚。

defeat
[dɪ`fit]
名 動 擊敗
colonel
[`kɝnḷ]
名 (陸軍) 上校
rescind
[rɪ`sɪnd]
動 撤銷
migrate
[`maɪˏgret]
動 移居

開口必備句

和老外聊開懷，就靠這幾句！

The American League and the National League are both in the MLB.

🔊 大聯盟裡分成美國聯盟和國家聯盟。

The MLB All-Star Game this year will be held in Miami.

🔊 今年的大聯盟明星賽將在邁阿密舉辦。

The Mets and the Yankees are both based in New York.

🔊 大都會隊和洋基隊都在紐約。

The Yankees and the Red Sox have been rivals for decades.

🔊 洋基隊和紅襪隊是數十年來的世仇。

Which team do you think might win the World Series?

🔊 你覺得哪一隊會贏得世界大賽？

Clayton Kershaw beat out many other great pitchers to win the Cy Young Award this year.

🔊 克雷頓・柯蕭擊敗許多優秀的投手，贏得今年的賽揚獎。

Ichiro Suzuki made a walk-off homerun and ended the game.

🔊 鈴木一朗擊出再見全壘打，結束了比賽。

Wang decided to join the Nationals after his contract with the Yankees expired.

🔊 與洋基隊的合約終止後，王建民決定加入華盛頓國民隊。

Kuo is warming up in the bullpen under the coach's instructions.

🔊 在教練的指導下，郭泓志正在牛棚進行熱身。

The coach asked the pitcher to do his best in the 9th inning.

🔊 教練要求投手在九局上半用盡全力。

Derek Holland, the White Sox's top pitcher, had a 2.5 ERA in 22 starts until last Friday.

🔊 直到上週五為止，白襪隊頂尖投手德瑞克・霍蘭德主投二十二場，自責分率僅二點五。

MP3 ▶ 043

★UNIT★ 06 旅遊
城市深度遊
Touring The City

 單字基本功 掌握關鍵字 = 開口第一步

核心聯想 搭乘地鐵 Taking the subway

conductor [kənˋdʌktɚ] 名 車掌	fare [fɛr] 名 票價；費用	platform [ˋplæt͵fɔrm] 名 月台；平台	subway [ˋsʌb͵we] 名 地鐵
one-way ticket 片 單程票	on schedule 片 準點	return ticket 片 來回票	second class 片 二等艙

 都市內部劃分 In the city **進階學習**

capital [ˋkæpətl̩] 名 首都 形 重要的	Chinatown [ˋtʃaɪnə͵taun] 名 中國城；唐人街	locality [loˋkælətɪ] 名 所在地	metropolis [məˋtrɑplɪs] 名 都會區
slum [slʌm] 名 貧民區	suburban [səˋbɝbən] 形 郊區的	urban [ˋɝbən] 形 市區的	town hall 片 市政廳

 深度追蹤 ♪ *Knowing More*

　　一般而言，觀光方式包含以下三大類，旅遊時可按照自己的行程和預算來做選擇：(1) 市區觀光（city tour）：以當地國家或地區的重點特色、古蹟文物或著名地標為主，行程通常安排半天或一天。(2) 夜間觀光（night tour）：夜間觀光行程像是精彩的歌舞秀、當地風味餐、眺望夜景……等等，常常可以讓人看到城市富有魅力的另外一面。(3) 市郊遊（excursion）：可參觀遠離市區的景點，通常會安排一整天，並為可當天來回的行程。

 套個單字,想說的都能表達!

be stuck between...and... 不知該選…還是…。

★ I am stuck between Bali and Paris.
我不知道該去峇里島還是巴黎。

★ The store owner is stuck between **surplus** and **shortage**.
店長不知該選擇讓產品過剩還是短缺。

★ Our nation is stuck between investors and **protesters**.
我國在投資者和抗議者之間進退兩難。

★ The freshmen are stuck between Korean and Japanese.
那名大一新生不知該學韓語還是日語。

★ That girl is stuck between her classmate and the **upperclassman**.
那位女孩不知該選擇同班同學還是學長。

surplus
[`sɝpləs]
名 過剩 形 多餘的
shortage
[`ʃɔrtɪdʒ]
名 短缺
protester
[pro`tɛstɚ]
名 抗議者
upperclassman
[ˏʌpɚ`klæsmən]
名 學長

sb. be looking for... 某人正在尋找…。

★ We are looking for the cheapest way to go to New York City.
我們正在查怎麼花最少錢去紐約。

★ A middle-aged man is looking for his wallet.
有一名中年男子正在找他的皮夾。

★ The collector is looking for **exquisite antiques**.
那名收藏家正在尋找精美的古董。

★ That old lady was looking for the telephone **directory**.
那位老婦人之前在找電話簿。

★ My grandfather was just looking for equipment for **calligraphy**.
我爺爺剛剛在找寫書法的用具。

exquisite
[`ɛkskwɪzɪt]
形 精緻的
antique
[æn`tik]
名 古董
directory
[də`rɛktərɪ]
名 電話簿
calligraphy
[kə`lɪgrəfɪ]
名 書法

MP3 ▶ 045

開口必備句 知老外聊開懷，就靠這幾句！

There are many beautiful buildings from the Renaissance era in this city.
這座城市裡有許多文藝復興時期的美麗建築。

Excuse me. Where is the nearest subway station?
不好意思，離這裡最近的地鐵站在哪裡？

Do you know the closest tube station to the London Eye?
你知道離倫敦眼最近的地鐵站是哪一站嗎？

How much is a round-trip ticket to Grand Central?
到大中央總站的來回票多少錢？

How long will it take if we travel by tube to King's Cross?
如果我們搭地鐵到國王十字站，要花多久時間？

If you want to visit the Louvre, take the metro to the Louvre-Rivoli stop.
若你想參觀羅浮宮，可搭乘地鐵至羅浮─里沃利站。

Never leave your bags unattended in a train station.
車站內，請隨時留意您的行李。

The train comes every twenty minutes.
火車每二十分鐘一班。

The train was late due to an accident at Times Square Station.
火車因時代廣場站的事故而誤點。

The subway is definitely the cheapest and the most convenient way to tour around a big city.
地鐵絕對是在大城市裡最便宜也最便利的旅遊方式。

A day pass is available to tourists for $5, which allows you to take the train an unlimited number of times within a 24-hour period.
遊客可購買五美元的一日票，二十四小時內可不限次數搭乘火車。

UNIT 07 旅遊

遊歷中國
Visiting China

單字基本功 掌握關鍵字 = 開口第一步

核心聯想 景色與地形 Different landscapes

basin
[`besn̩]
名 盆地

embankment
[ɪm`bæŋkmənt]
名 堤岸；河堤

glacier
[`gleʃɚ]
名 冰河

highland
[`haɪlənd]
名 高原地區

karst
[kɑrst]
名 石灰岩地形

lakebed
[`lek‚bɛd]
名 湖床

plateau
[plæ`to]
名 高原

rice terrace
片 水稻梯田

 形容美麗風景 Describing views **進階學習**

breathtaking
[`brɛθ‚tekɪŋ]
形 令人屏息的

fantastic
[fæn`tæstɪk]
形 奇妙的

gigantic
[dʒaɪ`gæntɪk]
形 巨大的

glamorous
[`glæmərəs]
形 迷人的

grand
[grænd]
形 雄偉的

picturesque
[‚pɪktʃɚ`rɛsk]
形 如畫一般的

spectacular
[spɛk`tækjəlɚ]
形 壯觀的

stunning
[`stʌnɪŋ]
形 令人讚嘆的

 深度追蹤 *Knowing More*

　　中國地大物博，有數不完的景點可以遊玩，除了像北京、上海、武漢、重慶……等大都市之外，在不同的季節不妨考慮探訪不同的地方！例如一月的哈爾濱每年都會舉辦冰雪節，可欣賞各式各樣的冰雕，還能體驗冰屋；在寒冷的二月，海南正是避寒的好去處；四月的黃山／盧山則是賞花的最佳季節，但到山林裡就要有走路的準備；七、八月則為西藏旅遊旺季，若走青藏公路進藏的話，雖比搭飛機辛苦，但沿途欣賞到的美景卻是非常值得一看的。

MP3 ▶ 047

句型偷吃步　套個單字，想說的都能表達！

How long will it take to...? …需要花多久時間？

★ How long will it take to fly from Taipei to Shanghai?
從台北到上海需要飛多久？

★ How long will it take to watch the movie?
看這部電影需要花多久時間？

★ How long will it take to **process** all of these applications?
處理完全部的申請書要花多久時間？

★ How long will it take to **form** a habit of regular exercise?
培養規律運動的習慣需要花多久時間？

★ How long will it take to **settle** Mr. Wang's case?
解決王先生的案子需要花多久時間？

> **process**
> [`prɑsɛs]
> 動 處理
> **form**
> [fɔrm]
> 動 養成
> **settle**
> [`sɛtl]
> 動 解決；安頓

sb. can...in the distance. 某人可以從遠處…。

★ Tourists can see the **dawn** sky in the distance.
觀光客可以從遠處觀賞黎明的景色。

★ The sailors on the deck can see **icebergs** in the distance.
在甲板上的船員可以從遠處看見冰山。

★ People can see fireworks **sparking** in the sky in the distance.
人們可以從遠處看見煙火在天空綻放。

★ All villagers can hear a **peal** of temple bells in the distance.
所有村民都能在遠處聽見寺廟的鐘聲。

★ Fishermen can see the lighthouse on the island in the distance.
漁民從遠處就能看到島上的燈塔。

> **dawn**
> [dɔn]
> 名 黎明
> **iceberg**
> [`aɪs,bɝg]
> 名 冰山
> **spark**
> [`spɑrk]
> 動 閃耀
> **peal**
> [pil]
> 名 鐘聲

 開口必備句　和老外聊開懷，就靠這幾句！

The Yangtze River offers a perfect escape for nature lovers.
長江是自然愛好者的絕佳去處。

The Great Wall of China was built for border control and defense.
萬里長城出於邊境控管和防禦目的而建造。

Rumor has it that the Great Wall can be seen from space.
謠傳從外太空就能看見萬里長城。

The Mogao Caves is listed as a World Heritage site.
莫高窟被列為世界遺產。

Being an important military gateway, Shanhaiguan Pass in Hebei is nicknamed "the First Pass of the World."
河北山海關因其防禦敵人入侵的重要性，而獲「天下第一關」的名號。

Zhangjiajie is the inspiration of the fictional landscape in Avatar.
張家界是電影《阿凡達》中場景的原型。

What do you think about taking a trip to Jiuzhaigou Valley?
去九寨溝旅行如何？

You can visit Yunnan to experience ethnic variety.
你可以造訪雲南，體驗多樣的民族風情。

What documents do I need to submit to apply for a tourist visa to China?
我需要繳交哪些文件來申請中國觀光簽證？

If you are traveling solo, you can hire a local tour guide downtown.
若你獨自旅行，可在市中心僱一位當地導遊。

Can you tell me about the guided tours to China your tour agency offers?
可以介紹我一些貴旅行社的中國團嗎？

MP3 ⊙ 049

職場

同事相處之道
Working Relationships

 單字基本功 掌握關鍵字 = 開口第一步

 核心聯想 | 與同事互動 Interacting with colleagues

bonding [`bandɪŋ] 名 聯繫感情	**communicate** [kə`mjunə‚ket] 動 溝通；交流	**frank** [fræŋk] 形 坦白的	**harmless** [`harmlɪs] 形 無害的
reserved [rɪ`z3vd] 形 有所保留的	**deal with** 片 應付；處理	**peer pressure** 片 同儕壓力	**tend to** 片 有…的傾向

 相處不來的苦 Nothing in common 進階學習

alert [ə`l3t] 名 動 警告 形 警覺的	**hardship** [`hardʃɪp] 名 艱難；辛苦	**hatred** [`hetrɪd] 名 憎惡；怨恨	**annoy** [ə`nɔɪ] 動 使惱怒
frown [fraun] 動 皺眉；表示不滿	**aggressive** [ə`grɛsɪv] 形 侵略的	**furious** [`fjurɪəs] 形 狂怒的	**passive** [`pæsɪv] 形 被動的

 深度追蹤 *Knowing More*

　　職場上應盡量避免以下行為，才能建立良好印象：(1) 愛找藉口：沒做到該做的，卻一味推託責任。(2) 不準時：經常遲到或工作常無法準時完成。(3) 開會沒準備：沒事先做準備的話，只會顯得專業度不夠。(4) 斤斤計較：對於工作職責或其他小事太過計較。(5) 無回應：應盡快處理別人寄的e-mail或要求，而不是看過、聽過就好。(6) 忽視細節：忽略小細節很有可能影響他人或無意間鑄成大錯。不時注意以上的要點，相信你的職場生活會更加順遂！

Do sb. have any idea of...? 　某人對…有無想法？

★ Do you have any idea of their proposal?
你對他們的提案有什麼想法嗎？

★ Do the **legislators** have any idea of the **bill of rights**?
立法委員對人權法案有什麼想法嗎？

★ Do your teammates have any idea of the reason why you lost?
你的隊友知道你們輸的原因嗎？

★ Do the judges have any idea of the skaters' performance?
評審對滑冰者的表演有什麼想法？

★ Did his parents have any idea of his **subscription** to the magazine?
他的父母知道他訂閱了雜誌嗎？

> **legislator**
> [`lɛdʒɪs‚letə]
> 名 立法委員；立法者
> **bill of rights**
> 片 (美) 人權法案
> **subscription**
> [səb`skrɪpʃən]
> 名 訂閱

...be superior to... 　…比…優秀。

★ Jade's sales performance is far superior to mine.
潔德的銷售業績比我的還要好。

★ Natural **fiber** is said to be superior to **synthetic** fiber.
據說天然纖維比人造纖維好。

★ The competitive markets are superior to **monopoly** ones.
自由競爭市場比獨佔市場好。

★ The author's latest novel is superior to her previous series.
那名作家最新的小說寫得比以前的系列精彩。

★ A **conceited** man isn't superior to a modest one.
驕傲自滿的人不會比謙虛的人優秀。

> **fiber**
> [`faɪbə]
> 名 纖維
> **synthetic**
> [sɪn`θɛtɪk]
> 形 人造的
> **monopoly**
> [mə`nɑplɪ]
> 名 獨佔；壟斷者
> **conceited**
> [kən`sitɪd]
> 形 自負的

MP3 ▶ 051

開口必備句　和老外聊開懷，就靠這幾句！

Jackson is always generous to his colleagues, which is why he has such a good reputation.
傑克森總對同事很慷慨，這也是他擁有好名聲的原因。

Do you want to come to our potluck party this Saturday?
這週六要來參加我們的聚餐派對嗎？

Do you want to grab some lunch with us?
你要不要和我們一起去吃午餐？

David is so arrogant that no one wants to work with him.
大衛太高傲了，所以沒人願意與他合作。

Some of our colleagues love to have a drink together every Friday night.
我們有些同事喜歡在每週五晚上相聚喝一杯。

I really need some advice on getting along with my coworkers.
我真的需要一些怎麼與同事和睦相處的建議。

Try to keep a good workplace relationship with your coworkers.
試著和你的同事保持良好的工作關係。

Do your best to avoid offending those who work with you.
盡力避免冒犯與你共事的人。

Judy is such a chatterbox, and she nags all the time.
茱蒂是個喋喋不休的人，總是在抱怨。

Many conflicts among colleagues arise from what starts out as harmless exchanges.
許多同事間的衝突都起因於無心之言。

How do you ask a chatterbox to stop interfering with your work?
該如何讓一個喋喋不休的人不再干擾你工作？

UNIT 09 職場
辦公室文化
Office Culture

 單字基本功 ✎ 掌握關鍵字 = 開口第一步

 核心聯想　　辦公室環境 What's in the office

division [dəˋvɪʒən] 名 部門；分開	**headquarters** [ˋhɛdˋkwɔrtəz] 名 總部	**office** [ˋɔfɪs] 名 辦公室；職務	**reception** [rɪˋsɛpʃən] 名 接待處
workplace [ˋwɜkˌples] 名 工作場所	**conference room** 片 會議室	**pantry room** 片 茶水間	**staff room** 片 員工休息室

 認真上班 Working & communicating 進階學習

deputy [ˋdɛpjətɪ] 名 代表；代理人	**disapprove** [ˌdɪsəˋpruv] 動 反對；不准許	**exchange** [ɪksˋtʃendʒ] 名 動 交換	**decisive** [dɪˋsaɪsɪv] 形 有決斷力的
diligent [ˋdɪlədʒnt] 形 勤勉的	**group purchase** 片 團購	**leave a note** 片 留下訊息	**pep talk** 片 鼓勵性演說

 深度追蹤 🔍　　Knowing More

　　相較於台灣辦公室重視人情味和輩分的觀念，美國的辦公室文化較重視個人的價值、機會公平原則和個人隱私。例如台灣人常以頭銜稱呼對方，美國人則直接以名字稱呼對方；美國人也很注重個人隱私權，因此詢問私事（例如薪水）是非常不禮貌的行為，還有可能損害對方對你的信賴度；另外，美國常強調效率以及個人主義，並讚美聰明的工作而非苦力，因此在採納意見時，會以意見內容、個人專業背景、實力和工作態度為準。

MP3 ▶ 053

套個單字，想說的都能表達！

Don't be late for...　…不要遲到。

★ Don't be late for work.
上班別遲到了。

★ Don't be late for the cherry blossom season.
別錯過櫻花季。

★ Don't be late for the English **proficiency** test tomorrow.
明天的英文程度測驗考試別遲到了。

★ Don't be late for the **medical qualification** examination.
醫師資格考試別遲到了。

★ Don't be late for the **casting audition** next Saturday.
下星期六的演員試鏡別遲到了。

proficiency
[prə`fɪʃənsɪ]
名 精通；熟練
medical
[`mɛdɪk]]
名 醫學的；醫療的
qualification
[ˌkwɑləfə`keʃən]
名 資格；取得資格
casting
[`kæstɪŋ]
名 角色分派
audition
[ɔ`dɪʃən]
名 試演

Let's keep on...　我們繼續…。

★ Let's keep on working on the project.
我們繼續處理這件企劃案吧。

★ Let's keep on developing new **technologies**.
我們繼續研發新的科技吧。

★ Let's keep on exercising till we feel **exhausted**.
我們繼續運動到體力用盡為止吧。

★ Let's keep on improving the quality of our machine.
我們繼續來提升機器的品質吧。

★ Let's keep on focusing on protecting cultural **heritage**.
我們繼續把焦點放在保護文化遺產上吧。

technology
[tɛk`nɑlədʒɪ]
名 科技
exhausted
[ɪg`zɔstɪd]
形 筋疲力竭的
heritage
[`hɛrɪtɪdʒ]
名 遺產

MP3 ► 054

開口必備句 和老外聊開懷，就靠這幾句！

It's our tradition that newbies have to buy everyone coffee on their first day at work.
新人上班第一天請大家喝杯咖啡是我們的傳統。

Every office has its unique office culture.
每間辦公室都有其獨特的辦公室文化。

It's our office tradition that we leave cards and candies on the birthday boy or girl's desk.
我們辦公室習慣在壽星的桌上留下卡片和糖果。

A positive office culture can motivate workers and improve work efficiency.
積極正面的辦公室文化能激勵員工並改善工作效率。

I really hate the backstabbing culture in my office.
我真的很討厭我們辦公室裡背後捅刀的文化。

Do you and your coworkers hang out after work?
你下班後會和同事一起出去嗎？

Instead of dressing too casually or too formally, try to blend in.
試著融入工作場合，穿著避免太過休閒或太過正式。

Jason always buys everyone dinner whenever a big deal is closed.
傑森總是在大案子結束後請大家吃晚餐。

Rumor has it that Chloe is seeing Andy, the team manager.
謠傳克蘿伊正在與團隊經理安迪約會。

Our leader tries to create a supportive office atmosphere.
我們組長試著建立一種「彼此扶持」的辦公室氛圍。

What do you think of leaving a thank-you note on your colleagues' desk?
你覺得在同事的桌上留一張感謝字條如何？

Part 03

放鬆身心充實三月

March Highlights:

Relaxing & Unwinding

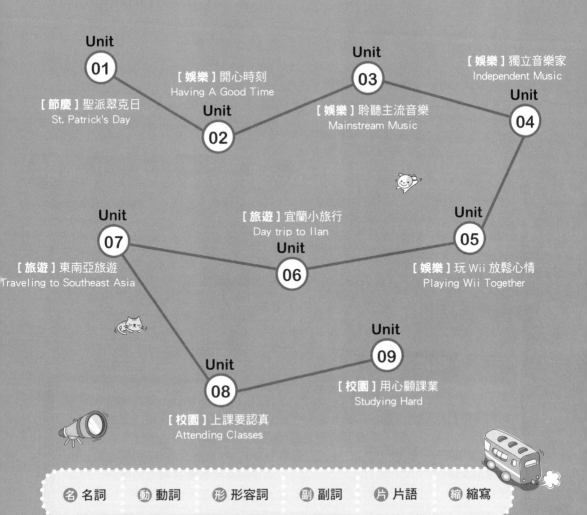

名 名詞　　動 動詞　　形 形容詞　　副 副詞　　片 片語　　縮 縮寫

UNIT 01 節慶 聖派翠克日
St. Patrick's Day

 單字基本功 ✏️ 掌握關鍵字＝開口第一步

 核心聯想 | 綠油油的標誌 Green everywhere

Irish [`aɪrɪʃ] 名 愛爾蘭人 形 愛爾蘭的	**jig** [dʒɪg] 名 吉格舞（三拍子快步舞）	**leprechaun** [`lɛprə,kɔn] 名 綠色小精靈	**rainbow** [`ren,bo] 名 彩虹
shamrock [`ʃæmrɑk] 名 三葉酢漿草	**Celtic** [`kɛltɪk] 形 凱爾特族的	**customary** [`kʌstəm,ɛrɪ] 形 習慣上的；習俗的	**emerald** [`ɛmərəld] 形 翡翠綠的

 參加綠色遊行 Parade of green 進階學習

applause [ə`plɔz] 名 喝采；稱讚	**bagpipe** [`bæg,paɪp] 名 風笛	**glee** [gli] 名 高興；喜悅	**parade** [pə`red] 名 遊行 動 參加遊行
stride [straɪd] 名 跨步 動 大步走	**whole** [hol] 名 全體 形 全部的	**divert** [daɪ`vɜt] 動 使轉向	**rejoice** [rɪ`dʒɔɪs] 動 歡喜；歡呼

 深度追蹤 🔍 Knowing More

聖派翠克日（St. Partick's Day）是傳統的愛爾蘭節日，同時也是愛爾蘭人的國慶日以及國定假日，最初是為了紀念將基督教帶入愛爾蘭的聖派翠克。每年到了三月十七日，愛爾蘭人便會舉辦盛大的遊行活動，並穿上代表性的綠色服飾和帽子，來慶祝聖派翠克節。據說身穿綠衣綠帽，可以吸引到古神話中熱愛收集黃金的小妖精（leprechaun），他會將黃金埋藏在彩虹的盡頭，只要抓住小妖精，他就會告訴你藏匿黃金的地方，便能一生不愁吃穿！

MP3 ⊙ 056

句型偷吃步　套個單字，想說的都能表達！

Nice to meet you. 　很高興認識你。

- ★ Nice to meet you. My name is Serena.
  很高興認識你，我叫瑟琳娜。

- ★ Nice to meet you. I am Steve, Christine's friend.
  很高興認識你，我是克莉絲汀的朋友，史蒂夫。

- ★ Nice to meet you. I'm Jane, the new **accountant**.
  很高興認識你，我是新的會計師，我叫珍。

- ★ Nice to meet you. I'm Tim. I'm here for **business**.
  很高興認識你，我叫提姆，我是為了公事來的。

- ★ Nice to meet you. I'm June. I haven't seen you around before.
  很高興認識你，我是茱恩，以前好像沒有看過你。

> **accountant**
> [ə`kauntənt]
> 名 會計師
> **business**
> [`bɪznɪs]
> 名 商業

sb. look forward to... 　某人期待…。

- ★ All of us look forward to the coming holiday.
  我們都很期待接下來的假期。

- ★ We look forward to **technological advances**, and we are open to any necessary changes.
  我們對技術上的進展充滿期待，而且我們也樂意接受改變。

- ★ My friends look forward to an **extension** of our holiday.
  我的朋友期待能延長我們的假期。

- ★ My parents look forward to seeing you again soon.
  我父母期待再次見到你。

- ★ Travelers look forward to going home after a long trip.
  旅行者們在長途旅行過後都很期待回家。

> **technological**
> [tɛknə`lɑdʒɪkl]
> 形 科技的
> **advance**
> [əd`væns]
> 名 發展
> **extension**
> [ɪk`stɛnʃən]
> 名 延期

開口必備句 和老外聊開懷，就靠這幾句！

St. Patrick's Day falls on March 17, which is also the day St. Patrick passed away.
三月十七日是聖派翠克日，也是聖派翠克逝世的日子。

St. Patrick's Day is the most important holiday in Irish culture.
聖派翠克日是愛爾蘭文化裡最重要的節日。

There will be great parades in Dublin on St. Patrick's Day.
聖派翠克日當天，在都柏林會有盛大的遊行。

The city will be painted green on St. Patrick's Day with people dressed in green.
整座城市在聖派翠克日會被穿著綠色的人們染成翠綠色。

Even landmarks are turned green for the day.
在當天，連地標都會被染成綠色。

Jessica tied an emerald ribbon on her ponytail and went towards the parade.
潔西卡在馬尾綁上翠綠色的緞帶，並走向遊行隊伍。

The St. Patrick's Day celebrations last for the whole day.
聖派翠克日的慶祝活動會持續一整天。

Green represents the coming of spring, and it is also the color of the country.
綠色代表著春天的來臨，同時也是這個國家的代表色。

Shamrocks are symbols of good luck.
三葉酢漿草是幸運的象徵。

Legend has it that green can attract leprechauns, who can lead you to pots of gold.
傳說綠色能吸引小精靈，他們會帶你找到裝滿黃金的罐子。

Would you like some St. Patrick's Day special green beer?
你想要來些聖派翠克日限定的綠啤酒嗎？

058

日常

開心時刻
Having A Good Time

 單字基本功 ▶ 掌握關鍵字 = 開口第一步

核心聯想 | 與人同享喜悅 Sharing joys

mood
[mud]
名 心情；情緒

share
[ʃɛr]
名 動 分享；分擔

overjoyed
[,ovə`dʒɔɪd]
形 狂喜的

be happy for
片 為…感到開心

buy sb. a drink
片 請某人喝飲料

foot the bill for
片 替…付賬

have fun
片 玩得開心

live it up
片 盡情享受

各種派對類型 Types of party | 進階學習

party
[`pɑrtɪ]
名 派對 動 開派對

baby shower
片 新生兒派對

pool party
片 泳池派對

slumber party
片 睡衣派對

theme party
片 主題派對

costume party
片 變裝派對

rave party
片 大型狂歡派對

farewell party
片 歡送會

 深度追蹤 *Knowing More*

　　中西的「送禮文化」差異甚大，像是美國人在送禮時，會特意強調為什麼選這個禮物，並希望這個禮物是對方喜歡的，也會當面把禮物打開，再好好誇讚一番，有些人還會在幾天後特地寫e-mail或打電話再次表示感謝。而表達喜悅之情時，不妨學著「說」出來，例如用「Awesome! / Great! / Wow! / Bravo! 超棒的！」來表示歡喜，或是活動結束說「I had a good time. 我玩得很開心。」適當地表達自己的情緒，也是溝通時很重要的一環呢！

套個單字，想說的都能表達！

sb. can't...more. 某人十分 / 非常…！

- ★ I can't love traveling with my family more.
  我非常喜愛和家人一起去旅行。

- ★ The photographer can't **enlarge** the picture more.
  攝影師已經把照片放到最大的尺寸了。

- ★ Mrs. Baker's **tenants** can't love their suites more.
  貝克太太的房客們非常喜歡他們的套房。

- ★ Those **delegates** can't agree with his theory more.
  那群會議代表十分贊同他的理論。

- ★ The charity can't help those **refugees** more.
  那個慈善機構十分幫助那群難民。

> **enlarge**
> [ɪn`lɑrdʒ]
> 動 放大
> **tenant**
> [`tɛnənt]
> 名 房客
> **delegate**
> [`dɛlə͵get]
> 名 代表
> **refugee**
> [͵rɛfjʊ`dʒi]
> 名 難民

What a surprise to...! …太讓人驚訝了！

- ★ What a surprise to **run into** you here!
  在這裡碰到你真令人驚訝！

- ★ What a surprise to get more **bonus** than I expected!
  拿到比我當初所預期還要更多的紅利，真令人驚訝！

- ★ What a surprise to be **selected** as the winner of the contest!
  在比賽中被選為優勝者真令人驚訝！

- ★ What a surprise to see my favorite **idol** at her party!
  在她的派對上看見我最愛的偶像真令人驚訝！

- ★ What a surprise to know that Luna speaks excellent French!
  之前都不知道露娜的法語說得這麼流利，真令人驚訝！

> **run into**
> 片 偶然碰到
> **bonus**
> [`bonəs]
> 名 紅利
> **select**
> [sə`lɛkt]
> 動 選擇
> **idol**
> [`aɪdl̩]
> 名 偶像

 開口必備句　和老外聊開懷，就靠這幾句！

Dave bought everyone a drink in celebration of his promotion.
戴夫為慶祝榮升，請每個人喝飲料。

Mila wants to throw a surprise party for Karen on her birthday.
米拉想要幫凱倫在生日那天辦個驚喜派對。

Do you know why Mr. Johnson looks so overjoyed?
你知道強生先生為什麼看起來那麼開心嗎？

Linda footed the bill for everyone at the table on her birthday.
琳達在她生日那天幫大家買單。

Audrey shouted for joy when she saw her favorite movie star, Jackie Chan, in front of her.
奧黛莉看見她最喜歡的電影明星—成龍站在面前時，開心地大叫。

On the day his child was born, Kenny was so excited that he immediately called everyone in his family.
肯尼在他孩子出生的那天，開心地打電話給每個家人。

Helen gleefully told her father that she got her dream job.
海倫開心地跟她父親說，她得到夢寐以求的工作了。

Does anyone have any good news to share?
誰有什麼好消息想要分享嗎？

The class jumped for joy when the teacher said there would be no test for today.
當老師說今天沒有考試時，全班開心地跳了起來。

I got a big raise last month. Let me buy you dinner.
我上個月加薪了，讓我請你吃晚飯吧。

Chris is on top of the world because his girlfriend just said yes when he popped the question.
克里斯非常開心，因為他女友答應了他的求婚。

How should we celebrate Ken's birthday?
我們要怎麼慶祝肯的生日？

UNIT 03 娛樂

聆聽主流音樂
Mainstream Music

 單字基本功 掌握關鍵字 = 開口第一步

 核心聯想　排行榜熱銷 Top-selling music

Billboard	**debut**	**sum**	**trend**
[`bɪl͵bord]	[dɪ`bju]	[`sʌm]	[trɛnd]
名 告示牌排行榜	名 初次登台；首次露面	名 總數 動 合計	名 趨勢；傾向

release	**hot**	**pop**	**reportedly**
[rɪ`lis]	[hɑt]	[pɑp]	[rɪ`portɪdlɪ]
動 發行；發表	形 受歡迎的；暢銷的	名 流行樂 形 流行的	副 據報導

　音樂類型 Various music genres　進階學習

blue	**classical**	**country**	**folk**
[blu]	[`klæsɪkḷ]	[`kʌntrɪ]	[fok]
名 藍調音樂	名 古典音樂	名 鄉村音樂	名 民謠；民族

hip-hop	**jazz**	**rock 'n' roll**	**R&B**
[`hɪp͵hɑp]	[dʒæz]	[`rɑkən`rol]	[`ɑr͵ænd`bi]
名 嘻哈音樂	名 爵士樂	名 搖滾樂	名 節奏藍調

 **深度追蹤**　Knowing More

　　除了經典的西洋情歌以及時下最熱門的西洋流行樂之外，亞洲也有讓全世界粉絲都瘋迷的日本流行樂（J-pop）以及韓國流行樂（K-pop）；其中日本常以獨特的電玩音樂風格及富有創意的MV拍攝手法來吸引觀眾，而韓國則常以整齊的「刀群舞」、電音曲風或是抒情唱腔取勝。另外，也出現愈來愈多的歌唱比賽節目，像是The Voice、American Idol、X Factor⋯⋯等等，挖掘出許多素人歌手，提供每個人在舞台上盡情歌唱、實現夢想的機會。

句型偷吃步　套個單字，想說的都能表達！

sb. be impressed by...　某人被…打動。

★ Dana's client was impressed by her **persistent** attitude.
黛娜的客戶被她堅持不懈的態度打動。

★ The director is impressed by that movie **extra**.
導演被那名電影臨時演員打動。

★ The producer is impressed by your scenario.
製作人被你的劇本打動了。

★ All the audience are impressed by your **superlative** performance.
全部的觀眾都被你們高超的表演打動了。

★ Don's supervisor was impressed by his efforts towards the case.
唐的主管被他對案子的付出打動。

> **persistent**
> [pəˋsɪstənt]
> 形 堅持不懈的
>
> **extra**
> [ˋɛkstrə]
> 名 臨時演員
>
> **superlative**
> [səˋpɜlətɪv]
> 形 最好的

Will...be refundable?　…是可以退錢的嗎？

★ Will the ticket be refundable?
門票是可以退錢的嗎？

★ Will this **security deposit** be refundable?
這筆保證金可以退費嗎？

★ Will the **unfitted topcoat** be refundable?
不合身的輕便大衣可以退錢嗎？

★ Will the **easel** I bought at your **stationer** be refundable?
在你文具店購買的畫架是可以退錢的嗎？

★ Will the deposits for the cottages be refundable?
度假別墅的押金是可以退的嗎？

> **security deposit**
> 片 保證金
>
> **unfitted**
> [ˌʌnˋfɪtɪd]
> 形 不適合的
>
> **topcoat**
> [ˋtɑp.kot]
> 名 輕便大衣
>
> **easel**
> [ˋizl]
> 名 畫架
>
> **stationer**
> [ˋsteʃənɚ]
> 名 文具店

開口必備句 和老外聊開懷，就靠這幾句！

Twenty One Pilots is one of my favorite bands.
🔊 「二十一名飛員樂團」是我最喜歡的樂團之一。

You can get the latest pop music updates on Billboard.com.
🔊 你可在告示牌排行榜的網頁上得到最新的流行音樂資訊。

Bruno Mars has been on the Billboard top 10 for 13 weeks!
🔊 火星人布魯諾在告示牌排行榜前十名已經十三週了！

Eminem is one of the biggest-selling hip-hop artists in the world.
🔊 阿姆是全世界最暢銷的嘻哈歌手之一。

I am a big fan of Sia, an inspirational singer and a song writer.
🔊 我是希雅的粉絲，她是一位啟發人心的歌手以及音樂創作者。

Judy enjoys indulging herself in jazz music after work.
🔊 茱蒂喜歡在下班後聽爵士樂放鬆。

Cats has been one of the most popular musicals for decades.
🔊 《貓》劇數十年來為最受歡迎的音樂劇之一。

Jenny is a huge fan of Justin Timberlake. She has a complete collection of his albums.
🔊 珍妮很喜歡大賈斯汀。她有他的全套專輯。

Lady Gaga's latest album will be released in early October this year.
🔊 女神卡卡的最新專輯預計於今年十月初發售。

If you order Katy Perry's concert ticket now, you can get a free limited edition poster.
🔊 如果您現在預購凱蒂‧佩芮的演唱會門票，就可獲得免費限量海報。

iTunes is an Internet platform where you can download the latest music at bargain prices.
🔊 iTunes 是個可讓你以優惠價格下載最新音樂的網路平台。

Mayday is going to give a live concert on New Year's Eve.
🔊 五月天將在跨年夜舉辦現場演唱會。

 MP3 ▶ 064

★UNIT★ 04

娛樂

獨立音樂家
Independent Music

 單字基本功 掌握關鍵字 = 開口第一步

 核心聯想 | 非主流印象 Independent labels

variety	arouse	pioneer	vary
[və`raɪətɪ]	[ə`rauz]	[ˌpaɪə`nɪr]	[`vɛrɪ]
名 多樣化	動 喚醒；激起	動 作為…的先驅	動 改變；使不同

innovative	unique	make skin crawl	remixed version
[`ɪnoˌvetɪv]	[ju`nik]		
形 創新的	形 獨特的	片 起雞皮疙瘩	片 混音版本

 用心製作音樂 Producing music | 進階學習

composer	concept	creation	creativity
[kəm`pozə]	[`kɑnsɛpt]	[krɪ`eʃən]	[ˌkrie`tɪvətɪ]
名 作曲家	名 概念；觀念	名 創作品；創造	名 創造力

studio	compose	convey	fulfill
[`stjudɪˌo]	[kəm`poz]	[kən`ve]	[ful`fɪl]
名 錄音室；工作室	動 組成；作曲	動 傳達；運送	動 實現；滿足

 深度追蹤 🔍

Knowing More

　　在音樂市場中，一般分為「主流」及「非主流」兩種，後者一般為獨立製作的音樂，但對許多人而言，很容易有種錯覺，認為非主流音樂就是「吵」；的確，有些走極端樂風的獨立樂團，傳達了較強烈的節奏為主打特色，也常以嘶吼的唱腔為主打特色，但是也有很多非主流樂團並不像大眾所想的那麼另類，他們常著重於情緒鋪陳、樂曲的創意、歌詞題材的創新……等等概念，試著走出自己的特色。除了最常聽到的主流風格之外，不妨也多涉獵不同類型的音樂吧！

sb. like...better 某人比較喜歡…。

★ My sister likes indie bands better.
我姐姐比較喜歡獨立樂團。

★ He likes summer better than winter.
比起冬天，他比較喜歡夏天。

★ I like heavy metal music better because of its **amplified distortion** in guitar solos.
我比較喜歡重金屬音樂，因為電吉他獨奏時的破音效果很吸引我。

★ I like this apartment better because the rent is **reasonable**.
我比較喜歡這間公寓，因為租金很合理。

★ I like the cocktail better because it tastes pretty **smooth**.
我比較喜歡這杯雞尾酒，因為它喝起來很順口。

amplify
[`æmplə͵faɪ]
⑩ 擴展；誇大
distortion
[dɪs`tɔrʃən]
⑧ 失真；變形
reasonable
[`riznəbl]
⑯ 合理的
smooth
[smuð]
⑯ 滑順的

sb. had a great time... 某人度過了一段很棒的時光…。

★ I had a great time going to the concert with you.
和你一起去聽音樂會很愉快。

★ The reporters had a great time interviewing the actor.
記者們與那名演員的訪談非常愉快。

★ The whole **crew** had a great time celebrating the success of the play.
全體工作人員都開心地慶祝演出成功。

★ The host had a great time speaking to the audience.
主持人和觀眾聊得很愉快。

★ Dan had a great time working with that **talented sculptor**.
和那名天才雕刻家工作的經驗對丹來說很愉快。

crew
[kru]
⑧ 工作人員
talented
[`tæləntɪd]
⑯ 有才華的
sculptor
[`skʌlptə]
⑧ 雕刻家

知老外聊開懷，就靠這幾句！

Let's enjoy the Swedish rock festival at the Wall Live House tonight.
今晚，一同享受在「這牆藝文展演空間」舉辦的瑞典搖滾音樂祭吧！

Music by Enigma always makes my skin crawl.
謎樂團的音樂總讓我起雞皮疙瘩。

Soul music is the combination of gospel music and R&B.
靈魂樂融合聖歌音樂和節奏藍調。

Which genre of music do you like the most?
你最喜歡的音樂類型是？

Mr. Thompson wants to introduce aboriginal music on his record.
湯普森先生想在他的專輯裡採用原住民音樂的概念。

The music of Mozart is an archetype of the Classical style.
莫札特的音樂是古典樂的代表。

I can hardly understand the concept behind Bjork's music.
碧玉歌曲的概念對我來說很難理解。

Baliwakes Lu is a famous aboriginal composer, whose music conveys the nature-loving spirit in aboriginal culture.
陸森寶是位著名的原住民編曲家，他的音樂傳達了原住民文化裡喜愛大自然的精神。

Because she has record-breaking album sales even though she's not well-known, Yozoh is the best singer I can think of.
不太有名卻能創造專輯銷售佳績的窈窕小姐，是我心中最棒的歌手。

I have a full collection of Radiohead's CDs.
我有收藏電台司令的全部專輯。

Can you tell me who the composer of the song is?
可以告訴我這首歌的作曲者是誰嗎？

★UNIT 05 娛樂

玩 Wii 放鬆心情
Playing Wii Together

單字基本功 ▶ 掌握關鍵字＝開口第一步

核心聯想 | 一起認識 Wii Introducing "Wii"

jab	Nunchuck	respond	multiplayer
[dʒæb]	[`nʌntʃʌk]	[rɪ`spɑnd]	[`mʌltɪ͵pleɚ]
動 以拳猛擊	名 Wii 左手操縱桿	動 反應；回應	形 多位玩家的

virtual	balance board	motion sensor	video game
[`vɝtʃʊəl]			
形 （電腦）虛擬的	片 平衡板	片 動作感測器	片 電動遊戲

玩賽車遊戲 Racing games | 進階學習

direction	position	transmission	racer
[də`rɛkʃən]	[pə`zɪʃən]	[træns`mɪʃən]	[`resɚ]
名 方向；指示	名 位置；立場	名 變速器；傳播	名 賽車手

rallycross	trophy	accelerate	a set of
[`rælɪ͵krɔs]	[`trofɪ]	[æk`sɛlə͵ret]	
名 汽車越野賽	名 獎盃；獎品	動 加速；促進	片 一組；一套

深度追蹤 🔍

Knowing More

　　Wii是任天堂公司推出的家用遊戲主機，而開發Wii的代號為「Revolution 革命」，象徵「電視遊戲的革命」。Wii不但聽起來像是We（我們），發音也相同，藉此傳達Wii老少咸宜、能讓一家大小都樂在其中的概念。另外，Wii的其中一項令人驚豔的創舉，就屬操縱桿上的創意了。Wii操縱桿的正式名稱叫做「Wii Remote」，其中內建麥克風與喇叭，還配合遊戲軟體設計來支援震動的功能，讓玩家能夠充分體驗遊戲的真實感！

MP3 ◉ 068

套個單字，想說的都能表達！

sb. be good at... 　某人擅長…。

★ My brother is really good at playing video games.
我的弟弟很擅長打電玩。

★ Mia's fiancé is good at cooking.
米雅的未婚夫很擅長烹飪。

★ That architect is good at renovation and **landscaping**.
那名建築師很擅長舊屋翻新和室外造景。

★ My advisor is good at analyzing the risk of investments.
我的顧問很會分析投資的風險。

★ That **surgeon** is good at **remedying cardiovascular** diseases.
那位外科醫生很會治療心血管疾病。

> **landscaping**
> [ˋlændskepɪŋ]
> 名 景觀美化
>
> **surgeon**
> [ˋsɝdʒən]
> 名 外科醫生
>
> **remedy**
> [ˋrɛmədɪ]
> 動 治療
>
> **cardiovascular**
> [ˌkɑrdɪoˋvæskjulə]
> 形 心血管的

What's the difference between...and...?

…和…之間有什麼區別？

★ What's the difference between PS4 and Wii?
PS4 和 Wii 有什麼不同？

★ What's the difference between you and your twin sister?
你和你的雙胞胎妹妹有什麼不同的地方？

★ What's the difference between a **dietitian** and a **nutritionist**?
營養師和營養學家有什麼不同？

★ What's the difference between a **helicopter** and a **jet fighter**?
直升機和戰鬥噴射機有何不同？

★ What's the difference between a deposit account and a checking account?
儲蓄存款帳戶和支票存款帳戶有什麼不一樣？

> **dietitian**
> [ˌdaɪəˋtɪʃən]
> 名 營養師
>
> **nutritionist**
> [njuˋtrɪʃənɪst]
> 名 營養學家
>
> **helicopter**
> [ˋhɛlɪkɑptə]
> 名 直升機
>
> **jet fighter**
> 片 噴射戰鬥機

開口必備句 和老外聊開懷，就靠這幾句！

There are five different games for your enjoyment in Wii Sports.

《Wii 運動》裡有五種不同的運動可供您遊樂。

Jimmy just bought Wii Sports Resort last weekend.

吉米上週末剛買了《Wii 運動：度假聖地》。

While bowling on Wii, just imagine the remote as an extremely light bowling ball, and then release the button like you're actually throwing the ball.

在玩 Wii 保齡球時，只要想像遙控器是顆非常輕的保齡球，再放開按鍵，像是你真的在投球一樣。

Wii is a lot of fun, and the boxing really gets the heart pumping.

Wii 非常有趣，拳擊遊戲也能讓心跳加速。

How about playing a baseball game on Wii, just you and me?

要不要來場 Wii 的棒球賽，就我們兩個？

Wii is actually a good exercise choice for those who don't like going out to the gym or exercising with other people.

對於那些不想去健身房或不喜歡和別人一起運動的人來說，Wii 其實是個很好的選擇。

Jeremy invited us to have a Wii fight with him at his place.

傑瑞米邀請我們去他家參與 Wii 大戰。

With Wii, you can canoe anytime at home just with a simple click on the remote.

有了 Wii，你只需操作遙控器，就能隨時在家裡划獨木舟。

Wii and Kinect are both ideal choices for a fun family reunion during the Chinese New Year.

Wii 和 Kinect 都是農曆新年期間，全家團聚歡樂的好選擇。

Both of my parents enjoy competing with each other on Wii.

我的父母很喜歡和對方玩 Wii 來比輸贏。

UNIT 06

旅遊

宜蘭小旅行
Day trip to Ilan

單字基本功 掌握關鍵字 = 開口第一步

 核心聯想　　宜蘭特色景點 Features of Ilan

architecture	estate	handicraft	rejuvenate
[`ɑrkə,tɛktʃ⁓]	[ɪs`tet]	[`hændɪ,kræft]	[rɪ`dʒuvənet]
名 建築物	名 遺產；財產	名 手工藝	動 恢復精神

guided tour	Lanyang Plain	Luodong Night Market	silver grass
片 導覽	片 蘭陽平原	片 羅東夜市	片 芒花

 宜蘭美食 Local foods in Ilan **進階學習**

pottage	ancient	century egg	food stand
[`pɑtɪdʒ]	[`enʃənt]	片 皮蛋	片 小吃攤
名 濃湯	形 古代的		

local snack	green onion pancake	sesame paste noodles	smoked duckling
片 當地小吃	片 蔥油餅	片 麻醬麵	片 鴨賞

 深度追蹤 🔍　　*Knowing More*

　　宜蘭四寶分別為膽肝、鴨賞、蜜餞、羊羹，其中最為人知的名產「鴨賞」是依古人智慧，醃製鴨肉來長久保存，後來便成為宜蘭的名產之一。除此之外，宜蘭的乾淨水質和季風帶來的豐富水氣，造就了「三星蔥」葉肉厚、纖維少、蔥味芬芳的特質，深受大眾喜愛。而其他特色小吃還包括了牛舌餅、糕渣、卜肉、溫泉空心菜、溫泉番茄……等等；若有機會去宜蘭玩，不妨逛逛羅東夜市、蘭陽觀光夜市或是東門夜市，嚐嚐在地的美食吧！

句型偷吃步 套個單字，想說的都能表達！

Will there be time to/for...? 會有時間…嗎？

- ★ Will there be time to watch a Taiwanese opera?
  會有時間看齣歌仔戲嗎？

- ★ Will there be time to go explore those **tribes**?
  會有時間去探訪那些部落嗎？

- ★ Will there be time for grocery shopping after we come back?
  回來之後會有時間去買日常用品嗎？

- ★ Will there be time to review a **full-length draft** of my essay?
  我會有複習整份論文草稿的時間嗎？

- ★ Will there be time for the **consultation** with the representative?
  會有時間和那名代表協商嗎？

tribe
[traɪb]
名 部落
full-length
[ˋfʊlˋlɛŋθ]
形 全長的；完整的
draft
[dræft]
名 草稿
consultation
[ˌkɑnsəlˋteʃən]
名 商議；諮詢

What is the operation hours of...?
請問…的營業時間是什麼時候？

- ★ What is the operation hours of National Center for Traditional Arts?
  傳統藝術中心的營業時間為何？

- ★ What is the operation hours of this boutique on weekends?
  這家精品店週末的營業時間是什麼時候？

- ★ What is the operation hours of that research **institute**?
  那間研究機構的營業時間為何？

- ★ What is the operation hours of the **post office**?
  郵局的營業時間為何？

- ★ What is the operation hours of the **district court** for receiving our application?
  地方法院收取申請書的時間為何？

institute
[ˋɪnstətjut]
名 機構
post office
片 郵局
district court
片 地方法院

MP3 ▶ 072

開口必備句 和老外聊開懷，就靠這幾句！

Ilan is a city with beautiful scenery and amicable people.
宜蘭是個擁有美景與友善居民的城市。

My solo trip to Ilan last week allowed me to relieve my stress and to enjoy delicious local cuisines.
我上週的宜蘭小旅行讓我可以紓解壓力以及享受在地美食。

Can you recommend some must-see places in Ilan?
你可以推薦一些宜蘭的必去景點嗎？

Caoling Historic Trail is excellent for people who love hiking.
草嶺古道對健行愛好者來說是極佳的選擇。

Gueishan Island is shaped like a sleeping turtle.
龜山島的外形像隻沈睡的烏龜。

You can book a room in Taipingshan online.
你可線上預約太平山住宿。

I bought snow chains for our trip to Taipingshan.
為了去太平山旅行，我買了雪鏈。

Camping is not allowed in the Taipingshan National Forest Recreation Area.
太平山國家森林遊樂區裡不能露營。

The National Center for Traditional Arts in Ilan preserves traditional Taiwanese culture and arts, such as Taiwanese opera.
宜蘭傳藝中心保存了台灣的傳統藝術，例如歌仔戲。

Many artistic groups put on shows at regular intervals in the National Center for Traditional Arts.
許多藝術團體會定期在傳藝中心表演。

I would really want to try the cold spring in Su-ao, Ilan.
我真的很想體驗蘇澳的冷泉。

UNIT 07 旅遊

東南亞旅遊
Traveling to Southeast Asia

 單字基本功 掌握關鍵字 = 開口第一步

核心聯想 探訪佛教國家 Buddhist culture

Buddha [`budə] 名 佛陀	**harmony** [`harmənɪ] 名 一致；和諧	**mercy** [`mɜsɪ] 名 慈悲	**monk** [mʌŋk] 名 僧侶
palace [`pælɪs] 名 宮殿	**temple** [`tɛmpl] 名 寺廟	**friendly** [`frɛndlɪ] 形 友善的	**Thao Maha Brahma** 片 四面佛

東南亞特色 Features **進階學習**

mosquito [məs`kito] 名 蚊子	**population** [ˌpɑpjə`leʃən] 名 人口	**tuk-tuk** [`tuktuk] 名 嘟嘟車（一種載客機車）	**humid** [`hjumɪd] 形 潮濕的
rainy [`renɪ] 形 多雨的	**coconut milk** 片 椰奶	**floating market** 片 水上市場	**paddy field** 片 水稻田

 **深度追蹤** 𝒦𝓃ℴ𝓌𝒾𝓃ℊ 𝑀ℴ𝓇ℯ

　　東南亞建築多以通風的「高腳屋」為主，而在水鄉澤國的區域還有特別的「水上屋」與「水上市場」。在文化方面，東南亞各國也都自成特色，例如在寮國，絕大多數男人都要經歷一次出家；越南人則最愛戴帽子、口罩、或以絲巾遮面來擋塵土和紫外線；菲律賓的少女在十二、三歲便為適婚年齡，實行早婚、多妻的制度；而汶萊禁賭、禁黃色（因黃色為皇室象徵），且因為汶萊人認為頭被觸摸會帶來災難，所以千萬不要隨便摸別人的頭。

套個單字，想說的都能表達！

sb. have decided to... 某人決定要⋯。

★ John has decided to go on a vacation next week.
約翰決定下週要去度假。

★ My father has decided to **retire** in May this year.
我父親決定在今年五月退休。

★ They have just decided to take the work home.
他們剛剛決定，要把工作帶回家做。

★ The government has decided to increase **minimum wage** for all **laborers**.
政府決定提高勞工的基本薪資。

★ My colleague has decided to accept an offer with a higher salary.
我的同事決定接受一份薪水更高的工作。

> **retire**
> [rɪ`taɪr]
> 動 退休
>
> **minimum wage**
> 片 法定最低薪資
>
> **laborer**
> [`lebərə]
> 名 勞工

sb. be lucky to... 某人很幸運⋯。

★ I am lucky to see the festival held at that night.
我真幸運能看到那天晚上舉辦的慶典。

★ I am lucky to get the **lion's share**.
我很幸運地得到最多的配額。

★ My sister is lucky to work with **renowned** artists from all over the world.
我妹妹很幸運，能和從世界各地來的知名藝術家一起工作。

★ I am lucky to read the novelist's early chapters in the **manuscript**.
能閱讀這位小說家的前幾章手稿真是太幸運了。

★ She is lucky to marry a **decent** gentleman like Mike.
她很幸運能和像麥克這樣正直的紳士結婚。

> **lion's share**
> 片 最大部分
>
> **renowned**
> [rɪ`naʊnd]
> 形 有名的
>
> **manuscript**
> [`mænjə,skrɪpt]
> 名 手稿
>
> **decent**
> [`disn̩t]
> 形 正派的

開口必備句 和老外聊開懷，就靠這幾句！

Thailand and Cambodia are both Buddhist countries.
泰國和柬埔寨皆屬佛教國家。

Do you know the difference between the temples and shrines in Thailand and in Cambodia?
你知道泰國和柬埔寨的佛寺有何差別嗎？

Thao Maha Brahma in Thailand is a must-see attraction for many tourists.
泰國的四面佛是許多觀光客的必訪景點。

Many visitors go to the floating market to gain some insight into the local culture.
許多觀光客會去水上市場體驗當地文化。

There are many vendors along the way to the Great Palace.
前往大皇宮的路上，沿途有許多小販。

The tuk-tuk is an iconic form of transportation in Thailand.
嘟嘟車是泰國最具代表性的交通工具。

There are many bars in Bangkok, the city that never sleeps.
曼谷是座酒吧林立的不夜城。

How much is the day tour to the Elephant Nature Park in Chiang Mai?
清邁大象自然公園一日遊的費用是多少？

Thailand is a paradise for massage and spa lovers.
泰國是喜愛按摩和三溫暖人士的天堂。

The magnificent Angkor Wat is one of the natural and cultural heritages around the world.
壯麗的吳哥窟是世界自然及文化遺產的其中之一。

Taking a cruise on Tonle Sap Lake is a popular day trip in Cambodia.
洞里薩湖一日遊在柬埔寨很受歡迎。

MP3 ▶ 076

UNIT 08 校園

上課要認真
Attending Classes

 單字基本功 | 掌握關鍵字 = 開口第一步

核心聯想 積極參與課堂 Participating in class

assignment
[ə`saɪnmənt]
名 作業；任務

comment
[`kɑmɛnt]
名 意見 動 評論

lecture
[`lɛktʃɚ]
名 動 授課

professor
[prə`fɛsɚ]
名 教授

seminar
[`sɛmənar]
名 研討會

subject
[`sʌbdʒɪkt]
名 科目；主題

speech
[spitʃ]
名 演講

participate
[par`tɪsə,pet]
動 參與；參加

 上課不小心遲到 Late for school **進階學習**

arrival
[ə`raɪvl]
名 到達；出現

oversleep
[`ovɚ`slip]
動 睡過頭

awake
[ə`wek]
動 喚醒 形 醒的

forget
[far`gɛt]
動 忘記；放棄

hurry
[`hɝɪ]
動 急忙；催促

within
[wɪ`ðɪn]
副 在…之內

dash
[dæʃ]
動 猛衝；急奔

nervous
[`nɝvəs]
形 緊張的

 深度追蹤 🔍 *Knowing More*

　　和台灣相比，國外的教授通常更重視學生在課堂上的參與度，也滿鼓勵學生在上課時勇於發表自己的看法。除此之外，上台做簡報的頻率也比台灣高出許多；相較於考試成績，國外教授其實更看重學生的簡報能力、服裝儀態以及報告的呈現方式，並常常要求大家分組討論，逐一發表自己的想法。就氣氛而言，也鼓吹「主動」的學習態度，因此，會要求學生做課前預習，事先準備下次要討論的主題，不加以準備的話，可是會跟不上同學的。

sb. had better...　某人最好⋯。

★ You had better settle down now and review the lessons.
你現在最好靜下心來複習功課。

★ You had better **put your heads together** about this matter.
你們最好花點時間好好地思考這個問題。

★ You had better get professional advice before investing.
你最好在投資之前取得專業建議。

★ You had better make sure that all guests will be **on time**.
你最好確定所有賓客都會準時抵達。

★ The dean had better gather all the students in the **auditorium** to announce the **renewed** policy.
院長最好召集所有學生到禮堂，再來宣布新政策。

> **put one's heads together**
> 片 集思廣益
> **on time**
> 片 準時
> **auditorium**
> [ˏɔdə`torɪəm]
> 名 禮堂
> **renewed**
> [rɪ`njud]
> 形 更新的

Have sb. considered...?　某人有考慮過⋯嗎？

★ Has Dr. Chen considered our new **proposal**?
陳教授有考慮過我們的新提案了嗎？

★ Have you considered your decision carefully?
你有仔細思考過你的決定嗎？

★ Has the economist considered the issues on **foreign trade**?
那位經濟學家有思考過外貿議題嗎？

★ Has the **loan** department considered the clients' financial situation?
放款部門有考慮過客戶的財務情況嗎？

★ Has your analyst considered our suggestion?
你的分析師有考慮過我們的建議嗎？

> **proposal**
> [prə`pozl]
> 名 提案；建議
> **foreign trade**
> 片 國際貿易
> **loan**
> [lon]
> 名 借出；貸款

MP3 ▶ 001

開口必備句 和老外聊開懷，就靠這幾句！

I am taking five courses this semester.
我這學期修了五門課。

Did you like Professor Coleman's speech?
你喜歡寇曼博士的演講嗎？

I didn't understand anything from Professor Madison's lecture.
我完全聽不懂麥迪森教授的課。

We're now doing the roll call. Answer if you hear your name, please.
現在要開始點名了，聽到你的名字請應聲。

Raise your hand if you have questions or comments.
如果你有問題或是意見，都可以舉手提出。

What chapter are we on?
我們上課上到哪一章了？

What class do you have next?
你下一堂是什麼課？

Why didn't you come to class this morning?
你為什麼今天早上沒來上課？

May I borrow your notes?
我能向你借筆記嗎？

I totally forgot to do my homework!
我完全忘記做功課了！

What is the assignment for today?
今天的作業是什麼？

I have to consult the teacher's assistant about the assignment since I'm not really sure if I'm on the right track.
因為我不太確定我作業寫的方向對不對，所以我得問一下助教。

UNIT 09 校園
用心顧課業
Studying Hard

單字基本功 掌握關鍵字＝開口第一步

核心聯想 課業表現 Academic performances

preview [`pri͵vju] 名動 預習	**review** [rɪ`vju] 名動 複習；回顧	**solve** [sɑlv] 動 解答；解決	**understand** [͵ʌndɚ`stænd] 動 了解；懂得
absent [`æbsn̩t] 形 缺席的	**outstanding** [`aut`stændɪŋ] 形 傑出的	**of course** 片 當然	**no wonder** 片 難怪

進階學習 參與小組討論 Group project

outline [`aut͵laɪn] 名 大綱 動 概述	**cooperate** [ko`ɑpə͵ret] 動 合作；配合	**discuss** [dɪ`skʌs] 動 討論；商談	**divide** [də`vaɪd] 動 劃分；分配
formulate [`fɔrmjə͵let] 動 明確陳述；公式化	**responsible** [rɪ`spɑnsəbl̩] 形 負責的	**meet up** 片 遇見；聚集	**team/group project** 片 小組報告

深度追蹤 🔍

Knowing More

　　國外大學圖書館的資源非常豐富，不只有一般書籍，也常包含期刊、研究成果、論文……等等可供參考。一般來說，學生都能用學生證來進入圖書館並免費借書，但教科書與雜誌通常只能在館內閱讀；找書時，可以請教圖書管理員，當然，如果教授提供完整的書單，也可以利用圖書館的搜尋系統找書。除了圖書館，現在美國很多學生也愛利用notehall.com搜尋各校的課堂筆記，甚至會彼此交易，藉此共享資源。

MP3 ▶ 080

句型偷吃步 套個單字，想說的都能表達！

I would like to start with... 我想先從…開始。

★ I would like to start with a **quote** from a famous **Athenian statesman**.
我想先從一位著名雅典政治家說的話談起。

★ I would like to start with a list of **rare** animals.
我想先從稀有動物的列表開始著手。

★ I would like to start with the outline.
我想先從大綱開始討論。

★ I would like to start with an important announcement.
我想先從一個重要的通知開始討論。

★ I would like to start with the explanation of my **delay**.
我想先解釋我遲到的理由。

> **quote**
> [kwot]
> 名 引言
>
> **Athenian**
> [ə`θinɪən]
> 形 雅典的
>
> **statesman**
> [`stetsmən]
> 名 政治家
>
> **rare**
> [rɛr]
> 形 稀有的
>
> **delay**
> [dɪ`le]
> 名 延遲；耽擱

sb. be engaged in... 某人在忙 / 正在從事…。

★ Professor Lee is engaged in a study on public issues.
李教授正在做一個有關公眾議題的研究。

★ My colleague wants to be engaged in that challenging project.
我同事想加入那個有挑戰性的專案。

★ The secret agent is engaged in **espionage**.
特務正在從事間諜活動。

★ The **advocates** of **free trade** are engaged in the consultation with the government.
提倡自由貿易的人們正忙著與政府協商。

★ They have been engaged in the **wholesale** business for three decades.
他們從事批發業已有三十年的時間了。

> **espionage**
> [`ɛspɪənɑʒ]
> 名 間諜活動
>
> **advocate**
> [`ædvəkɪt]
> 名 倡導者
>
> **free trade**
> 片 自由貿易
>
> **wholesale**
> [`hol,sel]
> 名 批發

開口必備句　和老外聊開懷，就靠這幾句！

The teacher asked us to preview lesson seven and eight.
老師要求我們預習第七課與第八課。

I don't understand this chapter. Can you explain it to me again, please?
我不了解這一章的內容，能請你再教我一次嗎？

What did the teacher say about this chapter? I don't remember at all!
關於這一章，老師說了什麼？我完全不記得了！

Have you finished reading chapter ten?
你讀完第十章了嗎？

Can you show me how to solve this math problem?
能不能請你教我解這道數學題目？

Do you have time later? I think we should spend more time working on the group project.
你等一下有時間嗎？我覺得我們得花點時間討論小組報告的事情。

Darrell is the most outstanding student in the class.
戴洛是班上最傑出的學生。

By reviewing what you learned after class, you can reduce the time needed to relearn the knowledge.
下課後複習所學的內容，可以讓你省下很多時間。

You'd better not watch TV and study at the same time if you want to achieve a higher grade.
如果你想要拿到高一點的分數，就最好不要邊看電視邊讀書。

Study harder and practice more, then you will get better grades.
再用功一點，並多做練習，你就會得到更好的成績。

I am so tired of pulling an all-nighter for the finals.
我已經厭倦為了期末考而熬夜唸書。

Part 04

歡樂滿滿四月生活

April Highlights:
Pranks, Foods, & Exams

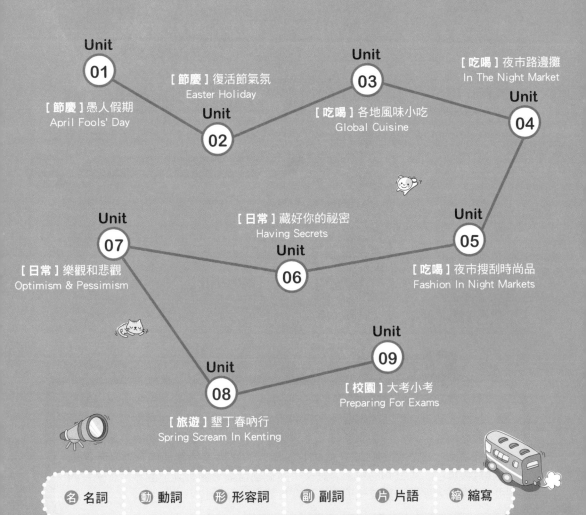

名 名詞　　動 動詞　　形 形容詞　　副 副詞　　片 片語　　縮 縮寫

★UNIT 01 節慶 愚人假期
April Fools' Day

單字基本功 掌握關鍵字 = 開口第一步

核心聯想 愚人節玩笑 Jokes on you

allow	hoax	prank	gullible
[ə`laʊ]	[hoks]	[præŋk]	[`gʌləbl̩]
動 允許;同意	名 惡作劇 動 欺騙	名 動 惡作劇	形 易受騙的

April fool	make fun of	monkey business	practical joke
片 在愚人節被整的人	片 開⋯玩笑	片 惡作劇	片 惡作劇

提高警覺 Being aware of pranks **進階學習**

April	idea	guide	believe
[`eprəl]	[aɪ`diə]	[gaɪd]	[bɪ`liv]
名 四月	名 主意;構想	名 嚮導 動 引導	動 相信;認為

join	amusing	careful	strange
[dʒɔɪn]	[ə`mjuzɪŋ]	[`kɛrfəl]	[strendʒ]
動 參加;連接	形 好笑的;有趣的	形 小心的	形 奇怪的

 深度追蹤 𝒦𝓃ℴ𝓌𝒾𝓃ℊ 𝑀ℴ𝓇ℯ

愚人節又稱作「萬愚節（All Fools' Day）」，據說是源自十六世紀的法國，當國王查理九世將原本四月一日的新年改到一月一日，守舊黨為了反對此舉，便堅持在四月一日慶祝新年及互送禮品，於是支持新曆法的改革派便藉此嘲笑守舊派，在四月一日贈送假禮物、舉辦假宴席來愚弄他們，並稱他們為「四月傻瓜」、「上鉤的魚」。之後，這個風俗漸漸遍布到全世界，於是在四月一日捉弄人就逐漸變成一項習俗，在世界各地盛行起來。

MP3 ▶ 083

套個單字，想說的都能表達！

...be (not) allowed to...　…（不）能／（不）被允許…。

★ People are allowed to play jokes on each other on April Fools' Day.
在愚人節這一天，人們可以互相開玩笑。

★ Children are allowed to fly kites at this park.
小孩子可以在這個公園裡放風箏。

★ The intern was allowed to give the patient an **injection**.
那名實習醫師已取得允許，可以替那位病人注射。

★ **Minors** who are under 18 are not allowed to smoke.
未滿十八歲的未成年人不能抽煙。

★ Models are not allowed to cheat in a **beauty contest**.
模特兒們不能在選美比賽作弊。

> **injection**
> [ɪnˋdʒɛkʃən]
> 名 注射
> **minor**
> [ˋmaɪnə]
> 名 未成年人
> **beauty contest**
> 片 選美比賽

either...or...　不是…就是…。／…或…。

★ What he said was either a joke or a **pick-up line**.
他之前說的話不是在開玩笑，就是用來搭訕的。

★ My aunt will take either a **coach** or the train.
我阿姨不是搭長途公車就是坐火車。

★ Visitors can either rent a car or take the MRT to tour around the city.
遊客可以用租車或搭捷運的方式來遊覽這個城市。

★ You can attend either **in person** or by a **proxy**.
你可以親自出席或請人代為出席。

★ I will buy my friend either a suitcase or some guide books.
我不是買行李箱就是買旅遊書籍來送我朋友。

> **pick-up line**
> 片 搭訕詞
> **coach**
> [kotʃ]
> 名 長途公車
> **in person**
> 片 親自
> **proxy**
> [ˋprɑksɪ]
> 名 代理人

 和老外聊開懷，就靠這幾句！

April Fools' Day is considered to be one of the most light-hearted holidays.
愚人節被認為是最輕鬆愉快的節日之一。

Practical jokes are a common practice on April Fools' Day.
惡作劇在愚人節是很常見的。

People always pull pranks on each other on April Fools' Day.
人們總是會在愚人節當天對彼此惡作劇。

Playing harmless pranks on April Fools' Day is a tradition widely recognized throughout the world.
在愚人節開開無傷大雅的玩笑，是全世界都認定的一項傳統。

You need to be prepared with hilarious pranks to play on friends.
你需要準備一些好笑的惡作劇來捉弄一下朋友們。

Some newspapers and magazines even play pranks by reporting fake stories on April Fools' Day.
在愚人節當天，有些報社和雜誌還會寫假故事來惡作劇。

Both Jessie and Owen fell victim to my pranks.
潔西和歐文都成為我惡作劇的受害者。

Robert tricked his parents by substituting a fake pull cord for the real one on the fan.
羅伯特把風扇的電源線換成一條假的，來捉弄他的父母。

People also pull pranks on their co-workers at the office.
人們也會對辦公室同事惡作劇。

A fool's errand is looking for things that don't exist.
呆瓜差事就是跑去找根本不存在的東西。

Though joking is acceptable, don't go too far.
雖然開玩笑是可以接受的，但不要開得太過火了。

MP3 ▶ 085

節慶

復活節氣氛
Easter Holiday

 單字基本功 ▷ 掌握關鍵字＝開口第一步

 核心聯想

復活節由來 Origin of Easter

miracle [`mɪrək!] 名 奇蹟	**origin** [`ɔrɪdʒɪn] 名 起源；來源

prayer [prɛr] 名 禱告	**religion** [rɪ`lɪdʒən] 名 宗教

relate [rɪ`let] 動 有關；敘述	**hidden** [`hɪdṇ] 形 隱藏的

original [ə`rɪdʒən!] 形 起初的	**Good Friday** 片 耶穌受難日（復活節前的週五）

 ### 復活節活動 Easter activities 進階學習

basket [`bæskɪt] 名 籃子	**jellybean** [`dʒɛlɪ, bin] 名 豆形糖果

search [sɝtʃ] 名 動 搜尋；尋找	**dye** [daɪ] 動 為…染色

colorful [`kʌləfəl] 形 彩色的；多彩多姿的	**Easter bunny** 片 復活節兔子

egg hunt 片 尋蛋活動	**egg rolling** 片 滾彩蛋活動

 深度追蹤🔍

Knowing More

　　復活節是紀念耶穌基督死而復生的基督教節日，象徵物包括了雞蛋、小雞、小兔子和百合花；其中，因為堅硬的蛋殼無法阻止裡面孕育的新生命，所以蛋和小雞都象徵孕育出的新生命；兔子則以贈送小朋友禮物的形象出現，帶著一籃彩蛋和糖果給乖孩子；而百合花在復活節時期盛開，象徵著神聖以及純潔，故常用來比喻死亡之後的復活。另外，人們會把各種糖果填入彩蛋裡面，所以美國的復活節就是僅次於萬聖節，糖果消費量第二大的節日！

sb. be familiar with...　某人對⋯熟悉。

★ Our professor is familiar with the history of Easter.
我們教授很了解復活節的歷史。

★ The cook is familiar with German cuisine.
那名廚師對德國菜餚很熟悉。

★ Few people are familiar with the **health care** system.
很少人熟悉醫療系統。

★ Successful sales would be familiar with their products **beforehand**.
成功的業務會預先熟悉他們的產品。

★ The **technician** is familiar with all the machines in the factory.
那位技師熟悉工廠內所有的機器設備。

health care
片 醫療保健
beforehand
[bɪˋfor͵hænd]
副 事先地
technician
[tɛkˋnɪʃən]
名 技術人員

sb. can try to...　某人可以試試⋯。

★ You can try to make Easter eggs with your kids.
你可以試著陪孩子製作彩蛋。

★ You can try to express your opinions **assertively**.
你可以試著有自信地陳述你的觀點。

★ You can try to write down your **objectives** on the list.
你可以試著在清單上寫下你的目標。

★ Actually, you can try to walk around the **corridor** if you feel bored.
如果你覺得無聊，其實可以去走廊那邊逛逛。

★ The technician can try to adjust the detail **settings** on the machine first.
技術工程師可以先試著調整機器的細部設定。

assertively
[əˋsɝtɪvlɪ]
副 有自信地
objective
[əbˋdʒɛktɪv]
名 目標
corridor
[ˋkɔrɪdə]
名 走廊
setting
[ˋsɛtɪŋ]
名 設定；背景

MP3 ◎ 087

開口必備句 和老外聊開懷，就靠這幾句！

Good Friday commemorates the crucifixion of Jesus.
耶穌受難日是紀念耶穌被釘在十字架上受難。

Easter is a three-day celebration, starting on Good Friday.
復活節是從耶穌受難日開始，為期三天的慶祝活動。

Easter is considered one of the most important Christian festivals.
復活節被視為最重要的基督教節日之一。

Easter is one of the most exciting holidays for children.
對孩子們來說，復活節是最令人興奮的節日之一。

Do you know how to make Easter eggs?
你知道怎麼製作復活節彩蛋嗎？

Ms. Chang taught the children to dye the eggs in preparation for Easter.
張老師教孩子們彩繪蛋，以為復活節做準備。

The Easter Bunny is an important symbol of Easter, symbolizing fertility.
復活節兔子是復活節的重要象徵，代表著「繁殖力」。

The custom calls for exchanging eggs at Easter, which symbolizes rebirth.
在復活節時交換蛋是個習俗，而蛋象徵著「重生」。

Children are all looking forward to the egg hunt.
小孩們都很期待找彩蛋遊戲。

When does the egg hunt start?
尋蛋遊戲什麼時候開始呢？

Easter egg roll is usually held on the White House South Lawn every year for children and their parents.
每年的復活節，在白宮的南草坪都會舉辦滾彩蛋遊戲，讓小朋友與家長們可以一起參加。

各地風味小吃
Global Cuisine

 單字基本功 ▶ 掌握關鍵字 = 開口第一步

 核心聯想 | 台灣特色小吃 Taiwanese snacks

braised pork rice 片 滷肉飯	bubble milk tea 片 珍珠奶茶	crispy fried chicken 片 鹽酥雞	fish ball soup 片 魚丸湯
fried rice noodles 片 炒米粉	hot and sour soup 片 酸辣湯	savory rice patty 片 豬血糕／米血	wonton soup 片 餛飩湯

 國外特色小吃 Exotic dishes 進階學習

crêpe [krep] 名（法）可麗餅	panini [pə`nini] 名（義）義式三明治	pretzel [`prɛtsl̩] 名（德）椒鹽脆餅	satay [`sɑrte] 名（印）沙嗲烤肉
taco [`tɑko] 名（墨）墨西哥捲餅	trifle [`traɪfl̩] 名（英）水果鬆糕	foreign [`fɔrɪn] 形 外國的；外來的	fish & chips 片（英）炸魚薯條

 深度追蹤 🔍 *Knowing More*

聯合國將以下六個國家的飲食納入「世界非物質文化遺產」：(1) 法國：因其高雅的用餐禮儀、對食材的重視，而被視為「世界上最優雅的美食」。(2) 傳統墨西哥飲食：彰顯全民共享性、無拘無束的用餐文化。(3) 土耳其小麥粥：將飲食和表演兩者融合在一起，並強調分享的概念。(4) 地中海飲食：講求均衡又健康的飲食概念。(5) 日本傳統和食：將色、香、味完美結合，被譽為「眼睛的料理」。(6) 韓國越冬泡菜：展現全民互助的飲食文化。

句型偷吃步　套個單字，想說的都能表達！

...be the ~est sb. have ever...

…是某人…過最…的。

★ Stinky tofu is the weirdest food I have ever tasted.
臭豆腐是我吃過最奇怪的食物。

★ Mr. Lee is the **toughest** boss I have ever worked for.
李先生是我所共事過，最難搞的老闆。

★ She is the **humblest** celebrity I have ever met.
她是我遇過最謙遜的名人。

★ My father is the strictest coach I have ever known.
我父親是我所知道的教練中，最嚴厲的一個。

★ The old man is the most **erudite** person I have ever talked to.
那位老先生是我遇過最博學的人。

> **tough**
> [tʌf]
> 形 棘手的；牢固的
> **humble**
> [`hʌmbl]
> 形 謙遜的
> **erudite**
> [`ɛru͵daɪt]
> 形 博學的

(It is) no wonder (that)...　難怪…。

★ No wonder you insisted to dine here.
難怪你堅持要在這裡用餐。

★ No wonder it **went to your head**.
難怪你被這件事沖昏頭了。

★ No wonder **Polaroid** sales keep on rising.
難怪拍立得的銷量一直在上升。

★ No wonder my cell didn't **ring** today.
難怪我的手機今天都沒有響過。

★ No wonder your brother doesn't have a girlfriend now.
難怪你哥現在沒有女朋友。

> **go to one's head**
> 片 沖昏某人的頭腦
> **Polaroid**
> [`polə͵rɔɪd]
> 名 拍立得
> **ring**
> [rɪŋ]
> 動 響；按鈴

Have you ever tried savory rice patties?
你吃過豬血糕嗎？

Fried chicken is a popular late-night snack among Taiwanese.
台灣人很喜歡把鹽酥雞當宵夜。

Sweet potato congee and braised pork rice are both traditional dishes in Taiwan.
地瓜稀飯與滷肉飯都是傳統的台灣料理。

Angelica duck is the best food to nourish human bodies in both winter and summer.
當歸鴨是夏天和冬天的滋補聖物。

Do your parents love rice tube pudding?
你的父母親喜歡吃筒仔米糕嗎？

Would you like to try some salty rice pudding or coffin bread?
你想不想吃點碗粿或棺材板？

Taiwanese beef noodles are world-famous!
台灣的牛肉麵世界聞名！

Every time Jane visits Hong Kong, she'll dine in her favorite dim sum restaurant.
珍每次去香港時，都會去她最喜歡的港式餐廳吃飯。

The escargot is usually served as a starter in France.
法國人常常以法國蝸牛當開胃菜。

Mexican foods such as tacos and burritos are popular worldwide, and they taste really good.
墨西哥食物像是玉米餅和捲餅都很受全球歡迎，也真的很好吃。

Fish and chips is a must-try in the UK.
到英國就一定要吃炸魚薯條。

MP3 ► 091

04 吃喝 夜市路邊攤
In The Night Market

單字基本功 掌握關鍵字 = 開口第一步

核心聯想 | 台灣夜市小吃 In night markets

stand
[stænd]
名 攤販

delicious
[dɪ`lɪʃəs]
形 美味的

packed
[pækt]
形 擁擠的；塞滿的

night market
片 夜市

oyster omelet
片 蚵仔煎

shaved ice
片 刨冰

stinky tofu
片 臭豆腐

tofu pudding
片 豆花

夜市文化 Night market culture | 進階學習

bargain
[`bɑrgɪn]
名 特價品 動 討價還價

civilian
[sə`vɪljən]
名 平民 形 平民的

diversity
[daɪ`vɝsətɪ]
名 多樣性

hawker
[`hɔkɚ]
名 叫賣小販

site
[saɪt]
名 位置；地點

vendor
[`vɛndɚ]
名 攤販

peddle
[`pɛdl]
動 叫賣；兜售

vend
[vɛnd]
動 叫賣；販賣

深度追蹤 🔍 *Knowing More*

　　夜市是「速食文化」的鼻祖，通常位於各區域發展最早且人潮最多的地方，並設在交通樞紐、廟會或市集的聚集處。夜市裡面不只有方便又快速、便宜又大碗的特色小吃，還有各種遊戲可以挑戰；每個夜市不同的特色小吃也反映出不同地區的文化背景，更是許多人從小到大的夜晚好去處。經過時間的考驗的小吃攤，由於大家的口耳相傳和捧場，這些有名的老店才得以繼續營業、滿足人們的口腹之慾，也成為陪伴人們一起長大的記憶之一。

 套個單字，想說的都能表達！

There is/are... 某處有⋯。

★ There are various stands at a night market.
在夜市裡有各式各樣的攤販。

★ There are many secret **tunnels** in the Pyramids.
金字塔裡有許多密道。

★ There are a variety of plants in the
botanical garden.
植物園中有各式各樣的植物。

★ There is definitely a **snitcher** in our
department.
我們部門裡面一定有個叛徒。

★ There are many recreation facilities in my
mansion.
我家公寓有附設許多休閒設施。

tunnel
[`tʌn]]
名 地道
botanical garden
片 植物園
snitcher
[`snɪtʃə]
名 告密者
mansion
[`mænʃən]
名 公寓；大廈

..., if possible. 可能的話，⋯。

★ Grace would come with us to the night market, if possible.
如果可以的話，葛雷絲會和我們一起去逛夜市。

★ That instructor will help you, if possible.
可能的話，那名指導員會幫忙你。

★ Rose would like to go on a two-month vacation,
if possible.
可能的話，蘿絲想要度假兩個月。

★ We hope to receive your **quotation** tomorrow
morning, if possible.
可能的話，我們希望明天一早就能收到你們的報價單。

★ We'll keep the **infectious** patients in
quarantine, if possible.
可能的話，我們會將得傳染病的病人安置在隔離區。

quotation
[kwo`teʃən]
名 報價單
infectious
[ɪn`fɛkʃəs]
形 傳染性的
quarantine
[`krɔrən,tin]
名 隔離區

開口必備句　和老外聊開懷，就靠這幾句！

I want to go to a night market and try some local snacks.
我想去逛夜市，嚐嚐一些道地的小吃。

Shi-Lin Night Market has some of the most famous food stands in Taiwan.
士林夜市裡有幾家台灣最知名的小吃攤。

Do you like the steamed spring roll at Ningxia night market?
你喜歡寧夏夜市裡賣的潤餅嗎？

My favorite food at this night market is tapioca milk tea.
在這個夜市裡，我最喜歡的是珍珠奶茶。

Many Japanese tourists especially love the pearl milk tea at this drink stand.
許多日本觀光客特別喜歡這個飲料攤賣的珍珠奶茶。

Have you tried chicken feet galantine before?
你吃過雞腳凍嗎？

I want to buy some pepper cakes for tomorrow's breakfast.
我想買一些胡椒餅當明天的早餐。

What is a double layer sausage?
什麼是大腸包小腸？

Though stinky tofu smells weird, it tastes quite good.
雖然臭豆腐聞起來有點奇怪，但還滿好吃的。

I want to order an oyster vermicelli and a hot and sour soup.
我想點一份蚵仔麵線和一碗酸辣湯。

Tofu pudding is a delicious dessert.
豆花是一道美味的甜點。

This Taiwanese meatball is extremely yummy.
這個肉圓真的超級好吃。

05 夜市搜刮時尚品
Fashion In Night Markets

吃喝

 單字基本功 掌握關鍵字 = 開口第一步

核心聯想 **夜市撿便宜 Making bargains**

earring [`ɪr,rɪŋ] 名 耳環	**foreigner** [`fɔrɪnɚ] 名 外國人	**necklace** [`nɛklɪs] 名 項鍊	**souvenir** [`suvə,nɪr] 名 紀念品
tourist [`tʊrɪst] 名 觀光客	**various** [`vɛrɪəs] 形 各式各樣的	**wonderful** [`wʌndəfəl] 形 極好的	**sell off** 片 廉價出售

夜市遊戲 Playing carnival games 進階學習

cast [kæst] 名 動 投擲	**exchange** [ɪks`tʃendʒ] 名 動 交換	**prize** [praɪz] 名 獎品 動 重視	**compete** [kəm`pit] 動 競爭；對抗
joyful [`dʒɔɪfəl] 形 愉快的	**goldfish scooping** 片 撈金魚	**pinball machine** 片 彈珠台	**ring toss** 片 套圈圈遊戲

 深度追蹤 𝒦𝓃ℴ𝓌𝒾𝓃ℊ 𝑀ℴ𝓇ℯ

　　台灣的「夜市文化」非常普遍，幾乎每個縣市，甚至小至鄉鎮、鄰里都會有夜市。夜市小吃攤聚集的人潮，更逐漸吸引愈來愈多的店家相繼在周邊設立，進而帶動周圍的服飾店、雜貨店、鞋店、以及各類餐飲的發展，而擴大夜市的商圈規模，所以夜市裡面販賣的物品應有盡有，匯聚美食小吃、雜貨、遊戲、休閒於一身。近年來，政府相關單位也輔導各大夜市轉化成「觀光夜市」，希望規劃出整齊的格局，讓外國觀光客也能深入認識台灣的在地風情。

套個單字，想說的都能表達！

sb. used to...　　某人以前…。

★ My colleagues and I used to go to the night market after work.
我和同事們以前下班後會都去夜市逛逛。

★ The president used to be an **eminent** linguist.
那位校長以前是著名的語言學家。

★ Skylar's mother used to **hum** her **lullabies** when she was little.
史嘉樂的母親在她小的時候會唱搖籃曲給她聽。

★ The comedian used to smoke a lot.
那名喜劇演員以前抽煙抽得很兇。

★ Our teacher used to **beguile** us with **fairy tales**.
我們老師以前會用童話故事吸引我們的注意。

eminent
[`ɛmənənt]
⑱ 著名的

hum
[hʌm]
⑩ 哼曲子

lullaby
[`lʌlə,baɪ]
⑭ 搖籃曲

beguile
[bɪ`gaɪl]
⑩ 吸引；使著迷

fairy tale
⑫ 童話故事

Is this one's first time...?　　某人第一次…嗎？

★ Is this your first time visiting Huaxi Street Night Market?
你是第一次來華西街夜市嗎？

★ Is this your first time experiencing **bungee jumping**?
這是你第一次體驗高空彈跳嗎？

★ Is this Jack's first time being an **examiner**?
這是傑克第一次擔任主考官嗎？

★ Is this the speaker's first time seeking a **postponement**?
這是那位講者第一次請求延期嗎？

★ Is this your company's first time holding a **conference**?
這是你們公司第一次舉辦研討會嗎？

bungee jumping
⑫ 高空彈跳

examiner
[ɪg`zæmɪnə]
⑭ 主考官

postponement
[post`ponmənt]
⑭ 延期

conference
[`kɑnfərəns]
⑭ 研討會；會議

This is my first time visiting a night market.
這是我第一次逛夜市。

Each night market has its own features and snacks that can be found in abundance.
每個夜市都有自己的特色，還可以在裡面找到許多小吃。

It's amazing how many different kinds of stands there are at this night market.
這個夜市裡有各式各樣的攤販，真令人大開眼界。

You can not only eat lots of foods at night markets, but also do some shopping.
在夜市裡，你不僅可以大吃一頓，還可以逛街買東西。

You can buy T-shirts, souvenirs, accessories, and so many more in night markets.
你可以在夜市裡買到 T 恤、紀念品、配件飾品……等等許多東西。

The best thing is, you can bargain.
最棒的是，你可以殺價。

I bought a pair of earrings at Shi-Da night market yesterday.
我昨天在師大夜市裡買了一副耳環。

The souvenir T-shirt I bought at the night market was not only cheap, but also very special.
我在夜市裡買的那件紀念 T 恤不但便宜，而且還非常特別。

This night market is always crowded with tourists from all over the world.
這個夜市裡總是擠滿了來自世界各地的觀光客。

I would love to come back and visit this night market again.
我希望有機會可以再回來逛逛這個夜市。

I ate a lot at Feng-Chia Night Market last week.
我上禮拜在逢甲夜市裡大吃特吃。

MP3 ▸ 097

日常 藏好你的祕密
Having Secrets

單字基本功 掌握關鍵字 = 開口第一步

核心聯想

傾訴心事 Pouring out your heart

advice
[əd`vaɪs]
名 建議；忠告

buddy
[`bʌdɪ]
名 好朋友

reaction
[rɪ`ækʃən]
名 反應；回應

relief
[rɪ`lif]
名 緩和；減輕

cheer sb. up
片 使某人開心起來

keep a secret
片 保守祕密

listen to
片 傾聽

open up to
片 對…敞開心胸

洩密或守密 Leaking or holding secrets

進階學習

apologize
[ə`pɑlə‚dʒaɪz]
動 道歉

chitchat
[`tʃɪt‚tʃæt]
動 閒談；聊天

clarify
[`klærə‚faɪ]
動 澄清；使清楚

confide
[kən`faɪd]
動 透露；吐露

mention
[`mɛnʃən]
動 提及；說起

peep
[pip]
名 動 偷看

harmful
[`hɑrmfəl]
形 有害的

spill the beans
片 洩密

深度追蹤 *Knowing More*

　　「祕密地；私下地」也可以用片語「under the rose」表示，這個片語來自於古羅馬神話，因為美神維納斯（Venus）偷情時被沉默之神（Harpocrates）發現，維納斯的兒子邱比特（Cupid）為了維護母親的名聲，便送了一朵白玫瑰給沉默之神，請祂保守這個祕密。因此，白玫瑰在古羅馬被視為「沉默」的象徵；若是到別人家中作客，發現天花板或桌上以玫瑰裝飾，就暗示在此的談話不能洩露出去，所有參與談話的人都必須保守祕密。

If you don't mind, ...　如果你不介意的話，…。

★ If you don't mind, you can tell me what keeps **bothering** you.
如果你不介意的話，可以和我說說你的心事。

★ If you don't mind, I've got another **appointment**.
如果你不介意的話，我另外還有約。

★ If you don't mind, Gina and I would like to join your team.
如果你不介意的話，吉娜和我想要加入你的團隊。

★ If you don't mind, please help me **proofread** my essay.
如果你不介意的話，請幫我校對我的論文。

★ If you don't mind, I have just a few quick questions for your son.
如果你不介意的話，我想要問你兒子一些簡短的問題。

> **bother**
> [`baðɚ]
> ⑩ 打擾；煩惱
> **appointment**
> [ə`pɔɪbtnəbt]
> 名 約定；約會
> **proofread**
> [`pruf, rid]
> ⑩ 校對

sb. apologize for...　某人為…道歉。

★ Dylan apologized for spilling the beans.
狄倫為了他洩密的行為道歉。

★ I must apologize for **disturbing** you like this.
我必須為了打擾您而致歉。

★ The politician apologized for taking **bribes** and lying to the public.
該名政客為了自己賄賂以及欺騙大眾的行為道歉。

★ My friend apologized for not telling me the truth.
我朋友因為沒有說實話，所以向我道歉。

★ The counselor apologized for **postponing** our appointment.
顧問為了延後會面的事而道歉。

> **disturb**
> [dɪs`tɜb]
> ⑩ 打擾
> **bribe**
> [braɪb]
> 名 賄賂
> ⑩ 收受賄賂
> **postpone**
> [post`pon]
> ⑩ 延後；延緩

MP3 099

開口必備句 和老外聊開懷，就靠這幾句！

What I'm going to tell you should stay between you and me.
我接下來要跟你說的事，不要跟別人講。

Nobody can know about this. Can you keep a secret?
誰都不能知道這件事。你可以保守秘密嗎？

My lips are sealed, so talk to me!
我的口風很緊，所以快跟我說！

I've been a bit depressed lately. Can I talk to you for a while?
我最近有點沮喪，可以跟你說說話嗎？

You can trust me and open up to me.
你可以相信我並對我坦誠。

True friends will listen to you when you are in trouble, and they will always keep your secrets.
當你有困難的時候，真正的朋友會聽你訴說，他們也會替你保守秘密。

Secrets are best shared only among close friends.
秘密最好只有密友知道就好。

Do you know who spread the confidential information about our company?
你知道是誰把我們公司的機密說出去的嗎？

Ryan confided in me that he was dating my sister.
萊恩跟我坦白說，他在和我的妹妹約會。

Andrew isn't good at keeping secrets at all. He'll be pouring his guts out after one shot of Tequila.
安德魯完全無法保守秘密，他只要喝一杯龍舌蘭，就什麼話都說出來了。

It had been a secret until Hannah brought it into the open.
到漢娜說出去之前，這一直是秘密。

Amy is such a blabbermouth, so no one trusts her.
愛咪是個大嘴巴，所以沒有人相信她。

UNIT 07

日常

樂觀和悲觀
Optimism & Pessimism

 單字基本功 ✏ 掌握關鍵字 = 開口第一步

核心聯想 **樂觀型人格 Optimistic people**

angle [`æŋgl] 名 角度；立場	**attitude** [`ætətjud] 名 態度；看法	**benefit** [`bɛnəfɪt] 名 好處 動 有益於	**challenge** [`tʃælɪndʒ] 名 動 挑戰
appreciate [ə`priʃɪˌet] 動 欣賞；感謝	**curious** [`kjʊrɪəs] 形 好奇的	**optimistic** [ˌɑptə`mɪstɪk] 形 樂觀的	**positive** [`pɑzətɪv] 形 正向的

 悲觀型人格 Pessimistic people 進階學習

burden [`bɜdən] 名 動 負擔	**lonely** [`lonlɪ] 形 孤單的	**negative** [`nɛgətɪv] 形 負面的	**painful** [`penfəl] 形 痛苦的
pessimistic [ˌpɛsə`mɪstɪk] 形 悲觀的	**hardly** [`hardlɪ] 副 幾乎不	**inherently** [ɪn`hɪrəntlɪ] 副 天性地	**stressed out** 片 壓力非常大的

深度追蹤 🔍 *Knowing More*

　　「悲觀」和「樂觀」都可以是一個人看待事物的態度，樂觀的人看任何事物總能想到好的一面，而悲觀的人則會先看到事物不好的一面，但這並不代表悲觀是不好的。著名的心理學家潘那貝克博士曾提出「建設性負面情緒」，在他的實驗中顯示，若讓悲觀性格的人用適合他們個性的「建設性方式」去解決問題，比強迫他們採取樂觀者的思考方式更有效，而此方法也常用來輔導重大心理創傷的患者，成功輔導沮喪的人運用建設性的思考方式解決問題。

MP3 ▶ 101

套個單字，想說的都能表達！

Please let me know when...

…的時候，請讓我知道。

★ Please let me know when you need someone to talk to.
當你需要找人聊聊的時候，請告訴我一聲。

★ Please let me know when your passport **expires**.
當你的護照過期時，請跟我說一聲。

★ Please let me know when the new law **takes effect**.
新法開始生效的時候，請告訴我一聲。

★ Please let me know when you arrive.
當你抵達時，請告訴我一聲。

★ Please let me know when you **make up your mind**.
當你下定決心時，請讓我知道你的決定。

> **expire**
> [ɪk`spaɪr]
> 動 過期
> **take effect**
> 片 生效
> **make up one's mind**
> 片 某人下定決心

All sb. need is... 某人需要的是…。

★ All you need is to take a good night's sleep.
你最需要的是好好睡一覺。

★ All you need is enough sleep and a **balanced** diet.
你需要足夠的睡眠和均衡的飲食。

★ All you need is an interesting topic and some **stimulations**.
你需要一個有趣的主題和一些激勵。

★ All you need is to arrange a stable **organizational** structure.
你需要安排一個穩定的組織架構。

★ All you need is a little instruction and a lot of practice.
你需要一些指導還有大量的練習。

> **balanced**
> [`bælənst]
> 形 平衡的
> **stimulation**
> [ˌstɪmjə`leʃən]
> 名 刺激；激勵
> **organizational**
> [ˌɔrgənaɪ`zeʃənl]
> 形 組織的

115

開口必備句

和老外聊開懷，就靠這幾句！

Happiness is not only an attitude but also a genetic disposition.

🔊 快樂不但是一種態度，也是一種天性。

Do you see the glass as half-full or half-empty?

🔊 你覺得杯內的水是半滿還是半空？

My teacher believes that people should always look on the bright side of life.

🔊 我的老師深信，人們應該要多看人生的光明面。

"Nothing is impossible" is Allison's motto.

🔊 「凡事都有可能」是愛麗森的座右銘。

"Whether you think you can or think you can't, you're right," once said Henry Ford, the founder of the Ford Motor Company.

🔊 福特汽車的創辦人亨利‧福特說過：「當你覺得你辦得到或者辦不到時，你永遠是對的。」

Pessimism may lead to failure, especially when you think things will turn out poorly and, as a result, take no action.

🔊 悲觀可能導致失敗，尤其當你覺得事情的結果會很糟，而因此不採取任何行動。

What kind of person are you, a pessimist or an optimist?

🔊 你是悲觀者還是樂觀者？

Which do you think is better, pessimism or optimism?

🔊 你覺得悲觀比較好，還是樂觀比較好？

Some people would rather expect the worst and be pleasantly surprised when things turn out fine.

🔊 有些人寧願把事情想到最糟，而當事情的結果還好時，便感到喜出望外。

An optimist is more likely to think he or she is always right.

🔊 樂觀者比較可能覺得自己總是對的。

UNIT 08

旅遊

墾丁春吶行
Spring Scream In Kenting

單字基本功 掌握關鍵字＝開口第一步

核心聯想

參加春吶活動 Spring Scream

beach [bitʃ] 名 海灘	**bikini** [bɪˋkinɪ] 名 比基尼泳裝
stage [stedʒ] 名 舞台 動 上演	**attend** [əˋtɛnd] 動 參加；出席

festive [ˋfɛstɪv] 形 喜慶的	**touching** [ˋtʌtʃɪŋ] 形 感人的
live band 片 現場演奏樂團	**Spring Scream** 片 春天吶喊

玩玩水上活動 Water activities 進階學習

snorkeling [ˋsnɔrklɪŋ] 名 浮潛	**surfing** [ˋsɜfɪŋ] 名 衝浪
paradise [ˋpærəˏdaɪs] 名 天堂	**parasailing** [ˋpærəˏselɪŋ] 名 拖曳傘

including [ɪnˋkludɪŋ] 介 包含；包括	**banana boating** 片 香蕉船
jet skis 片 水上摩托車	**water sports** 片 水上運動

深度追蹤

Knowing More

　　「春天吶喊」源起於一九九五年的春天，兩位住在墾丁的美國人——Wade和Jimi，他們決定把小型演奏會擴展成慶祝派對，於是邀請許多原創樂團一起到墾丁，用三天三夜盡情玩音樂，便開始了第一個春天吶喊音樂祭。遠離壓力、慵懶、貼近自然是春吶的三個核心元素，比起重視硬體設備的好壞，在這裡的演出推崇的是樂團獨創性，以及如何使用簡易器材把玩出有創意的音樂。而且除了音樂，還有許多美食攤位和表演活動來吸引遊客參加。

Is/Are sb. interested in...?　某人對…有興趣嗎？

★ Are you interested in electronic music?
你對電子音樂感興趣嗎？

★ Is your son interested in playing **Rubik's cube**?
你的兒子對魔術方塊有興趣嗎？

★ Are your friends interested in watching the **quiz show**?
你朋友對益智節目有興趣嗎？

★ Are you interested in applying for the **scholarship**?
你有興趣申請獎學金嗎？

★ Is your classmate interested in having **tattoos**?
你同學對刺青有興趣嗎？

> **Rubik's cube**
> 片 魔術方塊
> **quiz show**
> 片 問答節目
> **scholarship**
> [`skɑlə͵ʃɪp]
> 名 獎學金
> **tattoo**
> [tæ`tu]
> 名 刺青

As long as..., ...　只要… ，… 。

★ As long as you can play a guitar, you may join our band.
只要你會彈吉他，就能加入我們的樂團。

★ As long as you follow the **traffic rules**, you'll be safe.
只要遵守交通規則，你就會很安全。

★ As long as you continue exercising, you'll improve your health.
只要你持續運動，就能增進健康。

★ As long as you're **alive**, you'll have to face the reality.
只要你還活著，就得面對現實。

★ As long as we hang together, we'll **overcome** the difficulties.
只要我們團結一致，就能克服困難。

> **traffic rules**
> 片 交通規則
> **alive**
> [ə`laɪv]
> 形 活著的
> **overcome**
> [͵ovə`kʌm]
> 動 克服

MP3 ▶ 105

開口必備句　和老外聊開懷，就靠這幾句！

Band applications for the Spring Scream should be received by January 31.
想參加春天吶喊的樂團，必須在一月三十一日前提出申請。

Spring Scream is an outdoor music festival held in April.
春天吶喊是在四月舉辦的戶外音樂節。

Spring Scream was organized by two Americans in 1995.
春天吶喊在一九九五年由兩位美國人所創辦。

You will see lots of indie bands performing at Spring Scream every year.
每年的春天吶喊，你都會看到很多獨立樂團的表演。

Kenting is a paradise for young people with all its sunny beaches.
墾丁因為有陽光和沙灘，而成為年輕人的天堂。

Let's try a typical restaurant on Kenting's main street.
我們就在墾丁大街上選一家特色小吃店試試吧！

Have you ever been to Spring Scream?
你有去過春天吶喊嗎？

The National Museum of Marine Biology & Aquarium is a popular scenic spot for both children and adults.
國立海洋生物博物館是大人和小孩都喜愛的景點。

I am looking forward to the sleepover in the National Museum of Marine Biology & Aquarium.
我很期待夜宿海生館的行程。

My friend loves going surfing in Nanwan.
我朋友喜歡到南灣衝浪。

How can I sign up for surfing lessons?
我要怎麼報名衝浪課程呢？

UNIT 09 校園

大考小考
Preparing For Exams

單字基本功 掌握關鍵字 = 開口第一步

準備考試 Exam preparation

chapter [`tʃæptɚ] 名 章節	**a perfect score** 片 滿分	**final exam** 片 期末考	**midterm exam** 片 期中考
open-book exam 片 翻書考	**prepare for** 片 為…作準備	**stay up** 片 熬夜	**study group** 片 讀書小組

作弊與後果 Cheating & consequences

進階學習

cheating [`tʃitɪŋ] 名 作弊；欺騙	**excuse** [ɪk`skjuz] 名 藉口 動 原諒	**scold** [skold] 名 動 責罵	**shame** [ʃem] 名 羞愧 動 使羞愧
panic [`pænɪk] 動 使恐慌	**regret** [rɪ`grɛt] 動 後悔；感到遺憾	**dishonest** [dɪs`ɑnɪst] 形 不誠實的	**at all** 片 絲毫；根本

 深度追蹤

Knowing More

　　在國外，老師通常會先在第一堂課分發教學大綱（syllabus），上面會清楚註明課程介紹和分數比重。而學生最在意的分數比重，除了作業之外，通常還包含：(1) 課堂參與（class participation）：往往是決定學生成績的主要因素。(2) 期中考：考試形式常為紙筆考試或繳交論文（term papers）。(3) 小考（exam）或是隨堂測驗（pop quiz）：用來隨機測驗學生程度。(4) 期末考：通常是佔最大比例的一項，會在放暑假或寒假的前一周舉行。

MP3 ⊙ 107

套個單字，想說的都能表達！

...be supposed to...　…應該要…。

- ★ You are supposed to hand in your paper a week before the midterm.
  你們必須在期中考前一週繳交報告。

- ★ Everybody is supposed to be **equal** before the law.
  法律之前，人人平等。

- ★ Our class was supposed to begin at nine o'clock this morning.
  我們原本要在今天早上九點就開始上課的。

- ★ Journalists are supposed to **take the trouble to** check the facts.
  記者應該要不厭其煩地查明真相。

- ★ We are supposed to bring some souvenirs for the **hostess**.
  我們應該要帶一些伴手禮送給女主人。

equal
[`ikwəl]
形 平等的

take the trouble to...
片 不怕困難而去做…

hostess
[`hostɪs]
名 女主人

Is/are sb. done with...?　某人完成…了嗎？

- ★ Are you done with your assignment?
  你的作業做完了嗎？

- ★ Are the students done with their final papers?
  學生們都完成他們的期末報告了嗎？

- ★ Is the movie star done with her **press conference**?
  那位電影明星的記者會結束了嗎？

- ★ Is the engineer done with his **drawings**?
  那位工程師完成他的工程圖了嗎？

- ★ Is the statesman done with writing his **memoirs**?
  那位政治家寫完他的回憶錄了嗎？

press conference
片 記者會

drawing
[`drɔɪŋ]
名 製圖；圖形

memoir
[`mɛmwɑr]
名 回憶錄

121

開口必備句　和老外聊開懷，就靠這幾句！

The midterm exam will be next week.
下個星期是期中考。

The exam covers chapter one to ten, supplementary materials excluded.
考試範圍是第一章到第十章，不包括補充教材。

This is an open-book exam.
這次考試是開書考。

Let's form a study group and prepare for the exam together.
我們來組個讀書小組，一起準備考試吧。

I have three more chapters to study, so tonight I'll have to burn the midnight oil.
我還有三個章節要唸，所以今晚得熬夜讀書了。

Did you stay up all night studying for the exam?
你為了準備考試才整晚熬夜的嗎？

I reviewed my notes three times last night.
我昨晚將我的筆記複習了三次。

I am so doomed. I didn't study at all for the final exam!
我完蛋了，期末考我完全沒有準備！

Cheating on the exam is not allowed.
考試中不可作弊。

I got a perfect score on the quiz today.
今天的小考我得到滿分。

I'll forget everything after the exam.
我一考完試就會把所有東西都忘光。

Perhaps I should hire a tutor for my physics next semester.
或許下個學期，我應該請一位家教來教我物理。

Part 05

五月提升自我魅力

May Highlights:
Relationships, & Office Gossips

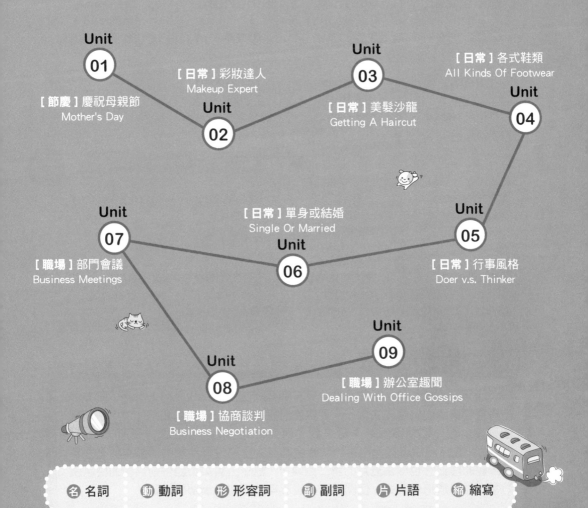

Unit 01
[節慶] 慶祝母親節
Mother's Day

[日常] 彩妝達人
Makeup Expert
Unit 02

Unit 03
[日常] 美髮沙龍
Getting A Haircut

[日常] 各式鞋類
All Kinds Of Footwear
Unit 04

Unit 05
[日常] 行事風格
Doer v.s. Thinker

[日常] 單身或結婚
Single Or Married
Unit 06

Unit 07
[職場] 部門會議
Business Meetings

Unit 09
[職場] 辦公室趣聞
Dealing With Office Gossips

Unit 08
[職場] 協商談判
Business Negotiation

名 名詞　動 動詞　形 形容詞　副 副詞　片 片語　縮 縮寫

UNIT 01 節慶

慶祝母親節
Mother's Day

單字基本功 掌握關鍵字＝開口第一步

母愛的光輝 Maternal love

patience [`peʃəns] 名 耐心；忍耐	warmth [wɔrmθ] 名 溫暖；暖意	nurture [`nɝtʃɚ] 動 養育；培育	beloved [bɪ`lʌvɪd] 形 親愛的；受喜愛的
caring [`kɛrɪŋ] 形 慈愛的；有愛心的	willing [`wɪlɪŋ] 形 心甘情願的	tenderly [`tɛndəlɪ] 副 溫柔地；體貼地	take care of 片 照顧

表達感謝 Sending thanks to mom

carnation [kɑr`neʃən] 名 康乃馨	gift [gɪft] 名 禮物；天賦	intimacy [`ɪntəməsɪ] 名 親密；私下	massage [mə`saʒ] 名 動 按摩
mother [`mʌðɚ] 名 母親 動 生產	sentiment [`sɛmtəmənt] 名 感情；多愁善感	surprise [sə`praɪz] 名 驚喜 動 使驚喜	special [`spɛʃəl] 形 特別的

 深度追蹤 🔎 Knowing More

　　西元一八七二年，美國女性作家茱莉亞赫薇（Julia Ward Howe）眼見許多母親在美國內戰中痛失愛子，便鼓吹訂定一個節日以提倡和平，但這個建議卻只有少數幾個地區採行；後來到了西元一九〇七年，安娜賈維斯（Anna Jarvis）在自己的母親過世後，決定發起訂定全國性母親節的活動，於是在自己母親的忌日，也就是五月的第二個週日，訂了五百朵母親生前最愛的白色康乃馨，並舉辦追思儀式，便開始了全世界第一個母親節慶祝活動。

MP3 ▶ 110

套個單字，想說的都能表達！

sb. feel like...　某人想要…。

★ My mother and I feel like going **skiing** in winter.
我媽媽和我想要在冬天的時候去滑雪。

★ My uncle feels like **hunting** in the mountains.
我叔叔想要在山裡打獵。

★ My parents feel like strolling in the park after dinner.
我爸媽想吃完晚餐後到公園散步。

★ Claire feels like going out tonight with her boyfriend.
克萊兒今晚想要和男友出門。

★ Ellie feels like starting a business with her friends.
愛莉想和朋友一起創業。

> **ski**
> [ski]
> ⑩ 滑雪
> **hunt**
> [hʌnt]
> ⑩ 打獵；追捕

sb. can/can't afford to...　某人負擔得起 / 負擔不起…。

★ We can **afford** to buy this necklace for Mom.
我們買得起這條項鍊送母親。

★ The poor student can't afford to go to the theater.
那名窮學生負擔不起看電影的錢。

★ Most **salarymen** can't afford to buy luxury goods.
大多數上班族買不起奢侈品。

★ Her **deputy** can't afford to make any mistake at this stage.
她的代理人在這個階段不能再犯任何錯誤。

★ My family can't afford to send me to the **private school**.
我家人負擔不起我去唸私立學校的學費。

> **afford**
> [ə`ford]
> ⑩ 買得起
> **salarymen**
> [`sælərɪ͵mɛn]
> ⑧ 上班族
> **deputy**
> [`dɛpjətɪ]
> ⑧ 代理人
> **private school**
> ⑮ 私立學校

開口必備句 和老外聊開懷，就靠這幾句！

Mother's Day is a day for every loving mother in the world.
母親節謹獻給世界上每一位慈愛的母親。

Mother's Day is celebrated on various days in different parts of the world.
世界各地會在不同的日子慶祝母親節。

Officially, Mother's Day was first celebrated in 1908 in the United States.
第一個正式母親節是在一九〇八年於美國慶祝的。

Do you know when Mother's Day was introduced in Taiwan?
你知道台灣是從何時開始慶祝母親節的嗎？

Mother's Day is a day to honor all the devotion and the sacrifices of every mother.
母親節是向每位母親的付出與犧牲表示敬意的日子。

What are you going to give Mom on Mother's Day?
你打算在母親節送媽媽什麼呢？

The carnation is the symbol of Mother's Day.
康乃馨是母親節的象徵。

A lot of schoolchildren will make cards for their mothers on Mother's Day.
許多學童會親手做卡片，在母親節送給媽媽。

A mother's hug always conveys the warmest care and love.
母親的擁抱總是傳遞著最溫暖的關心和愛意。

Most restaurants are fully booked on Mother's Day.
大多數餐廳在母親節都已被訂滿。

Some people would even make cakes by themselves on Mother's Day.
有些人在母親節的時候甚至會自己做蛋糕送給母親。

MP3 ▶ 112

02 日常 彩妝達人
Makeup Experts

單字基本功 掌握關鍵字 = 開口第一步

 核心聯想

化妝部位 Applying makeups

cheekbone [`tʃik͵bon] 名 顴骨	**chin** [tʃɪn] 名 下巴	**eyebrow** [`aɪ͵brau] 名 眉毛	**eyelash** [`aɪ͵læʃ] 名 眼睫毛
eyelid [`aɪ͵lɪd] 名 眼皮	**forehead** [`fɔr͵hɛd] 名 額頭	**lip** [lɪp] 名 嘴唇	**T-Zone** 片 T 字部位

 化妝品 All kinds of cosmetics **進階學習**

blush [blʌʃ] 名 腮紅；臉紅	**contour** [`kɑntur] 名 輪廓 動 畫輪廓	**concealer** [kən`silɚ] 名 遮瑕膏	**foundation** [faun`deʃən] 名 粉底
mascara [mæs`kærə] 名 睫毛膏	**highlight** [`haɪ͵laɪt] 動 打亮；強調	**waterproof** [`wɔtɚ͵pruf] 形 防水的	**lip gloss** 片 唇蜜

 深度追蹤 *Knowing More*

在伸展台或電影後台，常會看到彩妝師（makeup artist）穿梭其中、幫演員或模特兒化妝和補妝；不過，彩妝師還可分為較資淺的助理彩妝師（assistant makeup artist）和資深彩妝師（senior makeup artist），還有負責引領彩妝大小事的「首席彩妝師 key makeup artist」；從與導演、髮型設計師、服裝設計師一同訂定彩妝風格，到解決演員、模特兒或其他彩妝師的問題，都少不了首席彩妝師的功勞。

句型偷吃步　套個單字，想說的都能表達！

...compliment sb. on sth.　…稱讚某人做的某事。

★ The actress complimented the **makeup artist** on her techniques.
那位女演員對化妝師的技術讚許有加。

★ We complimented the dancer on her excellent performance.
我們都稱讚那名舞者的表演很完美。

★ My parents complimented the cook on his beautiful plate presentation.
我爸媽對那名廚師的擺盤藝術大加讚美。

★ People complimented the **firefighter** on his **courage**.
人們都稱讚那名消防員的勇氣。

★ The couple complimented Elena on the stunning **decor**.
那對夫婦對伊蓮娜完成的室內裝潢讚不絕口。

makeup artist
片 彩妝師
firefighter
[`faɪr͵faɪtɚ]
名 消防員
courage
[͵kɝɪdʒ]
名 勇氣；膽量
decor
[de`kɔr]
名 室內裝潢

What's one's opinion on...?　你對…的意見是什麼？

★ What's your opinion on this new concealer?
你對這支新的遮瑕膏有什麼意見？

★ What's that film critic's opinion on this horror movie?
那名影評家對這部恐怖片的看法是什麼？

★ What's the specialist's opinion on **grandparenting**?
那名專家對隔代教養有什麼看法？

★ What's our president's opinion on **corporal** punishment of children?
我們校長對於體罰孩子有什麼看法？

★ What's the director's opinion on the **malpractice**?
院長對於那件醫療過失事件有什麼看法？

grandparenting
[`grænd͵pɛrəntɪŋ]
名 隔代教養
corporal
[`kɔrpərəl]
形 肉體的
malpractice
[mæl`præktɪs]
名 醫療疏失；誤診

MP3 ▶ 114

和老外聊開懷，就靠這幾句！

We have lipsticks in a wide range of colors. Do you want to try one?

我們有多款顏色的唇膏，你想要試用嗎？

Do you have a base makeup in a lighter tone?

你有顏色亮一點的粉底嗎？

BB cream is popular among teenage girls.

BB 霜廣受青少女的歡迎。

Remember, just apply a thin layer of the foundation, or you may ruin all the makeup you apply on top.

記得，粉底只要上薄薄的一層就好，否則會毀了整個妝容。

The secret of putting on perfect makeup is to practice.

完美彩妝的秘訣就是要反覆練習。

Anna spends an hour doing her makeup every morning.

安娜每天早上都要花一個小時來化妝。

You can get free samples at the counter.

您可以在櫃檯索取免費的試用品。

It is extremely important for you to have a good powder brush.

擁有一支好用的蜜粉刷非常重要。

This specially-designed brush can lengthen your eyelashes beyond your imagination.

這支特製刷具可超乎想像地拉長您的睫毛。

This color palette features twelve gorgeous eye shadows, which are waterproof.

這個眼影盤有十二款亮彩防水眼影。

Gently remove your make-up with a cotton pad before washing your face.

洗臉之前，先用化妝棉輕輕地卸掉你的彩妝。

UNIT
日常

03 美髮沙龍
Getting A Haircut

單字基本功　掌握關鍵字＝開口第一步

核心聯想

多變髮型 Styling your hair

bang [bæŋ] 名 瀏海	**braid** [bred] 名 辮子	**dye** [daɪ] 名 染料 動 染髮	**perm** [pɜm] 名 動 燙髮
straight [stret] 形 直的；直率的	**ceramic perm** 片 陶瓷燙	**trim off** 片 修剪	**thin out** 片 打薄

 各種美髮工具 Hairstyling tools

進階學習

comb [kom] 名 梳子 動 梳頭髮	**clipper** [`klɪpə] 名 推剪；指甲剪	**scissor** [`sɪzə] 名 剪刀	**blow dryer** 片 吹風機
curling iron 片 電棒	**hair clip** 片 大髮夾	**hair spray** 片 定型液	**hair wax** 片 髮蠟

 深度追蹤 🔍 　　　　　Knowing More

　　說到染髮，就不得不知歐美髮型師常用的各種技巧，例如「漸層染髮 ombre hair」能讓髮色有深至淺的柔和漸層；「束挑 balayage」則是將頭髮分成一束束挑染，過程細膩繁複，但能平衡整頭的髮色，較有強烈的線條感。髮色方面，有可在黑暗中閃閃發亮的螢光色（neon glowing hair），最近還流行染成銀灰色，甚至有「星空混染 galaxy palette」能將星空的顏色染到頭髮上。想要改變個人風格，或許也可考慮換個適合自己的髮色呢！

句型偷吃步　套個單字，想說的都能表達！

How often do/does sb. ...? 某人多久…一次？

- ★ How often do you have a **haircut**?
  你多久剪一次頭髮？

- ★ How often do you go to a movie?
  你多久看一次電影？

- ★ How often do you **back up** your **database**?
  你多久備份一次你的電腦？

- ★ How often does your landlord replace the carpet?
  你的房東多久換一次地毯？

- ★ How often does the **association** hold an academic **forum**?
  協會多久舉辦一次學術講座？

> **haircut**
> [`hɛr,kʌt]
> 名 剪髮
> **back up**
> 片 備份
> **database**
> [`detə,bes]
> 名（電腦）資料庫
> **association**
> [ə,sosɪ`eʃən]
> 名 協會
> **forum**
> [`forəm]
> 名 討論會

What made sb. decide to...?

是什麼原因讓某人決定要…的？

- ★ What made you decide to cut your long hair?
  是什麼原因讓你決定剪掉那頭長髮呢？

- ★ What made you decide to study abroad?
  什麼原因讓你決定要到國外讀書的？

- ★ What made the couple decide to bury the hatchet?
  是什麼原因讓那對夫妻言歸於好呢？

- ★ What made the government decide to **amend** the **constitution**?
  是什麼原因讓政府決定要修改憲法的？

- ★ What made that judge decide to postpone the public **hearing**?
  是什麼原因讓那位法官把公聽會延期呢？

> **amend**
> [ə`mɛnd]
> 動 修改（法律）；修補
> **constitution**
> [,kɑnstə`tjuʃən]
> 名 憲法
> **hearing**
> [`hɪrɪŋ]
> 名（法）聽證會

開口必備句　和老外聊開懷，就靠這幾句！

I would like to make an appointment with my stylist for this Sunday afternoon.
🔊 我想和我的設計師預約本週日下午。

Do you know any good hair salons? I am thinking about changing my hairstyle.
🔊 你推薦哪家不錯的美髮沙龍嗎？我正考慮換個髮型。

I just want to get my hair trimmed a little bit.
🔊 我只想稍微修一下頭髮。

I would like a wash and a cut, please.
🔊 我要洗加剪，麻煩了。

How long will it take to perm my hair?
🔊 燙頭髮要花多久時間？

I'll cut your hair first, and then thin it out if necessary.
🔊 我會先剪短你的頭髮，如有需要的話也會打薄。

After lightening the base with smoky lavender, the hairstylist deepened her roots with a charcoal color.
🔊 設計師將她的頭髮先染成薰衣草紫色之後，再用木炭色加深了一點髮根的顏色。

My mother always gets a perm every other month.
🔊 我媽媽總是每兩個月燙一次頭髮。

Caroline's new hairdo is very cute. She looks just like Carey Mulligan.
🔊 卡洛琳的新髮型很可愛，她看起來就像凱芮 · 穆雷根。

Danny dyed his hair green, and it drives his father mad.
🔊 丹尼把頭髮染成綠色，所以他爸爸快氣瘋了。

Gary looks much younger with his new hairdo.
🔊 蓋瑞的新髮型讓他看起來更加年輕。

MP3 ▶ 118

日常

各式鞋類
All Kinds Of Footwear

單字基本功 掌握關鍵字 = 開口第一步

 核心聯想 **鞋子有哪些 Various shoes**

boot [but] 名 靴子	**flat** [flæt] 名 平底鞋 形 平的	**sandal** [`sændl̩] 名（露趾）涼鞋	**slipper** [`slɪpə] 名 拖鞋
sneaker [`snikə] 名 球鞋	**wellie** [`wɛlɪ] 名 橡膠靴	**high heels** 片 高跟鞋	**training shoes** 片 運動鞋

製作與保養 Making & preserving **進階學習**

leather [`lɛðə] 名 皮革	**sole** [sol] 名 鞋底	**stitch** [stɪtʃ] 名 針線 動 縫；繡	**measure** [`mɛʒə] 動 測量
polish [`palɪʃ] 動 擦亮	**smooth** [smuð] 動 使平滑 形 平滑的	**artificial** [ˌartə`fɪʃəl] 形 人工的	**sturdy** [`stɜdɪ] 形 耐用的

 深度追蹤 *Knowing More*

　　在國外，想進去鞋店逛逛的話，最常聽到以及用到的英文就一定要學起來！像是店員常會先問：「What size do you wear? 你穿幾號的鞋子？」；而試穿後若鞋子不合尺寸，可以說：「It doesn't fit me. / It's not my size. 這款不合我的腳」，再問店員有沒有合適尺寸：「Do you have it in any other sizes? 有其他尺寸嗎？ / What other sizes are available? 還有什麼尺寸呢？ / Have you got it in small, please? 有再小號一點的嗎？」。

Can/Could sb. have a look at...?
某人可以看一下…嗎?

- ★ Can I have a look at the smaller size?
  我可以看看小號一點的尺寸嗎?

- ★ Could you have a look at my broken watch?
  你可以看一下我壞掉的手錶嗎?

- ★ Can the freshmen have a look at the **laboratory** before class?
  在上課前,新生們可以先看一下實驗室嗎?

- ★ Could the **appraiser** have a look at the emeralds I bought?
  鑑定師可以看一下我買的綠寶石嗎?

- ★ Could you have a look at the news about the **conflagration**?
  你可以看一下這場大火的新聞嗎?

laboratory
[ˋlæbrə͵torɪ]
名 實驗室
appraiser
[əˋprezɚ]
名 鑑定者
conflagration
[͵kɑnfləˋgreʃən]
名 火災

Where can sb. get...?　某人能從哪裡取得…?

- ★ Where can I get the newest model?
  哪裡能買到最新的款式呢?

- ★ Where can the freshmen get their registration **slips**?
  新生要去哪裡領取註冊單呢?

- ★ Where can we get our train tickets?
  我們要到哪裡領我們的火車票呢?

- ★ Where can the users get the older **version** of this **software**?
  使用者們要去哪裡才能取得這個軟體以前的版本呢?

- ★ Where can we get information about the disease?
  我們要去哪裡才能取得這個疾病的資訊呢?

slip
[slɪp]
名 紙條
version
[ˋvɝʒən]
名 版本
software
[ˋsɔft͵wɛr]
名 軟體

MP3 ▶ 120

Running shoes provide more cushioning and support, which often translates into a higher heel drop.

慢跑鞋提供較多緩衝和支撐的功能，所以鞋底通常也會比較高。

Our son has outgrown his canvas shoes. Let's get him a new pair on Christmas.

我們兒子的帆布鞋已經不合腳了，耶誕節再送他一雙新的吧。

I am looking for a pair of all-weather shoes.

我正在找一雙適合各種天候穿的鞋。

Excuse me. I would like to try on these in a size six, please.

不好意思，我想要試穿這款的六號。

Sorry, but we don't have size five right now.

抱歉，我們目前沒有五號的尺寸。

We have three different colors: green, red, and black. Which one would you like?

我們有三款不同的顏色：綠色、紅色和黑色。您想要哪一款？

What is this pair of shoes made of, real or synthetic leather?

這雙鞋是以真皮還是合成皮製成的？

Aren't there too many lace holes in this shoe?

這隻鞋的鞋帶孔不會太多了嗎？

You'd better try the shoes on before you buy them.

你最好在購買前先試穿鞋子。

The new wedges fit Sarah like a glove.

這雙新的楔型鞋很合莎拉的腳。

Did you wear your boots in the rain?

你是不是穿著靴子淋雨？

How to prevent your new shoes from giving you blisters?

有什麼方法可以不讓新鞋咬腳呢？

05 日常 行事風格
Doer v.s. Thinker

 單字基本功 ▷ 掌握關鍵字 = 開口第一步

 核心聯想

積極熱血行動派 Being active

actionist	explore	observe	active
[`ækʃənɪst]	[ɪk`splor]	[əb`zɜv]	[`æktɪv]
名 行動派	動 探索；探究	動 觀察；注意到	形 主動的

inspiring	pay attention to	put into practice	take the initiative
[ɪn`spaɪrɪŋ]			
形 鼓舞人心的	片 注意…	片 付諸實行	片 採取主動

含蓄守舊保守派 Being reserved

進階學習

settlement	shrink	conservative	passive
[`sɛtḷmənt]	[ʃrɪŋk]	[kən`sɜvətɪv]	[`pæsɪv]
名 安排；解決	動 收縮；退縮	形 守舊的；傳統的	形 被動的

reserved	silent	studious	seldom
[rɪ`zɜvd]	[`saɪlənt]	[`stjudɪəs]	[`sɛldəm]
形 含蓄的；拘謹的	形 沉默的	形 一心一意的	副 不常；很少

 深度追蹤 🔍

Knowing More

　　「主動」在職場上，應是在職責範圍之外，再多做沒有人預期或要求你去做的事情，既不計較待遇，也不斤斤計較責任範圍。若只是把「該做的工作做完」，便不是主動，只是在盡本份而已；而在生活各方面的主動，應是積極閱讀、拓展人脈、嘗試新事物……等等，並從各種人生遭遇之中成長、獲得經驗。而「主動」與「被動」往往就在一念之間，若是在行動、精神層面都保持主動，相信每個人都能擁有充實又順利的人生以及職場生活！

MP3 ▶ 122

套個單字，想說的都能表達！

sb. have confidence in...　某人對…有信心。

★ I have confidence in what you suggested.
我對你的建議很有信心。

★ **Policemen** have confidence in discovering the truth.
警察有信心能找出真相。

★ That **delegate** had confidence in accomplishing his **mission**.
那名代表有信心能完成自己的使命。

★ The government has confidence in our country and its economic development.
政府對我們的國家以及經濟發展很有信心。

★ The coach has confidence in his strategies and his players.
教練對他的策略還有球員都很有信心。

> **policeman**
> [pə`lismən]
> 名 警察
> **delegate**
> [`dɛlə‚get]
> 名 代表
> **mission**
> [`mɪʃən]
> 名 使命；任務

sb. have difficulty in...　某人有…的困難。

★ Pete had difficulty in expressing his ideas at the meeting.
彼特在會議上難以表達自己的想法。

★ Perry has difficulty in **rewriting** the paper.
派瑞覺得重寫這份報告困難重重。

★ The girl used to have difficulty in **pronouncing** certain **vowels**.
那位女孩曾經發不太出幾個母音。

★ The widower has difficulty in receiving others' affection for him.
那名鰥夫難以接受他人的感情。

★ The **spoiled** kid had difficulty in adjusting to life in the army.
那名被寵壞的男孩難以適應軍中生活。

> **rewrite**
> [ri`raɪt]
> 動 重寫；改寫
> **pronounce**
> [prə`naʊns]
> 動 發音
> **vowel**
> [`vaʊəl]
> 名 母音
> **spoiled**
> [spɔɪlt]
> 形 被寵壞的

開口必備句 和老外聊開懷，就靠這幾句！

Actions speak louder than words.
坐而言不如起而行。

Alice always puts all of her ideas into practice.
愛麗絲總是將想法付諸實行。

Adam describes himself as an actionist who always focuses on inspiring people around to achieve their dreams.
亞當形容自己為行動派，並總是會鼓勵身邊的人去實踐他們的夢想。

Do you take action first, or watch and wait for a while?
你會先採取行動，還是會先稍微觀察？

There are no flies on Dianna.
黛安娜是個徹底的行動派。

An active doer usually likes to run a tight ship and keeps everything under control.
一個積極的行動派通常喜歡紀律嚴明，並掌握好所有事物。

Energetic people get their work done with enthusiasm and energy.
活力充沛的人會投注熱情和精力將工作完成。

Look before you leap.
三思而後行。

It takes time for an observer to figure out what to do.
觀察者需要一些時間來思考如何行動。

I evaluate what I can do and what I already have before taking any action.
我在行動前，總是會先謹慎評估我能做什麼、又擁有些什麼。

People with "owl personalities" tend to observe and even over-analyze before taking any action.
有「貓頭鷹性格」的人習慣在行動前先觀察，甚至會過度分析情況。

MP3 ▶ 124

06 日常 單身或結婚
Single Or Married

 單字基本功 掌握關鍵字 = 開口第一步

 核心聯想　黃金單身也不賴 Being single

bachelor	**bachelorette**	**widow**	**widower**
[`bætʃələ]	[ˌbætʃələ`rɛt]	[`wɪdo]	[`wɪdoə]
名 單身漢	名 單身女子	名 寡婦 動 使喪偶	名 鰥夫

divorce	**remain**	**eligible**	**separate**
[də`vors]	[rɪ`men]	[`ɛlɪdʒəbḷ]	[`sɛpəˌret]
動 離婚；使分離	動 保持；剩下	形 單身貴族的	形 分開的

 邁向幸福婚姻 Getting married 進階學習

couple	**difference**	**fidelity**	**duty**
[`kʌpḷ]	[`dɪfərəns]	[fɪ`dɛlətɪ]	[`djutɪ]
名 配偶；一對	名 差異；區別	名 忠誠	名 責任；職務

husband	**wife**	**depend**	**DINK**
[`hʌzbənd]	[`waɪf]	[dɪ`pɛnd]	縮 頂客族
名 丈夫	名 妻子	動 依賴；信賴	(Dual incomes, no kids)

 深度追蹤 Knowing More

　　在美國，五月是鮮花盛開的季節，故有所謂「四月雨帶來五月花 April showers bring May flowers.」的說法，而緊接著的六月便是結婚的黃道吉「月」，象徵諸事皆宜，故很多人都選在六月結婚，這也是英文中June Bride（六月新娘）的由來。另外，以前的婚紗並不拘泥於白色，穿白色婚紗是十九世紀末才開始出現的潮流，當時英國的維多利亞女王結婚時，就是穿著白色婚紗；而白色代表的聖潔純真，也使人們逐漸流行在婚禮穿上白色婚紗。

There's nothing sb. can do (about)...
對於…，某人無能為力。

- ★ There's nothing we can do to save their marriage.
  關於他們的婚姻，我們無力挽救。
- ★ There's nothing we can do about the accident.
  我們無法阻止那場意外的發生。
- ★ There's nothing the doctor can do about the **incurable** disease.
  那名醫師對於不治之症束手無策。
- ★ There's nothing the family members can do to help the **rescue** team.
  家屬們都幫不上搜救團隊。
- ★ There's nothing our manager can do about the **layoff** decision.
  關於裁員的決議，我們的經理也無能為力。

> **incurable**
> [ɪn`kjʊrəbl]
> 形 無法治癒的
> **rescue**
> [`rɛskju]
> 名 援救
> **layoff**
> [`le,ɔf]
> 名 解雇

sb. end up... 某人最後…。

- ★ Neil ended up marrying his first love.
  尼爾最後與他的初戀情人結婚了。
- ★ The couple ended up closing the door of communication.
  那對夫妻最終拒絕和彼此溝通。
- ★ The **culprit** will end up living the rest of his life in **jail**.
  那名罪犯將在監獄度過餘生。
- ★ Jennifer ended up auditioning for a **supporting role** in a musical.
  珍妮佛最後去了一齣音樂劇的配角試鏡。
- ★ Henry ended up becoming a **distinguished** scholar.
  亨利最終成為一位傑出的學者。

> **culprit**
> [`kʌlprɪt]
> 名 罪犯
> **jail**
> [dʒel]
> 名 監獄
> **supporting role**
> 片 配角
> **distinguished**
> [dɪ`stɪŋgwɪʃt]
> 形 卓越的

MP3 ▶ 126

開口必備句　和老外聊開懷，就靠這幾句！

Are you going to get married someday?
你將來想要結婚嗎？

He remains single in the end, realizing that marriage is not necessarily better.
他最後還是維持單身，了解到結婚不一定比較好。

Being single allows you to have more time to care for other people.
單身代表你有更多時間去關心其他人。

Ruby doesn't believe in love, hence she swears that she will never get married.
露比不相信愛情，因此她發誓永不結婚。

Some people live their happiest lives by marrying, whereas others live the most fulfilling lives by staying single.
有些人結婚之後過得最快樂，但也有人單身時才過得很充實。

Single life or married life, which one do you prefer?
單身或婚姻生活，你比較喜歡哪一種？

Do you think you are ready for marriage?
你覺得你已準備好進入婚姻了嗎？

What do you think of marriage?
你對於婚姻有什麼想法？

I would still want to maintain ties to my friends and family after getting married.
就算結婚了，我仍然會想要維持與朋友和家人的聯繫。

Married life is full of excitements and frustrations.
婚姻生活充滿了許多刺激和挫折。

Marriage is a magical thing that a single person may desire while a married person may regret.
婚姻是如此神奇，令單身的人嚮往，卻令已婚的人後悔。

UNIT 07 職場 部門會議
Business Meetings

會議中的大小事 In a meeting

agenda [ə`dʒɛndə] 名 議程；工作事項	**boardroom** [`bord͵rum] 名 會議室	**brainstorm** [`bren͵stɔrm] 名 集思廣益	**minutes** [`mɪnɪts] 名 會議紀錄
absent [`æbsn̩t] 形 缺席的	**punctual** [`pʌŋktʃuəl] 形 準時的	**recurring** [rɪ`kɝɪŋ] 形 循環的	**closing remark** 片 結語

決定事項 Important decisions

進階學習

boss [bɔs] 名 老闆 動 指揮	**charge** [tʃɑrdʒ] 名 費用 動 索價	**choice** [tʃɔɪs] 名 選擇	**avoid** [ə`vɔɪd] 動 避免；躲開
compare [kəm`pɛr] 動 比較；對照	**consider** [kən`sɪdɚ] 動 仔細考慮	**contain** [kən`ten] 動 包含；容納	**useful** [`jusfəl] 形 有用的

深度追蹤 🔍 Knowing More

　　「會議」其實隱藏了許多學問，從座位、當主持人、發言、到參加會議，都有需要注意的地方，例如發言方面，要注意會議中的發言分為「正式發言」與「自由發言」兩種；若為正式發言，須注意服裝，並盡量保持大方、自信的儀態，且需事先準備講稿，發言時千萬不要一直低頭讀稿，而發言結束後，也要記得對聽眾表達謝意；自由發言則主要為討論或提意見，態度不需過於嚴謹，但不要搶話、說出明確觀點，是兩個最重要的注意事項。

套個單字，想說的都能表達！

sb. make sure (that)... 某人確定⋯。

★ I'll make sure Mr. Austin gets the message as soon as possible.
我會儘快將消息轉達給奧斯丁先生。

★ You had better make sure everything is **on the right track**.
你最好確定每件事都正確。

★ You should make sure the sweater fits you well.
你應該要確定你穿得下這件毛衣。

★ I just want to make sure I get the correct information.
我只是想確定我收到的資訊無誤。

> **on the right track**
> 片 想法 / 作法正確
> **organic**
> [ɔrˋgænɪk]
> 形 有機的

★ I can make sure the vegetables they offer are **organic**.
我能確定他們供應的蔬菜都是有機的。

...be worth... ⋯值得⋯。

★ Andrea's **devotion** to the job is worth the high pay.
安德莉亞對工作全心奉獻，當然值得獲得高薪。

★ The **content** of this book is worth reading.
這本書的內容很值得一看。

★ The **Gothic abbey** is worth a visit.
那個哥德式教堂很值得造訪。

★ This single-lens **reflex** camera is worth five thousand dollars.
這個單眼相機值五千元。

★ No man or woman is worth your tears.
沒有人值得你為他 / 她流淚。

> **devotion**
> [dɪˋvoʃən]
> 名 奉獻
> **content**
> [ˋkɑntɛnt]
> 名 內容
> **Gothic**
> [ˋgɑθɪk]
> 形 哥德式的
> **abbey**
> [ˋæbɪ]
> 名 教堂；修道院
> **reflex**
> [ˋriflɛks]
> 名 反射；映像

開口必備句　和老外聊開懷，就靠這幾句！

The departmental meeting is a routine on every Monday.
🔈 部門會議是每週一的例行公事。

A reminder should be sent two days before the meeting.
🔈 會議提醒應於開會前兩天寄出。

Where is the cross-departmental meeting this morning?
🔈 今天早上的跨部門會議在哪裡舉行？

How should I organize a departmental meeting?
🔈 我該如何安排一場部門會議？

Who is the chairperson for today's meeting?
🔈 由誰擔任今天會議的主席？

Who is responsible for taking the minutes?
🔈 誰負責會議紀錄？

What are the questions under discussion for today's meeting?
🔈 今天會議中要討論的議題為何？

A cross-departmental meeting will be held in reaction to the latest company scandal.
🔈 為回應最近的醜聞，公司將召開跨部門會議。

Everyone should attend the departmental meeting on time.
🔈 每個人都應準時出席部門會議。

Aaron was sick and thus was absent from the departmental meeting this week.
🔈 亞倫生病了，因此缺席本周的部門會議。

Our annual meeting usually lasts for more than two hours, which always drives me crazy.
🔈 我們的年度會議通常持續兩個小時以上，這總是讓我抓狂。

Sometimes it's kind of hard to stay awake during meetings.
🔈 有時候，要在會議中保持清醒還真是困難。

MP3 ▶ 130

08 職場
協商談判
Business Negotiation

單字基本功 掌握關鍵字＝開口第一步

核心聯想 | 成功協商 Successful negotiations

proposal [prə`pozl] 名 提案；計畫	**task** [tæsk] 名 任務；工作	**accomplish** [ə`kamplɪʃ] 動 完成；實現	**conniving** [kə`naɪvɪŋ] 形 默許的
negotiate [nɪ`goʃɪˏet] 動 協商；洽談	**satisfy** [`sætɪsˏfaɪ] 動 使滿意	**settle down** 片 塵埃落定	**turn out** 片 結果是；證明是

協商中間人 Being a middleman **進階學習**

alternative [ɔl`tɜnətɪv] 名 選擇 形 替代的	**argument** [`argjʊmənt] 名 論點；爭執	**contact** [`kantækt] 名 連絡 動 接觸	**conversation** [ˏkanvə`seʃən] 名 交談；談話
strategy [`strætədʒɪ] 名 策略；對策	**disagree** [ˏdɪsə`gri] 動 不同意	**believable** [bɪ`livəbl] 形 可信任的	**bottom line** 片 底線

深度追蹤 Knowing More

　　協商時，若當事人雙方無法直接接觸到對方或是協商停擺時，常會請「中間人」來居中協調；而中間人的立場須中立且客觀，需要從中找到利於雙方的折衷點，來促進協商成功。另外，統計結果指出，若協商雙方本來就有交情，雖可建立信任感，但也因為友誼，而傾向用「資源均分」來解決，所以經常錯失一些更好的方案。不過，無論是面對誰，協商時都要溝通清楚、事先準備，只要掌握好自己的協商籌碼，並適時讓步，就能創造雙贏局面。

句型偷吃步　套個單字，想說的都能表達！

sb. can hardly believe...　某人幾乎無法相信…。

★ I can hardly believe that Rick settled the **case** within one week.
我幾乎不敢相信瑞克在一週內就解決這個案子了。

★ We can hardly believe the **accident** that happened last week.
我們幾乎無法相信上星期所發生的那件意外。

★ The woman can hardly believe what she read in the letter.
那名女性簡直不敢相信她在信上所看到的內容。

★ The **defendant** could hardly believe what he heard in court.
被告簡直不敢相信他在法庭上聽到的事情。

★ The **stockbroker** can hardly believe that the price has gone down within two hours.
股票經紀人幾乎無法相信價格在兩小時內就下跌了。

> **accident**
> [`æksədənt]
> 名 事故；災禍
>
> **case**
> [kes]
> 名 案件
>
> **defendant**
> [dɪ`fɛndənt]
> 名 被告人
>
> **stockbroker**
> [`stɑk͵brokɚ]
> 名 股票／證券經紀人

sb. be wondering if...(or not)
某人在思考是否能…。

★ I was wondering if you could **pay a visit to** the client with me.
不知道你可否和我一起去拜訪客戶。

★ I was wondering if we can have lunch tomorrow.
不知道我們明天能不能一起吃午餐。

★ I was wondering if you feel like going to a movie tonight.
不知道你今晚想不想去看電影。

★ Our manager was wondering if Thomas and his client are around.
我們的經理想知道湯姆斯和他的客戶在不在。

★ He was wondering if I have time to discuss our **dissertation**.
他想知道我有沒有時間來討論我們的畢業論文。

> **pay a visit to**
> 片 拜訪
>
> **dissertation**
> [͵dɪsɚ`teʃən]
> 名 畢業論文

MP3 ▶ 132

開口必備句　和老外聊開懷，就靠這幾句！

I really need your tips on negotiating with clients.
📣 我很需要你給我一些跟客戶談判的小撇步。

Being afraid of negotiations won't help you get the job done.
📣 害怕協商的心態無法讓你完成工作。

You have to know your bottom line before every negotiation.
📣 每場談判之前，你都必須要很清楚你的底線。

First, know what your customers want and what you can provide.
📣 首先，要理解客戶的需求，也要清楚你能提供什麼。

Knowing the right time to negotiate is also very important.
📣 知道適當的協商時機，也是非常重要的。

Is that compatible with what you would like to see?
📣 這與你想看到的相符嗎？

Is there anything on the contract that you would like to change?
📣 合約上有任何您想更改的地方嗎？

In fact, your negotiation style can suggest what type of person you are.
📣 其實個人的協商風格，可以暗示你是怎樣的人。

Kenny just earned us two more days to complete the project.
📣 肯尼剛剛幫我們的計劃多爭取了兩天的時間。

List the least desirable but tolerable terms that you'd be willing to take, which will be your walk-away point.
📣 列出最不想要但還能接受的條件，做為你的停損點。

Instead of focusing on what you want, consider what the client needs and aim to work toward a compromise.
📣 與其著眼於你的需求，不如考慮客戶的需求，並致力於彼此妥協。

UNIT
09
職場
辦公室趣聞
Dealing With Office Gossips

 單字基本功 掌握關鍵字＝開口第一步

核心聯想

休息時聊八卦 Gossiping around

fault [fɔlt] 名 錯誤	**gossip** [`gɑsəp] 名 八卦 動 聊八卦

reality [rɪ`æləti] 名 真實；事實	**reputation** [ˌrɛpjə`teʃən] 名 名譽

bad-mouth [`bæd͵maʊθ] 動 講壞話；批評	**ruin** [`ruɪn] 動 破壞；毀壞

exact [ɪg`zækt] 形 確切的	**open secret** 片 公開的秘密

對流言的態度 Facing rumors 進階學習

doubt [daʊt] 名 動 懷疑	**influence** [`ɪnfluəns] 名 動 影響

reply [rɪ`plaɪ] 名 動 回答	**silence** [`saɪləns] 名 沉默 動 使沉默

spread [sprɛd] 名 動 散佈	**disappear** [͵dɪsə`pɪr] 動 消失；不見

explain [ɪk`splen] 動 解釋；說明	**ignore** [ɪg`nor] 動 忽視；不理會

 深度追蹤 *Knowing More*

　　一位知名心理學家曾說過：「八卦是人性根深蒂固的一部份，無論如何是擋不住的。」而俗話也說：「有人就有是非，有是非就有八卦。」可見八卦是每個人都會接觸到的。八卦一詞其實源自於德文「Klatsch」，是以前的德國人形容婦女們洗衣時拿著棒子用力拍打衣服的聲音；而洗衣婦們聚集在河邊洗衣，因為一直做著重複性的工作，便開始聊起各家的大小事，甚至加入自己的揣測，所以這個字後來被引申成為「無中生有的小道消息」，也就是八卦。

MP3 ⏵ 134

套個單字，想說的都能表達！

sb. didn't mean to...　某人不是故意…的。

★ I didn't mean to lie about what happened.
我不是故意要說謊的。

★ Nicole didn't mean to embarrass you.
妮可不是故意要讓你難堪的。

★ The speaker didn't mean to **engender controversies**.
講者不是有意要引起爭論的。

★ Our boss didn't mean to pick on the proposal you wrote.
我們老闆並不是有意要挑你寫的提案的毛病。

★ The candidate didn't mean to **offend** the **electoral** law.
那名候選人並非有意觸犯選舉法。

> **engender**
> [ɪn`dʒɛndə]
> 動 引起
> **controversy**
> [`kɑntrə,vɜsɪ]
> 名 爭議
> **offend**
> [ə`fɛnd]
> 動 觸犯；冒犯
> **electoral**
> [ɪ`lɛktərəl]
> 形 選舉的

In one's opinion, ...　在某人看來，…。

★ In my opinion, what Nina said is just a rumor.
在我看來，妮娜說的不過是傳聞罷了。

★ In my opinion, a wise man doesn't **glory** in his **wisdom**.
在我看來，真正的智者不會誇耀自己多有智慧。

★ In the critic's opinion, the movie **lacks** content and a creative ending.
就那位評論家看來，那部電影沒什麼內容，結局也沒有創意。

★ In my friend's opinion, Japanese are generally **modest**.
在我朋友看來，日本人通常都滿謙遜的。

★ In my sister's opinion, it is better for me to stay single.
在我妹看來，維持單身對我比較好。

> **glory**
> [`glorɪ]
> 動 為…感到驕傲
> **wisdom**
> [`wɪzdəm]
> 名 智慧
> **lack**
> [læk]
> 動 缺少
> **modest**
> [`mɑdɪst]
> 名 謙遜

開口必備句　和老外聊開懷，就靠這幾句！

Gossips seem to be unavoidable in all workplaces.
流言似乎在所有工作場所都無法避免。

It's almost impossible to eliminate gossip in the office.
要消滅辦公室流言幾乎是不可能的。

Many companies prevent employees from disclosing sensitive and personal information to others.
很多公司會禁止員工洩露敏感的個人資訊給他人。

I enjoy chatting with my colleagues in the coffee room from time to time.
我很喜歡偶爾與同事在茶水間閒聊。

Rose and her colleagues usually have lunch together and talk about their coworkers.
蘿絲和同事們常常一起吃午餐、談論其他的同事。

Is it true that Nick and Lynn went out on a date last night?
尼克跟琳恩昨晚去約會了，是真的嗎？

That publicist resigned over a financial scandal.
那位公關因為一樁金融弊案而辭職了。

It's an open secret that Frank always slips out the door a little too quickly every day.
法蘭克每天總是提早下班，這已經不是秘密了。

The rumor of her dating our boss was bandied about in the office.
她與我們老闆約會的傳言已經在辦公室裡傳的沸沸揚揚。

It made Jim bristle with rage when he heard his colleague spoke ill of him.
當吉米聽到同事講他壞話時，氣地火冒三丈。

I want to keep my distance from a gossipmonger like Diana.
我想和像黛安娜那樣愛說閒話的人保持距離。

Part 06

六月兼顧校園職場

June Highlights:
Farewell, School!

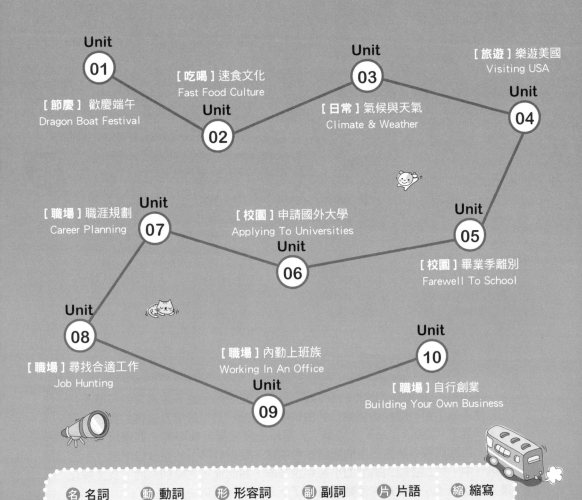

Unit 01
[節慶] 歡慶端午
Dragon Boat Festival

[吃喝] 速食文化
Fast Food Culture
Unit 02

Unit 03
[日常] 氣候與天氣
Climate & Weather

[旅遊] 樂遊美國
Visiting USA
Unit 04

[職場] 職涯規劃
Career Planning
Unit 07

[校園] 申請國外大學
Applying To Universities
Unit 06

Unit 05
[校園] 畢業季離別
Farewell To School

Unit 08
[職場] 尋找合適工作
Job Hunting

[職場] 內勤上班族
Working In An Office
Unit 09

Unit 10
[職場] 自行創業
Building Your Own Business

名 名詞　　動 動詞　　形 形容詞　　副 副詞　　片 片語　　縮 縮寫

UNIT 01 節慶

歡慶端午
Dragon Boat Festival

 單字基本功 掌握關鍵字 = 開口第一步

 核心聯想 端午節習俗 Customs & traditions

calamus [ˋkæləməs] 名 菖蒲	**mugwort** [ˋmʌɡˏwɜt] 名 艾草	**race** [res] 名 比賽；賽跑	**reunion** [riˋjunjən] 名 重聚；集合
bamboo leaf 片 竹葉	**dragon boat** 片 龍舟	**perfume pouch** 片 香包	**rice dumpling** 片 粽子

 端午節由來 History of Dragon Boat Festival 進階學習

despair [dɪˋspɛr] 名 動 絕望	**drown** [draʊn] 動 把…淹死	**folklore** [ˋfokˏlor] 名 民間傳說	**patriot** [ˋpetrɪət] 名 愛國者
poet [ˋpoɪt] 名 詩人	**imperial** [ɪmˋpɪrɪəl] 形 帝國的	**valiant** [ˋvæljənt] 形 英勇的	**over the years** 片 數年來

 深度追蹤 Knowing More

　　端午節（Dragon Boat Festival）為華人三大節慶之一，每年的農曆五月五日就是端午節。關於這個節日的由來眾說紛紜，其中最廣為流傳的就是愛國詩人—屈原（Qu Yuan）的故事了。屈原上諫言卻反被陷害，最後投江自盡之後，百姓們擔心這位忠臣的屍體被魚啃食，便用竹筒及竹葉裝盛米飯，丟至汨羅江中，並划著龍頭造型的小船嚇跑魚群，藉此保護屈原的身體。於是每年端午節吃粽子、划龍舟的活動就流傳了下來，成為習俗之一。

MP3 ▶ 137

套個單字，想說的都能表達！

...is a great way to...

…是…的好方法。

★ Going on a vacation is a great way to enjoy your annual leave.
度假是個享受年假的好方法。

★ Exercise is a great way to reduce **stress**.
運動是減壓的好方法。

stress
[stɛs]
名 壓力

★ Swimming is a great way to stay in good shape.
游泳是維持身材的好方法。

★ Keeping a **budget** is a great way to **cut down** expense.
維持預算是節省開支的好方法。

budget
[`bʌdʒɪt]
名 預算

cut down
片 削減

★ Using **eco-friendly** product is a great way to solve environmental problems.
使用環保產品是個解決環境問題的好方法。

eco-friendly
[`iko, frɛndlɪ]
形 環保的

Can you tell me something about...?

你可以告訴我一些關於…的事嗎？

★ Can you tell me something about the customs of Dragon Boat Festival?
你能告訴我一些端午節的習俗嗎？

★ Can you tell me something about my weaknesses?
你能和我講一下我有哪些缺點嗎？

★ Can you tell me something about your work experiences?
你能談談你的工作經驗嗎？

★ Can you tell me something about the supporting **evidence** in your study?
你能告訴我你研究中的支持證據嗎？

evidence
[`ɛvədəns]
名 證據

performance
[pɚ`fɔrməns]
名 成果

★ Can you tell me something about your team's **performance**?
你能告訴我你的團隊績效怎麼樣嗎？

開口必備句　知老外聊開懷，就靠這幾句！

The Dragon Boat Festival is one of the most important traditional holidays.

端午節是最重要的傳統節日之一。

The Dragon Boat Festival honors an ancient patriotic poet, Qu Yuan.

端午節紀念一位古代的愛國詩人——屈原。

To keep Qu Yuan from being eaten by fish, people threw rice dumplings in the river.

為了讓屈原不被魚啃食，人們把粽子丟進河裡。

The Dragon Boat Festival is also called Double Fifth Day.

端午節又稱作五五節。

Fillings in rice dumpling differ from area to area.

每個地區的粽子餡料不盡相同。

My grandma makes the most delicious rice dumplings in the world.

我奶奶做的粽子是世界上最美味的。

The Dragon Boat Race in Hsinchu always attracts many visitors.

新竹的划龍舟競賽總是吸引許多的遊客。

Andy shouted for joy when they won the Dragon Boat race.

安迪在贏得龍舟比賽的時候開心大叫。

Besides eating rice dumplings, people hang calamus or mugwort on their doors and drink realgar wine to keep out evil nemesis.

除了吃粽子，人們會掛菖蒲或艾草在門上，也會喝雄黃酒來驅邪。

It is said that people who manage to stand an egg at exactly 12 o'clock noon, the following year will be a lucky one.

傳說若能在當天中午十二點把蛋立起來，隔一年就會很幸運。

MP3 ▶ 139

UNIT 02

吃喝

速食文化
Fast Food Culture

單字基本功 掌握關鍵字 ＝ 開口第一步

核心聯想

來份速食 In a fast food restaurant

dressing
[`drɛsɪŋ]
名 沙拉醬；調料

ketchup
[`kɛtʃəp]
名 番茄醬

teenager
[`tin͵edʒɚ]
名 青少年

convenient
[kən`vinjənt]
形 方便的

fast food
片 速食

French fries
片 炸薯條

milk shake
片 奶昔

to go
片 外帶

香酥油炸食品 Deep-fried foods

進階學習

fry
[fraɪ]
名 油炸物 動 油炸

grease
[gris]
名 油脂 動 塗油於

heat
[hit]
名 熱度 動 加熱

oil
[ɔɪl]
名 油 動 塗油於

pepper
[`pɛpɚ]
名 胡椒；辣椒粉

crispy
[`krɪspɪ]
形 脆的

crunchy
[`krʌntʃɪ]
形 鬆脆的

spicy
[`spaɪsɪ]
形 辛辣的

深度追蹤

Knowing More

　　在速食店快速解決一餐，是許多上班族的生活寫照，然而工業社會下產生的速食文化，卻容易對環境和健康造成傷害。為了對抗速食文化，義大利人卡爾洛‧佩特里尼（Carlo Petrini）創立了「慢食 Slow Food」，呼籲人們重視食物的挑選、來源及食物製造時對環境的影響，且只享受「好」的食物；所以對「慢食者」來說，吃飯就不再只是一個消極行為，而是藉由選用製造過程中對環境無害且健康的食材，來間接保護環境。

sb. can't live without... 某人的生活中不能缺少…。

- ★ My brother can't live without fast food.
  我哥不能沒有速食。

- ★ Derek can't live without his tablet.
  德瑞克的生活中不能缺少平板電腦。

- ★ The **handicapped** man can't live without his wife.
  那位肢體殘障的男士不能沒有他的太太。

- ★ All **creatures** in the world can't live without **oxygen**.
  世界上所有的生物都不能缺少氧氣。

- ★ Modern people can't live without Internet and their cellphones.
  現代人的生活不能缺少網路以及手機。

> **handicapped**
> [`hændɪ͵kæpt]
> 形 肢體殘障的
> **creature**
> [`kritʃə]
> 名 生物
> **oxygen**
> [`ɑksədʒən]
> 名 氧氣

...go perfectly with... …和…是絕配。

- ★ French fries go perfectly with ketchup.
  薯條和蕃茄醬是絕配。

- ★ **Pickle** salads go perfectly with barbecue ribs.
  醃黃瓜沙拉和烤肋排非常配。

- ★ The black **bowler hat** goes perfectly with your **double-breasted** coat.
  那頂黑色禮帽和你的雙排釦大衣真是絕配。

- ★ This dress goes perfectly with the white boots you bought yesterday.
  這件洋裝和你昨天買的白色靴子很搭。

- ★ This **appetizer** goes perfectly with the **aperitif** you ordered.
  這道開胃菜和你點的餐前酒真是絕配。

> **pickle**
> [`pɪkḷ]
> 名 醃小黃瓜
> **bowler hat**
> 片 禮帽
> **double-breasted**
> [`dʌbḷ`brɛstɪd]
> 形 雙排扣的
> **appetizer**
> [`æpə͵taɪzə]
> 名 開胃菜
> **aperitif**
> [ɑperi`tif]
> 名 餐前酒

141

Fast food restaurants are literally everywhere nowadays.
現在，速食餐廳幾乎每個地方都有。

I am a big fan of fast food because it's really convenient.
我很喜歡速食，因為速食真的很方便。

I eat fast food three meals a day.
我一天三餐都吃速食。

I hate greasy food, so I don't really like to eat fast food.
我討厭油膩的食物，所以我不太喜歡吃速食。

Teenagers and children love fried chicken and sundae.
青少年與孩童都很愛吃炸雞和聖代。

Do you want some chicken nuggets?
你要點些雞塊嗎？

Do you want your fried chicken spicy or with green onions?
你要辣味還是青蔥口味的炸雞？

Do you want to make it a meal?
你要升級成套餐嗎？

Can I have some ketchup and honey mustard, please?
可以麻煩給我一些番茄醬和蜂蜜芥末醬嗎？

I'd like to have a small salad with Japanese dressing, please.
我要一份小的沙拉，醬料要日式和風醬。

May I have a quarter pounder with cheese and a filet-o-fish to go, please?
我要外帶一份四盎司牛肉堡和一份麥香魚。

It's so convenient that we can order our meals at the drive-through without getting out of the car.
在快取車道不用下車就能完成點餐，真的很方便。

UNIT 03

氣候與天氣
Climate & Weather

單字基本功 ✏ 掌握關鍵字＝開口第一步

核心聯想 氣象預報 Weather forecast

blizzard [`blɪzəd] 名 暴風雪	**forecast** [`for͵kæst] 名 動 預報	**snow** [sno] 名 雪 動 下雪	**temperature** [`tɛmprətʃə] 名 氣溫
typhoon [taɪ`fun] 名 颱風	**heat wave** 片 熱浪	**thunder shower** 片 雷陣雨	**weather condition** 片 天氣狀況

特殊的沙漠景觀 Desert climate

進階學習

boundary [`baʊndrɪ] 名 邊界；範圍	**cactus** [`kæktəs] 名 仙人掌	**desert** [`dɛzɜt] 名 沙漠	**dune** [djun] 名 沙丘
oasis [o`esɪs] 名 綠洲	**sand** [sænd] 名 沙子；沙地	**barren** [`bærən] 形 荒蕪的	**dry** [draɪ] 形 乾燥的；乾旱的

 深度追蹤 🔎

Knowing More

　　美國幅員廣大造成各州氣候的差異，所以考慮在美國攻讀學位時，除了學校的名氣，還得先了解一下當地的氣候。一般而言，華人學生最常選擇的幾個州為：(1) California（加州）：大部份地區只有乾季與濕季，冬季較冷但夏季氣候宜人。(2) Illinois（伊利諾州）：以芝加哥為最大城市，全年皆為暖和的天氣。(3) Georgia（喬治亞州）：氣候溫和，北部高山區的夏季尤為涼爽。(4) Ohio（俄亥俄州）：氣候溫和，冬季較冷但夏季溫暖且潮濕。

MP3 ⊙ 143

套個單字，想說的都能表達！

regarding...　關於…。

★ Prof. Barren answered a question regarding the climate change.
拜倫教授回答了一個關於氣候變遷的問題。

★ I **brought up** some new solutions regarding your request.
關於你的要求，我提出了一些新的解決方案。

★ Our manager announced a few things regarding his decision this morning.
我們經理今天早上宣布了一些決定。

★ My boss threw out a **hint** regarding our bonuses.
關於我們的獎金，老闆丟出了一些暗示。

★ The scholar proposed a hypothesis regarding the origin of wars.
關於戰爭的起源，那名學者提出了一個假說。

bring up
片 提出；談到
hint
[hɪnt]
名 提示

How much do/does sb. know about...?

某人對…了解多少？

★ How much do people know about the climate change?
人們對氣候變遷的了解有多少呢？

★ How much do you know about **endangered species**?
你對瀕臨絕種的動物有什麼了解呢？

★ How much does your supervisor know about his background?
你的主管對他的背景了解多少呢？

★ How much do **astronomers** know about other planets and the **galaxy**?
天文學家對其他行星與銀河的了解有多少呢？

★ How much do businessmen know about the **emerging** markets?
商人們對新興市場的了解有多少呢？

endangered species
片 瀕臨絕種的動植物
astronomer
[ə`strɑnəmə]
名 天文學家
galaxy
[`gæləksɪ]
名 銀河
emerging
[ɪ`mɝdʒɪŋ]
形 新興的

開口必備句　和老外聊開懷，就靠這幾句！

Do you know the difference between a typhoon and a hurricane?
你知道颱風和颶風的差別嗎？

What is the weather like in June in California?
加州六月的天氣怎麼樣？

Taipei has high humidity all year round.
台北一年四季都非常潮溼。

Most foreigners can't stand the heat and the humid weather in Taiwan.
大多數的外國人無法忍受台灣炎熱又潮溼的氣候。

The temperate climate in Vancouver attracts many tourists.
溫哥華的溫和氣候吸引了許多遊客。

One of the biggest challenges of living abroad is to adapt oneself to the local weather.
住在國外最大的挑戰之一，就是適應當地的天氣。

Be sure to check the local weather forecast before traveling.
在出發旅遊之前，一定要先看一下當地的天氣預報。

Remember to bring lotion with you to cope with the dry climate in London.
記得帶乳液，這樣才能應付倫敦乾燥的氣候。

It seldom snows in Taiwan in the winter, except in the high mountains.
台灣很少在冬天下雪，除非在高山上才會降雪。

Monsoon usually brings heavy rainfall to the area.
季風通常會為地方帶來大量的降雨。

Most tourists choose to visit Southeast Asia during dry season instead of in the wet season.
很多觀光客選擇乾季去東南亞玩，而不是雨季。

MP3 ▶ 145

UNIT 04

旅遊

樂遊美國
Visiting USA

單字基本功 ▸ 掌握關鍵字 = 開口第一步

核心聯想 | **美國景點 Famous attractions in USA**

Hollywood [`halɪ, wud] 名 好萊塢	Central Park 片 中央公園	Fifth Avenue 片 第五大道	Grand Canyon 片 大峽谷
Las Vegas 片 拉斯維加斯	Niagara Falls 片 尼加拉瀑布	Statue of Liberty 片 自由女神像	Times Square 片 時代廣場

觀賞百老匯 Broadway shows | 進階學習

alternative [ɔl`tɝnətɪv] 名 輪班演員	Broadway [`brɔd, we] 名 百老匯	ensemble [ɑn`samb!] 名 合唱；劇團	prologue [`pro, lɔg] 名 序幕；前言
revival [rɪ`vaɪv!] 名 重演；復活	crowded [`kraudɪd] 形 擁擠的	entrance fee 片 入場費	plenty of 片 許多

深度追蹤 🔍

Knowing More

　　美國的百老匯是許多人必訪之地，但在觀賞音樂劇的同時，也要注意以下細節，才能讓自己有個美好的百老匯之夜：(1) 確認開演時間：一定要看清楚時間，並將交通時間考慮進去。(2) 提早到劇院：除了領票之外，還要找位子，所以最好提早半小時抵達。(3) 穿著得體：雖然不需要穿西裝或禮服，但穿背心、拖鞋也不適當。(4) 提早用餐：如果是看晚場，建議先吃過晚餐再進場。(5) 拍照禮儀：進入劇院後就不得拍照，開演之後更是嚴禁照相。

Have sb. got a chance to...? 某人有機會…嗎？

★ Have you got a chance to go shopping at Fifth Avenue?
你有機會去第五大道逛街嗎？

★ Has the artist got a chance to exhibit his artworks?
那位藝術家有機會展示他的作品嗎？

★ Has your sister got a chance to take a picture with the singer?
你的妹妹有機會和那位歌手一起拍照嗎？

★ Has the **proponent** got a chance to take an **affirmative** action?
那名提案人有機會採取積極的行動嗎？

★ Have the **unions** got a chance to **conciliate** with the government?
公會有機會和政府和解嗎？

> **proponent**
> [prə`ponənt]
> 名 提案者
> **affirmative**
> [ə`fɜmətɪv]
> 形 肯定的
> **union**
> [`junjən]
> 名 公會
> **conciliate**
> [kən`sɪlɪ͵et]
> 動 使和解

Have sb. been to...? 某人曾經去過…嗎？

★ Have you been to the United States?
你去過美國嗎？

★ Has your family been to the Egyptian pyramids?
你家人去過埃及金字塔嗎？

★ Has any of your friends been to Europe lately?
你的朋友之中有人最近去過歐洲嗎？

★ Has the **archaeologist** been to the Roman **amphitheater**?
那名考古學家去過羅馬競技場嗎？

★ Have the explorers been to the Amazon **rainforest**?
那群探險家去過亞馬遜的熱帶雨林區嗎？

> **archaeologist**
> [͵ɑrkɪ`ɑlədʒɪst]
> 名 考古學家
> **amphitheater**
> [͵æmfɪ`θɪətə]
> 名 競技場
> **rainforest**
> [`ren͵fɑrɪst]
> 名 熱帶雨林

MP3 ▶ 147

開口必備句　和老外聊開懷，就靠這幾句！

New York, the Big Apple, is the most populous city in the United States.
紐約又稱作「大蘋果」，是全美人口最多的都市。

Times Square is always crowded with people 24/7.
時代廣場不管什麼時候都擠滿了人。（24/7：24 小時 / 7 天）

The Statue of Liberty is one of the most famous landmarks in New York City.
自由女神像是紐約市最著名的其中一個地標。

Taking the hop-on and hop-off bus is the fastest and the cheapest way to tour the city.
搭乘觀光巴士是遊覽市區最快又最便宜的方式。

What is the best way to get to the Statue of Liberty?
到自由女神像的最佳方式是什麼呢？

If you're lucky, you might run into movie stars in Beverly Hills.
如果你運氣好，或許可以在比佛利山莊遇見電影明星。

What's your favorite place in San Francisco?
你最喜歡舊金山的什麼地方？

Los Angeles is a dynamic city featuring a wide variety of tours and attractions.
多樣化的觀光行程和景點是「活力之都」洛杉磯的特色。

Do you know any unique restaurants in Chicago?
你知道芝加哥有哪些特別的餐廳嗎？

Universal Studios is a popular theme park featuring scenes from movies where you can get a sense of filmmaking.
環球影城是個受歡迎的電影主題樂園，你可以在那裡體驗電影製作。

Maybe we can schedule a trip to Yellowstone this summer.
今年夏天，我們或許可以安排一趟黃石公園之旅。

UNIT 05 校園

畢業季離別
Farewell To School

單字基本功 掌握關鍵字＝開口第一步

核心聯想 **離別時刻 Saying goodbye**

goodbye [ˌɡʊd`baɪ] 名 再見	**promise** [`prɑmɪs] 名 動 承諾	**regard** [rɪ`ɡɑrd] 名 問候；關心	**support** [sə`port] 名 動 支持
leave [liv] 動 離開；留下	**sometime** [`sʌmˌtaɪm] 副 改天；某時間	**stay in touch** 片 保持聯絡	**take care** 片 珍重

依依不捨 Being reluctant to part 進階學習

depression [dɪ`prɛʃən] 名 沮喪；降低	**grip** [ɡrɪp] 名 緊握 動 抓住	**tear** [tɪr] 名 眼淚 動 流淚	**blur** [blɝ] 動 使模糊
relieve [rɪ`liv] 動 減緩；解除	**reluctant** [rɪ`lʌktənt] 形 不情願的	**mild** [maɪld] 形 溫和的	**memorable** [`mɛmərəbḷ] 形 值得紀念的

深度追蹤 *Knowing More*

　　在離別之際，除了簡單地說「Goodbye! 再見！」之外，想要表達自己的不捨之情，還有以下幾種簡單又好記的日常說法，例如「I'll miss you. 我會想念你的。」、「Call me sometime. 有時間打個電話給我吧。」、「Let's get together again sometime. 我們有時間再聚聚吧。」而所謂天下無不散的筵席，每個人都會經歷離別，但有些離別只是暫時的，若是想要好好珍惜友情，不妨主動聯絡朋友們，來鞏固彼此的友誼！

▶ 149

句型偷吃步 套個單字，想說的都能表達！

No matter what/who/how/where... 無論…。

★ No matter where you are, I'll keep in touch with you.
不管你人在哪裡，我都會和你保持聯繫。

★ No matter what may come, we must overcome it.
無論接下來會發生什麼事，我們都必須戰勝它。

★ No matter how bad your day is, just be grateful that you still have one.
不管你的一天有多糟糕，只要還活著就要心存感恩。

★ No matter what **channel** we **switch** to, we're **bound to** see a Christmas movie.
無論轉到哪一台，都在播聖誕節的電影。

★ No matter who you are, you can always change and become a better version of yourself.
無論你是誰，你都可以做出改變，並且成為一個更好的人。

> **channel**
> [ˋtʃænḷ]
> 名 頻道
> **switch**
> [swɪtʃ]
> 動 轉換
> **be bound to**
> 片 必定

sb. be about to... 某人差不多 / 即將要…。

★ All the **seniors** are about to graduate.
所有的大四生都即將畢業。

★ I think I'm about to catch a cold.
我覺得我快要感冒了。

★ The government is about to **ban gambling**.
政府即將要禁止賭博這件事。

★ Staple goods is about to get a little more expensive.
民生用品的價格即將要微幅調漲。

★ The author is about to **adapt** his novels into films.
那名作家即將把他的小說改編成電影。

> **senior**
> [ˋsinjɚ]
> 名 大學四年級生
> **ban**
> [bæn]
> 動 禁止
> **gambling**
> [ˋgæmblɪŋ]
> 名 賭博
> **adapt**
> [əˋdæpt]
> 動 改編

I really appreciate all your help.
謝謝你的全力協助。

I am deeply grateful for your support.
我真的很感激你的支持。

Thank you for being there for me all this time.
謝謝你這段時間都一直挺我。

I really hate to say goodbye.
我真的很討厭說再見。

Best of luck in the future, and keep in touch!
祝你有個美好的未來，務必保持聯絡！

Don't forget to give me a call sometime.
有空別忘了打電話給我。

It's really hard to say goodbye to such a good friend like you. All my best wishes are with you!
真捨不得跟像你這樣的好朋友說再見，在此送上我最真誠的祝福！

I wish I could stay longer, but I'm afraid I have to go now.
我真希望可以待久一點，但我必須要走了。

Remember to send my regards to your family.
請記得代我向你的家人問安。

When will I see you again?
我何時能再見到你呢？

Do take good care of yourself.
你一定要好好照顧自己。

How lucky I am to have friends that make saying goodbye so hard. I'll always remember you!
很幸運能認識這些朋友，雖然離別很難，但我會永遠記得你們的！

MP3 ▶ 151

UNIT 06 校園 申請國外大學
Applying To Universities

 單字基本功 掌握關鍵字 ＝ 開口第一步

核心聯想 備齊資料 Application materials

application [ˌæpləˋkeʃən] 名 申請表	**deadline** [ˋdɛdˌlaɪn] 名 截止日期	**essay** [ˋɛse] 名 論文；作文	**form** [fɔrm] 名 表格；形式
major [ˋmedʒɚ] 名 動 主修	**recommendation** [ˌrɛkəmɛnˋdeʃən] 名 推薦信	**specific** [spɪˋsɪfɪk] 形 特定的	**TOEFL** 縮 托福考試

 開始申請學校 Ready to apply **進階學習**

data [ˋdetə] 名 資料；數據	**examination** [ɪgˌzæməˋneʃən] 名 考試	**organization** [ˌɔrgənəˋzeʃən] 名 機構	**school** [skul] 名 學校 動 教育
season [ˋsizṇ] 名 季節；時節	**apply** [əˋplaɪ] 動 申請；應用	**check** [tʃɛk] 動 核對；檢查	**provide** [prəˋvaɪd] 動 提供

 深度追蹤 Knowing More

　　申請國外學校時，除了必備的基本資料之外，向學校描述自己的綜合能力也非常重要，尤其美國大學在招生過程中，更喜歡能力全面的學生，而不是只會讀書和考試的「書呆子」，所以除了學科成績之外，通常也會要求申請者有各種課外活動的經驗；因此在申請時，務必描述參與過的課外活動，從體育到文藝、公司實習、暑期打工、甚至是社區公益活動，只要是曾經參加過的，都可以寫在申請表裡面，並適度地描述自己的經驗。

句型偷吃步　套個單字，想說的都能表達！

sb. find sth./sb. ...　某人發覺某事 / 某人⋯。

★ My brother found his grades not high enough to apply to the merit-based scholarship.
我弟弟發現他的成績不夠好，無法申請優異獎學金。

★ I found the operator's voice charming and a little bit **husky**.
我發現那名接線生的聲音很有磁性、有一點沙啞。

★ Liam found himself **trembling** with anger.
里姆發現自己憤怒到全身發抖。

★ She found her new hair color strange.
她發現自己的新髮色很奇怪。

★ The **jury** found the witness's words too **vague**.
陪審團發現證人的證詞太模糊。

> **husky**
> [ˋhʌskɪ]
> 形（聲音）沙啞的
> **tremble**
> [ˋtrɛmbl]
> 動 顫抖
> **jury**
> [ˋdʒʊrɪ]
> 名（律）陪審團
> **vague**
> [veg]
> 形 模糊的

I'm calling to...　我來電是為了⋯。

★ I'm calling to accept the **admission** offer.
我來電是為了接受錄取通知。

★ I'm calling to make a reservation for tomorrow night.
我來電是為了預約餐廳明天晚上的位子。

★ I'm calling to **fill you in** on the updates in today's meeting.
我來電是為了告訴你今天開會的最新消息。

★ I'm calling to report a lost wallet I found at the **petrol station**.
我來電是因為在加油站撿到皮夾，想要報案。

★ I'm calling to ask you some questions about Sam.
我來電是為了問你關於山姆的事。

> **admission**
> [ədˋmɪʃən]
> 名（學校的）入學許可
> **fill sb. in**
> 片 提供某人最新消息
> **petrol station**
> 片（英）加油站

MP3 ▶ 153

開口必備句　和老外聊開懷，就靠這幾句！

I am thinking about studying in the United States.
我打算要到美國唸書。

Which school are you going to apply to?
你打算申請哪一所學校？

I am applying for business school in Harvard University.
我要申請哈佛大學的商學院。

First, you'll need to check if you're eligible to apply to certain departments.
首先，你必須先確定你是否有資格申請那些系所。

I really need some advice on how to prepare for the TOEFL and the GRE.
我很需要托福和美國研究生入學考試的一些準備建議。

Is there any state or city in particular that you are thinking of going?
你有沒有特別想去的州或是城市呢？

I've heard that there are several reputed schools in Boston.
我聽說波士頓有幾所名氣不錯的學校。

You can apply via online application or by mailing your application forms.
你可以透過線上申請，或直接郵寄申請表給對方。

When is the application deadline?
申請的截止日期是什麼時候？

You need to submit the online application form, three recommendations and two essays before the deadline.
你必須在截止日前繳交線上申請表、三封推薦信以及兩份論文。

I've got the admission letter from Stanford yesterday!
我昨天收到史丹佛大學的入學許可了！

UNIT 07 職場 職涯規劃
Career Planning

 單字基本功 掌握關鍵字 = 開口第一步

 核心聯想 探尋未來方向 Future paths

outlook [`aʊt͵lʊk] 名 願景；看法	**possibility** [͵pɑsə`bɪlətɪ] 名 可能性	**consult** [kən`sʌlt] 動 請教；查閱	**fulfill** [fʊl`fɪl] 動 實現；完成
ideal [aɪ`diəl] 形 理想的	**aptitude test** 片 性向測驗	**career advice** 片 職涯建議	**go after** 片 追求；追逐

職業百百種 All walks of life 進階學習

architect [`ɑrkə͵tɛkt] 名 建築師	**engineer** [͵ɛndʒə`nɪr] 名 工程師	**hairdresser** [`hɛr͵drɛsə] 名 理髮師	**model** [`mɑdl̩] 名 模特兒
musician [mju`zɪʃən] 名 音樂家	**painter** [`pentə] 名 畫家	**photographer** [fə`tɑgrəfə] 名 攝影師	**reporter** [rɪ`portə] 名 記者

 深度追蹤 *Knowing More*

　　職涯方向對許多人來說，往往很難決定，有些畢業生甚至花了好幾年，也無法確立自己的職涯方向。若要探索適合自己的職業，不妨試試以下幾種方式：(1) 學校輔導／職涯中心：若學校或任何機構舉辦與求職有關的活動，都可以去聽聽看。(2) 政府設立的就業服務站：會提供性向測驗以及諮商服務。(3) 職場實習：利用寒暑假實習，能幫助自己挑選有興趣的領域。(4) 參考親朋好友的經驗：可藉此獲取資訊，但最重要的還是自己做出決定。

MP3 ▶ 155

sth. play an important role in...
某事 / 物在…方面扮演重要的角色。

- ★ My university days play an important role in my life.
  我的大學生活在我的生命中扮演很重要的角色。

- ★ Exports play an important role in our country's economy.
  出口貿易在我們國家的經濟上扮演重要的角色。

- ★ Departmental characteristics play an important role in **determining** the **productivity**.
  部門特質能左右生產力。

- ★ These samples play an important role in my study.
  這些樣本在我的研究中扮演很重要的角色。

- ★ These new **bills** will play an important role in health care **reform**.
  這幾項新法案將會在醫療改革扮演很重要的角色。

determine
[dɪˋtɝmɪn]
🔟 決定

productivity
[͵prodʌkˋtɪvətɪ]
🔢 生產力

bill
[bɪl]
🔢 法案

reform
[͵rɪˋfɔrm]
🔢 改革

It's really hard to...　　…真的很困難。

- ★ It's really hard to make up my mind whether I should accept the job offer or not.
  要不要接受這個工作機會,是個很困難的決定。

- ★ It's really hard to say that I've got a new position at another company.
  要和對方說我已經在另一家公司找到職位,真的很困難。

- ★ It's really hard to **copy** another actor in order to be successful.
  模仿另一個演員並獲得成功很困難。

- ★ It's really hard to start my second novel at this moment.
  要在現在這種時刻撰寫我的第二本小說實在很困難。

- ★ It's really hard to **convince** her husband to retire by May this year.
  要說服她先生在今年五月前退休真的很困難。

copy
[ˋkɑpɪ]
🔟 複製

convince
[kənˋvɪns]
🔟 說服

開口必備句　和老外聊開懷，就靠這幾句！

Susan can't decide which career path to take after graduation.
蘇珊不知道畢業後究竟要從事什麼工作。

The first step towards finding the right career path is to know yourself.
尋找合適職業的第一步，就是了解自己。

What career suits your personality the best?
什麼職業最適合你的個性？

A personality assessment can help you find out who you are.
性格評量可幫助你了解自己。

Where should I start in order to find my ideal job?
我應該從何處著手才能找到理想的工作？

It takes time and effort to find the career that best suits you.
要找到最適合自己的職業，往往需要花費時間與精力。

You can consult someone who is now in the field of your interest.
你可以請教那些現在正在你感興趣的領域工作的人。

You can also map out where you want to go and life goals.
你也可以列出你想要達成的事物以及人生目標。

The right job can satisfy you both financially and psychologically.
一份適合的工作，能讓你在經濟和心理方面都得到滿足。

Although your family's expectations are important, it is your own desires that matter the most.
雖然家人的期望很重要，但最要緊的還是你自己的想法。

The perfect situation is to make a living at what you are both good at and interested in.
最好的情況是，靠你既擅長又有興趣的工作謀生。

UNIT 08

職場

尋找合適工作
Job Hunting

單字基本功 ✏ 掌握關鍵字 = 開口第一步

核心聯想 | 準備求職資料 Preparing for interviews

education
[ˌɛdʒəˈkeʃən]
名 學歷；教育

referee
[ˌrɛfəˈri]
名 推薦人

resume
[ˌrɛzjuˈme]
名 履歷表

specialty
[ˈspɛʃəltɪ]
名 專長；專業

testimonial
[ˌtɛstəˈmonɪəl]
名 證明書

cover letter
片 求職信

job objective
片 應徵職務

work experience
片 工作經驗

找工作管道 Looking for jobs | **進階學習**

headhunter
[ˈhɛdˌhʌntɚ]
名 獵頭公司

newspaper
[ˈnjuzˌpepɚ]
名 報紙

website
[ˈwɛbˌsaɪt]
名 網站

background check
片 背景調查

career field
片 職業領域

human resource agency
片 人力資源仲介

job fair
片 就業博覽會

job search engine
片 工作搜尋網站

 深度追蹤 🔍　*Knowing More*

　　在美國找工作的常見管道有以下四種：(1) 徵才網站：類似台灣的人力銀行網站，可以線上投遞履歷和申請面試機會。(2) 獵頭公司：若是透過獵人頭公司申請職位，之後不管你想詢問任何事情，都一定要透過獵頭公司，否則再有能力，也會被公司除名。(3) 公司的官方網站：愈大的公司就愈需要直接到公司網站查詢徵才訊息及投遞履歷。(4) 人脈介紹：除了直接介紹，在履歷當中也可以提及自己在該公司認識的人，以提高面試的機會。

May I speak to...?　請問我是否能與…通話呢？

★ May I speak to Mr. Baker in **Personnel**?
請問我是否能與人事部的貝克先生通話呢？

★ May I speak to your **section chief**?
請問我是否能與你們的科長通話呢？

★ May I speak to someone in the sales department?
請問我是否能與業務部的人通話呢？

★ May I speak to the person who handles this account?
請問我是否能與負責這個帳號的人通話呢？

★ May I speak to the person **in charge of** the electric bills?
我是否能與負責電費帳單的人通話呢？

> **personnel**
> [ˌpɝsn̩ˋɛl]
> 名 人事部門
> **section**
> [ˋsɛkʃən]
> 名 科；部門
> **chief**
> [tʃif]
> 名 長官
> **in charge of**
> 片 負責

Hold on, please.　請稍候（打電話專用）。

★ Hold on, please. Let me see if she is in.
請稍候，讓我看看她在不在。

★ Hold on, please. Let me see if I can **put you through**.
請稍等，讓我看看是否能為您轉接。

★ Hold on, please. I'll put you through to Amanda.
請稍候，我將替您轉接給亞曼達。

★ Hold on, please. Let me get a pencil and paper.
請稍等，讓我拿個紙和筆。

★ Hold on, please. Let me **double-check** your personal data.
請稍等，讓我核對一下您的個人資料。

> **put sb. through**
> 片 替某人接通電話
> **double-check**
> [ˋdʌblˋtʃɛk]
> 動 再次確認

MP3 ▶ 159

開口必備句

和老外聊開懷，就靠這幾句！

Each June, thousands of graduates are in search of jobs.
每年六月都會有數以千計的大學畢業生在找工作。

It is expected to be more than 10,000 job seekers this month.
這個月預期會有超過一萬名求職者。

There will be a job fair on campus in early June, and more than 500 jobs are available.
六月初學校會有就業博覽會，提供超過五百個工作機會。

You can ask Mr. Watson to proofread your resume.
你可以請華生先生校閱你的履歷表。

Nowadays, most people check out job bank websites for job openings.
現在，人們大多都是在人力銀行網站查詢工作職缺。

By joining GiveMeJobs.com, you will be updated with more than 5,000 jobs every week.
加入「給我工作網」，你每週就能收到超過五千筆的新工作資訊。

I have been looking for a job for two months.
我找工作已經找了兩個月了。

Can you give me some suggestions on job searching?
你可以給我一些找工作的建議嗎？

You can start by developing your job searching skills, which can help you find your dream job.
你可以先培養找工作的技巧，這能幫你找到理想的工作。

Please enclose your C.V. with the application form. Also, make sure you bring a copy of your resume to the interview.
請在申請書中附上你的履歷表，面試時也請務必帶一份履歷過來。

Is there anything I should know about phone interviews?
進行電話面試需要注意些什麼嗎？

UNIT 09 職場

內勤工作
Working In An Office

 單字基本功 ✏ 掌握關鍵字 = 開口第一步

 核心聯想 🐌 辦公室內 Office environment

cubicle [`kjubɪk] 名 小隔間	**department** [dɪ`partmənt] 名 部門	**divide** [də`vaɪd] 動 劃分;使隔開	**entrance** [`ɛntrəns] 名 入口
office [`ɔfɪs] 名 辦公室	**restroom** [`rɛst͵rum] 名 洗手間	**socket** [`sakɪt] 名 插座	**corporate** [`kɔrpərɪt] 形 公司的

文書作業 Deskwork & paperwork   **進階學習**

accurate [`ækjərɪt] 形 準確的	**depend on** 片 信賴;依靠	**file documents** 片 歸檔文件	**incoming call** 片 來電
job description 片 職務說明	**key in** 片 輸入資料	**run errand** 片 跑腿	**word processing** 片 文字處理

 深度追蹤 🔍 *Knowing More*

　　一般而言,工作分為「內勤」和「外務」兩種。所謂的外務,簡單來說就是「在公司外的時間較長的工作」,最常見的就是業務人員,他們經常需要去拜訪客戶與廠商;相反地,內勤則為在辦公室內的工作,像是祕書、助理、會計……等等,都是內勤的一環。另外,在確定錄取之後,最好先認識工作內容,並判斷自己的工作權責和範圍,尤其是遇到涉及跨部門的工作時,一定要弄清楚責任範圍並報告上級,以免日後發生推諉的情況。

MP3 ▶ 161

套個單字，想說的都能表達！

sb. need a hand with... 某人需要他人幫忙…。

★ Mr. Johnson needs a hand with getting an assistant.
強生先生需要人幫他找一名助理。

★ The customer needs a hand with selecting a **proper laptop**.
那名顧客需要有人幫他挑選適合的筆記型電腦。

★ I need a hand with my luggage, please.
我需要有人幫我搬行李，謝謝。

★ She might need a hand with **fundraising**.
她也許需要有人幫忙募款。

★ Our client needs a hand with his financial plan.
我們的客戶需要人幫忙規劃財務。

> **proper**
> [ˋprɑpɚ]
> 形 合適的
> **laptop**
> [ˋlæptɑp]
> 名 筆記型電腦
> **fundraising**
> [ˋfʌnd͵rezɪŋ]
> 名 募款

...as soon as possible. …愈快愈好。

★ Ms. Davis asked her secretary to make a reservation as soon as possible.
戴維斯小姐要她的祕書儘早完成預約。

★ You should finish your assignment as soon as possible.
你應該要盡快完成你的作業。

★ The **inspectors** should **resolve** the problems as soon as possible.
檢測員必須儘早解決問題。

★ You should **turn down** that request as soon as possible.
你應該儘早拒絕那項要求。

★ We should get the report done as soon as possible.
我們應該儘早完成報告。

> **inspector**
> [ɪnˋspɛktɚ]
> 名 檢查員
> **resolve**
> [rɪˋzɑlv]
> 動 解決；決定
> **turn down**
> 片 拒絕

開口必備句

和老外聊開懷，就靠這幾句！

Gina found an ideal desk job in an international firm.
吉娜在一間跨國公司找到一份理想的文書工作。

Staying in the office all day long sometimes bores me a lot.
整天待在辦公室，有時實在非常無聊。

Who can copy these files for me?
誰可以幫我影印這些文件？

Julian is responsible for organizing our boss's schedule.
朱利安負責安排我們老闆的行程。

Mr. Smith always has his secretary answer his phone calls.
史密斯先生總是讓祕書替他接聽電話。

Cindy answers incoming calls and takes messages for us.
辛蒂負責替我們接聽電話並記下留言。

It's enough for me for a job that I don't have to sweat under the sun all day long.
只要工作無須整日待在戶外、揮汗如雨，對我而言就已經夠了。

What's the job description of an office manager?
辦公室經理的工作內容是什麼？

What does a human resources manager do?
人資經理要做些什麼？

Typical duties of an office manager vary according to the size of the organization and the management structure.
辦公室經理的常態工作，隨著組織大小以及管理架構而有所變化。

Most office jobs nowadays involve computer skills.
現今大多數的內勤工作都涉及電腦使用技巧。

Cathy is looking for a new secretary who can help her organize meetings with clients.
凱西正在找新祕書，對方必須要能替她安排與客戶開會的時間。

MP3 ▶ 163

UNIT 10 職場

自行創業
Building Your Own Business

 單字基本功 掌握關鍵字＝開口第一步

核心聯想 **決心創業 Starting a business**

tycoon [tar`kun] 名 企業大亨	**evaluate** [r`vælju‚et] 動 評估；估價	**oversee** [`ovɚ`si] 動 監督；管理	**necessary** [`nɛsə‚sɛrɪ] 形 必要的
budget control 片 預算控制	**make decision** 片 下決定	**run a business** 片 經營事業	**set up the goal** 片 設立目標

 管理公司 Running a company **進階學習**

coalition [‚koə`lɪʃən] 名 結合；聯合	**cooperation** [ko‚apɚ`reʃən] 名 合作	**deploy** [dɪ`plɔɪ] 名 動 展開；部署	**administer** [əd`mɪnəstɚ] 動 管理；實施
announce [ə`nauns] 動 宣布；發布	**dominate** [`damə‚net] 動 支配；統治	**entitle** [ɪn`taɪtḷ] 動 給予權力或資格	**supervise** [`supɚvaɪz] 動 管理；監督

 深度追蹤 Knowing More

　　大多數的創業者在行動之前，都會寫「創業計畫書（business plan）」，不但能幫助創業家將所有環節思考過一次，在面對投資人、政府機關或金融機構時，也能成為彼此溝通的書面資料。計畫書中必須包含公司的基本資料、營運組織、產品、特點、資金規劃……等重點，涵蓋的細節愈多，之後失誤就愈少。不過，細節雖然重要，卻不需要長篇大論，只要抓到創業的要點，並用可與業界溝通的形式呈現，就是一份好的計畫書。

 套個單字，想說的都能表達！

sb. would rather...　某人寧願…。

★ I would rather start a new business on my own.
我寧願自行創業。

★ I would rather go shopping at **outlets**.
我寧願到暢貨中心逛街。

★ I would rather work in the **cinema** throughout my life.
我寧願一生從事電影業。

★ I would rather **reschedule** the press conference.
我寧願重新安排記者會的時間。

★ I would rather **sacrifice** my free time to help people.
我寧願把時間奉獻在幫助他人的事情上。

> **outlet**
> [`aut,lɛt]
> 名 商店
>
> **cinema**
> [`sɪnəmə]
> 名 電影業；電影院
>
> **reschedule**
> [ri`skɛdʒul]
> 動 重新安排時間
>
> **sacrifice**
> [`sækrə,faɪs]
> 動 犧牲

It cost sb. ...to...　某人花了（錢）去…。

★ It cost Jim a fortune to start his business.
創業花了吉姆一大筆錢。

★ It cost him 100 thousand dollars to buy the **roadster**.
那輛跑車花了他十萬元美金。

★ It cost my sister two hundred dollars to buy the perfume.
我姐姐花了兩百元美金買那瓶香水。

★ It cost me a lot to buy this **ornament**.
這個裝飾品花了我很多錢。

★ It only cost me five dollars to buy this **overcoat** in a **thrift shop**.
我只花了五塊錢就在二手商店買到這件大衣。

> **roadster**
> [`rodstə]
> 名 跑車
>
> **ornament**
> [`ɔrnəmənt]
> 名 裝飾品
>
> **overcoat**
> [`ovə,kot]
> 名 大衣
>
> **thrift shop**
> 片 二手商店

開口必備句　和老外聊開懷，就靠這幾句！

Building a business of your own takes a lot of effort, and money of course.
自己創業會耗費許多精力，當然也得花很多錢。

Jack was a passionate young lad who started his own computer business after graduating from university.
傑克是個有抱負的青年，他大學畢業後就自己創立了電腦公司。

You should start planning before you actually start a business.
實際創業前，你應該先擬定計畫。

What should I do to start a business of my own?
我該如何創業呢？

Have you decided what type of business you're going to run?
你已經決定要經營何種生意了嗎？

I read many books and online articles to get some tips on starting up a business.
為了得知創業的技巧，我讀了很多書和網路上的文章。

Eve is thinking about starting a bakery in a building on the street corner.
伊芙考慮在街角的那棟房子開麵包店。

What are the risks of starting my own business?
自行創業有哪些風險？

The bank won't give you a loan unless a detailed financial plan is provided.
除非你提供詳細的財務計劃書，否則銀行不會核貸。

Chris's father agreed to give his son's company financial support.
克里斯的爸爸同意提供經濟援助給他的公司。

Running your own business is a rewarding choice.
經營自己的生意是個有回報的選擇。

NOTE

Part 07

炎炎七月夏日消暑

July Highlights:
Summer Is Coming!

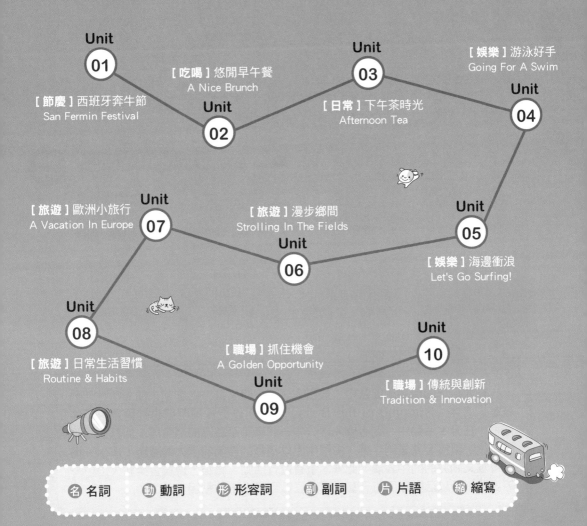

Unit
01
[節慶] 西班牙奔牛節
San Fermin Festival

[吃喝] 悠閒早午餐
A Nice Brunch

Unit
02

Unit
03
[日常] 下午茶時光
Afternoon Tea

[娛樂] 游泳好手
Going For A Swim

Unit
04

Unit
05
[娛樂] 海邊衝浪
Let's Go Surfing!

[旅遊] 歐洲小旅行
A Vacation In Europe

Unit
07

[旅遊] 漫步鄉間
Strolling In The Fields

Unit
06

Unit
08
[旅遊] 日常生活習慣
Routine & Habits

[職場] 抓住機會
A Golden Opportunity

Unit
09

Unit
10
[職場] 傳統與創新
Tradition & Innovation

名 名詞　　動 動詞　　形 形容詞　　副 副詞　　片 片語　　縮 縮寫

節慶
UNIT 01
西班牙奔牛節
San Fermin Festival

 單字基本功 ▷ 掌握關鍵字＝開口第一步

 核心聯想 傳統鬥牛賽 Exciting bullfights

bull	**bullfight**	**bullring**	**matador**
[bʊl]	[`bʊl.faɪt]	[`bʊlrɪŋ]	[`mætədor]
名 公牛	名 鬥牛賽	名 鬥牛場	名 鬥牛士

lure	**courageous**	**get oneself hurt**	**rush into**
[lʊr]	[kə`redʒəs]		
動 誘惑；引誘	形 勇敢的	片 使…受傷	片 一湧而進

 奔牛活動 Running of the bulls **進階學習**

haste	**race**	**speed**	**exceed**
[hest]	[res]	[spid]	[ɪk`sid]
名 急忙；急速	名 動 賽跑	名 速度 動 加速	動 超過；勝過

reach	**fast**	**final**	**rapid**
[ritʃ]	[fæst]	[`faɪnl]	[`ræpɪd]
動 到達；伸手拿	形 快速的 副 很快地	形 最終的	形 迅速的

 深度追蹤 ♪ *Knowing More*

　　在西班牙的聖佛明節當中，最引人注目、吸引最多遊客前來的象徵性活動就是「奔牛（Running of the Bulls）」，所以聖費爾明節也被稱為「奔牛節」。在奔牛活動中，跑者會先與公牛一起奔跑至終點的鬥牛場；而抵達鬥牛場之後，緊接著就是鬥牛賽，由鬥牛士以精彩的技術和過人的膽識，演出一場既優雅又刺激的鬥牛表演。此外，還有遊行活動、舞蹈、傳統音樂和火焰……等表演，所以活動期間每天都從早上狂歡到晚上十二點呢！

MP3 ▶ 167

套個單字，想說的都能表達！

In case of sth., ...　如果發生…，就要…。

★ In case of **urgency**, keep an extra careful watch.
如果發生緊急情況，就要加強戒備。

★ In case of fire, open this safety door and dial 911 **at once**.
一旦發生火災，請打開這扇安全門並立即撥打 911。

★ In case of a drought, we need to conserve water.
如果發生旱災，我們就必須節約用水。

★ In case of an **outage**, they'll set up backup generator.
如果跳電的話，他們就會設置備用的發電機。

★ In case of an explosion, they'd **monitor** the warship by helicopter.
如果爆炸的話，他們會搭直昇機查看軍艦的情況。

> **urgency**
> [`ɜdʒənsɪ]
> 名 緊急事件
>
> **at once**
> 片 馬上
>
> **outage**
> [`aʊtɪdʒ]
> 名 停電
>
> **monitor**
> [`mɑnətə]
> 動 監督

How (adj.) sb./sth. be!　某人 / 事 / 物多麼…！

★ How exciting the bullfight is!
多令人興奮的鬥牛賽啊！

★ How beautiful the scenery was!
那個景色多美啊！

★ How **marvelous** the **waterfall** was!
那個瀑布真是令人嘆為觀止！

★ How friendly your neighbor is!
你的鄰居真友善！

★ How **sheepish** that **craven** is!
那個膽小鬼真懦弱！

> **marvelous**
> [`mɑrvələs]
> 形 令人驚嘆的
>
> **waterfall**
> [`wɔtə‚fɔl]
> 名 瀑布
>
> **sheepish**
> [`ʃipɪʃ]
> 形 懦弱的
>
> **craven**
> [`krevən]
> 名 膽小鬼

開口必備句 和老外聊開懷，就靠這幾句！

The San Fermin Festival is also known as the Running of the Bulls.

聖費爾明節也被稱作奔牛節。

San Fermin is said to be the protector of the city of Pamplona.

聖費爾明據說是潘普洛納市的守護者。

The San Fermin Festival also features exciting bullfights.

聖費爾明節也以刺激的鬥牛賽為特色。

Tourists crowded into Pamplona to experience being a matador.

遊客們擁入潘普洛納市，體驗成為一名鬥牛士的感覺。

Thousands of tourists came for the thrill of running with herds of bulls.

數以千計的遊客為了體驗與牛群同奔的快感而來。

There have been thirteen deaths during the Festival of San Fermin as of yet.

至今已有十三人在奔牛節期間死亡。

People run with frantic bulls to the bullring on the rumbly marble lanes.

人群跟發狂的牛群一起，在崎嶇不平的大理石路上奔向鬥牛場。

The matador waved the red cape, which provoked the frenzied bull.

鬥牛士揮舞著紅色斗篷，激怒了狂牛。

Every year, thrill-seekers join in the event with red handkerchiefs around necks.

每年都會有追求快感的人，在脖子上綁著紅手帕來參加節慶。

The San Fermin Festival is not only about the Running of the Bulls, but also music, dancing, and singing.

聖費爾明節不只有奔牛活動，也充滿音樂、舞蹈和歌聲。

MP3 ⏵ 169

02 吃喝 悠閒早午餐
A Nice Brunch

單字基本功 ➤ 掌握關鍵字 = 開口第一步

核心聯想 | 西式早午餐 Western style brunch

omelet [`ɑmlɪt] 名 煎蛋捲；歐姆蛋	pancake [`pæn͵kek] 名 薄煎餅	waffle [`wɑfḷ] 名 鬆餅	baked beans 片 焗豆
eggs Benedict 片 班尼迪克蛋	French toast 片 法式吐司	grilled tomato 片 烤番茄	sunny-side- up egg 片 單面煎蛋

 中式早午餐 Chinese style brunch | 進階學習

porridge [`pɔrɪdʒ] 名 粥；稀飯	Chinese omelet 片 蛋餅	clay oven rolls 片 燒餅	fried bread stick 片 油條
radish cake 片 蘿蔔糕	scallion pancake 片 蔥油餅	soy milk 片 豆漿	steamed bun 片 饅頭

 深度追蹤 🔍 ~~~~~~~~~ *Knowing More*

　　早午餐（brunch）的起源眾說紛紜，有一說主張其源自於天主教徒彌撒後的聚餐；也有人說是來自於英國的一九八〇年代，為了讓早起的獵人一回來就有餐點享用，才開始出現；後來此風氣漸漸傳到美國，還成為新紐奧良的傳統。早午餐歷史大致分為三階段：(1) 一九二〇年代禁酒令時期：早午餐成為上流階級白天喝酒的好藉口。(2) 一九五〇年代：因職業婦女增加而帶起此風潮。(3) 一九八〇年代之後：人們會藉此炫耀財力。

套個單字，想說的都能表達！

When is a good time to...? 什麼時候可以…？

★ When is a good time to have brunch?
什麼時候適合去吃早午餐呢？

★ When is a good time to take these **diet supplements**?
什麼時候該服用這些飲食補給品呢？

★ When is a good time to wake Teddy up?
什麼時候能叫泰迪起床呢？

★ When is a good time to **inform** Nina our new schedule?
什麼時候能告訴妮娜我們的新日程呢？

★ When is a good time to call the author?
什麼時候方便打給那位作家呢？

diet
[`daɪət]
名 食物；飲食
supplement
[`sʌpləmənt]
名 補給品
inform
[ɪn`fɔrm]
動 通知；告知

Is/Are sb. able to...in time? 某人來得及…嗎？

★ Is Frank able to get on the bus **in time**?
法蘭克趕得上公車嗎？

★ Are you able to attend the party in time?
你來得及出席派對嗎？

★ Are your team members able to prepare everything for the feast in time?
你的組員來得及準備好宴會事宜嗎？

★ Are you able to **dispatch** a **shuttle bus** to the **terminal** in time?
你來得及派接駁車到機場航廈嗎？

★ Is our **supplier** able to deliver the **components** in time?
我們的供應商來得及遞送零件嗎？

in time
片 及時；趕上
dispatch
[dɪ`spætʃ]
動 派遣
shuttle bus
片 接駁車
terminal
[`tɜmənḷ]
名 航廈
supplier
[sə`plaɪɚ]
名 供應商
component
[kəm`ponənt]
名 零件

MP3 ▶ 171

開口必備句　和老外聊開懷，就靠這幾句！

I usually get up late, and then have brunch during weekends.
我週末通常都很晚起床，再去吃個早午餐。

My mom always starts her weekend morning with a sunny-side-up egg and some cucumber sandwiches.
只要是週末的早晨，我媽媽都會以荷包蛋和小黃瓜三明治開始她的一天。

I will have brunch with my friends next Saturday. Would you like to join us?
我下星期六要和朋友們一起吃早午餐，你要不要一起來？

Thanks for inviting me, but I guess I'll have to pass.
謝謝你的邀請，但我應該去不了。

My family likes to have a dim sum brunch together every Sunday.
我家每週日都喜歡一起吃港式早午餐。（dim sum：廣東話的「點心」）

They serve American brunch from 10:30 a.m. to 3:00 p.m.
他們從早上十點半到下午三點都會提供美式早午餐。

I really love the eggs Benedict and cinnamon rolls in this brunch restaurant.
我真的很愛這間早午餐店的班尼迪克蛋和肉桂捲。

Do you prefer pancakes, waffles, or English muffins?
你比較喜歡吃薄煎餅、格子鬆餅、還是英式鬆餅呢？

I would like to have a cheese omelet with ham and onions.
我要一份火腿洋蔥起司蛋捲。

Can I add some cream cheese and smoked salmon in my bagel, please?
我的貝果裡面可以加奶油起司跟煙燻鮭魚嗎？

I'll have a French toast with grilled cheese, please.
請給我一份法式吐司加烤起司。

UNIT

03 吃喝 下午茶時光
Afternoon Tea

單字基本功　掌握關鍵字 = 開口第一步

核心聯想　可口小點心 Delicious snacks

biscuit [`bɪskɪt] 名（英）餅乾	**cinnamon** [`sɪnəmən] 名 肉桂	**cupcake** [`kʌp͵kek] 名 杯子蛋糕	**raisin** [`rezn̩] 名 葡萄乾
scone [skon] 名 英國司康餅	**tart** [tɑrt] 名 水果塔	**Boston cream pie** 片 波士頓派	**cheese cake** 片 起司蛋糕

 香氣四溢的茶 Fragrant tea　進階學習

teapot [`ti͵pɑt] 名 茶壺	**strainer** [`strenɚ] 名 過濾器	**afternoon tea** 片 下午茶	**black tea** 片 紅茶
chamomile tea 片 洋甘菊茶	**Earl Grey tea** 片 伯爵茶	**fruit tea** 片 水果茶	**herbal tea** 片 花草茶

 深度追蹤　　　　　Knowing More

　　下午茶源於西元一八四〇年，英國維多利亞時代的女爵－安娜貝佛七世（7th Duchess of Bedford）。因為每到下午時刻，她就感到意興闌珊，便請女僕準備烤麵包、奶油和茶來果腹，後來更邀請好友同享愜意的午後時光，於是這種悠閒的下午茶習慣便漸漸蔚為風尚。正統的英式下午茶一般以三層（tier）的瓷盤盛裝，要注意正確吃法是由下至上、鹹至甜，從最下層的三明治往上吃到最上層的甜點，並配合水果茶或紅茶一起享用。

套個單字，想說的都能表達！

sb. have an eye for...　某人有識別⋯的眼光。

★ The lady over there has an eye for successful marketing strategies for tea houses.
那位小姐對下午茶館的行銷策略很有眼光。

★ Ms. Johnson has an eye for the quality of **imports**.
強森小姐很能辨別舶來品的品質。

★ Mr. Jackson has an eye for a good bargain.
對於買賣，傑克森先生很有眼光。

★ The jeweler has an eye for red **rubies** and **emeralds**.
那名珠寶商對紅寶石和綠寶石很有眼光。

★ The peasant has an eye for agricultural **shoots**.
那名農夫很能辨別農作物幼苗的好壞。

> **import**
> [`ɪmport]
> 名 進口品
> **ruby**
> [`rubɪ]
> 名 紅寶石
> **emerald**
> [`ɛmərəld]
> 名 綠寶石
> **shoot**
> [ʃut]
> 名 幼芽

sth. be beneficial to...　某事 / 物對⋯有益。

★ Taking a break from time to time is beneficial to your health.
適度休息一下有益身體健康。

★ The new drug will be beneficial to these patients.
新藥將對這些病人有幫助。

★ This plan is beneficial to many universities.
這項計畫對許多大學都有助益。

★ The unemployment insurance is beneficial to the **jobless**.
失業保險會對失業者有幫助。

★ A **mobile clinic** would be beneficial to the remote area.
行動診療車對偏遠地區的人有幫助。

> **jobless**
> [`dʒɑblɪs]
> 形 失業的
> **mobile**
> [`mobɪl]
> 形 可移動的
> **clinic**
> [`klɪnɪk]
> 名 診所

開口必備句　和老外聊開懷，就靠這幾句！

This coffee shop has great afternoon tea and a relaxing atmosphere.
這間咖啡廳有很不錯的下午茶和輕鬆的氛圍。

More and more hotels are starting to serve afternoon tea at an affordable price to their guests.
愈來愈多的旅館開始提供平價的下午茶給客人。

The signature here is cinnamon scones with raisins.
他們的招牌餐點是肉桂葡萄乾司康。

They serve afternoon tea from 2:00 p.m. to 5:00 p.m. every day.
他們每天下午兩點至五點都會提供下午茶。

Our afternoon tea set includes finger sandwiches, scones, homemade cakes, and your choice from a range of teas.
我們的下午茶套餐包含小三明治、司康餅、自製蛋糕，還能從眾多的茶品中選擇其中一項。

What kind of black tea would you like? We have Earl Grey, Assam, and Darjeeling.
您要點哪一種紅茶？我們有伯爵茶、阿薩姆、和大吉嶺。

I'd like a tea and scone set, with hot Lady Grey tea, please.
我要一份司康套餐，飲料選熱的仕女伯爵茶。

Please give me a piece of Boston cream pie and a cup of hot rose tea.
請給我一塊波士頓派和一杯熱的玫瑰茶。

We're going to throw a tea party next Saturday at 3 p.m. Please do come!
我們會在下週六的下午三點舉行下午茶派對，一定要來參加喔！

My sister is going to put her handmade pastries on the topmost tier of the cake stand.
我姐姐會把她的手作糕點放到蛋糕架的最上層。

MP3 ▷ 175

UNIT
04
娛樂

游泳好手
Going For A Swim

單字基本功 掌握關鍵字＝開口第一步

游泳裝備 Swimming gears

earplug [`ɪr͵plʌg] 名 耳塞	**floaty** [`flotɪ] 名 浮圈；浮板	**swimsuit** [`swɪmsut] 名（女）泳衣	**kick board** 片 浮板
swimming cap 片 泳帽	**swim goggles** 片 蛙鏡	**swim ring** 片 游泳圈	**swim trunks** 片（男）泳褲

游泳技巧 Swimming styles　進階學習

backstroke [`bæk͵stok] 名 仰式	**breaststroke** [`brɛst͵strok] 名 蛙式	**freestyle** [`fri͵staɪl] 名 自由式	**lifeguard** [`laɪf͵gɑrd] 名 救生員
sidestroke [`saɪd͵strok] 名 狗爬式	**dive** [daɪv] 動 跳水	**butterfly stroke** 片 蝶式	**survival floating** 片 水母漂

深度追蹤　　Knowing More

　　在古希臘的文物與作品中，經常可以看到描述水中活動的紀錄，像是在希臘的索倫法律中，就規定兒童必須學習希臘文及游泳，同時也鼓勵女性學習游泳，而上流社會也認為不會游泳的人就像是沒有知識一樣愚昧無知，所以大部分的希臘人在小時候，因為規定和觀念，就將游泳視為鍛鍊健全身心的活動，同時也是不可或缺的休閒活動。同樣重視游泳的還有古羅馬，青年都必須接受訓練，尤其是羅馬戰士，須具備就算全副甲冑還是能游泳的能力。

sb. make it a habit to... 某人使…成為習慣。

★ I make it a habit to swim 30 **laps** every day.
我養成每天游泳三十趟的習慣。

★ The author makes it a habit to proofread what she writes.
那名作家養成校對自己文章的習慣。

★ The boy makes it a habit to **declaim** loudly in class.
那名男孩養成在課堂上大聲朗讀的習慣。

★ Andy makes it a habit to walk to work.
安迪養成走路上班的習慣。

★ The teacher makes it a habit to read something **inspiring**.
那位老師培養了閱讀勵志書籍的習慣。

> **lap**
> [læp]
> 名 (一) 圈
> **declaim**
> [dɪ`klem]
> 動 朗讀
> **inspiring**
> [ɪn`spaɪrɪŋ]
> 形 激勵人心的

The more/~er..., the more/~er...

愈…，就愈…。

★ The more you practice, the better you will be.
你練習得愈多，就會變得愈厲害。

★ The brighter the sun, the happier my kids would be.
太陽愈大，我的孩子們就愈開心。

★ The healthier you eat, the longer you will live.
你吃得愈健康，就會愈長壽。

★ The more sleep he gets, the more tired he feels.
他睡得愈多，就愈覺得累。

★ The more he drinks, the more **terrible hangover** he will have.
他喝得愈多，宿醉的情形就愈嚴重。

> **terrible**
> [`tɛrəbl̩]
> 形 嚴重的
> **hangover**
> [`hæŋ͵ovɚ]
> 名 宿醉

MP3 ● 177

開口必備句 和老外聊開懷，就靠這幾句！

Swimming is one of my favorite exercises. How about you?
游泳是我最愛的運動之一，你呢？

You can rent a locker for two dollars at the counter.
你可以花兩塊錢在櫃檯租用置物櫃。

Remember to warm up before you get into the pool.
下水前記得先暖身。

Lots of people are sunbathing at the pool side.
很多人正在泳池邊做日光浴。

Young kids love the water slide most.
滑水道一向是小孩子的最愛。

Excuse me. Where can I get an extra starting block?
不好意思，我可以在哪取得多的出發台？

Joseph is good at swimming, especially the freestyle and backstroke.
約瑟夫擅長游泳，尤其是自由式和仰式。

Don't forget to dry yourself off when you get out of the pool so you don't catch a cold.
從游泳池上來的時候別忘了擦乾身體，以免感冒。

What are the advantages of swimming?
游泳的好處有哪些？

My father swims at least twenty laps each morning, which is the secret to his excellent health.
我的父親每天早上至少會游二十趟來回，這就是他健康的祕訣。

Just relax your body, and you can float in the water.
只要放鬆身體，你就能漂浮在水中。

The lifeguard was absent when the accident happened.
意外發生時，那名救生員不在現場。

UNIT 05　娛樂　**海邊衝浪**
Let's Go Surfing!

 單字基本功　掌握關鍵字＝開口第一步

核心聯想　衝浪必知術語 Surfing terms

cutback [`kʌt, bæk] 名 切迴轉彎；減少	**current** [`kɜənt] 名 洋流　形 當前的	**surfboard** [`sɜf, bord] 名 衝浪板	**surfer** [`sɜfɚ] 名 衝浪者
wave [wev] 名 海浪	**paddle out** 片 向外滑行	**seize the timing** 片 把握時機	**stand up** 片 站立

 享受海邊和沙灘 On the beach　進階學習

cover-up [`kʌvɚ, ʌp] 名 罩衫（女生會穿在泳衣外）	**flip-flop** [`flɪp, flɑp] 名 夾腳拖鞋	**parasailing** [`pærə, selɪŋ] 名 拖曳傘	**snorkeling** [`snɔrkl̩ɪŋ] 名 浮潛
sunscreen [`sʌn, skrin] 名 防曬乳	**beach umbrella** 片 海灘傘	**jet skiing** 片 騎水上摩托車	**scuba diving** 片 潛水

 深度追蹤　　　　　Knowing More

　　講到衝浪，就不可不知來自於一千多年前的木製衝浪板「Alaia」，在現今玻璃纖維衝浪板盛行的年代，它代表整個衝浪文化的起源，有著不可抹滅的地位。在階級制度嚴格的古夏威夷，如果衝浪技巧無法服眾，在部族中就只能當個平民，只能在岸邊使用 Alaia 玩「岸邊浪（shore break）」（浪到岸邊會突然拉高之後再重重蓋下），也不能駕乘夏威夷外海的大浪。但現在的 Alaia已經跳脫平民的象徵，代表的是無拘無束的衝浪方式和生活態度。

MP3 ▶ 179

套個單字，想說的都能表達！

... I (just) can't wait!　…，真期待！

★ We are going to the beach this weekend. I can't wait!
我們這個週末要去海邊，真期待！

★ Dad said he will bring home lots of **souvenirs** he bought from France. I just can't wait!
我爸說他會帶很多從法國買的紀念品回來，真期待！

★ The annual sale will begin next week. I just can't wait!
週年慶下週開跑，真期待！

★ My sister will be the leading role of the **musical**. I can't wait!
我姐姐將飾演那齣音樂劇的主角，真期待！

★ My favorite **author** is going to **publish** his new novel. I can't wait!
我最愛的作家即將出版新小說，真期待！

> **souvenir**
> [`suvə,nɪr]
> 名 紀念品
> **musical**
> [`mjuzɪk]]
> 名 音樂劇
> **author**
> [`ɔθə]
> 名 作者；作家
> **publish**
> [`pʌblɪʃ]
> 動 出版

sb. like sth. the best.　某人最喜歡某物 / 某事。

★ My brother likes surfing the best.
我哥哥最愛衝浪。

★ Tony likes **hang gliding** the best.
東尼最愛玩滑翔翼了。

★ I like **extreme sports** the best.
我最愛玩極限運動。

★ My foreign friends liked Beitou the best.
我的外國朋友們最喜歡北投了。

★ Most of the **natives** like winter the best.
大部分的本地人都最愛冬天。

> **hang gliding**
> 片 滑翔翼
> **extreme sport**
> 片 極限運動
> **native**
> [`netɪv]
> 名 本土人

 開口必備句　知老外聊開懷，就靠這幾句！

Penghu Island is ideal for surfing because of its sandy beach breaks.
澎湖島因為有沙質海灘，而成為理想的衝浪地點。

Queensland, Australia is called a paradise for surfers.
澳洲的昆士蘭享有衝浪天堂的美名。

Do you know any good surf spots around here?
你知道這附近哪裡有適合衝浪的好地點嗎？

You can rent a surfboard from any surf school by the beach and take lessons to experience the excitement of surfing.
你可以在海灘邊任何一家衝浪學校租借衝浪板，也能參加課程，體驗衝浪的刺激。

Matt has been into surfing ever since he was 14.
麥特從他十四歲起就愛上了衝浪。

Surf safety and awareness are of great importance to every surfer.
對衝浪者來說，時時注意衝浪安全是十分重要的。

Never let go of your surfboard and be aware of other surfers.
絕對不要放開你的衝浪板，並同時留意其他衝浪者。

Wearing a leash can keep your board close to you and keep it from becoming a hazard to other surfers.
戴著鏈繩可以確保衝浪板離你最近，避免對其他衝浪者造成危險。

Every surfer should be certified in CPR and basic first aid.
每一名衝浪者都應該要通過心肺復甦術和基本急救法的認證。

A good surfer always keeps an eye on changing weather conditions and the danger of sun exposure.
一名好的衝浪者會隨時留意天氣的變化以及太陽曝晒的危險。

What are the requirements for a good surfboard?
好的衝浪板應該具備哪些條件呢？

UNIT 06 旅遊
漫步鄉間
Strolling In The Fields

 單字基本功 掌握關鍵字 = 開口第一步

 核心聯想 走訪鄉間 The countryside

agriculture	cottage	countryside	farm
[`ægrɪˏkʌltʃɚ]	[`katɪdʒ]	[`kʌntrɪˏsaɪd]	[farm]
名 農業；農耕	名 農舍	名 鄉間	名 農場

farmhouse	hometown	meadow	produce
[ˏfarmˏhaʊs]	[`homˋtaʊn]	[`mɛdo]	[`pradjus]
名 農舍；農家	名 家鄉	名 草地	名 農產品

 採果樂趣 Picking fruits **進階學習**

grape	guava	mango	papaya
[grep]	[`gwavə]	[`mæŋgo]	[pəˋpaɪə]
名 葡萄（常用複數形）	名 番石榴；芭樂	名 芒果	名 木瓜

peach	pineapple	tangerine	watermelon
[pitʃ]	[`paɪnˏæpḷ]	[`tændʒəˏrin]	[`wɔtɚˏmɛlən]
名 桃子	形 鳳梨	名 橘子	名 西瓜

 **深度追蹤** 🔍

Knowing More

　　在美國，若想要到果園採果、體驗鄉間風情，就一定要知道幾種常見的水果：(1) 奇異果（kiwi），原產於中國，西元十九世紀時才從中國輸出到紐西蘭和歐洲，而美國到二十世紀才從中國進口奇異果。（2）白甜桃（nectarine），果皮顏色淡、酸度也較低，摸起來較硬，但可立即食用，無須等它變軟。(3) 石榴（pomegranate），原產於伊朗和北印度地區，是世界最古老的水果之一，且用途廣泛，常被做成果汁、藥品、染料或裝飾品。

 套個單字,想說的都能表達!

Why don't/doesn't sb. ...? 為什麼某人不…呢?

★ Why don't we spend a day in this lovely village?
我們何不在這迷人的村落裡待一天呢?

★ Why don't you bring the umbrella?
你為什麼不帶傘呢?

★ Why doesn't the **peddler** sell his products at a lower price?
那名小販為何不降低他產品的價格呢?

★ Why didn't the painter exhibit her paintings in the **gallery**?
為什麼那名畫家不在畫廊展示她的作品呢?

★ Why didn't the couple go out and take a **stroll**?
那對情侶為什麼沒有出門散步呢?

> **peddler**
> [`pɛdlɚ]
> 名 小販
> **gallery**
> [`gælərɪ]
> 名 畫廊
> **stroll**
> [strol]
> 名 散步

sb. be getting used to... 某人漸漸習慣…。

★ My aunt is getting used to the **frugal** and simple life here.
我的阿姨漸漸習慣這裡簡單質樸的生活。

★ The workers are getting used to the climate on this island.
工人們漸漸習慣了這座島上的氣候。

★ My **elder** sister is getting used to her new job.
我姐姐漸漸習慣她的新工作。

★ The actor is getting used to signing **autographs**.
那位演員漸漸習慣了簽名這件事。

★ The **graduate** is getting used to **public speaking**.
那名研究生漸漸習慣在公眾場合演說。

> **frugal**
> [`frugl]
> 形 簡樸的
> **elder**
> [`ɛldɚ]
> 形 年長的
> **autograph**
> [`ɔtə.græf]
> 名 親筆簽名
> **graduate**
> [`grædʒu.et]
> 名 研究生
> **public speaking**
> 片 公眾演說

MP3 ▶ 183

開口必備句 和老外聊開懷，就靠這幾句！

Traveling in the countryside is always relaxing.
到鄉間旅行總是很放鬆。

I suggest you rent a car to explore the countryside.
我建議你租輛車來探索鄉間。

It is a perfect time to bond with your family while enjoying a country tour.
享受鄉村之旅，是聯繫家庭感情的絕佳時機。

How about a trip to get closer to Mother Nature?
何不來段與大自然更親近的旅行？

I'm looking for a quick getaway to a beautiful countryside in California this fall.
我正在尋找這個秋天可以前往旅遊的加州美麗鄉間。

You can also enjoy a multi-course lunch at a scenic winery with guests from all over the world.
你也可以和來自世界各地的客人，在風景優美的釀酒廠享受正式午餐。

Strolling through the grape yards and smelling the fragrance of mellow wine is one of the biggest delights in life.
漫步在葡萄園區、聞著醇厚的酒香，是人生一大樂事。

My niece had a great weekend picking baskets of fresh fruits in the orchard.
我的姪女在果園裡摘了一籃又一籃的新鮮水果，度過了一個美好的週末。

They always spend their weekends at the lake house.
他們週末總是會去湖邊的別墅休息。

I relieve my stress by biking around the countryside and exploring in the forest on weekends.
我會在週末假期時，到鄉間騎腳踏車和走訪森林，以紓解壓力。

I like to visit my uncle's farm whenever I have free time.
我一有時間，就喜歡到叔叔的農場玩。

UNIT 07 旅遊

歐洲小旅行
A Vacation In Europe

單字基本功 掌握關鍵字 = 開口第一步

核心聯想 旅歐須知 Some travel tips

double-decker [`dʌbl̩`dɛkɚ] 名 雙層巴士	**express** [ɪk`sprɛs] 名 快車	**Euro** [`jʊro] 名 歐元	**Eurostar** [`jʊrostɑr] 名 歐洲之星列車
Channel Tunnel 片 英法海底隧道	**budget airline** 片 廉價航空	**plug adapter** 片 插座轉換接頭	**overnight train** 片 過夜火車（通常會提供臥鋪的長途火車）

參訪文化遺產 Cultural heritages **進階學習**

Stonehenge [`ston`hɛndʒ] 名（英）史前巨石柱群	**Buckingham Palace** 片（英）白金漢宮	**cultural heritage** 片 文化遺產	**Eiffel Tower** 片（法）艾菲爾鐵塔
New Swanstone Castle 片（德）新天鵝堡	**Palace of Versailles** 片（法）凡爾賽宮	**Rhein River** 片 萊茵河	**Windsor Castle** 片（英）溫莎堡

 深度追蹤 *Knowing More*

　　「歐洲文化遺產日（European Heritage Days）」是歐洲的象徵性活動其中之一。這個活動最初是由法國文化部鼓勵國人認識境內的遺產而設立，很快地便有熱烈的迴響，還有許多國家爭相效仿。之後，歐洲理事會便正式推廣歐洲文化遺產日，把活動時間訂為每年九月的第三個週末，讓人們可以用一個週末的時間來了解歐洲文化遺產、重溫歐洲的遺產瑰寶；且活動期間還會推出超過兩萬場講座、音樂會和課堂，來宣揚當地的文化遺產。

句型偷吃步　　套個單字，想說的都能表達！

...is between A and B. ...在 A 和 B 之間。

★ Switzerland is between Austria and France.
瑞士位於奧地利與法國之間。

★ The post office is between the breakfast shop and the tea house.
郵局位於早餐店和飲料店之間。

★ The pool is between the **sauna** and the **steam room**.
泳池位於烤箱和蒸氣室之間。

★ The **fresco** is between the sculpture and graphic arts.
壁畫介於雕刻和版畫之間。

★ The **castle** is between the luxury apartments and the slum.
那座城堡位在豪宅區與貧民區之間。

sauna
[ˋsaʊnə]
名 桑拿；三溫暖

steam room
片 蒸氣室

fresco
[ˋfrɛsko]
名 壁畫

castle
[ˋkæsḷ]
名 城堡

sb. pay the cost of sth. 某人支付了某物的費用。

★ Liliana sent her son to France and paid the cost of his trip.
莉莉安娜送她兒子去法國，並支付了他的旅行費用。

★ Jeff's parents sent him to the United States and paid the cost of his **tuition**.
傑夫的父母送他去美國，並支付了他的學費。

★ She rent a house in town and paid the cost of all the fees.
她在鎮上租了一棟房子，並支付了所有的費用。

★ Our boss held an **incentive** tour and paid the cost of everyone else's airline tickets.
我們老闆舉辦了員工旅遊，還付了大家的機票錢。

★ Alex took the responsibility and paid the cost of **maintenance**.
艾利克斯承擔了責任，並支付了維修費。

tuition
[tjuˋɪʃən]
名 學費

incentive
[ɪnˋsɛntɪv]
名 刺激；鼓勵

maintenance
[ˋmentənəs]
名 維修

開口必備句

Edinburgh, the capital of Scotland, has been a popular tourist spot for a long time.

蘇格蘭的首都——愛丁堡，一直都是熱門的觀光景點。

Have you ever heard of Loch Ness and Nessie?

你聽說過尼斯湖和水怪嗎？

The changing of the Guard at Buckingham Palace takes place at 11:30 every other day from May till the end of July.

白金漢宮的守衛交接從五月至七月底，每兩天於十一點半舉行。

The Castle of Versailles used to be a royal castle, and it is one of the most popular scenic spots now.

凡爾賽宮曾是皇家城堡，現在則是最熱門的觀光景點之一。

There are more than thirty museums in Paris.

超過三十座博物館坐落於巴黎。

Excuse me. Do you know where the Sherlock Holmes Museum is located?

不好意思，你知道福爾摩斯博物館在哪嗎？

It takes only two hours by Eurostar from Paris to London.

搭乘歐洲之星列車，從巴黎到倫敦僅需兩小時。

Cotswolds, a countryside village in England, always impresses people with its tranquil atmosphere and old-fashioned spirit.

柯茲窩——一個英國的鄉村小鎮，常以其寧靜的氣氛和古典情懷帶給人們深刻的印象。

I am definitely going to the Louvre Museum to appreciate the Mona Lisa.

我一定要去羅浮宮欣賞《蒙娜麗莎的微笑》。

If you love Peter Rabbit, you shouldn't miss the Lake District.

若你喜愛彼得兔，你就絕不能錯過湖區。

MP3 ▶ 187

日常生活習慣
Routine & Habits

 單字基本功 掌握關鍵字＝開口第一步

 悠閒的生活步調 Slow pace

leisure [`lidʒɚ] 名 閒暇 形 空閒的	**teatime** [`ti,taɪm] 名 下午茶時間	**laid-back** [`led,bæk] 形 悠閒的	**scenic** [`sinɪk] 形 風景優美的
serene [sə`rin] 形 寧靜的；安詳的	**suburban** [sə`bɝbən] 形 郊外的	**lunch break** 片 午休時間	**take a break** 片 休息片刻

 規律的日常生活 Regular life 進階學習

punctuality [,pʌŋktʃu`ælətɪ] 名 準時	**continuous** [kən`tɪnjuəs] 形 連續的	**hourly** [`auɚlɪ] 形 每小時的 副 每小時地	**punctual** [`pʌŋktʃuəl] 形 準時的
regular [`rɛgjəlɚ] 形 規律的	**rigid** [`rɪdʒɪd] 形 嚴格的	**alarm clock** 片 鬧鐘	**stick to schedule** 片 遵守表定時間

 深度追蹤 Knowing More

　　無論你習慣早睡早起或「晚睡晚起」，都可有計畫地分配時間，把生理時鐘（internal clock）調整到最佳狀態！統計顯示，早起的人最有創意是上午，但在下午大約一點半時，因體溫下降、腦部進入休息狀態，常導致注意力不集中；而下午五點，手部與眼部的協調性達到最佳狀態，是最好的運動時間。至於習慣晚起的人，雖然在晚上比較有精神，但也不宜太晚睡而影響腦部的活動力，且就算早上趕著上班，也要記得吃早餐、提供腦部所需的營養喔！

 套個單字，想說的都能表達！

It is about time to/for... 該是…的時間了。

- ★ It is about time to go to bed.
  睡覺的時間到了。

- ★ It is about time to change your lifestyle.
  該是改變你生活型態的時候了。

- ★ It is about time to **upgrade** our skills.
  該是提升我們技術的時候了。

- ★ It is about time for **revising** our rules and **regulations**.
  該是修正我們規章制度的時候了。

- ★ It is about time to think about the **implementation**.
  該是思考執行方法的時候了。

upgrade
[`ʌp`gred]
⑩ 升級
revise
[rɪ`vaɪz]
⑩ 修正
regulation
[ˌrɛgjə`leʃən]
⑧ 規章
implementation
[ˌɪmpləmɛn`teʃən]
⑧ 實施

Needless to say, ... 不用說，…。

- ★ Needless to say, health is more important than **wealth**.
  不用說，健康比財富重要。

- ★ Needless to say, learning without thinking is useless.
  不用說，學而不思是沒有用的。

- ★ Needless to say, **assiduous** working leads a man to success.
  不用說，辛勤工作才能引導人走向成功。

- ★ Needless to say, that **sincere** man **kept his promise**.
  不用說，那名正直的男性守住了他的承諾。

- ★ Needless to say, **biodiversity** is gradually declining because of climate change.
  不用說，生物多樣性因為氣候變化而逐漸減少。

wealth
[wɛlθ]
⑧ 財富
assiduous
[ə`sidʒuəs]
⑱ 勤勞刻苦的
sincere
[sɪn`sɪr]
⑱ 真誠的
keep one's promise
⑪ 遵守諾言
biodiversity
[baɪo͵daɪ`vɝsətɪ]
⑧ 生物多樣性

開口必備句　和老外聊開懷，就靠這幾句！

Most Western people prefer taking a shower in the morning.
大部分的西方人喜歡在早上淋浴。

Parents always ask their children to maintain a regular routine.
父母總會要求小孩維持規律的生活。

You can find balance in life if you plan your personalized daily routine and stick to it.
如果你規劃每日作息並嚴格執行，就能找到生活的重心。

I'm not used to the busy pace of life in Taipei city.
我還不習慣台北市忙碌的生活步調。

In Chinese culture, punctuality is considered a virtue.
在中華文化，準時是一種美德。

Chinese people tend to arrive a bit earlier than the scheduled time to show their earnestness.
中國人會提早一些赴約，以表示他們的誠意。

My Korean friend is a "chimaek" fanatic. He always has Korean-style fried chicken and beer after work.
我的韓國朋友是個「雞啤」迷，他每次下班都會去買韓式炸雞配啤酒。

I have been longing for the laid-back lifestyle in Spain.
我一直很嚮往西班牙的悠閒生活。

Do you usually have snacks before going to bed?
你睡前通常會吃宵夜嗎？

Most Taiwanese enjoy going to night markets for late-night snacks.
大部分台灣人都喜歡去夜市買小吃來當宵夜。

In some European countries, people don't have dinner until eight in the evening.
在一些歐洲國家，不到晚上八點不會吃晚餐。

★UNIT★ **09** 職場

抓住機會
A Golden Opportunity

 單字基本功 ▶ 掌握關鍵字 = 開口第一步

 核心聯想　當機會來敲門 Seizing opportunities

luck [lʌk] 名 運氣；好運	**capture** [`kæptʃɚ] 動 把握；捕捉	**seize** [siz] 動 抓住；逮捕	**accidental** [ˌæksə`dɛntḷ] 形 偶然的
likely [`laɪklɪ] 形 有可能的	**fight for** 片 努力爭取…	**knock on** 片 敲門（形容機會來臨）	**in the future** 片 在未來

 命定的未來 A bright future　進階學習

destiny [`dɛstənɪ] 名 命運；宿命	**doom** [dum] 名 厄運 動 註定	**eternity** [ɪ`tɜnətɪ] 名 永遠；永恆	**prophet** [`prɑfɪt] 名 先知
prospect [`prɑspɛkt] 名 期望；前景 動 勘查	**disciple** [dɪ`saɪpḷ] 名 信徒	**precise** [prɪ`saɪs] 形 精確的	**lifetime** [`laɪfˌtaɪm] 名 一生

 深度追蹤 🔍　　　　Knowing More

　　與「機會」有關的英文諺語，也可學學以下說法：(1) Actions speak louder than words. 坐而言不如起而行。(2) Example is better than precept. 身教勝於言教。(3) You can't have your cake and eat it. 魚與熊掌不可兼得。(4) Make hay while the sun shines. 把握時機。另外，常聽到的「Carpe diem.」，中文常譯為「把握光陰、及時行樂」，鼓勵人不要太過盲目追求看不見的未來，要在今天就盡力活出自我、做出實際行動。

句型偷吃步　套個單字，想說的都能表達！

not only...but (also)...　不僅…，而且…。

★ Johnny is not only lucky but also **hard-working**.
強尼不僅很幸運，而且也很努力。

★ The projector is not only environmental friendly but also cheap.
這台投影機不僅很環保，價格還很便宜。

★ Adam is **in pursuit of** not only wealth but also a sense of achievement.
亞當不僅追求財富，還很重視成就感。

★ Getting **kickbacks** is not only **immoral** but also illegal.
收取回扣不僅不道德，而且是違法的。

★ The pesticides affect not only pests but also wildlife.
殺蟲劑不僅會除掉害蟲，還會影響其他野生動植物。

hard-working
[ˌhɑrdˈwɜkɪŋ]
形 勤勉的

in pursuit of
片 追求

kickback
[ˈkɪkˌbæk]
名 回扣；佣金

immoral
[ɪˈmɔrəl]
形 不道德的

sb. have a feeling that...　某人覺得 / 感覺…。

★ I have a feeling that I did well on the interview.
我覺得我在面試中表現得很好。

★ He has a feeling that this project would be a huge success.
他覺得這項企劃將會非常成功。

★ She has a feeling that something is missing at the **scene**.
她覺得現場好像少了些什麼。

★ I have a feeling that Abby is not as close to Oliver as she used to be.
我覺得艾比和奧利佛沒有以前那麼親密。

★ The **detective** has a feeling that the real **murderer** is still **at large**.
那位偵探覺得真兇仍逍遙法外。

scene
[sin]
名 案發現場

detective
[dɪˈtɛktɪv]
名 偵探

murderer
[ˈmɝdərə]
名 兇手

at large
片 逍遙法外

Men propose, God disposes.
謀事在人，成事在天。

William McFee once said, "If fate means you to lose, give him a good fight anyhow."
威廉‧麥克菲曾說：「如果命運要你認輸，總要好好抵抗。」

What do you believe in, fate or opportunity?
你相信機會還是命運？

When the time comes, seize your chance and choose your destiny.
當時機來臨，要把握機會、選擇你的命運。

I don't believe in fate, only in my devotion and myself.
我不相信命運，只相信付出和相信自己。

Be open to opportunity and embrace it while you can.
接受機會，並好好把握機會。

Having the chance to work for such a well-known company is definitely the opportunity of a lifetime for me.
能在如此知名的公司工作，絕對是我一生僅有一次的機會。

Positive thinking can lead to more opportunities.
正向思考可讓你有更多好機會。

Opportunity likely depends upon the effort you make.
機會來自於你所付出的努力。

You can't sit back like a turtle, waiting for a chance to come.
你不能像隻烏龜，整天坐著等待機會降臨。

What would you do if you got a lucky break?
當你認為機會來臨時，你會怎麼做？

Success in life doesn't just happen. You have to fight for it.
成功不會自然發生，你得努力爭取。

MP3 ▶ 193

UNIT 10 職場

傳統與創新
Tradition & Innovation

單字基本功 掌握關鍵字 = 開口第一步

核心聯想 維持傳統 Keeping traditions

importance	precedent	symbol	accustomed
[ɪmˋpɔrtn̩s]	[ˋprɛsədənt]	[ˋsɪmbl̩]	[əˋkʌstəmd]
名 重要性	名 前例 形 前面的	名 象徵；標誌	形 習慣的；通常的

former	as usual	comply with	used to
[ˋfɔrmɚ]	片 照例；如常	片 順應	片 習慣於；過去曾經
形 以前的			

創新思維 Being innovative 進階學習

aspect	exploit	create	improve
[ˋæspɛkt]	[ˋɛksplɔɪt]	[krɪˋet]	[ɪmˋpruv]
名 方面；觀點	名 功績 動 開發	動 創造；創作	動 改善；增進

reform	innovative	novel	break with tradition
[ˌrɪˋfɔrm]	[ˋɪnoˌvetɪv]	[ˋnavl̩]	片 打破傳統
動 改革	形 創新的	形 新穎的	

深度追蹤 Knowing More

　　世界級權威的「破壞式創新大師」克雷頓・克里斯汀生（Clayton Christensen）曾提出五種訓練創意的方法：(1) 聯想（associating）：從行不通的情況開始發想，並把看似無關的點子相互連結。（2）疑問（questioning）：活用問句來思考問題。(3) 觀察（observing）：仔細觀察身邊所有的人事物。(4) 社交（networking）：和各種人交流，並擴大朋友圈。(5) 實驗（experimenting）：親身經歷新事物並學習新知。

套個單字，想說的都能表達！

...be familiar to sb. ⋯對某人來說很熟悉。

★ Developing an effective integrating strategy is familiar to our manager.
規劃一個有效的併購計畫對我們經理來說很熟悉。

★ The one-and-only "home button" is familiar to iPhone users.
這個獨一無二的「Home 鍵」對 iPhone 使用者來說很熟悉。

★ All articles in the old man's **will** are familiar to his **attorney**.
那位老人的律師很熟悉他遺囑內的所有條款。

★ Current issues on Internet safety are familiar to most people.
最近的網路安全議題對大多數人來說都很熟悉。

★ **Baroque**-style design is familiar to that **architect**.
那名建築師很熟悉巴洛克風格的設計。

> **will**
> [wɪl]
> 名 遺囑
> **attorney**
> [ə`tɜnɪ]
> 名 律師
> **Baroque**
> [bə`rok]
> 形 巴洛克式的
> **architect**
> [`ɑrkə‚tɛkt]
> 名 建築師

Is it possible to...? ⋯是可能的嗎？

★ Is it possible to keep the tradition under this situation?
在這種情況下，有可能維持傳統嗎？

★ Is it possible to control the high **blood pressure** without drugs?
不用藥物就控制住高血壓是有可能的嗎？

★ Is it possible to **educate** a child without any scold?
以完全不責罵的方式去教育孩子是有可能的嗎？

★ Is it possible to change one's habit and personality?
改變一個人的習慣與性格是有可能的嗎？

★ Is it possible to promote the product with a small amount of **advertisement**?
只依靠少量廣告來行銷這個產品是有可能的嗎？

> **blood pressure**
> 片 血壓
> **educate**
> [`ɛdʒə‚ket]
> 動 教育；培養
> **advertisement**
> [‚ædvə`taɪzmənt]
> 名 廣告；宣傳

MP3 ▶ 195

開口必備句 和老外聊開懷，就靠這幾句！

Innovation and tradition are both important for a company.
對一家公司而言，創新和傳統都很重要。

Without traditions, we wouldn't know where we came from.
沒有傳統的話，我們就不會知道自己從何而來。

Most of the time, innovation brings new ideas and products, while tradition is the keeper of our past.
大多時候，創新帶來新想法和新素材，而傳統則守護著我們的過去。

Usually, innovation is defined as the exploitation of new ideas, leading to the creation of new products, processes, or services.
創新通常被定義為替產品、過程、或服務注入新想法。

What do you think is more important, innovation or tradition?
你覺得哪個比較重要，創新還是傳統？

Our boss considers innovation a vital element to the prosperity of our company.
我們老闆覺得創新在我們公司的發展過程中非常重要。

Try thinking out of the box, and you'll find more possibilities.
試著跳脫傳統，你會發現更多的可能性。

The local government is trying to preserve tradition in an innovative way in order to attract the tourists.
當地政府為了吸引旅客，正試著以創新的方式保存傳統。

Joe is the first to adopt the symbolism of wind in architecture.
喬是第一個在建築界採納風的象徵含義的人。

Jason's sculpture successfully displayed a combination of innovation and tradition by using clay and aluminum.
藉由結合使用粘土和鋁，傑森的雕塑品成功地顯現出創新與傳統的融合。

Laura is innovative, and thus qualified for this position.
蘿拉很勇於創新，因此很適合這個職務。

NOTE

Part 08

濃情八月約會作戰

August Highlights:
From Lovers To Couples

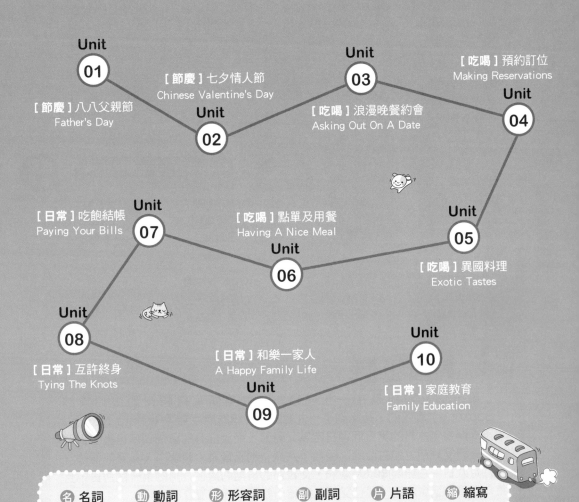

Unit 01
[節慶] 八八父親節
Father's Day

[節慶] 七夕情人節
Chinese Valentine's Day

Unit 02

Unit 03
[吃喝] 浪漫晚餐約會
Asking Out On A Date

[吃喝] 預約訂位
Making Reservations

Unit 04

[日常] 吃飽結帳
Paying Your Bills

Unit 07

[吃喝] 點單及用餐
Having A Nice Meal

Unit 06

Unit 05

[吃喝] 異國料理
Exotic Tastes

Unit 08

[日常] 互許終身
Tying The Knots

[日常] 和樂一家人
A Happy Family Life

Unit 09

Unit 10

[日常] 家庭教育
Family Education

名 名詞　動 動詞　形 形容詞　副 副詞　片 片語　縮 縮寫

★UNIT★ 01 節慶 八八父親節
Father's Day

 單字基本功 掌握關鍵字 = 開口第一步

核心聯想 感謝父親 Thanking your dad

commitment [kə`mɪtmənt] 名 承諾；責任感	**contribution** [ˌkɑntrə`bjuʃən] 名 貢獻；捐助
discipline [`dɪsəplɪn] 名 紀律；訓練	**admire** [əd`maɪr] 動 欣賞；欽佩

beloved [bɪ`lʌvɪd] 形 摯愛的	**be held on** 片 在⋯舉行
bring up 片 撫養	**devote...to** 片 將⋯奉獻給⋯

 父親節禮物 Presents for Dad **進階學習**

briefcase [`brif͵kes] 名 公事包	**e-card** [`ikɑrd] 名 電子賀卡
necktie [`nɛk͵taɪ] 名 領帶	**razor** [`rezɚ] 名 刮鬍刀

tablet [`tæblɪt] 名 平板電腦	**watch** [`watʃ] 名 手錶
electronic gadget 片 電子產品	**fishing rod** 片 釣魚竿

 深度追蹤 Knowing More

　　第一個父親節是在一九一○年，於美國華盛頓州的史伯坎鎮（Spokane）慶祝的，後來到了一九七二年，總統尼克森（Richard Nixon）才正式將每年六月的第三個週日定為父親節，而大部分的歐洲國家也是在這個時間慶祝父親節。但在亞洲，因為「八八」的諧音為「爸爸」，父親節便被訂為八月八日。在紐西蘭以及澳洲，父親節的日期則落在九月的第一個週日，且每年在澳洲還會評選「最佳父親」並給予當選父親榮譽嘉獎。

MP3 ▶ 197

 套個單字，想說的都能表達！

A and B are (adv.) alike. A 和 B（很）相似。

★ My personality and my father's are so much alike.
我的個性和我爸爸很像。

★ A **hostage** and a prisoner are too much alike.
人質和囚犯太相似了。

★ His **handwriting** and mine are pretty much alike.
他的筆跡和我的筆跡還滿相似的。

★ **Indifference** and pride are very alike.
漠不關心和傲慢看起來非常相似。

★ Conservatives and liberals are actually alike.
保守人士和自由主義者其實很相似。

> **hostage**
> [`hɑstɪdʒ]
> 名 人質
> **handwriting**
> [`hænd,raɪtɪŋ]
> 名 筆跡
> **indifference**
> [ɪn`dɪfərəns]
> 名 漠不關心

sb. express one's gratitude to... 某人感謝…。

★ I would like to express my gratitude to my dear father.
我想對我親愛的父親表達感謝之情。

★ My grandparents expressed their gratitude to the nurses for their **meticulous** care.
我祖父母對那些護士無微不至的照顧很感謝。

★ Our manager would like to express her gratitude to these new customers for their support and frequent **patronage**.
我們經理想要感謝這些新顧客的支持和時常的光顧。

★ We want to express our gratitude to your **foundation** for the **generosity** you've shown us.
我們想要對你們基金會的慷慨對待表示感謝。

★ All the attendees expressed their gratitude to the initiator of this annual meeting.
所有與會者都對這場年會的發起人表示感謝。

> **meticulous**
> [mə`tɪkjələs]
> 形 無微不至的
> **patronage**
> [`pætrənɪdʒ]
> 名 光顧
> **foundation**
> [faun`deʃən]
> 名 基金會
> **generosity**
> [,dʒɛnə`rɑsətɪ]
> 名 慷慨

開口必備句 和老外聊開懷，就靠這幾句！

Father's Day is the day to honor fathers' love and devotion to their family.

父親節是表揚父親對家庭的愛與奉獻的節日。

Father's Day falls on the third Sunday in June in both the U.S. and Canada.

在美國和加拿大，父親節是六月的第三個週日。

Father's Day is celebrated on August 8 in Asia.

在亞洲，父親節是在八月八日慶祝。

Father's Day is the fourth-largest day of sending cards.

父親節是卡片寄送量第四大的節日。

In honor of all the father figures, many activities are held on Father's Day.

為了向所有父執輩致敬，父親節當天會舉辦許多活動。

What are you going to buy your father as a Father's Day gift?

你想為你父親準備什麼樣的禮物呢？

What do you think would be the best gift for Dad?

你覺得送給爸爸最棒的禮物是什麼呢？

Let's take Dad out for a fancy dinner on Father's Day.

我們帶爸爸出去吃頓父親節大餐吧。

It is my father's love and care that has nourished me through all these years.

是父親的愛與關懷滋養著我，讓我年年成長苗壯。

Sons and daughters send greeting cards or make a simple phone call to their sweet fathers on Father's Day.

兒女們會在父親節寄送卡片，或是簡單打通電話給親愛的父親。

I'm sure my dad is going to love the gift I bought for him.

我覺得我爸一定會很喜歡他的禮物。

UNIT 02

節慶
七夕情人節
Chinese Valentine's Day

單字基本功 ▶ 掌握關鍵字＝開口第一步

 核心聯想 七夕由來 Stories of Qixi Festival

cowherd [`kaʊˌhɜd] 名 牛郎	**magpie** [`mægˌpaɪ] 名 喜鵲	**moved** [muvd] 形 被感動的	**fall in love with** 片 與⋯陷入愛河
folk legend 片 民間傳說	**lunar calendar** 片 農曆	**Milky Way** 片 銀河	**weaver girl** 片 織女

甜蜜時光 Sweet time together **進階學習**

caress [kə`rɛs] 名 動 愛撫	**clench** [klɛntʃ] 名 動 緊握	**enhancement** [ɪn`hænsmənt] 名 增進；提高	**maiden** [`medn̩] 名 少女 形 少女的
chuckle [`tʃʌkl̩] 動 輕笑；竊笑	**indispensable** [ˌɪndɪ`spɛnsəbl̩] 形 不可缺少的	**naive** [nɑ`iv] 形 天真的	**tender** [`tɛndɚ] 形 溫柔的

 深度追蹤 🔍

Knowing More

　　源於牛郎織女愛情故事的七夕（Chinese Valentine's Day/Double Seventh Festival），落在農曆的七月七日。與西洋情人節的不同之處在於，七夕不僅是屬於戀人的節日，對少女來說也相當重要；除了拜織女以求好姻緣之外，少女們會在這天進行許多「乞巧」遊戲，像是比賽誰最快將線穿入針裡面，或把平日縫衣的針投入碗中，若呈現像花朵鳥獸的影子，表示織女賜了一根靈巧的繡花針、能有像織女一樣的好手藝，故七夕又稱「乞巧節」。

 句型偷吃步　套個單字，想說的都能表達！

Do you happen to know...? 你碰巧知道…嗎？

★ Do you happen to know the origin of Chinese Valentine's Day?
你碰巧知道七夕的起源嗎？

★ Do you happen to know the meaning of this **slang**?
你碰巧知道這句俚語的由來和意思嗎？

★ Do you happen to know how to **deactivate** the **siren**?
你碰巧知道怎麼關掉警報器嗎？

★ Do you happen to know where the new shopping **plaza** is?
你碰巧知道新的購物廣場在哪裡嗎？

★ Do you happen to know how the couple started **quarrelling**?
你碰巧知道那對夫妻爭吵的原因嗎？

slang
[slæŋ]
名 俚語

deactivate
[di`æktə‚vet]
動 撤銷；使無效

siren
[`saɪrən]
名 警報器

plaza
[`plæzə]
名 廣場

quarrel
[`krɔrəl]
動 吵架

so...that... 太…以致於…。

★ He is so in love with her that he would give up everything just for her.
他太愛她了，以致於可以為她放棄所有事情。

★ It is so late that we cannot go sightseeing.
時間太晚了，以致於我們無法繼續遊覽。

★ The car stopped so suddenly that it caused a serious **pileup**.
車子急停而引起連環相撞。

★ The woman is so **picky** that nobody would work for her.
那名女子太挑剔，以致於沒有人要為她工作。

★ The scenery was so stunning that we decided to stay there for at least a year.
那邊的景色優美到讓我們決定至少在那住個一年。

pileup
[`paɪl‚ʌp]
名 （交通事故）連環相撞

picky
[`pɪkɪ]
形 吹毛求疵的

開口必備句 和老外聊開懷，就靠這幾句！

Chinese Valentine's Day celebrates the meeting of the cowherd and weaver girl in Chinese mythology.

🔊 七夕情人節是為了慶祝牛郎與織女的重逢。

Tens of thousands of magpies built a bridge for the long-separated couple.

🔊 成千上萬的喜鵲為這對長久分隔的情侶搭了一座橋。

The sky is dotted with stars, and people can see the Milky Way as well.

🔊 天空佈滿了星星，人們也可以看見銀河。

Legend has it that Altair symbolizes the cowherd, while Vega represents the weaver girl.

🔊 傳說中，牛郎星代表著牛郎，而織女星則代表織女。

How are you going to celebrate Chinese Valentine's Day?

🔊 你打算怎麼慶祝七夕情人節呢？

People will give their lovers flowers and chocolates.

🔊 人們會送他們的愛人鮮花和巧克力。

Girls worship the weaver girl and pray for a good marriage on Chinese Valentine's Day.

🔊 女孩們會在七夕情人節拜織女，並祈求好婚姻。

Single and newlywed women make offerings to the weaver girl, which usually includes fruits, flower, and face powder.

🔊 單身以及新婚的女性通常會用水果、鮮花和脂粉當作祭品來祭拜織女。

It's a tradition for girls to throw needles into a basin for divination of dexterity in needlework.

🔊 傳統上，女孩們會把針線投入水盆中來占卜是否能得到靈巧的針線手藝。

Many florists offer customized bouquets for lovers on Chinese Valentine's Day.

🔊 許多花商在七夕情人節供應情人特製花束。

UNIT 03 日常 浪漫晚餐約會
Asking Out On A Date

單字基本功 掌握關鍵字 = 開口第一步

核心聯想 主動邀約 Asking someone out

couple [`kʌpļ]	date [det]	relationship [rɪ`leʃən`ʃɪp]	flirt [flɜt]
名 情侶；夫妻	名 動 約會	名 關係；戀愛關係	動 調情

woo [wu]	romantic [rə`mæntɪk]	single [`sɪŋgļ]	ask sb. out
動 追求；求婚	形 浪漫的	形 單身的	片 邀約某人約會

 小鹿亂撞 Butterflies in the stomach **進階學習**

chemistry [`kɛmɪstrɪ]	crush [krʌʃ]	infatuate [ɪn`fætʃʊ,et]	be infatuated with sb.
名 曖昧；（男女間的）來電	名 熱戀；迷戀對象	動 使著迷	片 為某人著迷

fall for sb.	love at first sight	sweep sb. off their feet	unrequited love
片 迷戀某人	片 一見鍾情	片 使某人為之傾倒	片 單戀

 深度追蹤 *Knowing More*

　　約會通常是男女進入戀愛關係的第一步，而兩人的單獨約會稱為「single date」，「double date」則指兩對男女一起約會；其他約會方式還有相親（blind date）、網路約會（cyber date）、聯誼（group dating）和快速約會（speed dating）。至於對方之後突然消失（ghosting）或是漸漸斷了聯絡（slow fade）的話也不要太傷心，而還未確定彼此的感覺之前，也別急著在臉書公開感情狀態（FBO / Facebook Official）囉。

MP3 ▶ 203

套個單字，想說的都能表達！

sb. should try one's best to...
某人應該盡最大的努力去…。

- ★ You should try your best to ask her out.
  你應該努力約她出去。

- ★ People should try their best to get rid of bad habits.
  人們應該盡最大的努力戒除壞習慣。

- ★ Parents should try their best to communicate with their children.
  父母應該盡最大的努力與孩子溝通。

- ★ **Pharmacists** should try their best to explain the use of this **ointment**.
  藥劑師應該盡最大的努力來解釋這款藥膏的用途。

  pharmacist
  [`fɑrməsɪst]
  名 藥劑師
  ointment
  [`ɔɪntmənt]
  名 藥膏

- ★ Governors should try their best to support the national economic reforms.
  州長應該盡最大的努力來支持國家的經濟改革。

If..., sb./sth. will/may/can...
如果…，某人 / 某事會 / 也許 / 可以…。

- ★ If she has a good impression on you, she may go out on a second date with you.
  如果她對你有好印象，她或許會答應跟你再次約會。

- ★ If you get up early, you can exercise more.
  如果你很早起，你就可以多運動了。

- ★ If I do well on the exam, dad will buy me a gift.
  如果我這次考得不錯，爸就會買禮物給我。

- ★ If you add that much salt, it will be too **salty**.
  如果你加那麼多鹽，可能會太鹹。

  salty
  [`sɔltɪ]
  形 鹹的
  rotten
  [`rɑtn̩]
  形 壞掉的
  food poisoning
  片 食物中毒

- ★ If you eat **rotten** food, you may get **food poisoning**.
  如果你吃到壞掉的食物，你可能會食物中毒。

開口必備句 和老外聊開懷，就靠這幾句！

My mom tried to set my brother up with our neighbor, Ella.

我媽媽試著想幫我哥和鄰居艾拉牽紅線。

Eve is definitely his type of girl.

依芙絕對是他的理想型。

Alan had a crush on Lily, so he decided to ask her out.

艾倫被莉莉煞到，所以決定約她出去。

It never occurred to Nick that he would ever have the chance to date the girl of his dreams.

尼克從沒想過他會有和夢中情人約會的機會。

Do you know who Janet's date is tonight?

你知道珍妮絲今晚要和誰約會嗎？

When should I pick you up, seven or eight?

我該幾點去接你，七點還是八點？

Tommy always takes a girl to that famous Italian restaurant on the first date.

湯米第一次約會總是帶女生去那間有名的義式餐廳。

It's my sister's first date with her crush, so she couldn't be more nervous.

這是我妹第一次和暗戀對象約會，所以她非常緊張。

They had a romantic candlelight dinner at a fancy French restaurant last night.

他們昨晚在一間高級的法式餐廳，享用了一頓浪漫的燭光晚餐。

Victoria was touched when she saw her boyfriend carrying a bunch of red roses, her favorite flower.

當維多利亞看到她男友捧著一束她最愛的紅玫瑰時，她非常感動。

Frank is such a gentleman because he always opens the car door for his date.

法蘭克很有紳士風度，他總是會幫約會對象開車門。

MP3 ▶ 205

04 吃喝 預約訂位

Making Reservations

單字基本功 ▷ 掌握關鍵字 = 開口第一步

核心聯想

預約必知 Reserving a table

booth [buθ] 名 雅座；攤販	**table** [`tebḷ] 名 桌子；一桌人
vacancy [`vekənsɪ] 名 空位；空間	**reserve** [rɪ`zɜv] 動 預約；保留
book [bʊk] 動 預定；登記	**cancel** [`kænsḷ] 動 取消；刪除
postpone [post`pon] 動 推遲；使延期	**available** [ə`veləbḷ] 形 有空的；可用的

吃喝地點 Plenty of places to eat

進階學習

bistro [`bistro] 名 小酒館；小餐廳	**buffet** [bu`fe] 名 自助餐
café [kə`fe] 名 咖啡廳	**cafeteria** [ˌkæfə`tɪrɪə] 名 食堂
diner [`daɪnə] 名 小餐館	**fast food restaurant** 片 速食餐廳
food court 片 美食街	**snack bar** 片 快餐店

深度追蹤 🔍

Knowing More

　　想要預約餐廳，除了打通電話，也可以下載餐廳業者開發的應用程式，只要註冊並登入會員，動動手指就可以完成預約，也有餐廳設立自己的網站，提供客人線上訂位的功能。而預約當然是盡早完成才好，要不然想要預約知名餐廳的話，說不定要等好幾個月才有空位；另外，也有一些餐廳不接受預約，只接受現場排隊，甚至還有餐廳怕客人突然消失，請客人預約時就先付一筆訂金。所以在預約之前，可別忘記要先查看餐廳資訊和訂位政策囉。

Is there any possibility...? 有機會可以⋯嗎？

★ Is there any possibility that I can change my reservation to tomorrow?
可以把我的預約改成明天嗎？

★ Is there any possibility that I can go with you?
我可以跟你一起去嗎？

★ Is there any possibility that we can meet the **specialist** in person?
我們有與專科醫師見面的機會嗎？

★ Is there any possibility for the defendant to **appeal** to the **Supreme Court**?
那位被告人有機會向最高法院上訴嗎？

★ Is there any possibility of canceling Mr. Watson's order now?
有可能現在馬上取消華生先生的訂單嗎？

> **specialist**
> [ˋspɛʃəlɪst]
> 名 專科醫生
> **appeal**
> [əˋpil]
> 動（法）上訴
> **Supreme Court**
> 片 最高法院

with a variety of... 富含各式各樣的⋯。

★ The chef offered customers with a variety of local cuisines.
那位主廚提供顧客各式各樣的在地菜餚。

★ A newer version of the product was released with a variety of **add-ons**.
新版本的軟體上市，內建許多附加功能。

★ The controversy occurred with a variety of **misconceptions**.
許多誤解造成了這項爭議的發生。

★ Our team comes together with a variety of people of **solid** skills.
我們的團隊是由各種專業人才組成的。

★ Seniors seek to stay active with a variety of exercise programs.
老年人試圖用各種運動計畫來維持活力。

> **add-on**
> [ˋædˏɑn]
> 名 附加物
> **misconception**
> [ˏmɪskənˋsɛpʃən]
> 名 誤解
> **solid**
> [ˋsɑlɪd]
> 形 可信賴的

 知老外聊開懷，就靠這幾句！

Have you made the reservation for our anniversary dinner?
你訂好我們紀念日晚餐的位子了嗎？

Do you know the number of that restaurant?
你知道那間餐廳的電話號碼嗎？

That Japanese restaurant accepts reservations via emails.
那間日式餐廳接受 email 訂位。

That famous dim sum restaurant only takes 100 customers per day, so we'd better hurry up.
那間有名的港式茶餐廳一天只限一百位客人，所以我們得趕快過去啦。

This restaurant is very popular. You'll have to make reservations one month in advance.
這間餐廳非常受歡迎，你必須在一個月前就訂好位子。

I'd like to make a reservation for two on Saturday at 7 p.m.
我想預約星期六晚上七點，兩個人的位子。

Do you still have a table available at 6 p.m. tonight?
你們今天晚上六點還有空位嗎？

We would like a table by the window, if possible.
如果可以的話，我們想要靠窗的位子。

We're fully booked at 7 p.m. Do you want to reserve a table for 8 p.m.?
晚上七點的位子已經訂滿了，您要不要改訂晚上八點？

That restaurant is fully booked. How about eating somewhere else?
那間餐廳客滿了，要不要到別的地方吃呢？

There are three groups ahead of you, and it'll be a 30-minute wait.
您們前面還有三組客人在候位，候位時間大約三十分鐘。

UNIT 05

吃喝

異國料理
Exotic Tastes

 單字基本功 掌握關鍵字 = 開口第一步

 核心聯想

豪華大餐 A full-course meal

appetizer [`æpə,taɪzə] 名 開胃菜	**dessert** [dɪ`zɜt] 名 甜品	**entrée** [`ɑntre] 名 前菜	**meal** [mil] 名 一餐
salad [`sæləd] 名 沙拉	**starter** [`stɑrtə] 名 開胃菜	**main course** 片 主菜	**side dish** 片 配菜；小菜

 伴佐料調味 Seasoning & flavoring

進階學習

basil [`bæzɪl] 名 羅勒；九層塔	**condiment** [`kɑndəmənt] 名 調味料	**dip** [dɪp] 名 調味醬料	**herb** [hɜb] 名 香草；藥草
season [`sizn̩] 名 季節 動 調味	**spice** [spaɪs] 名 香料	**topping** [`tɑpɪŋ] 名 配料	**MSG** 縮 味精

 深度追蹤 🔍

Knowing More

　　每個國家對於食材的選用及烹調方式，都自成特色；許多報章雜誌還列出了另類食物，最常上榜的不外乎是在東南亞國家的炸昆蟲、日本的河豚生魚片、韓國生吃活章魚、墨西哥的「龍舌蘭蟲」、挪威的醃鯊魚……等等，台灣的豬血糕甚至被列入最另類食物的第一名呢。另外，要注意各國的餐桌禮儀也有所不同，例如印度及中東地區將左手視為不潔淨的，所以不用左手拿取食物；而智利人幾乎不用手拿食物吃，連吃薯條時也會使用餐具。

套個單字，想說的都能表達！

There is/are...(V-ing)　那裡有⋯正在⋯

★ There are lots of people lining up for an **exotic** taste.
那裡有很多人在排隊，想嚐嚐異國風味。

★ There are monkeys climbing up to the tree.
那裡有猴子正在爬樹。

★ There are **gangsters** giving **hush money** to the witness.
那邊有流氓正在給目擊證人封口費。

★ There are models standing on the **runway** in **outlandish** clothes.
那裡的模特兒在伸展台上展示異國風格的服飾。

★ There is a desperate guy trying to jump off a high building.
那邊有個絕望的人想要從高樓上跳下來。

exotic
[ɛg`zɑtɪk]
形 異國的

gangster
[`gæŋstə]
名 流氓

hush money
片 封口費

runway
[`rʌn, we]
名 伸展台

outlandish
[aut`lændɪʃ]
形 異國風格的

sb. have the right to...　某人有權利⋯。

★ You have the right to ask for a refund if you are not satisfied with the service.
如果你對服務不滿意，就有權利要求退費。

★ Our CEO has the right to cut the commercial budget.
我們的執行長有權利削減廣告預算。

★ You don't have the right to **retrieve** the **victim**'s file.
你沒有權利調閱被害者的檔案。

★ Administrators have the right to delete articles that **violating** the regulations.
管理人有權刪除違反規定的文章。

★ Legislators have the right to **take measures** to amend an **enactment**.
立法委員有權採取措施來修訂法規。

retrieve
[rɪ`triv]
動 擷取資訊

victim
[`vɪktɪm]
名 被害者

violate
[`vaɪə, let]
動 違反

take measures
片 採取措施

enactment
[ɪn`æktmənt]
名 法令

開口必備句

和老外聊開懷，就靠這幾句！

Have you ever been to a Mexican restaurant?
你去過墨西哥餐廳嗎？

What is your favorite Spanish dish?
你最喜歡哪一道西班牙菜？

I would really want to try escargot when I travel to France.
去法國旅遊的時候，我真的很想吃吃看法國蝸牛。

The French have exquisite taste in food.
法國人對於食物有著極為精緻的品味。

The three French national culinary treasures are caviar, foie gras, and truffles.
法國有三寶，魚子醬、鵝肝醬與松露。

My family is going to have fondue at a Swedish restaurant next Friday.
我們家下禮拜五要去一家瑞典餐廳吃起司火鍋。

That Korean barbecue restaurant is always crowded.
那間韓式烤肉店的客人一直都很多。

Many Chinese dishes are actually world-renowned delicacies.
許多中式菜餚其實都是世界聞名的美食。

You should spread some cream cheese on crackers, and then add some caviar on top.
你應該先在餅乾上塗抹一些奶油乳酪，再把魚子醬鋪在最上面。

At most restaurants, food is served as a set menu or a la carte.
大部分的餐廳會提供套餐或單點給顧客選擇。

Many restaurants in Japan display plastic or wax replicas of their dishes in a window near the entrance.
日本有很多餐廳會在入口處擺放塑膠製或蠟製的食品模型。

MP3 ▶ 211

UNIT 06 吃喝

點單及用餐
Having A Nice Meal

單字基本功 　掌握關鍵字 = 開口第一步

核心聯想

來點熱門菜色 Popular dishes

menu	server	special	order
[`mɛnju]	[`sɝvɚ]	[`spɛʃəl]	[`ɔrdɚ]
名 菜單	名 服務生	名 特餐 形 特別的	動 點餐;指揮

recommend	starving	tuck into	wine list
[ˏrɛkə`mɛnd]	[`stɑrvɪŋ]	片 狼吞虎嚥	片 酒單
動 推薦;建議	形 飢餓的		

 驚艷味覺 Describing taste

進階學習

describe	delicate	delicious	flavorful
[dɪ`skraɪb]	[`dɛləkɪt]	[dɪ`lɪʃəs]	[`flevɚfəl]
動 描述;形容	形 精緻的;嬌弱的	形 美味的	形 有風味的

rich	tasty	tender	taste bud
[rɪtʃ]	[`testɪ]	[`tɛndɚ]	片 味蕾
形 (食物)味濃的	形 美味的	形 軟嫩的	

 深度追蹤

Knowing More

　　世界上最具代表性的餐廳評比,就屬「米其林指南 Michelin」了。最早的米其林指南其實是由法國的米其林兄弟看好汽車行業的未來,而提供的免費旅遊指南;一九二〇年之後,才建立起嚴格的星級制度,並開始出售這本指南,同時在歐洲、美國、日本、中國等地的餐廳評級。評等的符號包括星星(食物美味的等級)、叉匙(用餐環境)、人頭標誌(Bib Gourmand;米其林推薦的道地餐廳)、和兩個銅板(指有提供不超過16歐元的餐點)。

be good enough to...　好到足以…。

★ The dishes here are good enough to compete with those in a Michelin restaurant.
這裡的菜好吃到可以跟米其林餐廳競爭。

★ The experienced singer is good enough to be the judge.
那名老練的歌手足以擔任評審。

★ This **enzyme** is good enough to **mend** your **indigestion**.
這種酵素足以改善消化不良的問題。

★ Her resume is good enough to make a strong impression to the interviewers.
她的履歷好到讓面試官留下深刻的印象。

★ This draft is good enough to meet their **criteria**.
這份草案足以達到他們的標準。

> **enzyme**
> [`ɛnzaɪm]
> 名 酵素
> **mend**
> [mɛnd]
> 動 改善；修補
> **indigestion**
> [ˌɪndə`dʒɛstʃən]
> 名 消化不良
> **criteria**
> [kraɪ`tɛrɪə]
> 名 標準（單數為 criterion）

give sb. credit for...　讚許某人的…。

★ She gives the manager credit for their healthful and sanitary catering.
她對經理讚許他們餐廳健康又衛生的餐飲服務。

★ Mr. Chen gave those **newcomers** credit for their work.
陳先生讚許那群新人的工作表現。

★ The banker gives credit for the **derivatives** his consultant suggested.
那位銀行家很滿意顧問推薦的衍生性金融商品。

★ Our boss gave the proponent credit for this **feasible** plan.
我們老闆讚許提案人提出的可行計畫。

★ The manager gave those architects credit for the floor plan of the **arcade**.
經理對建築師提供的商場平面圖讚許有加。

> **newcomer**
> [`nju`kʌmɚ]
> 名 新進人員
> **derivative**
> [də`rɪvətɪv]
> 形 衍生的
> **feasible**
> [`fizəbl]
> 形 可行的
> **arcade**
> [ɑr`ked]
> 名 商場

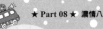

MP3 ▶ 213

知老外聊開懷，就靠這幾句！

Can I have a menu, please?
可以給我菜單嗎？

Would you like to take a look at our wine list?
您要參考一下我們的酒單嗎？

Are you ready to order?
您準備好要點菜了嗎？

We still need a few minutes to decide what to order.
我們還需要幾分鐘的時間來決定點什麼菜。

What is the lunch special?
中午的特餐是什麼？

What do you recommend?
你推薦哪道菜？

There's basil, rosemary, and parsley added in this dish.
這道菜有加羅勒、迷迭香和荷蘭芹。

My sister always adds a lot of chili pepper on every dish she orders.
我妹妹總是加很多的辣椒粉在每樣菜裡面。

Do you have vegetarian dishes?
你們提供素食餐點嗎？

We'd like to have a cheeseburger, some fajitas and a salad.
我們要點一份起司漢堡、一份法士達以及一份沙拉。

I was really impressed by the lasagna in this Italian restaurant. It's so delicious!
我對這間義式餐廳的千層麵印象很深，因為它真的太好吃了！

My mom gave her compliments to the chef for his excellent culinary skills.
我媽非常讚賞主廚高超的廚藝。

*UNIT 07

日常

吃飽結帳
Paying Your Bills

單字基本功 ✏ 掌握關鍵字 = 開口第一步

核心聯想 | 拍拍肚皮吃飽了 Full & satisfied

counter [`kaʊntə] 名 櫃台	**complimentary** [ˌkɑnplə`mɛntərɪ] 形 贈送的	**comment card** 片 意見卡	**customer service** 片 服務顧客
credit card 片 信用卡	**doggie bag** 片 打包袋	**pack up** 片 打包	**take out** 片 外帶

進階學習 | 結帳去 Paying the bill & tipping

amount [ə`maʊnt] 名 總額；總數	**bill** [bɪl] 名 帳單 動 開立帳單	**charge** [tʃɑrdʒ] 名 費用 動 收費	**check** [tʃɛk] 名 帳單
gratuity [grə`tjuətɪ] 名 小費	**overcharge** [`ovə`tʃɑrdʒ] 名 過高的要價 動 索價過高	**separate** [`sɛpə,ret] 動 分開 形 分開的	**pay the bill** 片 付款

深度追蹤 🔍

Knowing More

　　到美國餐廳用餐的時候，就一定要知道美國的小費文化！通常在速食餐廳只要付帳單上面加稅的總金額就好，而一般餐廳則是會給15%到20%的小費，如果真的非常滿意服務生的服務，當然也可以視滿意度增加小費。另外，因為有些服務生的薪水是依賴小費的，除非服務生態度極差，都最好不要低於10%；若是覺得食物難吃，就算是吃到一半了，也可以跟服務生反應，請他們幫你換掉，可別因為廚師的失誤，而減少服務生的小費囉。

句型偷吃步 套個單字，想說的都能表達！

in response to...　對…做出反應。

- ★ The server gave us some coupons in response to our generous tips.
  服務生為了回應我們慷慨的小費，便給了我們一些優惠券。

- ★ The audience laughed in response to the comedian' performance.
  那位喜劇演員的表演引起觀眾大笑。

- ★ I **implemented** the policy in response to the public pressure.
  我實行這項政策是因為公眾壓力的關係。

- ★ Products were improved in response to people's various preferences.
  為迎合人們不同的偏好，產品被改良過了。

- ★ The results changed in response to the **manipulated variables**.
  因為控制了可變因素，結果便因此產生變化。

> **implement**
> [`ɪmplə‚mɛnt]
> 動 執行
> **manipulate**
> [mə`nɪpjə‚let]
> 動 操作
> **variable**
> [`vɛrɪəbl]
> 名 可變因素

I am sorry, but...　我很抱歉，但是…。

- ★ I am sorry, but we only take cash here.
  不好意思，我們這邊只收現金。

- ★ I am sorry, but I need to point out the incorrect **estimation**.
  我很抱歉，但我必須指出不正確的估計值。

- ★ I am sorry, but my client wants you to pay for the damages.
  我很抱歉，但我的客戶要你負責賠償損害。

- ★ I am sorry, but I can't be friends with such an **unscrupulous** person.
  我很抱歉，但我無法和這麼不擇手段的人做朋友。

- ★ I am sorry, but we still have to make a claim for **compensation**.
  我很抱歉，但我們仍必須索賠。

> **estimation**
> [‚ɛstə`meʃən]
> 名 估計
> **unscrupulous**
> [ʌn`skrupjələs]
> 形 無恥的
> **compensation**
> [‚kɑmpən`seʃən]
> 名 賠償

開口必備句 知老外聊開懷，就靠這幾句！

MP3 ▶ 216

May I have the check, please?
請給我帳單好嗎？（表示想要結帳了）

Do you accept credit cards?
你們收信用卡嗎？

Do you want separate checks?
您們要分開算嗎？

Let's go Dutch!
我們各付各的吧！

Let's split the check evenly! / Let's share the bill.
我們各付一半吧！／我們一起分攤費用吧。

I insist on paying my half.
我堅持付我的部分。

It's on me. / It's my treat.
我請客。

May I have the receipt, please?
可以給我收據嗎？

It's gratuity included, so you don't have to tip the server.
帳單已經有加服務費了，所以你不需要再另外給服務生小費。

A fifteen-percent service charge will be added to the check.
我們會多收百分之十五的服務費。

Larry always tips generously every time he eats out.
賴瑞每次出門外食，都會給慷慨的小費。

The waiter complained about the low tips he received from that couple.
服務生抱怨那對情侶給的小費太低了。

MP3 ▶ 217

日常
互許終身
Tying The Knots

單字基本功 ▸ 掌握關鍵字 = 開口第一步

核心聯想 · 結婚準備 Preparing weddings

engagement [ɪn`gedʒmənt] 名 訂婚；約定	**fiancé** [ˌfiən`se] 名 未婚夫	**fiancée** [ˌfiən`se] 名 未婚妻	**officiant** [ə`fɪʃɪənt] 名 公證人
wedding [`wɛdɪŋ] 名 婚禮	**marry** [`mærɪ] 動 結婚	**propose** [prə`poz] 動 求婚；提議	**wedding bands** 片 結婚對戒

婚宴邀請 Wedding reception

進階學習

bridegroom [`braɪdˏgrum] 名 新郎	**bridesmaid** [`braɪdzˏmed] 名 伴娘	**ceremony** [`sɛrəˏmonɪ] 名 典禮；儀式	**invitation** [ˌɪnvə`teʃən] 名 邀請函
reception [rɪ`sɛpʃən] 名 婚宴接待	**best man** 片 首席伴郎	**guest list** 片 賓客名單	**maid of honor** 片 首席伴娘

深度追蹤 🔍

Knowing More

　　在西洋婚禮中，新郎（groom/bridegroom）會找四位好友當伴郎（groomsmen），再請一位最好的朋友當首席伴郎（best man）；新娘（bride）同時也會邀請四位朋友作為伴娘（bridesmaid），和一位單身朋友為首席伴娘（maid of honor）。而且結婚之前，男性通常都會舉辦單身派對（bachelor party）狂歡一天，女性則是辦單身女子派對（bachelorette party）或是溫馨的bridal shower，來告別單身、慶祝即將進入的婚姻大事。

It is essential for...to...   …對…是必要的。

★ It is essential for a wedding to invite all of your friends and relatives.
邀請所有的親朋好友來參加婚禮，是一定要做的事。

★ It is essential for us to include **protein** in our diet.
攝取含蛋白質的食物對我們來說是必要的。

★ It is essential for every kid to receive education.
讓每個孩子都接受教育是必要的。

★ It is essential for candidates to be **conversant** with the procedures.
候選人必須要熟悉競選程序。

★ It is essential for **residents** to know about their patients' **doses**:
住院醫生必須要知道病人藥物的劑量。

> **protein**
> [`protiɪn]
> 名 蛋白質
>
> **conversant**
> [`kɑnvəsṇt]
> 形 熟悉的
>
> **resident**
> [`rɛzədənt]
> 名 住院醫生
>
> **dose**
> [dos]
> 名（藥物）一劑

sth. be designed to...   某物被設計成…。

★ Their wedding is designed to be a fairy tale party on a **cruiser**.
他們將婚禮設計成童話故事風格的遊艇派對。

★ This software is designed to provide online trading.
這個軟體是為了提供線上交易而設計的。

★ This training is designed to promote their work efficiency.
這個訓練是為了要提升他們的工作效率。

★ The legislation is designed to **boycott sexual discrimination**.
這個法規是要用來抵制性別歧視的。

★ This scene is designed to **imitate** a jail under **surveillance**.
這一幕被設計成模仿被監控的牢房。

> **cruiser**
> [`kruzə]
> 名 遊艇
>
> **boycott**
> [`bɔɪˌkɑt]
> 動 杯葛；抵制
>
> **sexual discrimination**
> 片 性別歧視
>
> **imitate**
> [`ɪməˌtet]
> 動 模仿
>
> **surveillance**
> [sɝ`veləns]
> 名 監視；看守

開口必備句

跟老外聊開懷，就靠這幾句！

Most young people tend to choose love over money.
大多數年輕人會選愛情，而非麵包。

Janet thinks basing a decision on money is too materialistic, and what matters most is how your heart feels.
珍妮特覺得選麵包太現實，最重要的是自己的感覺。

It is true that money cannot buy happiness, but without money it's hard to survive in the real world.
金錢的確不能買到快樂；但若沒有錢，也很難在現實世界中存活。

Even if you had all the money in the world, without love, you would not be able to enjoy it.
沒有愛情的話，即使你擁有世界上的所有財富，你也無法享受。

Michelle believes that money, like bread, is the staff of life.
蜜雪兒相信金錢好比麵包，對生活很重要。

As an old saying goes, "Poverty makes a couple pessimistic."
諺語說得好：「貧賤夫妻百事哀。」

There goes an old saying, money cannot do everything, but you can do nothing without it.
俗話說：「錢不是萬能，但是沒有錢萬萬不能。」

Is it true that no matter how strong a love is, it will finally be destroyed by reality?
不論愛情多穩定，最後都會被現實打敗嗎？

Love what you choose and choose what you love.
愛你所擇，擇你所愛。

Why can't you have both money and love?
你為什麼不能同時擁有愛情與麵包？

Kelly would never marry someone just for his wealth.
凱莉絕對不會只因為財產而結婚。

和樂一家人
A Happy Family Life

MP3 ▶ 220

單字基本功 — 掌握關鍵字 = 開口第一步

核心聯想

組成一家人 Forming a family

anniversary [ˌænəˋvɝsərɪ] 名 周年紀念日	**honeymoon** [ˋhʌnɪˌmun] 名 蜜月	**household** [ˋhausˌhold] 名 家庭；一家人	**inheritance** [ɪnˋhɛrɪtəns] 名 遺傳；繼承物
newlywed [ˋnjulɪˌwɛd] 名 新婚夫婦	**spouse** [spauz] 名 配偶	**extended family** 片 大家庭（三代同堂）	**nuclear family** 片 核心家庭

歡樂大家族 Related by blood or marriage

進階學習

generation [ˌdʒɛnəˋreʃən] 名 世代；同時代的人	**in-law** [ˋɪnˌlɔ] 名 姻親	**kinship** [ˋkɪnʃɪp] 名 親屬關係	**relative** [ˋrɛlətɪv] 名 親戚
sibling [ˋsɪblɪŋ] 名 兄弟姊妹	**blood relative** 片 血親	**maiden name** 片（女子）娘家姓； 婚前姓	**next of kin** 片 直系血親

深度追蹤

Knowing More

根據世界衛生組織（WTO）的定義，當國家65歲以上的人口超過7%，就屬於「高齡化（population aging）」，且各國家庭結構也因高齡化而改變，從以前的大家庭變為最常見的核心家庭或頂客族（DINK；雙薪但無小孩）；再加上離婚率的增加，由兩個家庭組成的繼親家庭（stepfamily）及單親家庭（single-parent family）也愈來愈常見；也有許多人選擇不生小孩而收養孩子（adoption）、組成收養家庭（blended family）。

MP3 ▶ 221

套個單字，想說的都能表達！

sth. should always come before...
某事永遠都應該比…重要。

★ Your family should always come before your job.
家人永遠都應該比你的工作重要。

★ Family teaching should always come before education in school.
家庭教育應該要比學校教育還重要。

★ Integrity should always come before all other kinds of **ideologies**.
正直與誠實永遠應該比其他各種意識形態還要重要。

★ The welfare of citizen should always come before political **infighting**.
人民福利永遠都應該比政治內鬥還要重要。

★ Reducing energy consumption should always come before building more **nuclear power plants**.
節約能源應永遠都比興建更多核電廠還重要。

> **ideology**
> [ˌaɪdɪˈɑlədʒɪ]
> 名 意識形態
> **infighting**
> [ˋɪnˌfaɪtɪŋ]
> 名 內鬥
> **nuclear**
> [ˋnjuklɪə]
> 形 核能的
> **power plant**
> 片 發電廠

Would sb. mind...?　某人介意…嗎？

★ Would your parents mind us dropping by their house for a while?
你的父母介意我們順道去拜訪一下嗎？

★ Would you mind repeating that again?
你介意再說一次嗎？

★ Would everyone mind leaving Peggy and me alone for a few minutes?
大家能給我跟佩姬一些私人時間嗎？

★ Would you mind handing in the **embarkation card** to me now, please?
可以麻煩你現在拿給我入境登記卡嗎？

★ Would you mind unpacking your luggage for a routine **inspection**?
你介意把你的行李打開做例行性檢查嗎？

> **embarkation card**
> 片 入境表格
> **inspection**
> [ɪnˈspɛkʃən]
> 名 檢查

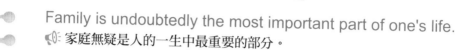

開口必備句　和老外聊開懷，就靠這幾句！

Family is undoubtedly the most important part of one's life.
家庭無疑是人的一生中最重要的部分。

Strong and close ties among family members can help raise well-adjusted and confident children.
家人間強而緊密的聯繫可培養出適應力強且有自信的孩子。

How often do you go traveling with your family?
你多常和家人一同旅遊？

What do you usually do with your kids on the weekends?
週末時，你通常都和孩子做些什麼？

Do you have a good relationship with your grandparents?
你和祖父母的關係好嗎？

My mom insists that the whole family has dinner together every day.
我媽堅持全家人每天都要一起吃晚餐。

My father used to spend some quality time with us before we went to bed.
我父親過去在睡前，會特別花時間與我們相處。

Every family has problems, but they can be solved with love and respect.
每個家庭都有他的問題，但都可用愛和尊重來解決。

My mother tries her best to provide care and safety for our family.
我媽媽盡全力提供家人關懷和確保安全。

Despite all the conflicts, the love in our family remains strong.
儘管有衝突，我們家人仍然以愛緊密相繫。

The City Council offers free counseling sessions for couples who need advice on relationships and child-raising.
市議會提供免費諮商講座給需要婚姻諮詢和教養建議的夫妻。

MP3 ▶ 223

UNIT 10 日常 家庭教育
Family Education

單字基本功 掌握關鍵字 = 開口第一步

核心聯想　照顧及養育 Raising kids

babysitter [`bebɪsɪtɚ] 名 保姆	**custody** [`kʌstədɪ] 名 撫養權	**adopt** [ə`dɑpt] 動 收養；採納	**foster** [`fɔstɚ] 動 領養；培養
nurture [`nɝtʃɚ] 動 養育	**raise** [rez] 動 撫養；提高	**bring up** 片 養育	**tuck in** 片 幫（小孩）蓋被子

　溝通和教養 Family education **進階學習**

adolescence [ˏædl̩`ɛsn̩s] 名 青春期	**adolescent** [ˏædl̩`ɛsn̩t] 名 青少年	**communicate** [kə`mjunəˏket] 動 溝通；交流	**spoil** [spɔɪl] 動 寵壞；損壞
naughty [`nɔtɪ] 形 淘氣的	**overprotective** [ˏovɚprə`tɛktɪv] 形 過度保護的	**strict** [strɪkt] 形 嚴格的	**formative years** 片 成長期

 深度追蹤 🔍 *Knowing More*

　　西方文化大多鼓勵孩子自立自強、積極自主，同時也會注重以下幾點：(1) 傾聽並支持子女的夢想；(2) 提供磨練的機會，例如讓孩子們多參加運動校隊、童子軍或課外活動；(3) 充分鼓勵但不過度稱讚，藉此建立孩子的自信心；(4) 多問「假如」，培養孩子思考一件事的前因後果；(5) 鼓勵探險，建立孩子勇於冒險和應付挑戰的精神；(6) 學會「3R」—Respect（尊重）、Resourcefulness（機智）和Responsibility（責任心）。

 套個單字，想說的都能表達！

set a good example for... 替…樹立好榜樣。

- ★ Parents should always set a good example for their children.
  父母應該要替自己的孩子樹立好榜樣。
- ★ Our CEO sets a good example for all the managers.
  我們的執行長為所有經理人立下良好的典範。
- ★ The lady's **goodwill** sets a good example for the next generation.
  這位婦人的善心為下一代立下良好的典範。
- ★ The senior citizen sets a good example for the teenagers in the city.
  那位年長市民為該城市的青少年立下良好的典範。
- ★ His **sportsmanship** sets a good example for all athletes on the baseball team.
  他的運動員精神為棒球隊員立下良好的典範。

goodwill
[ˋgʊdˋwɪl]
名 善心
sportsmanship
[ˋsportsmən͵ʃɪp]
名 運動家精神

There's no doubt that... …是毫無疑問的。

- ★ There's no doubt that parents play a crucial role in their children's life.
  家長無疑地在小孩的人生中扮演重要的角色。
- ★ There's no doubt that we live in an era of technology advancement.
  毫無疑問，我們正身處一個科技進步的時代。
- ★ There's no doubt that the damages will be **compensated** in **due** time.
  損害必在期限內獲得賠償。
- ★ There's no doubt that most people dislike traffic **congestion** in big cities.
  毫無疑問地，大多數人都不喜歡大城市交通堵塞的現象。
- ★ There's no doubt that globalization affects global economy in various aspects.
  全球化對全球經濟各方面都有影響是毫無疑問的。

compensate
[ˋkɑnpən͵set]
動 補償；賠償
due
[dju]
形 到期的
congestion
[kənˋdʒɛstʃən]
名 堵塞

244

開口必備句 和老外聊開懷，就靠這幾句！

How do you think a great parent would do to educate their children?

你覺得稱職的父母應該會怎麼教育他們的小孩？

The best way to teach your child is to be a good role model yourself.

教育孩子最好的方式就是以身作則。

The first step of interacting with your child is to express love.

與你的小孩互動的第一步，就是表達愛。

Even a gentle cuddle can fill your kid's life with sunshine and love.

即使是一個溫暖的擁抱，也能讓你孩子的生命中充滿陽光和愛。

Avoid comparing your children with others, especially with siblings.

避免拿你的孩子跟其他人做比較，尤其是手足間相互比較。

Criticism will not only hurt your children's feelings but also your relationship with them.

批評不只會傷了孩子的心，也會傷了你們的關係。

Try to be assertive yet kind when pointing out what your children have done wrong.

試著堅定但和善地指出孩子的錯誤。

Don't be too quick to rescue your child from a problem because life itself is the best teacher.

不要太快幫你的孩子解決問題，因為生命本身就是最好的老師。

Keep in mind that your child is not an extension of yourself, but an individual who is dependent upon your care.

要牢記孩子並不是你，而是仰賴你的照顧而成長的個體。

Cassie expects her son to be a doctor in the future.

凱西期待她的兒子將來成為一位醫生。

NOTE

Part 09

暑假結束九月收心
September Highlights:
Starting A New Chapter

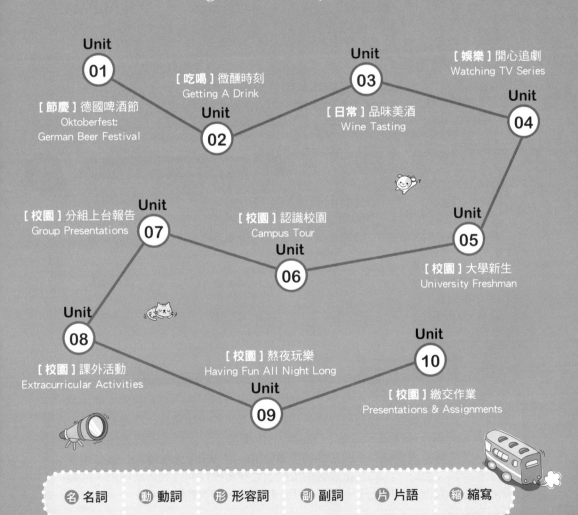

Unit 01
[節慶] 德國啤酒節
Oktoberfest:
German Beer Festival

[吃喝] 微醺時刻
Getting A Drink
Unit 02

Unit 03
[日常] 品味美酒
Wine Tasting

[娛樂] 開心追劇
Watching TV Series

Unit 04

[校園] 分組上台報告
Group Presentations
Unit 07

[校園] 認識校園
Campus Tour
Unit 06

Unit 05
[校園] 大學新生
University Freshman

Unit 08
[校園] 課外活動
Extracurricular Activities

[校園] 熬夜玩樂
Having Fun All Night Long
Unit 09

Unit 10
[校園] 繳交作業
Presentations & Assignments

名 名詞　　動 動詞　　形 形容詞　　副 副詞　　片 片語　　縮 縮寫

★UNIT★ 01 節慶

德國啤酒節
Oktoberfest: German Beer Festival

 單字基本功　掌握關鍵字＝開口第一步

 核心聯想　德國必吃 Must-eat foods in Germany

beer [bɪr] 名 啤酒	sauerkraut [`saʊr͵kraʊt] 名 德國酸菜	sausage [`sɔsɪdʒ] 名 香腸	ferment [fɝ`mɛnt] 動 使發酵
smoked [smokt] 形 煙燻的	ham hock/ pork knuckle 片 豬腳	sweet mustard 片 甜芥末醬	white sausage 片 白香腸

 啤酒節活動 At the beer festival　進階學習

Bavarian [bə`vɛrɪən] 形 巴伐利亞的	bouncer [`baʊnsɚ] 名 門衛	brewery [`bruərɪ] 名 釀酒廠	delicacy [`dɛləkəsɪ] 名 佳餚
fairground [`fɛr͵graʊnd] 名 露天遊樂場	hail [hel] 動 歡呼	keg [kɛg] 名 小桶	tent [tɛnt] 名 帳篷

 深度追蹤　Knowing More

　　德國啤酒節又稱為「十月節」，通常於每年九月底到十月初舉辦；原本是巴伐利亞的皇家婚禮，現在則變成德國最具代表性的傳統慶典。而慶典在慕尼黑市長敲開第一桶啤酒，高喊「Ozapft ist! 開桶了！」就正式揭開序幕；園區內，各大啤酒廠會設有不同主題的啤酒帳篷，但想要進入帳篷內，就必須事先上網申請；另外，人們在這幾天的慶典還會穿著巴伐利亞的傳統服飾，活動則從早上十點進行到晚上十一點，人手一杯啤酒，氣氛熱鬧非凡！

句型偷吃步　套個單字，想說的都能表達！

It is good for sb. to...　…對某人來說很好。

★ It is good for tourists to join all kinds of local festivities.
參加各種當地慶典對遊客來說很好。

★ It is good for you to keep early hours.
早睡早起對你來說是好的。

★ It is good for fresh graduates to learn more by practicing **vocational** skills.
在練習職業技能的過程中學習，對社會新鮮人是好的。

★ It is good for **illiterates** to go to night schools to get knowledge.
到夜校上課以獲取知識對文盲來說是好的。

★ It is good for children to read **picture books**.
閱讀繪本對小孩來說是很好的。

> **illiterate**
> [ɪˋlɪtərɪt]
> 名 文盲
> **vocational**
> [voˋkeʃən]
> 形 職業的
> **picture book**
> 片 繪本

sb. can't help but...　某人忍不住…。

★ My friend can't help but order another liter of beer.
我的朋友忍不住又點了一升的啤酒。

★ We can't help but be **overwhelmed** by the bad news.
我們聽到了壞消息，不禁感到非常震驚。

★ That heir can't help but keep thinking about her after she left.
她離開後，那名繼承人忍不住一直想著她。

★ Some viewers can't help but **sob** after watching that **touching** movie.
有些觀眾看完那部感人的電影後，就忍不住哭了。

★ He can't help but **snicker** when **overhearing** his brother's secrets.
當他無意間聽到他哥的秘密，就忍不住竊笑。

> **overwhelm**
> [͵ovɚˋhwɛlm]
> 動 使驚訝
> **sob**
> [sɑb]
> 動 啜泣
> **touching**
> [ˋtʌtʃɪŋ]
> 形 感人的
> **snicker**
> [ˋsnɪkɚ]
> 動 竊笑
> **overhear**
> [͵ovɚˋhɪr]
> 動 偶然聽到

開口必備句　和老外聊開懷，就靠這幾句！

"Wiesn", meaning "meadow" in German dialect, is another name for Oktoberfest.

「Wiesn」是德國方言中的「牧草地」，也是德國啤酒節的別名。

Oktoberfest usually takes place in late September.

德國啤酒節通常於九月底舉行。

Munich is always crowed with people in traditional Bavarian costumes during Oktoberfest.

啤酒節期間，慕尼黑總會擠滿身穿巴伐利亞傳統服飾的人們。

In the 2016 Munich Oktoberfest, over 7.7 million liters of beer were consumed.

二〇一六年的慕尼黑啤酒節，總計消耗了超過七百七十萬公升的啤酒。

The food stalls along the sides make Oktoberfest a giant amusement park.

各式各樣的小吃攤讓德國啤酒節成為一座大型的遊樂場。

Visitors can enter into the tents and enjoy liters of beer for free during Oktoberfest.

德國啤酒節期間，遊客可以進入帳篷裡，享用免費的啤酒。

In addition to beer, you can't miss all kinds of German specialties such as pretzels and white sausages.

除了啤酒外，千萬別錯過像是脆餅和白香腸等德國特色小吃。

You must try roast chicken and various kinds of sausages in Oktoberfest as well!

在啤酒節當中，你也一定要來嚐嚐烤雞和各式各樣的香腸！

Oktoberfest is not only for beer lovers but for children.

德國啤酒節受到貪杯者和小孩們的喜愛。

My friend finally had a chance to live her dream of tasting the world's best beer.

我的朋友終於有機會可以實現她的夢想—品嚐世上最棒的啤酒。

229

吃喝
微醺時刻
Getting A Drink

 單字基本功 ▶ 掌握關鍵字 = 開口第一步

核心
聯想 | 喝點什麼好 All kinds of drinks

alcohol [`ælkə,hɔl] 名 酒精	**booze** [buz] 名 (口)酒	**cocktail** [`kak,tel] 名 雞尾酒	**cider** [`saɪdə] 名 蘋果酒
tonic [`tɑnɪk] 名 通寧水	**tipsy** [`tɪpsɪ] 形 微醉的	**bottoms up** 片 乾杯	**mixed drink** 片 混酒

如何點酒 Ordering drinks at a bar | 進階學習

bartender [`bɑr,tɛndə] 名 酒保	**neat** [nit] 名 純酒精	**shot** [ʃat] 名 一小杯（烈酒）	**shooter** [`ʃutə] 名 小杯的分層調酒
designated driver 片 代駕	**on the rocks** 片 加冰塊	**straight up** 片 不加冰塊	**well drink** 片 （以最便宜的酒調成的）調酒

 深度追蹤🔍 ⟁⟁⟁⟁ Knowing More

　　酒吧（bar/pub）分為很多種類，像是「country bar」，裡面娛樂設施較多且設有舞池，角落也常有鬥牛的機器可以玩，為年輕人常去的地方；還有播放運動賽事的「sports bar」，大家會一起觀看、熱烈討論各大比賽；「music bar」店內則會定期邀請樂團演出，曲風從搖滾到爵士音樂都有；而「lounge」店內氣氛輕鬆，適合與朋友一同聊天、喝酒；至於到「club」的人則是主要去跳舞，大多配合震耳欲聾的電子音樂，徹夜狂歡到天亮。

套個單字,想說的都能表達!

...be just too much for sb.   …對某人而言太超過了。

★ The loud music in clubs is just too much for me.
我覺得夜店震耳欲聾的音樂太大聲了。

★ The **abductor**'s demand is just too much for the boy's guardian.
對那名男孩的監護人來說,綁架犯的要求實在太多了。

★ The **roller coaster** ride is just too much for Janet.
坐雲霄飛車對珍妮特來說太激烈了。

★ Blaming people like that is just too much for your **subordinates**.
對你的部屬來說,像那樣責備人也太超過了吧。

★ The **opponents'** offense is just too much for our team's defense.
對我們隊的防守來說,對手的攻勢太強了。

abductor
[æb`dʌktɚ]
名 綁架者
roller coaster
片 雲霄飛車
subordinate
[sə`bɔtdɪnɪt]
名 屬下
opponent
[ə`ponənt]
名 對手

sb. have no choice but to...   某人只能…。

★ Kate has no choice but to call a designated driver.
凱特別無選擇,只能找一位代駕。

★ We have no choice but to **obey** the rules of the competition.
我們除了遵守競賽規則外,別無選擇。

★ The staff has no choice but to submit a dispute to **arbitration**.
全體員工除了把爭議訴諸仲裁,別無選擇。

★ The tour guide has no choice but to postpone all the tourist itineraries.
導遊別無選擇,只能推遲旅遊行程。

★ All visitors have no choice but to **abide by** the rules and directions.
所有參觀者都只能遵守規則和指揮。

obey
[ə`be]
動 服從;遵從
arbitration
[ˌɑrbə`treʃən]
名 仲裁
abide by
片 遵守

開口必備句 和老外聊開懷，就靠這幾句！

The bartender here is my close friend, so I can get free drinks.
我跟這裡的酒保很熟，所以我可以免費喝酒。

It is very enjoyable to have drinks with a couple of friends in a cocktail lounge.
和三五好友一起在酒吧喝點雞尾酒，真是一大享受。

I am a social drinker only.
我只在社交場合淺嚐幾口。

If you are looking for a place to relax, Ray's Lounge Bar is your best choice.
如果你想找個地方放鬆一下，雷酒吧就是你的首選。

Don't forget your ID! You have to show it to the bouncer before entering night clubs.
別忘了你的身分證！你必須給門衛看過之後才能進去夜店。

Whoever joins the pole dance competition can have a cocktail on the house.
凡是參加鋼管舞競賽的人，都可以得到一杯本店招待的雞尾酒。

I am going to get a drink. Can I get you one?
我要去點飲料喝。要幫你點一杯嗎？

A dry martini, shaken not stirred, please.
我要一杯馬丁尼，麻煩用搖盪法調，不要用攪拌的。

How about grabbing something to eat after we finish this drink?
喝完這杯後，要不要一起去吃些東西？

The girl Jack hit on at the bar last night happened to be my sister.
傑克昨天晚上在酒吧搭訕的女孩剛好是我妹妹。

I think Janice has a crush on the guy dancing with her at the club yesterday.
我覺得珍妮絲看上昨天在夜店跟她一起跳舞的那個人。

UNIT 03 日常

品味美酒
Wine Tasting

單字基本功 掌握關鍵字 = 開口第一步

核心聯想　常見酒類一覽 List of wines

brandy	Champaign	mead	whisky/whiskey
[`brændɪ]	[ʃæm`pen]	[mid]	[`hwɪskɪ]
名 白蘭地	名 香檳	名 蜂蜜酒	名 威士忌

house wine	red wine	rosé wine	white wine
片 招牌酒	片 紅酒	片 粉紅酒	片 白酒

 酒莊巡禮 Visiting the winery　進階學習

barrel	brew	vintage	warehouse
[`bærəl]	[bru]	[`vɪntɪdʒ]	[`wɛr,haʊs]
名 木桶	名 啤酒 動 釀造	名 釀酒；優良葡萄酒	名 倉庫

winemaker	winery	vineyard	distill
[`waɪnmekɚ]	[`waɪnərɪ]	[`vɪnjəd]	[dɪs`tɪl]
名 製酒者	名 釀酒廠	名 葡萄園	動 蒸餾

深度追蹤 🔍　　　Knowing More

　　品酒的四大步驟為 (1) 見（look）：以顏色來判斷口感和味道，例如紅酒顏色若是有點透明的櫻桃色，喝起來通常較清爽，而色深的酒則口感較濃稠。(2) 聞（smell）：先轉杯（swirl）、輕輕地旋轉並搖晃杯子3到5秒，再細聞酒香，若是經過橡木桶成年的酒就會有煙燻味。(3) 嚐（taste）：讓酒在口腔中停留幾秒，充分感受酒的味道和口感。(4) 吞／吐酒（swallow/spit）：可以吞一點酒來感受尾韻，或是吐到酒桶內，保持清醒以迎接下一瓶酒。

MP3 ▶ 233

sb. keep...in mind.　某人將…記在心裡。

★ I kept the five important steps of wine tasting in mind.
我已記熟了品酒的五大步驟。

★ The philosopher keeps the life **aphorism** in mind.
那名哲學家把人生箴言記在心上。

★ The young man keeps his past **failures** in mind.
那位年輕人把他過去的失敗記在心上。

★ The **apprentice** keeps these valuable experiences in mind.
那位學徒把這些寶貴經驗記在心上。

★ My students keep the mathematical **formulas** in mind.
我的學生都把數學公式記在心上。

> **aphorism**
> [`æfə͵rɪzəm]
> 名 格言
>
> **failure**
> [`feljə]
> 名 失敗
>
> **apprentice**
> [ə`prɛntɪs]
> 名 學徒
>
> **formula**
> [`fɔrmjələ]
> 名 公式

introduce...to sb.　把…介紹給某人。

★ Thanks for introducing the tasting room to me!
謝謝你介紹那間品酒店給我！

★ Let me introduce my friend to you.
讓我介紹我的朋友給你認識。

★ The new **correspondent** was introduced to the manager this morning.
今天早上，這位新進特派員被介紹給經理認識了。

★ The writer would like to introduce her **best seller** to those graduates.
那位作者想要把她的暢銷書介紹給那些研究生。

★ Allow me to introduce the latest **nanotechnology** to you.
讓我來跟你們介紹一下最新的奈米技術吧！

> **correspondent**
> [͵kɔrɪ`spandənt]
> 名 特派員
>
> **best seller**
> 片 暢銷書
>
> **nanotechnology**
> [͵nænotɛk`naləd͵ʒɪ]
> 名 奈米技術

開口必備句 和老外聊開懷，就靠這幾句！

I like to visit wineries and have some red wine with my friends on weekends.

每逢假日，我都喜歡和朋友們一起到酒莊品嚐紅酒。

They will teach you how to taste wine and even provide a wine-tasting course.

他們會教你怎麼品酒，甚至還有提供品酒課程。

Can I taste some of the 1990 Chardonnay, please?

我可以試喝一九九〇年份的夏多內嗎？

Be sure to decant the wine first so that aromas and flavors will be more vibrant upon serving.

記得要先醒酒，喝的時候酒的香氣和味道才會比較突出。

Appearance, aroma, in-mouth sensations, and finish are the four important elements to wine tasting.

外觀、香氣、口中的感受和餘味，是品酒中四個重要的元素。

You can assess a wine's overall quality by its taste, scent, texture and length.

你可以用酒的味道、香味、口感跟餘味來評估酒的品質。

You should first take a sip, let the liquid move around your tongue, and then spit it out.

你應該先啜飲一小口，好好用舌頭感受一下味道，然後再把酒吐出來。

Wines with high acidity are often tart and zesty.

高酸度的酒嚐起來通常都很酸，也有點辣。

This wine was aged in oak, thus gave it a buttery characteristic and a rich flavor.

這支酒存放在橡木桶裡面，所以有一種奶油柔滑的口感和豐富的味道。

My dad really loves this fruit-forward wine because of its big and rich taste.

我爸很喜歡這個有果味的紅酒，因為喝起來的味道很圓潤、豐富。

▶ 235

04 開心追劇

娛樂

Watching TV Series

單字基本功 ✎ 掌握關鍵字 = 開口第一步

核心
聯想

追劇術語 Must-know terms

anime
[`ænɪˌme]
名 動畫

drama
[`drɑmə]
名 戲劇；連續劇

episode
[`ɛpəˌsod]
名 一集；事件

season
[`sizn̩]
名 季；季節

sequel
[`sikwəl]
名 續集

series
[`siriz]
名 一系列

special
[`spɛʃəl]
名 特別篇；番外篇

computer graphic
片 電腦動畫技術

各種電視劇 Types of drama

進階
學習

crime
[kraɪm]
名 犯罪；罪行

sitcom
[`sɪtˌkɑm]
名 情境喜劇

tragedy
[`trædʒədɪ]
名 悲劇；災難

epic
[`ɛpɪk]
形 史詩的

medical
[`mɛdɪkl̩]
片 醫學的

reality show
片 實境節目

science fiction
片 科幻片

talk show
片 脫口秀

深度追蹤 🔍

Knowing More

　　歐美影集在製作方面就與亞洲有很大的不同，且通常分為以下三種：(1) 試映集（pilot）：電影製作人先將題材交給電視台，若電視台願意投資才開始撰寫劇本，接著若劇本符合電視台的期待才會正式開拍，但被採用的試映集，通常只有不到一半的數量。(2) 衍生劇（spinoff）：從一部已經成名的影集再衍生出另一部類似的影集。(3) 斷尾劇：若電視台認為影集沒有再播放下去的價值、無法回收成本的話，不管劇情進行到哪裡都會直接停播。

 套個單字，想說的都能表達！

sb. make an excuse to/for...　某人找藉口⋯。

★ Max made an excuse for taking a leave just to finish watching the series.
麥克斯為了看完連續劇，就隨便編了個請假理由。

★ The learner made an excuse for her lack of preparation.
那名學習者找藉口說明她的準備不足。

★ The **novelist** made an excuse just to reject our invitation.
那位小說家編了一個理由拒絕我們的邀請。

★ The critic made an excuse for his **subjective appraisals**.
那名評論家為了他主觀的評價找了藉口。

★ Kevin shouldn't make an excuse to skip the conference.
凱文不該找藉口缺席研討會。

> **novelist**
> [ˋnɑvl̩ɪst]
> 名 小說家
> **subjective**
> [səbˋdʒɛktɪv]
> 形 主觀的
> **appraisal**
> [əˋprezl̩]
> 名 評價

sb./sth. ...for no reason.　某人／事莫名奇妙地⋯。

★ The popular drama was suddenly ended for no reason.
那部熱門劇不知道為什麼突然被停掉了。

★ Over forty workers were made **compulsively redundant** for no reason.
四十多名員工毫無理由地遭到強制性裁員。

★ Her dog **streaked** across the street for no reason.
她的狗莫名其妙地突然飛奔過街。

★ My opponent gave me another clue for no reason.
我的對手不知道為什麼要提供我其他的線索。

★ Most users' accounts got **suspended** for no reason.
大部分使用者的帳號都莫名其妙被停權了。

> **compulsively**
> [kəmˋpʌlsɪvlɪ]
> 副 強制性地
> **redundant**
> [rɪˋdʌndənt]
> 形 被解雇的
> **streak**
> [strik]
> 動 飛奔
> **suspend**
> [səˋspɛnd]
> 動 使終止

MP3 ▶ 237

知老外聊開懷，就靠這幾句！

What's your favorite TV series?
你最喜歡的電視影集是什麼？

Nick always fights over the remote control with his sister.
尼克和他妹妹總是互搶電視遙控器。

"Friends" is said to be the most successful sitcom in the U.S.
《六人行》被譽為全美最成功的情境喜劇。

The finale of "Friends," a popular TV series, had an amazingly high viewership rate of 22%.
熱門影集《六人行》，在完結篇創下了百分之二十二的驚人收視率。

My friend loves "The Big Bang Theory", a series about four geeky scientists.
我朋友很愛看《宅男行不行》，這是部描述四位怪胎科學家的影集。

"The Walking Dead" is one of the most-viewed horror series worldwide.
《陰屍路》是部受全球歡迎的恐怖影集。

"Breaking Bad" has been successful since it came out.
絕命毒師一上映就大獲成功。

Who will be the guests on the Ellen Show next week?
《艾倫秀》下一周的嘉賓是誰呢？

The Emmy Awards is an award recognizing excellence in the television industry in the U.S.
艾美獎是美國為了獎勵在電視業的傑出人士的獎項。

Who do you think will be voted the Best Actor at the Emmys?
你覺得今年誰會贏得艾美獎最佳男演員？

Frank's wife divorced him because she couldn't stand a couch potato like him anymore.
法蘭克的太太再也無法忍受他如此愛看電視又懶散，因而和他離婚。

UNIT 05 校園
大學新生
University Freshman

 單字基本功 掌握關鍵字 = 開口第一步

核心聯想 踏入校園 Entering university

academy [əˋkædəmɪ] 名 學院	**college** [ˋkɑlɪdʒ] 名 學院；大專院校	**department** [dɪˋpɑrtmənt] 名 系所	**freshman** [ˋfrɛʃmən] 名 大一新生
peer [pɪr] 名 同儕	**university** [͵junəˋvɝsətɪ] 名 大學	**enroll** [ɪnˋrol] 動 註冊	**peer group** 片 同儕團體

攻讀學位 Pursuing a degree **進階學習**

diploma [dɪˋplomə] 名 畢業證書	**graduate** [ˋgrædʒʊ͵et] 名 研究生 動 畢業	**study** [ˋstʌdɪ] 名 動 研究；學習	**undergraduate** [͵ʌndəˋgrædʒuɪt] 名 大學生
bachelor's degree 片 學士學位	**doctor's degree** 片 博士學位	**master's degree** 片 碩士學位	**PhD** 縮 哲學博士；博士學位

 深度追蹤 Knowing More

　　收到國外學校的錄取通知（admission offer）之後，第一件事就是回覆入學的意願，有些學校可以直接回覆通知錄取的e-mail，有的學校則需要到網頁進行確認。接下來便能申請住宿，通常可在學校網站申請校內住宿，或是開始尋找周圍的校外住宿。再來才是購買機票到美國，並至學校完成註冊，要注意的是，留學生同時也必須到國際學生中心報到。另外，學校通常也會要求保學生保險，因為國外看病費用較高，有學生保險的話才能省下花費。

MP3 ▶ 239

套個單字，想說的都能表達！

sb. adjust oneself to... 某人使自己適應⋯。

★ I hope I'll soon adjust myself to my university life.
我希望我能很快就適應我的大學生活。

★ The **veteran** just can't adjust himself to the ordinary life now.
那位老兵無法適應現在的平凡生活。

★ **Chameleons** can adjust themselves to match the surroundings.
變色龍能主動適應周遭環境。

★ Those employees need to adjust themselves to the working environment.
那些員工必須自己去適應工作環境。

★ The **reformer** must try to adjust himself to difficult conditions.
那位改革家必須試著去適應最艱困的情況。

> **veteran**
> [`vɛtərən]
> 名 老兵；退役軍人
>
> **chameleon**
> [kə`miljən]
> 名 變色龍
>
> **reformer**
> [rɪ`fɔrmɚ]
> 名 改革者

sb. have no idea... 某人不知道⋯。

★ I have no idea how to enroll in a course online.
我不知道怎樣線上選課。

★ She has no idea how the **accident** happened.
她不知道這個事故是怎麼發生的。

★ Her family have no idea why depression has **struck** her.
她的家人不知道為什麼憂鬱症會找上她。

★ Jane has no idea how to react to his **offensive** words.
珍不知道該如何回應他無禮的對待。

★ My colleagues have no idea why Emily insists on **ratifying** this agreement.
我的同事們都不知道為什麼愛蜜莉堅持批准這項協議。

> **accident**
> [`æksədənt]
> 名 意外
>
> **strike**
> [straɪk]
> 動 （疾病）侵襲
>
> **offensive**
> [ə`fɛnsɪv]
> 形 冒犯的
>
> **ratify**
> [`rætə,faɪ]
> 動 正式批准

開口必備句 和老外聊開懷，就靠這幾句！

I finally get my student visa two months after my visa application.
申請兩個月之後，我終於拿到我的學生簽證了。

You'll receive an email regarding orientation dates in advance of the start of the semester.
在學期開始之前，你會收到一封 email 通知新生訓練的時間。

Don't forget to go to the International Student Service to check in first.
別忘了要先到國際學生事務處報到。

There will be a one-week orientation for you to know more about the lives here and some university policy.
將會有為期一周的新生訓練，介紹這邊的生活還有一些學校的政策。

Students generally register for classes during the orientation through your online student account.
在新生訓練期間，學生通常可以用線上學生系統來選課。

Health insurance coverage is compulsory before being allowed to register for classes.
在可以開始選課之前，一定要先保好健康保險。

Tuition and fees can be paid through wire transfer.
學雜費可以透過匯款方式繳交。

You need to go to building C12 to collect your student ID card before classes commence.
在課程開始之前，你必須到 C12 棟去領取你的學生證。

I am so excited about meeting all the newcomers.
即將與新生相見，讓我感到相當興奮。

I met an old friend at the welcome party. I didn't know that we go to the same school.
我在迎新派對上遇見一位老朋友，我不知道我們竟然讀同一所學校。

UNIT 06

校園

認識校園
Campus Tour

單字基本功 掌握關鍵字 = 開口第一步

核心聯想

校園設備 Campus facilities

campus [`kæmpəs] 名 校園	**cafeteria** [ˌkæfə`tırıə] 名 學生餐廳	**gymnasium** [dʒɪm`nezɪəm] 名 健身房	**identification** [aɪˌdɛntəfə`keʃən] 名 身分證明
bulletin board 片 布告欄	**lecture hall** 片 大講堂	**on campus** 片 校內的	**off campus** 片 校外的

深入認識 Knowing more about the school

進階學習

dean [din] 名 院長	**faculty** [`fækḷtɪ] 名 教職員工	**major** [`medʒɚ] 名 動 主修	**minor** [`maɪnɚ] 名 動 副修
professor [prə`fɛsɚ] 名 教授	**term** [tɝm] 名 學期	**academic** [ˌækə`dɛmɪk] 形 學術性的	**teaching assistant** 片 助教

深度追蹤

Knowing More

　　關於美國名校的校園風光，以下為簡單的介紹：(1) 哈佛大學（Harvard University）中紅色的建築及低矮簡約的樓房，反映出對傳統的尊崇和對學術的無限追逐。(2) 康奈爾大學（Cornell University）的校舍被譽為維多利亞式建築的經典，且當地風景優美。(3) 耶魯大學（Yale University）中的建築物，則包含了各式各樣的設計風格。(4) 麻省理工學院（Massachusetts Institute of Technology）則是個充滿新古典主義建築的校園。

句型偷吃步　套個單字，想說的都能表達！

Please feel free to...　請儘管…。

★ Please feel free to consult your academic advisor about any problems you may have.
如果有任何問題，請儘管詢問你的導師。

★ Please feel free to **elaborate** on your proposals at the meeting.
請儘量在會議中詳細說明你的提案。

★ Please feel free to participate in this international **symposium**.
請自由參加這個國際座談會。

★ Please feel free to **browse** through the articles and leave comments.
請儘管瀏覽文章並給予評論。

★ Please feel free to send us your specific enquiries and quotation.
請儘管將你們具體的問題及報價寄給我們。

> **elaborate**
> [ɪˋlæbə͵ret]
> 動 詳細說明
> **symposium**
> [sɪmˋpozɪəm]
> 名 座談會
> **browse**
> [brauz]
> 動 瀏覽

sb. can't...until...　某人在…之前不能…。

★ You can't enter the lab until you get your student ID card.
你要拿到學生證之後才能進入實驗室。

★ Erin and I can't go to L.A. until next month.
艾琳和我下個月才能去洛杉磯。

★ The **plumber** can't fix the **leak** until tomorrow.
水管工明天才能修理漏水。

★ His team can't finish this project until November.
他的團隊十一月之前無法完成這份企劃。

★ I can't see why she decided to **take the blame** until she explained everything to me yesterday.
在昨天她跟我解釋之前，我不懂為什麼她要背黑鍋。

> **plumber**
> [ˋplʌmə]
> 名 水管工
> **leak**
> [lik]
> 名（水、瓦斯等）漏出
> **take the blame**
> 片 背黑鍋

開口必備句

和老外聊開懷，就靠這幾句！

How do you like our campus?
你覺得我們的校園如何？

Your campus is really big and beautiful.
你們的校園真大，也很美。

Where is the administration office?
教務處在哪裡？

The library is right next to the swimming pool.
圖書館就在游泳池的旁邊。

I have to return these books to the library before tomorrow.
我必須在明天之前把這些書還回圖書館。

You have to show your student ID to get into the library.
你必須出示學生證才能進入圖書館。

The cafeteria is always crowded during lunch time.
學校的自助餐廳在午餐時間總是非常擁擠。

Can you meet me at the student lounge at four-thirty?
你四點半的時候可以在學生交誼廳跟我碰面嗎？

That building over there is the gymnasium.
那棟建築物是體育館。

Some students are having physical training in the gymnasium.
有些學生正在體育館裡進行體能訓練。

If you need anything, you can go to the student center and ask for help.
如果你有需要，你可以到學生中心去詢問。

We offer 24-hour computer access available at computer labs across the campuses.
我們校園內的電腦教室二十四小時都可以使用電腦。

UNIT 07 校園
分組上台報告
Group Presentations

單字基本功 掌握關鍵字 = 開口第一步

核心聯想 分組組員 Teaming up with classmates

classmate [`klæs͵met] 名 同學	**cohort** [`kohɔrt] 名 一隊人;同伴	**partner** [`pɑrtnɚ] 名 夥伴	**teammate** [`tim͵met] 名 隊友
teamwork [`tim͵wɝk] 名 合作;協力	**coordinate** [ko`ɔrdnet] 動 協調	**pair up with sb.** 片(因工作或比賽) 與某人結成搭檔	**team up** 片 合作

分配工作 Working together **進階學習**

feedback [`fid͵bæk] 名 回饋	**cooperate** [ko`ɑpə͵ret] 動 合作;配合	**collaborate** [kə`læbə͵ret] 動 合作	**delegate** [`dɛlə͵get] 名 委派(某人)做
distribute [dɪ`strɪbjut] 動 分配;分開	**emulate** [`ɛmjə͵let] 動 與…競爭	**refine** [rɪ`faɪn] 動 改善;提煉	**tackle** [`tækḷ] 動 應付;抓住

 **深度追蹤** ♪♪♪♪♪ Knowing More

> 　　許多人認為,在外求學感受到的文化衝擊就是上台發表意見。不同於台灣,每學期的口頭報告可能只有一、兩次而已,在國外的課堂中,常常需要發表自己的意見,同時也必須在上課之前就先把資料查好,養成主動學習的習慣,這樣上課中才能表達出自己的想法。值得一提的是,分組討論時通常要主動尋找隊友,甚至還有人會先提出自己的想法,再邀請別人一起合作,於是有更多的機會可以與不同專長的人交流,藉此開拓視野和人脈。

 套個單字，想說的都能表達！

Who is...with...?　那個…的人是誰？

★ Who is that **lecturer** with a white suitcase?
那位手上拿著白色手提箱的講者是誰？

★ Who is the boy with a blue **cap** and a yellow jacket?
那個戴藍色帽子、穿黃色外套的男孩是誰？

★ Who is that student with a novel in his hand?
那位手裡拿著小說的學生是誰？

★ Who is the speaker with the black **tuxedo**?
那名穿白色晚禮服的講者是誰？

★ Who is that runner with a funny **mask** and costume?
那名戴滑稽面具還穿奇異服裝的跑者是誰？

lecturer
[ˈlɛktʃərə]
名 講師

cap
[kæp]
名 帽子

tuxedo
[tʌkˈsido]
名 （男式）禮服

mask
[mæsk]
名 面具；口罩

...would like sb. to...　…想要某人…。

★ The teacher would like everyone in the class to introduce themselves before the class begins.
老師想請班上每一個人在上課之前都先自我介紹。

★ I would like you to be the most popular singer in the world.
我希望你能成為世界上最受歡迎的歌手。

★ Jimmy would like his assistant to pass him some **envelopes**.
吉米請他的助理給他一些信封。

★ Our manager would like the **developer** to take the responsibility for this project.
我們經理請那位開發者負責本次的企劃。

★ Our boss would like all staff to share their **verdicts** on this matter.
我們老闆想請所有員工分享他們對這件事的看法。

envelop
[ˈɛnvə‚lop]
名 信封

developer
[dɪˈvɛləpə]
名 開發者

verdict
[ˈvɝdɪkt]
名 （口）意見

The teacher divided the class into a total of twelve groups.
老師把全班分成總共十二個小組。

This week's assignment is a team project.
這個星期的作業是要撰寫分組報告。

There should be four people on our team, with one of us a team leader.
我們組應該要有四個人，其中一個為組長。

Neil wanted to know more people, so he chose to team up with other classmates rather than his friends.
尼爾想認識多一點人，所以選擇跟其他同學合作，而不是他的朋友們。

It is important to cooperate and communicate with your team members.
與小組成員合作、溝通都是很重要的。

I like to work in teams and also to fly solo.
我喜歡團隊合作，也喜歡一個人做事。

Our team will meet up this afternoon to discuss our project.
我們小組今天下午會碰面，一起討論我們的報告。

During our discussion, there were some disagreements.
我們討論的過程中，有一些意見不合的情況。

When there is a disagreement, the majority rules.
有意見不合的情況時，都是少數服從多數。

Kate made no contributions to her team, and she never shows up during discussions.
凱特對她的小組沒有貢獻，而且從不參加小組討論。

Being part of a team will help you develop interpersonal skills as well as leadership skills.
融入小組討論可以培養人際溝通技巧以及領導技巧。

MP3 ▶ 247

UNIT 08 校園 課外活動
Extracurricular Activities

單字基本功 掌握關鍵字 = 開口第一步

核心聯想 各種社團 Various clubs to join

alumni
[ə`lʌmnaɪ]
名 校友（單數為 alumnus）

club
[klʌb]
名 社團

toastmasters
[`tost͵mæstə]
名 英語演講社

varsity
[`vɑrsətɪ]
名 校隊

extracurricular
[͵ɛkstrəkə`rɪkələ]
形 課外的

cheering squad
片 啦啦隊

debate team
片 辯論社

student association
片 學生會

進階學習 參與社團 Taking part in the clubs

chief
[tʃif]
名 長官 形 主要的

coordinator
[ko`ordn͵etə]
名 協調者

director
[də`rɛktə]
名 社長；主管

president
[`prɛzədənt]
名 會長；主席

competitive
[kəm`pɛtətɪv]
形 競爭性的

executive
[ɪg`zɛkjutɪv]
形 執行的

vice
[vaɪs]
形 副的

public relations
片 公關

深度追蹤 🔍

Knowing More

　　在美國電影中，常看到所謂的「兄弟會 fraternity」和「姊妹會 sorority」，但想要入會就必須通過一連串的篩選，像是學業成績、家世背景、身分地位……等等；篩選過後，還要通過許多關卡來證明自己加入的決心和忠誠度，經過重重考驗後，才能進入代代相傳的別墅會館，與會員們一同交流、玩樂。入會雖然是拓展人脈、訓練與人應對的軟能力（soft skills）的好機會，但也經常舉辦各種派對，所以更常給人一種花花世界的既定印象。

sb. adjust to... 　某人適應⋯。

★ Jane adjusts to her university life by attending all kinds of extracurricular activities.
珍妮以參加許多課外活動的方式來適應她的大學生活。

★ The **toddlers** try to adjust to the **day-care center**.
孩子們試著適應托兒所的環境。

★ The tourists can't adjust to the harsh winters here.
旅客無法適應這邊的寒冬。

★ Astronauts must adjust to a weightless state.
太空人必須適應無重力狀態。

★ The man can hardly adjust to the **withdrawal symptoms**.
男子幾乎無法適應這些戒斷症狀。

> **toddler**
> [`tɑdlə]
> 名 兒童
> **day-care center**
> 片 托兒所
> **withdrawal symptoms**
> 片 戒斷症狀

sb. be known as... 　某人以⋯聞名。

★ Daniel is known as a gold-winning star in the swimming team.
丹尼爾是游泳隊的金牌明星。

★ Puccini is known as an excellent composer of operas.
普契尼以其優秀歌劇創作者的身份聞名。

★ That **corpulent** man is known as a **tenor**.
那位胖男人以男高音成名。

★ The **disheveled** man is known as a **cartoonist**.
那個邋遢的男人是位有名的漫畫家。

★ The man who won the prize in literature is known as an up-and-coming writer.
那位贏得文學獎的男性以新銳作家身分聞名。

> **corpulent**
> [`kɔrpjələnt]
> 形 肥胖的
> **tenor**
> [`tɛnə]
> 名 男高音
> **disheveled**
> [dɪ`ʃɛvld]
> 形 衣冠不整的
> **cartoonist**
> [kɑr`tunɪst]
> 名 漫畫家

MP3 ▶ 249

開口必備句　和老外聊開懷，就靠這幾句！

There will be a freshers' fair during orientation for clubs to take in new members.
🔊 新生訓練期間，會有一場可讓社團招收新成員的介紹會。

I am thinking about joining a club and meet more people.
🔊 我想要加入一個社團，認識更多的人。

Which club do you want to join?
🔊 你想參加什麼社團？

Are you interested in joining the astrology club?
🔊 你想參加占星社嗎？

The hiking club meets every Saturday at 8:00 a.m. They always organize a trip into the mountains on weekends.
🔊 健行社每週六早上八點鐘聚會，他們每當假日總是會相約去爬山。

He is a member of this fraternity.
🔊 他是這個兄弟會的會員。

Do you want to go to that sorority party?
🔊 你想去參加那個姊妹會的派對嗎？

I signed up for the movie club yesterday.
🔊 我昨天加入了電影社。

Cassie joined the tennis club to improve her tennis skills.
🔊 凱西為了增進網球實力而參加了網球社。

Do you know anyone in the art club?
🔊 你認識美術社的人嗎？

I am the president of the singing club.
🔊 我是合唱社的社長。

I have no idea what that club is.
🔊 我完全不知道那個社團是做什麼的。

UNIT 09 校園

熬夜玩樂
Having Fun All Night Long

 單字基本功 ➤ 掌握關鍵字 = 開口第一步

 核心聯想 　夜遊行程 Fun activities at night

karaoke [ˌkɑrəˈoke] 名 卡拉 OK	**motorbike** [ˈmotəˌbaɪk] 名 摩托車	**nightlife** [ˈnaɪtlaɪf] 名 夜生活	**scooter** [ˈskutə] 名 小型摩托車
haunted house 片 鬼屋	**night owl** 片 夜貓子	**night view** 片 夜景	**trivia night** 片 機智問答之夜

 　整晚熬夜不睡覺 Staying up late　**進階學習**

ghost [gost] 名 鬼魂	**insomnia** [ɪnˈsɑmnɪə] 名 失眠	**crawl back in bed** 片 賴床	**energy drink** 片 能量飲料
pull an all-nighter 片 熬夜	**sleep over** 片 在別人家過夜	**sleep walk** 片 夢遊	**stay up late** 片 熬夜

 **深度追蹤** 　　　　*Knowing More*

　　你是否聽過美國大學的「3S魔咒」？這個詞其實是指study（學習）、social（社交）、和sleep（睡覺）；選擇學習和睡覺的人為「書呆子」，選擇社交和睡覺的則被稱為「遊蕩者」，而選擇學習和社交的被叫做不需要睡覺的「殭屍」。人的一天雖只有二十四小時，且體力也有限，大部份的美國學生都會三者兼顧，再根據自己的需求做調整。另外，他們也常投資自己、培養交際能力，一有時間便去實習或做社區服務，積極地拓展自己的競爭力。

 **套個單字，想說的都能表達！**

sb. had a great time...　　某人很愉快地度過…。

- ★ My friends and I had a great time singing karaoke last night.
  我跟我的朋友昨晚度過了一個愉快的卡拉 OK 之夜。
- ★ The high school students had a great time at the **field trip**.
  那些高中生們度過了愉快的校外教學。
- ★ My date and I had a great time at the party on Tuesday.
  我的約會對象和我星期二度過了一個愉快的派對。
- ★ The boy **scouts** had a great time up in the mountains this weekend.
  童子軍在山上度過了一個愉快的周末。
- ★ My family had a great time in Las Vegas during our vacation.
  我的家人在拉斯維加斯度過了愉快的假期。

> **field trip**
> 片 校外教學
> **scout**
> [skaut]
> 名 童子軍

sb. be afraid that...　　某人認為…恐怕得…。

- ★ I'm afraid that Frank might get expelled if he keeps skipping classes.
  我想如果法蘭克一直翹課，他恐怕會被退學。
- ★ The analyst is afraid that this is a risky investment.
  分析師覺得這恐怕是項冒險的投資。
- ★ My director is afraid that Bill **underrated** the difficulty of the task.
  我的主任覺得比爾或許低估了任務的困難度。
- ★ His mother is afraid that the scar on his cheek may be **permanent**.
  他的母親認為他臉上的傷疤恐怕得永遠留在臉上。
- ★ That doctor is afraid that there will be a **fatal outbreak** of the disease.
  那名醫生認為致命疾病恐怕會流行。

> **underrate**
> [ˌʌndəˋret]
> 動 低估；輕視
> **permanent**
> [ˋpɝmənənt]
> 形 永久的
> **fatal**
> [ˌfet!]
> 形 致命的
> **outbreak**
> [ˋautˏbrek]
> 名 爆發

Young people love to ride scooters in groups all night and have fun together.
年輕人喜歡在晚上成群結隊，騎著摩托車一起去玩樂。

Do you want to join us for a night ride?
你想跟我們去夜遊嗎？

Let's go for a night ride after the midterm exam!
我們期中考過後去夜遊吧！

I guess I'll pass. I am afraid of ghosts.
我想我還是不去好了，我真的很怕鬼。

I want to join you guys, but I'll have to borrow a helmet first.
我想跟你們去，但是我得先借頂安全帽。

They plan to depart from the Shi-lin Night Market at 11 p.m. and then ride all the way to Tam-shui.
他們計畫晚上十一點從士林夜市出發，接著再一路騎車到淡水。

Don't forget to fill up the tank before we depart.
別忘了在出發前要先加滿油。

You have to be very careful when riding at night.
晚上騎車要非常小心。

We decided to go to Yang-ming Mountain and enjoy the sunrise.
我們決定在陽明山上看日出。

I went on a ride last night, so I'm so exhausted now.
我昨晚去夜衝，所以現在累得要命。

They like to hang out at bars and drink their nights away every Friday.
他們每逢星期五，就喜歡到酒吧整晚暢飲。

MP3 ▶ 253

單字基本功 掌握關鍵字 = 開口第一步

核心聯想　**繳交作業 Submitting reports**

assessment
[ə`sɛsmənt]
名 作業；評估

assignment
[ə`saɪnmənt]
名 作業；任務

dissertation
[ˌdɪsə`teʃən]
名 畢業論文

report
[rɪ`port]
名 動 報告

research
[rɪ`sɝtʃ]
名 動 研究

thesis
[`θisɪs]
名 論文

submit
[səb`mɪt]
動 繳交；屈服

hand in
片 繳交

朝目標邁進 Grades & goals 進階學習

credit
[`krɛdɪt]
名 學分

prerequisite
[ˌpri`rɛkwəzɪt]
名 先修課程

requisite
[`rɛkwəzɪt]
名 必修課

scholarship
[`skalə`ʃɪp]
名 獎學金

transcript
[`træn͵skrɪpt]
名 成績單

flunk
[flʌŋk]
動 不及格

dean's list
片 優秀學生名單

student loan
片 學生貸款

深度追蹤  Knowing More

　　上台報告時，只要多加注意以下幾點，就不怕拿不到分數：(1) 充分準備、事先規劃好要講的內容，且演講時最好避免一直低頭讀稿。(2) 上台報告時，專心在傳達自己的想法來緩解緊張，也可用熱情、信心帶動自己的表現，用適當的音量以及肢體語言展現自信，並適時與台下的觀眾多多互動。(3) 多累積經驗，因為講得愈多，下次上台就不會再那麼緊張。(4) 注意服裝儀容以及報告細節，服裝須整齊乾淨，同時也要掌握好報告的時間。

句型偷吃步　套個單字，想說的都能表達！

sb. like A more than B. 比起 B，某人比較喜歡 A。

- ★ Most students like handing in papers more than giving presentations.
  比起上台報告，大部分學生還是比較喜歡交報告。

- ★ My sister likes jazz more than pop music.
  比起流行音樂，我的妹妹比較喜歡爵士音樂。

- ★ I like creative **pedagogy** more than **spoon-fed education**.
  比起填鴨式教育，我比較喜歡有創意的教學法。

- ★ Most of the locals here like winter more than any other seasons.
  大部分的本地人比起其他季節，還是比較喜歡冬天。

- ★ The millionaire likes to stay in his **villa** in the countryside more than in his mansion in the city.
  那位億萬富翁比較喜歡待在郊外的別墅，而不是他在城市的大宅院。

> **pedagogy**
> [`pɛdə͵godʒɪ]
> 名 教學法
> **spoon-fed education**
> 片 填鴨式教育
> **villa**
> [`vɪlə]
> 名 別墅

sb. have got to... 某人必須…。

- ★ I have got to study hard to get higher grades for the scholarship.
  我必須努力提高成績才能獲得獎學金。

- ★ We have got to **cut back on** our expenses.
  我們必須減少花費。

- ★ I have got to figure out what happened recently.
  我一定要了解最近到底發生了什麼事。

- ★ We have got to pay attention to personal **grooming** when going on stage.
  我們在舞台上一定要多注意服裝儀容。

- ★ The teacher has got to tolerate their **foibles** and focus on their strengths.
  那位老師必須包容他們的缺點，並多注意他們的優點。

> **cut back on sth.**
> 片 削減某事／物
> **grooming**
> [`grumɪŋ]
> 名 打扮
> **foible**
> [`fɔɪbl]
> 名 弱點

MP3 ▶ 255

開口必備句　和老外聊開懷，就靠這幾句！

It is important to make eye-contact with the audience during presentations.

報告時，與觀眾眼神交流是很重要的。

The opening of your presentation is very interesting.

你報告的開頭部份很有趣。

I think your presentation was well-organized.

我覺得你的報告內容很有組織。

You shouldn't use too many hand gestures.

你不該使用太多手勢。

Can you speak louder? We can't hear you in the back.

可以請你大聲一點嗎？我們坐在後面都聽不到你的聲音。

While giving presentations, don't forget to have eye contact with your audience.

上台報告時，別忘了要適度與觀眾交流眼神。

Be sure to make your point of view clear and strong in your report.

你的報告裡面必須堅定且清晰地表達出你的觀點。

What did the professor say about my dissertation?

教授有說我的研究論文寫得怎麼樣嗎？

If you emphasized that issue more, your essay would be much better.

如果你能夠再強調一下那個主題，你的論文就會出色許多。

Ella has made it on the dean's list again this semester.

艾拉這學期仍然是班上的前幾名。

Henry was not satisfied with his grades, so he decided to study harder from now on.

亨利對他的成績不滿意，所以他決定從現在開始要更用功讀書。

NOTE

Part 10

十月好個出遊時節

October Highlights:
Time To Travel

Unit 01
[節慶] 中秋賞月
Mid-Autumn Festival

[節慶] 萬聖節氣息
Halloween:
Trick Or Treats!

Unit 02

Unit 03
[娛樂] 街頭藝人藝術
Street Artists & Street Arts

[校園] 宿舍生活
Living On Campus

Unit 04

[旅遊] 跟團或自助
Tour Groups & Self-
guided Tours

Unit 07

[旅遊] 想飛的心
Planning Your Vacation

Unit 06

Unit 05
[校園] 租屋生活
Living Off Campus

Unit 08

[旅遊] 出入境大廳
Arrival & Departure

[旅遊] 飛機上放鬆
Relaxing On The Plane

Unit 09

Unit 10
[旅遊] 入住及退房
Checking In & Checking Out

名 名詞　　動 動詞　　形 形容詞　　副 副詞　　片 片語　　縮 縮寫

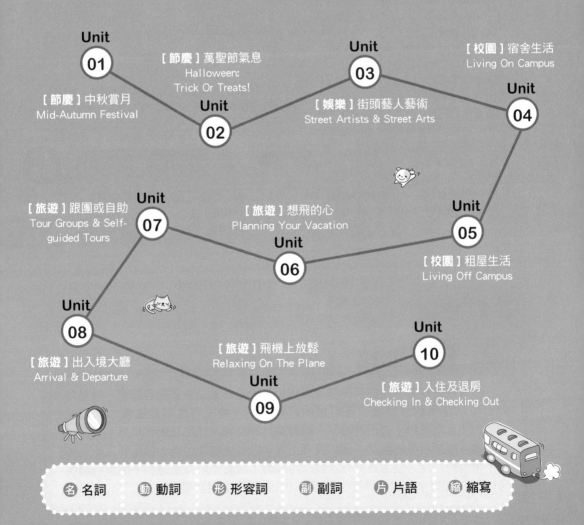

UNIT 01 節慶 中秋賞月
Mid-Autumn Festival

 單字基本功 掌握關鍵字 = 開口第一步

 核心聯想 吃月餅聽故事 Moon cakes & folktales

barbecue [ˋbɑrbɪkju] 名 動 烤肉	**elixir** [ɪˋlɪksɚ] 名 仙藥	**lantern** [ˋlæntɚn] 名 燈籠	**pomelo** [ˋpɑmǝlo] 名 柚子
worship [ˋwɝʃɪp] 動 崇拜；景仰	**drool with envy** 片 垂涎三尺	**folk tales** 片 民間故事	**moon cake** 片 月餅

 大家齊賞月 In the moonlight 進階學習

crescent [ˋkrɛsn̩t] 名 弦月	**moonlight** [ˋmun͵laɪt] 名 月光	**wane** [wen] 動 月虧	**wax** [wæks] 動 月亮漸滿
bright [braɪt] 形 明亮的	**full moon** 片 滿月	**lunar eclipse** 片 月蝕	**new moon** 片 新月

 深度追蹤 *Knowing More*

　　古今中外有許多關於月亮的民間傳說，像是如果幼童多病難養育，或是年輕女子期望得到好姻緣，都可以向月亮祈求，故人們也稱月亮為「太陰星君」、「太陰娘娘」或「月娘」，認為有月亮之神，並加以膜拜月亮。另外，也有很多關於月亮的揣測，例如月亮上面早已有生物居住過，甚至有人認為美國不再登陸月球，是因為第一次登陸月球時，所有宇航員都遇到不明飛行物體（UFO）而對未知的世界產生恐懼、中止之後的登月計畫。

MP3 ▶ 257

套個單字，想說的都能表達！

People say/It is said that... 聽說 / 俗話說…。

★ People say that your ears will be cut off if you point at the moon.
聽說如果用手指月亮，你的耳朵就會被割掉。

★ People say that ghosts **haunt** that old lodge.
聽說那個小木屋在鬧鬼。

★ People say that she used **witchcraft** to **lure** those young men.
有人說她用妖術去誘騙那些年輕人。

★ It is said that Guilin's scenery is **unrivaled** in the world
俗話說：「桂林山水甲天下。」

★ It is said that the number thirteen is often considered unlucky
數字十三經常被認為是不吉利的數字。

haunt
[hɔnt]
動 (鬼魂等) 常出沒於

witchcraft
[`wɪtʃ͵kræft]
名 巫術

lure
[lur]
動 引誘；誘惑

unrivaled
[ʌn`raɪvld]
形 無對手的

Could you do sb. a favor and...?
你可以幫忙某人…嗎？

★ Could you do me a favor and bring me some more **charcoals**?
你可以幫我多拿些木炭嗎？

★ Could you do me a favor and clean the bathroom?
你可以幫我清理一下浴室嗎？

★ Could you do your brothers a favor and **redress** the scales?
你可以幫你弟弟們主持公道嗎？

★ Could you do the babysitter a favor and **coddle** the baby for a while?
你可以幫媬姆照顧一下嬰兒嗎？

★ Could you do our manager a favor and **verify** every article of this contract?
你可以幫我們經理確認合約條款嗎？

charcoal
[`tʃɑr͵kol]
名 木炭

redress
[rɪ`drɛs]
動 糾正；矯正

coddle
[`kɑdl]
動 悉心照料

verify
[`vɛrə͵faɪ]
動 核實

281

MP3 ▸ 258

 開口必備句 和老外聊開懷，就靠這幾句！

The full moon on Moon Festival symbolizes the reunion of family members.
🔊 中秋節的滿月象徵著一家團聚。

My family always gather together and watches the bright moon on Moon Festival.
🔊 我們一家總是在中秋節聚在一起，一同欣賞明月。

There are many folk tales about the Moon Festival, such as Chang-Er flying to the moon.
🔊 關於中秋節的民間傳說有很多，例如嫦娥奔月。

It is said that Chang-Er took the pills for immortality and flew into the sky.
🔊 傳說嫦娥吃了長生不老之藥後，便飛上天空。

According to the folktale, there is a hare pounding medicine with Chang-Er on the moon.
🔊 根據民間傳說，月亮上除了嫦娥之外，還有一隻搗藥的月兔。

The rebels against Mongol rule hid messages in moon cakes and distributed to their allies.
🔊 對抗蒙古統治的反叛軍，將訊息藏在月餅裡，並把月餅分送給盟軍。

How about coming to my barbecue party next week?
🔊 下星期想來參加我的烤肉派對嗎？

What kind of moon cake do you like the best?
🔊 你最喜歡哪種月餅呢？

Where is the Moon Festival barbecue?
🔊 中秋節烤肉派對在哪裡舉辦呢？

Jenny cut the pomelo peel into a hat and put it on Jack's head, which was hilarious.
🔊 珍妮把柚子皮切成帽子的形狀戴在傑克頭上，真的很好笑。

MP3 ◉ 259

02

節慶

萬聖節氣息
Halloween: Trick Or Treats!

單字基本功 ▷ 掌握關鍵字＝開口第一步

核心聯想

萬聖節變裝 Dressing up for Halloween

beast [bist] 名 野獸	**phantom** [ˋfæntəm] 名 幽靈	**skull** [skʌl] 名 骷髏頭	**vampire** [ˋvæmpaɪr] 名 吸血鬼
werewolf [ˋwɪrˏwʊlf] 名 狼人	**witch** [wɪtʃ] 名（女）巫師	**wizard** [ˋwɪzəd] 名（男）巫師	**zombie** [ˋzɑmbɪ] 名 殭屍

起源與活動 Origin & activities 進階學習

afterlife [ˋæftəˏlaɪf] 名 來世	**pumpkin** [ˋpʌmpkɪn] 名 南瓜	**disguise** [dɪsˋgaɪz] 動 喬裝	**petrify** [ˋpɛtrəˏfaɪ] 動 使驚呆
dreadful [ˋdrɛdfəl] 形 可怕的	**gruesome** [ˋgrusəm] 形 恐怖的	**thrilling** [ˋθrɪlɪŋ] 形 毛骨悚然的	**trick or treat** 片 不給糖就搗蛋

深度追蹤 🔍

Knowing More

在萬聖夜當天，常會見到鄰里間舉辦「街區舞會 block party」，且人們打扮成各種各樣的造型，像是殭屍、鬼魂、木乃伊……等來參加舞會，而街上也裝飾著用南瓜做的「南瓜燈 Jack O'Lantern」；其他慶祝方式還有玩「釘上驢尾巴 pin the tail on the donkey」，參加者須矇上雙眼轉圈後，再把釘子釘到紙驢子的尾巴上面；另一個受歡迎的遊戲為「咬蘋果 apple bobbing」，要把蘋果從裝滿水的桶子裡拿出來，但過程中不能用雙手。

 套個單字，想說的都能表達！

...in the end. …最後…。

★ Mandy picked her Halloween costume for three hours, and she chose to dress as a zombie in the end.
曼蒂挑萬聖節服裝挑了三個小時，而最後還是選擇扮成一個殭屍。

★ The audience in the movie theater wept in the end.
電影院內的觀眾最後都落淚了。

★ The troops were forced to **surrender** in the end.
軍隊最後被迫投降。

surrender
[sə`rɛndə]
働 使投降

★ All the experiments proved my **assumption** false in the end.
最後，所有實驗都證明我的假設是錯誤的。

assumption
[ə`sʌmpʃən]
图 設想；假定

★ The soldier had no choice but to **amputate** his foot in the end.
那名士兵最後別無選擇，只能截肢他的雙腳。

amputate
[`æmpjə‚tet]
働 (醫) 截肢

sb. be good in sth. 某人很擅長做某事。

★ Actually, Jennifer is really good in special effects makeup.
珍妮佛其實很擅長特效化妝。

★ The student sitting next to me is good in math.
坐在我隔壁的學生數學很好。

★ Our professor is good in **geomechanics**.
我們教授很精通地球力學。

geomechanics
[‚dʒiəmɪ`kænɪks]
图 地球力學

★ Doctor Lee is good at **repairing** nerve damages.
李醫生很擅長修復神經損傷。

repair
[rɪ`pɛr]
働 修補

★ That **geneticist** is good in gene **transplantation**, and his researches are all published in academic journals.
那位遺傳學家很精通基因移植，而且他的研究都有發布在學術期刊上面。

geneticist
[dʒə`nɛtɪsɪst]
图 遺傳學家

transplantation
[‚trænsplæn`teʃən]
图 移植

MP3 ▶ 261

和老外聊開懷，就靠這幾句！

Halloween is the night before All Saints' Day.
萬聖節是諸聖節的前一晚。

Folklore has it that Stingy Jack was refused to enter heaven nor to hell because he lied to the Devil.
傳說傑克因為戲弄惡魔，死後無法到天堂也無法入地獄。

People put out Jack-o'-lanterns as decorations on Halloween.
萬聖節時，人們會擺設南瓜燈做為裝飾。

Mrs. Lee will teach us how to carve a pumpkin lantern.
李老師會教我們如何雕刻南瓜燈。

Trick-or-treating is one of the most popular festive Halloween activities.
「不給糖，就搗蛋！」是萬聖節最受歡迎的慶祝活動之一。

There are many kids asking for candy along the street on Halloween.
萬聖節當天，沿街有很多孩童向住戶要糖果。

What do you want to dress up as for the Halloween party?
萬聖節派對你想做什麼樣的打扮呢？

Do you know anywhere to rent Halloween costumes?
你知道哪裡可以租借萬聖節服裝嗎？

Jack dressed up as Iron Man for the Halloween party.
傑克在萬聖節派對上裝扮成鋼鐵人。

Jason and his friends played a prank and changed some of the house numbers on the street.
傑森和朋友們玩惡作劇，調換了一些門牌的位置。

My grandma always makes a lot of delicious toffee apples before Halloween.
我的奶奶在萬聖節之前，總是會做很多好吃的太妃糖蘋果。

UNIT 03 娛樂

街頭藝人藝術
Street Artists & Street Arts

單字基本功 掌握關鍵字 = 開口第一步

核心聯想

街頭作品形式 Forms of arts

busker [`bʌskɚ] 名 街頭藝人	**graffiti** [græˋfitɪ] 名 塗鴉（單數為 graffito）	**stencil** [ˋstɛnsḷ] 名 模板；圖案	**sticker** [ˋstɪkɚ] 名 貼紙
installation art 片 裝置藝術	**spray paint** 片 噴漆	**street art** 片 街頭藝術	**street artist** 片 街頭藝人

藝術 vs 法律 Arts and the law

進階學習

connotation [͵kɑnəˋteʃən] 名 含蓄；言外之意	**controversy** [ˋkɑntrə͵vɝsɪ] 名 爭論；爭議	**vandalism** [ˋvændḷɪzəm] 名 破壞公物	**anonymous** [əˋnɑnəməs] 形 匿名的
illegal [ɪˋligḷ] 形 違法的	**subversive** [səbˋvɝsɪv] 形 破壞性的	**thought-provoking** [ˋθɔtprə͵vokɪŋ] 形 令人深思的	**incognito** [ɪnˋkɑgnɪ͵to] 副 隱藏身分地

深度追蹤 🔍

Knowing More

　　要當街頭藝人的話，就要先通過考試、並拿到街頭藝人的證照之後，才能在街上表演。而各個國家對於考試規定及考試項目都不同，例如若在台灣考試，可先選定一個地點，再由考試主辦單位安排一個指定位置以及時間，考生到現場表演之後，由評審們根據各自的評分標準，例如技巧、互動、熟練度……等等，來決定是否通過考試。另外，國外街上常見到的塗鴉也是街頭藝術的一種，而且世界上的塗鴉藝術也愈來愈風行，甚至有商業化的趨勢。

MP3 ▶ 263

套個單字，想說的都能表達！

Let sb. see if... 讓某人確認 / 看看…。

★ Let me see if we are qualified to apply for a **busking permit**.
讓我來看看我們符不符合申請街頭藝人執照的資格。

★ Let me see if there are available seats on Sunday.
讓我查一查星期日是否有空位。

★ Let the **official** see if the local artist can display his work at the **fair**.
讓官員看看那位當地藝術家能否在市集展示他的作品。

★ Let the **clerk** see if you have made a reservation for the VIP box.
讓店員查查你們是否有預約 VIP 包廂。

★ Let us see if there is any chance to make up for our mistakes.
讓我們看看是否有彌補錯誤的機會。

> **busking permit**
> 片 街頭藝人執照
> **official**
> [əˋfɪʃəl]
> 名 官員
> **fair**
> [fɛr]
> 名 市集
> **clerk**
> [klɜk]
> 名 店員；銷售員

sb. run out of... 某人用光…了。

★ That street artist ran out of his spray paints.
那位街頭藝術家的噴漆用完了。

★ The old engine has run out of fuel in an hour.
那個老舊引擎一個小時內就用完了燃料。

★ The **playwright** ran out of ideas for his latest musical
那名劇作家已經想不出最新音樂劇的構想了。

★ These victims will run out of water if the **drought** continues.
若乾旱持續，這些災民將會缺水。

★ Our agent has run out of **stock** and needs to replenish the **reserves**.
我們的代理商沒有庫存了，所以需要先進貨。

> **playwright**
> [ˋple͵raɪt]
> 名 劇作家
> **drought**
> [draut]
> 名 乾旱；旱災
> **stock**
> [stɑk]
> 名 庫存；存貨
> **reserve**
> [rɪˋzɝv]
> 名 儲藏量

開口必備句

和老外聊開懷，就靠這幾句！

There are many street performers on High Street in Edinburgh.

愛丁堡的「高街」上有許多街頭表演者。

Performances in public places by street musicians and mime performers are very entertaining.

由街頭音樂家和默劇表演者在公眾場所進行的街頭表演，非常有趣。

Olivia used to be a street violinist in the park on weekends.

以前奧莉維亞在週末時，會到公園表演小提琴。

The British singer Sting was once a street performer.

英國歌手史汀以前當過街頭藝人。

The street performers along the River Thames are unforgettable.

泰晤士河沿岸的街頭表演者令人難忘。

There are many fiddlers performing along the river.

有很多小提琴手在河邊演奏著。

The performer pretends to be a statue, which makes many passersby gasp at each of his movements.

那個表演者扮成一座雕像，在他移動時嚇到許多路過的民眾。

There is a huge graffiti of Obama on the back of the building.

這棟大樓後方有一幅歐巴馬的大型塗鴉。

You can get a glimpse of teenage subculture by the graffiti they paint.

從街頭塗鴉中，你可以窺見青少年的次文化。

The city is always bristling with buskers and tourists on holidays.

這座城市每逢假日總是充斥著街頭藝人和觀光客。

How can I apply for a busking permit?

我該如何申請街頭表演許可證？

UNIT 04 校園

宿舍生活
Living On Campus

單字基本功 掌握關鍵字＝開口第一步

核心聯想

學校宿舍 In the dormitory

amenity
[əˋmɛnətɪ]
名 便利設施（常用複數 amenities）

dormitory
[ˋdɔrmə͵torɪ]
名 宿舍

lounge
[laʊndʒ]
名 交誼廳；休息室

roommate
[ˋrum͵met]
名 室友

coed
[ˋkoˋɛd]
形 男女同住的

single-sex
[ˋsɪŋglˋsɛks]
形 單一性別的

dining hall
片 學生餐廳

residence hall
片 宿舍樓

宵禁及注意事項 Terms & regulations

進階學習

policy
[ˋpɑləsɪ]
名 政策；原則

curfew
[ˋkɝfju]
名 宵禁

comply
[kəmˋplaɪ]
動 遵從

collegiate
[kəˋlidʒɪɪt]
形 大學生的

communal
[ˋkɑmjunl̩]
形 公共的

resident advisor/ assistant
片 舍長

resident director
片 舍監

proximity card
片 感應卡

深度追蹤 🔍

Knowing More

　　在國外求學時，最常選擇的住宿方式不外乎是學校宿舍，而各國大學宿舍其實都各有特色，例如美國大學大多要求一年級新生住校，且通常有單人房或雙人房可以選擇；而英國大學宿舍主要分為共用衛浴的單人房（single room）、有洗漱台的單人房（single room with basin），以及有個人衛浴設備的套房（en suite）；赴日留學的學生則常選擇住學校宿舍或學生交流會館（為學生公寓，費用便宜但有人數及申請資格限制）。

句型偷吃步　套個單字，想說的都能表達！

sb. be (not) permitted to...　某人（不）被准許…

- ★ You will be **permitted** to use all the facilities after checking in.
  在登記入住後，你就能使用所有的設備。

- ★ Students are not permitted to do drugs nor to consume alcohol in the residence hall.
  學生宿舍內，一律禁止吸毒以及飲酒。

- ★ The administrator is permitted to **disable** the computer if necessary.
  管理員在必要的時候可以關掉電腦。

- ★ That negotiation expert is permitted to talk to the **terrorists**.
  那個協商專家被准許與恐怖份子溝通。

- ★ No one is permitted to look into this classified case until the captain gave his orders.
  在上校下令之前，沒有人能調查這件機密的案子。

> **permit**
> [pə`mɪt]
> 働 允許；准許
> **disable**
> [dɪs`ebḷ]
> 働 使…不能正常運轉
> **terrorist**
> [`tɛrərɪst]
> 名 恐怖份子

sb. ...on purpose.　某人故意…。

- ★ Jack's roommate locked him out of their dorm room on purpose.
  傑克的室友故意把他鎖在宿舍外面。

- ★ The naughty boy kicked the front door on purpose.
  那名頑皮的男孩故意踢大門。

- ★ Those **mean** girls **taunted** Amy on purpose yesterday.
  昨天，那些壞女孩故意嘲笑愛咪。

- ★ The **egocentric** manager hurt his subordinates' pride on purpose.
  那名自我中心的經理故意去傷害部屬的自尊。

- ★ Danny dyed his hair green on purpose.
  丹尼故意把頭髮染成綠色。

> **mean**
> [min]
> 形 刻薄的
> **taunt**
> [tɔnt]
> 働 嘲笑；奚落
> **egocentric**
> [ˏigo`sɛntrɪk]
> 形 自我中心的

開口必備句 和老外聊開懷，就靠這幾句！

Do you live in a co-ed dorm or a single-sex one?
你住的宿舍是男女混宿還是單一性別的呢？

To many students, dorm is like a home away from home.
對很多學生來說，宿舍就像是第二個家一樣。

There is a student lounge and a kitchen on each floor.
宿舍中，每一層樓都有交誼廳以及廚房。

There is also a laundry room in the basement of our dorm.
我們宿舍的地下室有一間洗衣房。

The cafeteria is right next to our dorm.
學校的自助餐廳就在我們宿舍隔壁。

Students can use their proximity cards to enter the residence hall after 11 p.m.
晚上十一點過後，學生們可以用感應卡進入宿舍大樓。

It's hard to have privacy in the dorms.
在宿舍裡面很難擁有隱私權。

Melody decided to apply for a single room so that she could sing in her room all night without any disturbance.
美樂蒂決定申請單人宿舍，這樣徹夜高歌時就不會被打擾。

I live in the dormitory on campus with two roommates.
我跟兩位室友一起住在學校宿舍。

I can't put up with my messy roommate anymore.
我再也無法忍受那個髒亂的室友了。

I'm glad that my roommates and I get along very well.
我很高興我的室友們與我相處都很愉快。

Living with different types of people allows an individual to see the world with a whole new perspective.
跟不同的人住在一起，能讓你看事情的角度更不一樣。

UNIT 05 校園 租屋生活
Living Off Campus

單字基本功　掌握關鍵字 = 開口第一步

核心聯想

入住選擇 Off-campus housing

apartment [ə`pɑrtmənt] 名 公寓	condo [`kɑndo] 名 公寓大樓	flat [flæt] 名 （英）公寓	loft [lɔft] 名 頂樓；閣樓
suite [swit] 名 套房	townhouse [`taun͵haus] 名 連棟式房屋	homestay [`hom͵ste] 名 寄宿家庭	single room 片 單人房

 租屋注意 Renting an apartment

進階學習

deposit [dɪ`pɑzɪt] 名 保證金；存款	furniture [`fɜnɪtʃɚ] 名 家具	guarantor [`gærəntɚ] 名 保證人	lease [lis] 名 租約 動 出租
rent [rɛnt] 名 房租 動 租屋	utilities [ju`tɪlətɪz] 名 水電費	sublet [sʌb`lɛt] 動 轉租	spacious [`speʃəs] 形 空間大的

深度追蹤　Knowing More

　　在美國租房子時，須注意以下幾個隱藏費用：(1) 搬家費用：請搬家公司時，要注意關於服務方面的收費規定。(2) 倉庫租賃：若搬到新家之前需存放物品，可選擇租一個臨時倉庫；但如果遷入和遷出在一天之內，也可以將東西放在租來的卡車裡即可。(3) 申請費：通常房東收取申請費是為了對租戶進行背景和信用檢查。(4) 保證金：大部分的州法律都規定房東可收取一個月或兩個月的租金為保證金，用於賠償租住期間租戶造成的損壞。

sb. be careful with...　某人要小心⋯。

★ You should be careful with every item on the lease before signing it.
簽約之前，你應該要注意看租約上面每一個項目。

★ We'll have to be careful with these **antique** vases.
我們必須格外小心這些古董花瓶。

★ The journalist should be careful with his words while interviewing that politician.
那名記者訪問那位政客時，必須要注意措辭。

★ Experimenters have to be careful with the **flammable chemicals**.
實驗者必須要小心易燃的化學物品。

★ A good detective should be careful with every piece of evidence at the crime scene.
一位好偵探必須小心查看在犯罪現場的所有證據。

> **antique**
> [æn`tik]
> 名 古董 形 古董的
> **flammable**
> [`flæməbḷ]
> 形 易燃的
> **chemical**
> [`kɛmɪkḷ]
> 名 化學製品

sb. can/can't get sth. (V-pp)

某人能 / 不能讓某物⋯。

★ I'll ask the **landlord** if he could get the pump fixed by tomorrow.
我會問問看房東能否再明天之前修好抽水馬達。

★ Our repairman can get your car started right away.
我們的修理工現在就能讓你的車子發動。

★ The farmer can't get these sacks of potatoes sold.
那位農夫賣不掉這幾袋馬鈴薯。

★ My partner wish to get our business started as soon as possible.
我的合夥人希望可以盡早開辦我們的公司。

★ Mike's team is supposed to get this **urgent** project finished by the end of this month.
麥克的團隊應當在這個月底之前完成這份緊急企劃。

> **landlord**
> [`lænd.lɔrd]
> 名 房東
> **urgent**
> [`ɜdʒənt]
> 形 緊急的

開口必備句 和老外聊開懷，就靠這幾句！

The website of our university provides students with detailed information on living off-campus.
🔊 我們學校的網站提供學生有關校外住宿的詳細資訊。

How much is the rent and the security deposit?
🔊 房租跟押金各是多少錢呢？

I see that it's fully furnished. But, are utilities included as well?
🔊 我了解這邊有附全部的家具，但水電費也包含在內嗎？

We would probably rent for at least a year.
🔊 我們可能至少會租個一年。

A six-month lease is the minimum.
🔊 至少要租六個月。

Would you like to renew the lease?
🔊 你要續約嗎？

The lease will expire on August 31, 2018.
🔊 租約將在二〇一八年八月三十一日到期。

When can I move in?
🔊 我什麼時候可以搬進來？

I'd like to move in as soon as possible.
🔊 我想趕快搬進去。

The penalty for breaking the lease is clearly stated on the lease.
🔊 租約裡面有清楚地註明違反租約的罰金。

Make sure you keep a copy of all the paperwork that you and the landlord sign.
🔊 務必要把你跟房東都有簽名的所有文件留下來。

Can I go visit your place sometime?
🔊 我什麼時候可以過去看看你住的地方？

MP3 ⏵ 271

旅遊

想飛的心

Planning Your Vacation

單字基本功 掌握關鍵字 = 開口第一步

核心聯想

開始規劃 Start planning your trip

accommodation [ə͵kɑməˋdeʃən] 名 住宿	**airline** [ˋɛr͵laɪn] 名 航空公司；航線	**flight** [flaɪt] 名 班機	**itinerary** [aɪˋtɪnə͵rɛrɪ] 名 行程
journey [ˋdʒɜnɪ] 名 動（長途）旅行	**route** [rut] 名 路線；路程	**transportation** [͵trænspɚˋteʃən] 名 交通	**organize** [ˋɔrgə͵naɪz] 動 組織；安排

準備妥當 Packing up & ready to go

進階學習

luggage [ˋlʌgɪdʒ] 名（英）行李	**passport** [ˋpæs͵port] 名 護照	**suitcase** [ˋsut͵kes] 名 行李箱	**ticket** [ˋtɪkɪt] 名 票券 動 給…票
visa [ˋvizə] 名 簽證	**one-way** [ˋwʌn͵we] 形 單程的	**round-trip** [ˋraʊnd͵trɪp] 形 來回的	**carry-on bag** 片 隨身行李

 深度追蹤 Knowing More

　　自己規劃行程時，可以先想清楚自己喜歡看哪種類型的景點，像是喜歡歷史人文的人，都會探訪世界遺產或古蹟，喜歡逛街的人則是會排較多的購物行程，而熱愛美食的人則會想要嚐遍特色小吃。再來，就可以決定目的地與天數，並多參加國際旅展和旅遊講座分享，來獲取旅遊資訊。同時，一定要根據自己的預算，參考旅遊網站或書籍列出的物價，像是飛機票、交通費、食宿、參觀門票……等等，根據預算來規劃出最適合自己的行程！

句型偷吃步　　套個單字，想說的都能表達！

How do sb. get to...from...?
某人要如何從…抵達…？

★ How do we get to The London Eye from British Museum?
我們要怎麼從倫敦眼過去大英博物館？

★ How do the **attendees** get to the conference hall from the train station?
與會者要怎麼從會場到火車站？

★ How did he get to the **stadium** from here?
他是怎麼從這裡到體育館的？

★ How do I get to that restaurant from the **intersection** I met you at before?
怎麼從那間餐廳到我之前遇到你的那個十字路口？

★ How did she get to the department store from the bus stop?
她是怎麼從公車站到百貨公司的？

> **attendee**
> [ə`tɛndi]
> 名 出席者
> **stadium**
> [`stedɪəm]
> 名 體育館
> **intersection**
> [ˌɪntə`sɛkʃən]
> 名 十字路口

...sure enough. 一定會…。

★ We'll have plenty of time to visit all the must-see attractions in New York sure enough.
我們一定會有足夠的時間來欣賞紐約所有的必去景點。

★ Our lecturer will come sure enough.
我們的講師一定會來。

★ The new **therapy** will be effective after the operation sure enough.
手術之後，這個新治療法的效果一定會很有效。

★ The result of the election will be a **landslide** sure enough.
選舉的結果一定會是一面倒的勝利。

★ **Protest** isn't the only resolution of this problem sure enough.
抗議一定不是解決問題的唯一方法。

> **therapy**
> [`θɛrəpɪ]
> 名 治療法
> **operation**
> [ˌɑpə`reʃən]
> 名（醫）手術
> **landslide**
> [`lænd‚slaɪd]
> 名 壓倒性的勝利
> **protest**
> [`protɪst]
> 名 抗議；反對

開口必備句

和老外聊開懷，就靠這幾句！

Do you have any plans for the coming holiday?

接下來的假期你有什麼計劃？

Are you planning to go anywhere during the Chinese New Year holiday?

你春假有要去什麼地方嗎？

Do you have any places of interest in mind?

你有沒有想去什麼地方玩？

If you book your tickets online, you can get an early-bird price!

如果你線上訂票，就可享有早鳥優惠價！

Have you made hotel reservations yet?

你訂好旅館了嗎？

Matt likes to plan a trip by himself and travel solo.

麥特喜歡自己規劃旅程並獨自旅行。

I like to travel light and make a list of must-see places before every trip.

我喜歡輕便旅行，並且在旅行之前列張「必去地點」的清單。

It is essential to make sure that you have all your travel documents, including your passport and travel visa.

一定要確認是否備齊所有旅行文件，包括你的護照和觀光簽證。

Perhaps it is a good idea to buy a guidebook or even a phrase book before your tour.

或許在出發旅行前買本旅遊書、甚至是外語手冊，都是個好主意。

It is also a good idea to exchange local currency in advance.

預先換好當地貨幣也是個好主意。

You can buy traveler's checks at a bank, so you won't have to carry too much cash with you during the trip.

你也可以在銀行購買旅行支票，這樣旅途中就不用攜帶太多現金。

★UNIT★
07 旅遊
跟團或自助
Tour Groups & Self-guided Tours

單字基本功 　掌握關鍵字＝開口第一步

核心聯想 ┃ **報名旅行團 Joining tour groups**

brochure [broˋʃʊr] 名 小冊子	**leaflet** [ˋliflɪt] 名 傳單	**tour** [tʊr] 名 動 旅行	**all-inclusive** [ˋɔlɪnˋklusɪv] 形 包括一切的
day tour 片 一日遊	**travel agency** 片 旅行社	**escorted tour** 片（有導遊的）旅遊團	**tour guide** 片 導遊

自助旅遊 Planning on your own **進階學習**

detour [ˋditʊr] 名 動 繞道	**navigation** [͵nævəˋgeʃən] 名 導航；航行	**extensive** [ɪkˋstɛnsɪv] 形 廣泛的；大量的	**free** [fri] 形 自由的 副 自由地
seamless [ˋsimlɪs] 形 無縫的；連續的	**self-guided** [ˋsɛlfgaɪdɪd] 形 自助的	**breakfast and bed** 片 民宿	**look forward to** 片 期待…

深度追蹤 　　　　　　　　　　*Knowing More*

　　出國旅行最常見的方式就是跟團旅行以及自助旅行。「團體旅遊」人數一般在十五人以上，團費已含交通、餐飲、住宿和門票，但導遊及領隊的小費需另計；而近年來，為因應客製化的旅遊需求，也出現「迷你小團 mini tour」的選擇，兩人即可成行且天天都能出發，常配有專車和導遊，行程也可彈性調整。「自助旅行」則是部分依賴旅行社，一般會自行安排住宿、交通、景點和行程，當然也可透過旅行社代辦簽證、機票或是預訂旅館。

 套個單字，想說的都能表達！

...tell the difference between A and B

…區別 A 與 B 不同的地方。

★ Can you tell the difference between a package tour and an escorted tour?
你能分辨自由行和團體旅遊嗎？

★ Many people can't tell the difference between an **interior** designer and a **decorator**.
許多人無法區分室內設計師與室內裝潢師。

★ My daughter can't tell the difference between cabbage and lettuce.
我的女兒無法分辨高麗菜和萵苣。

★ That camper can't tell the difference between poisonous mushrooms and **edible** ones.
那名露營者無法區別毒香菇與可食用香菇。

★ That buyer can tell the difference between natural and **synthetic** supplements.
那名買主可以分辨出天然與人造補給品。

> **interior**
> [ɪn`tɪrɪə]
> 形 內部的
>
> **decorator**
> [`dɛkə͵retə]
> 名 室內裝潢師
>
> **edible**
> [`ɛdəbḷ]
> 形 可食的
>
> **synthetic**
> [sɪn`θɛtɪk]
> 形 人造的

one's opinion is that...　某人認為…。

★ That backpacker's opinion is that people should travel light.
那位背包客認為人們應該要輕裝旅行。

★ My opinion is that her project should be practical.
我認為她的企劃應該可行。

★ Her opinion is that he is just **asking for trouble**.
她覺得他只是在自討苦吃。

★ Our professor's opinion is that the critic's comments are not that professional.
我們教授認為那位論家的意見並沒有很專業。

★ The teacher's opinion is that **vulgar** TV programs will be a bad influence to the children.
那位老師認為內容粗俗的電視節目對孩子來說有不好的影響。

> **ask for trouble**
> 片 自討苦吃
>
> **vulgar**
> [`vʌlgə]
> 形 粗俗的；下流的

開口必備句

和老外聊開懷，就靠這幾句！

We have several tour packages. Which one do you prefer?
我們有很多套裝行程，您比較喜歡哪一個行程呢？

Do you know any great places to go around here?
你知道這附近有什麼好玩的地方嗎？

The tour guide was so funny that everyone on the bus burst into laughter after hearing his joke.
導遊很風趣，讓遊覽車上每個人聽了他的笑話都開懷大笑。

Please meet up in the hotel lobby at seven tomorrow morning.
明天早上七點請到旅館大廳集合。

Let's exchange some travel information with other travelers in the lobby!
我們和其他旅客在大廳交換旅遊情報吧！

Michael is an experienced tour guide who is always able to satisfy everyone in his group.
麥可是個很有經驗的導遊，他總是可以滿足每一位團員的要求。

Remember to keep your passport with you at all times.
記得隨身攜帶護照。

The couple tipped the tour guide 20 US dollars after the trip.
旅行結束後，那對夫妻付給導遊二十美金的小費。

Candice is going on a solo trip to Europe for three months.
坎蒂絲即將前往歐洲自助旅行三個月。

This is my first time traveling alone.
這是我第一次獨自旅行。

Backpacking in New Zealand for half a year is the most unforgettable experience I have ever had.
在紐西蘭背包旅行的半年期間，是我最難忘的經驗。

MP3 ▶ 277

UNIT 08 旅遊

出入境大廳
Arrival & Departure

單字基本功 ▶ 掌握關鍵字 ＝ 開口第一步

核心聯想

出入境須知 Must-know tips

arrival [ə`raɪvḷ] 名 進站；到達	**airport** [`ɛr͵port] 名 機場	**gate** [get] 名 登機門	**terminal** [`tɝmənḷ] 名 航廈
domestic [də`mɛstɪk] 形 國內的	**baggage claim** 片 提領行李處	**departure hall** 片 出境大廳	**immigration hall** 片 入境大廳

 過海關 Going through customs 進階學習

customs [`kʌstəmz] 名 海關	**inspection** [ɪn`spɛkʃən] 名 檢查	**proceed** [prə`sid] 動 繼續進行；開始	**duty-free** [`djutɪ`fri] 形 免稅的
boarding pass 片 登機證	**declaration form** 片 申報單	**passport control** 片（出入境的）護照檢查處	**security check** 片 安全檢查

 深度追蹤

Knowing More

　　入境美國時，一定要注意以下幾件事：(1) 下機後須先排隊等候檢查，持非移民簽證者應排在「nonresidents 非移民」的隊伍，持移民簽證或綠卡者則在「citizens/residents 居民」的行列。(2) 須將相關資料如護照、入境表格、報關單……等文件交給移民官。(3) 簡單陳述來訪的目的或預計逗留時間，回答只要簡短即可。(4) 若海關人員要求檢查行李，須遞上證件，並立刻打開行李接受檢查，驗關人員表示沒問題後，才可提出行李離開。

套個單字，想說的都能表達！

sb. be in a hurry to...　某人急切地…。

★ We are in a hurry to get to the transfer desk.
我們正趕著去轉機櫃檯。

★ The movie star is in a hurry to leave for Hong Kong.
那個電影明星急著要前往香港。

★ The **merchant** is in a hurry to participate in the **auction**.
那位商人趕著去參加拍賣會。

★ All policemen are in a hurry hunting down the **fugitive**.
所有警察都急著搜捕那個逃犯。

★ That man is in a hurry to get his car started and leave **hastily**.
那個男人急著發動車子並趕緊離開。

merchant
[`mɝtʃənt]
名 商人

auction
[`ɔkʃən]
名 拍賣會

fugitive
[`fjudʒətɪv]
名 逃犯

hastily
[`hestɪlɪ]
副 匆忙地

prevent sb./sth. from...　使某人／事／物無法…。

★ The sniffer dogs prevent illegal drugs from entering a country.
緝毒犬使毒品無法走私進入國家。

★ A storm prevented the plane from **taking off**.
暴風雨讓飛機無法起飛。

★ **Urgent** business prevented him from continuing his vacation.
緊急事件讓他無法繼續享受度假。

★ They set a sign to prevent people from falling off the **cliff**.
他們設立了一個警告標誌，以防人們跌落懸崖。

★ The prison guard could have prevented him from escaping.
獄警原本可以防止他逃出去的。

take off
片 （飛機）起飛

urgent
[`ɝdʒənt]
形 緊急的

cliff
[klɪf]
名 懸崖

開口必備句　和老外聊開懷，就靠這幾句！

Tourists are not allowed to stay beyond three months.
旅客不得停留超過三個月。

I am sorry, but no liquids over 100 ml. can be taken on board.
很抱歉，但超過一百毫升的液體不得帶上飛機。

Please take off your shoes before passing through the X-ray checkpoint.
通過 X 光掃瞄機前，請脫掉您的鞋子。

Please have your passport ready before going through the security.
通過安檢處之前，請先準備好你的護照。

Do you have anything to declare?
你需要申報任何物品嗎？

What is the purpose of your visit?
你這次旅行的目的是什麼？

Where will you be staying?
你將會入住哪裡？

I am here on business/for pleasure.
我是來出差 / 旅遊的。

How long will you stay in this country?
你會在這個國家待多久？

Have you ever been to this country before?
你來過這個國家嗎？

Our luggage will be at carrousel 14.
我們的行李會在幾號轉盤？

Make sure you have your luggage claim ticket with you.
確認你持有行李收據。

303

UNIT 09 旅遊
飛機上放鬆
Relaxing On The Plane

 單字基本功 掌握關鍵字 = 開口第一步

 核心聯想　　麻煩空服員服務 Needing help

blanket [`blæŋkɪt] 名 毛毯	**headphone** [`hɛd‚fon] 名 耳機	**pillow** [`pɪlo] 名 枕頭	**press** [prɛs] 動 壓下;按
in-flight [`ɪn`flaɪt] 形 飛行中的	**cabin crew** 片 機組人員	**call button** 片 服務鈴	**flight attendant** 片 空服員

機上娛樂 In-flight entertainment　進階學習

device [dɪ`vaɪs] 名 設備;裝置	**entertainment** [‚ɛntə`tenmənt] 名 娛樂	**monitor** [`manətə] 名 螢幕	**poker** [`pokə] 名 撲克牌
Wi-Fi 縮 無線上網	**audio** [`ɔdɪ‚o] 形 聲音的	**touch screen** 片 觸控螢幕	**reading light** 片 閱讀燈

 **深度追蹤** *Knowing More*

　　知名的阿提哈德航空公司（Etihad）為滿足顧客，創造了一架豪華的空中巴士（A380），機內分成兩層樓及四種座位─經濟艙、商務艙、頭等艙和居住艙。最豪華的居住艙位於飛機的上層，有客廳、臥室和浴室；頭等艙除了配有洗手間，特色其中之一就是每個艙房之間的分隔可以滑動，讓乘客可以和旁邊的人聊天；而商務艙的乘客則有可以完全躺下的大空間；即使是經濟艙，航空公司也提供了墊子和枕頭，讓旅客能夠更舒適地度過飛行時間。

套個單字，想說的都能表達！

...provide sb. with sth.

…提供某人某物。

★ The flight attendants can provide you with an extra blanket.
空服員可以再多給你一條毛毯。

★ They will provide you with a local map and a bus schedule.
他們對提供您當地地圖以及公車時刻表。

★ The experience of being an **intern** provided him with a better chance to enter the company.
企業實習的經驗讓他有更多的機會可以進入公司。

★ We will provide all participants a name **badge**.
我們會提供名牌給所有參加者。

★ The hotel provides customers with a luxury dinner at the top of the floor.
飯店提供客人在頂樓享受豪華晚餐。

> **intern**
> [ɪn`tɜn]
> 名 實習生
> **badge**
> [bædʒ]
> 名 名牌

Please let me know what time…

請讓我知道…的時間。

★ Please let me know what time the meal will be served.
請跟我說一下正餐的供應時間。

★ Please let me know what time our first class begins.
請讓我知道我們的第一堂課幾點開始。

★ Please let me know what time the artist will show us her **portfolio**.
請讓我知道那個藝術家什麼時候會展示她的代表作給我們看。

★ Please let me know what time the baby will get his last **vaccination** today.
請跟我說那個寶寶今天哪個時候打最後一劑預防針。

★ Please let me know what time he will be online for our **videoconference**.
請讓我知道他什麼時候會上線到我們的視訊會議。

> **portfolio**
> [port`folɪ͵o]
> 名 代表作品集
> **vaccination**
> [͵væksn̩`eʃən]
> 名 預防接種
> **videoconference**
> [`vɪdɪo͵kɑnfərəns]
> 名 視訊會議

開口必備句 和老外聊開懷，就靠這幾句！

Can I see your passport and boarding pass, please?
可以看一下您的護照以及登機證嗎？

I need a hand putting my luggage into the overhead compartment.
麻煩幫我把行李放到上面的置物艙裡面。

You are in row twelve, seat E.
您的座位在第十二排，座位 E。

When does the in-flight duty-free sale start?
機上免稅品何時會開始銷售？

Since it's a short flight, we will be serving light refreshments instead of a meal.
由於本航班為短程飛行，機組人員將提供小點心，而不會提供正餐。

Excuse me. Can I have some more chips and a soda, please?
不好意思，可以再給我一些洋芋片和一罐蘇打水嗎？

Would you like something to drink?
您想喝點什麼嗎？

You can always ask the flight attendant for a pillow if you're tired.
您如果累了，可隨時向空服員索取枕頭。

It is a little bit cold in the cabin. Can I have an extra blanket?
機艙內有點冷。可以再給我一條毯子嗎？

The lavatory is occupied.
洗手間有人。

Please remain in your seat until we taxi to the gate.
在飛機滑行至機艙口前，請您留在座位上。

Do you need a Customs and Immigration Form?
您需要一張入境卡嗎？

入住及退房
Checking In & Checking Out

 單字基本功 ▸ 掌握關鍵字 = 開口第一步

 旅館服務 Hotel services

concierge
[ˌkɑnsɪˋɛrʒ]
名 門房;禮賓

doorman
[ˋdor͵mæn]
名 門僮

porter
[ˋportɚ]
名 (提行李的) 服務員

valet
[ˋvælɪt]
名 泊車人員

lobby
[ˋlɑbɪ]
名 大廳

reception
[rɪˋsɛpʃən]
名 (旅館) 大廳接待

check in
片 辦理入住

check out
片 退房

房型選擇 Choosing a hotel room
進階學習

double
[ˋdʌbl̩]
名 雙人房
(一張雙人床)

facility
[fəˋsɪlətɪ]
名 設備;設施

family
[ˋfæməlɪ]
名 家庭房;家庭

single
[ˋsɪŋgl̩]
名 單人房 形 單人的

twin
[twɪn]
名 雙人房
(兩張單人床)

deluxe
[dɪˋlʌks]
形 豪華的

non-smoking
[͵nɑnˋsmokɪŋ]
形 禁菸的

junior suite
片 標準套房 (含床、
餐桌、起居空間)

 深度追蹤 🔍 *Knowing More*

　　除了常見的住宿選擇，像是一般旅館（hotel）、精品旅館（boutique hotel）、套房飯店（suite hotel）和汽車旅館（motel）……等等之外，若預算比較有限，也可以選擇青年旅館（hostel）、民宿（B&B/bed and breakfast）、小型家庭旅館（guesthouse）或是旅店（inn）；想要入住特色住宿的話，則可以考慮膠囊旅館（capsule hotel）、水上流動旅館（floatel），甚至還有火車上的移動旅館（rotel）……等等可供選擇。

As soon as sb. ...., ...   某人一…，就…。

★ As soon as we arrived at the airport, we took a taxi to our hotel.
我們一到機場，就叫了一台計程車過去飯店。

★ As soon as the ship reached the harbor, all the passengers got off immediately.
船一靠岸，所有乘客就馬上下船了。

★ As soon as the time and **venue** were decided, they sent out the invitations.
他們一確定時間和地點，就寄出邀請函了。

★ As soon as I entered the room, I sensed a joyful **atmosphere**.
我一走進房間，就感受到愉悅的氣氛。

★ As soon as the **tsunami** came, it formed a **terrifying** wall of water
海嘯一來，就形成一堵堵可怕的水牆。

> **venue**
> [`vɛnju]
> 名 場地
> **atmosphere**
> [`ætməs,fɪr]
> 名 氣氛
> **tsunami**
> [tsu`nɑmi]
> 名 海嘯
> **terrifying**
> [`tɛrə,faɪɪŋ]
> 形 極可怕的

sb. find it...   某人發覺/認為…。

★ She found it easy to get from the hostel to the city center.
她發現要從旅館到市中心其實很簡單。

★ Most users found it **annoying** to receive junk mails.
許多使用者覺得收到垃圾信件很煩人。

★ My brother found it important to make good use of time.
我的哥哥認為善用時間很重要。

★ Teachers find it helpful to know their students' parents.
教師們覺得認識學生的家長會很有幫助。

★ My nephew found it interesting to see gold fishes swimming in the **fish bowl**.
我的姪子覺得看著金魚在魚缸裡面游泳很有趣。

> **annoying**
> [ə`nɔɪɪŋ]
> 形 惱人的
> **fish bowl**
> 片 魚缸

開口必備句　知老外聊開懷，就靠這幾句！

I will book two adjoining rooms for my parents and myself.
我會替爸媽和自己訂兩間相鄰的房間。

How much is a twin room?
雙床房一晚多少錢？

I would like a room with a king-size bed.
我要一間加大床的房間。

Do you still have rooms with a lake view?
你們還有湖景房嗎？

I am afraid that the hotel is fully booked tonight.
飯店今晚恐怕已全數客滿。

The bellboy will take your bags to your room for you now.
門僮現在會替您把行李拿到房間裡。

Your room number is 512. Please take the lift on the right to the fifth floor.
您的房號是 512，請搭乘右手邊的電梯至五樓。

You can check in any time after three in the afternoon.
下午三點後隨時都能入住。

What time would you like your wake-up call?
您希望明天早上幾點叫您起床？

We should call the room service and order something to eat. I'm starving!
我們應該叫一下客房服務、點些東西來吃，我快餓昏啦！

When is check-out time?
退房時間是什麼時候？

The towels in the room are hotel property and should not be taken as you leave.
房間內的毛巾屬於飯店財產，離開時不得帶走。

NOTE

Part 11

十一月聚焦職場力

November Highlights:

Focusing On Career

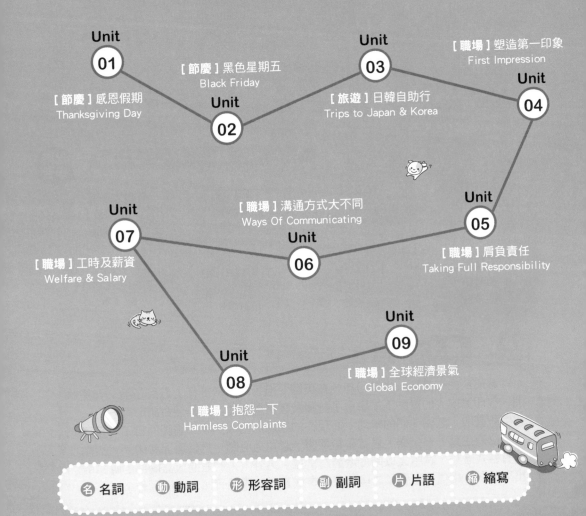
名 名詞　　動 動詞　　形 形容詞　　副 副詞　　片 片語　　縮 縮寫

UNIT 01

感恩假期
Thanksgiving Day

單字基本功 掌握關鍵字 = 開口第一步

核心聯想 感恩節由來 Origin of Thanksgiving

settler [`sɛtlə] 名 移居者；開拓者	**Indian** [`ɪndɪən] 名 印第安人 形 印第安的	**Mayflower** [`me͵flauə] 名 五月花號	**native** [`netɪv] 名 原住民；本地人
pilgrim [`pɪlgrɪm] 名 清教徒；朝聖者	**sail** [sel] 動 （乘船）航行	**give thanks to** 片 感謝…	**settle down** 片 定居；安頓下來

傳統感恩節大餐 Traditional foods　**進階學習**

casserole [`kæsə͵rol] 名 砂鍋；燉菜	**feast** [fist] 名 大餐；盛宴	**gravy** [`grevɪ] 名 肉汁	**harvest** [`hɑrvɪst] 名 動 收穫
stuffing [`stʌfɪŋ] 名 填料	**turkey** [`tɜkɪ] 名 火雞	**wishbone** [`wɪʃ͵bon] 名 許願骨	**sweet corn** 片 玉米

深度追蹤 Knowing More

　　感恩節由來是於一六二〇年，在英國受迫害的清教徒搭上五月花號來到美洲，在印第安人的幫助下才學會了狩獵及種植農作物，於是便邀請印第安人一起慶祝豐收，感謝他們的幫助。而現在的感恩節已成為闔家團圓的日子，且餐桌上必有主菜——火雞，還有蔓越莓醬、起司通心麵、馬鈴薯泥和肉汁，甜點則有各式派類，其中又以南瓜派最為常見。另外，人們會將火雞胸部的骨頭取出來許願，相信拉斷骨頭之後願望就會成真，故稱此骨頭為「許願骨」。

MP3 ⊙ 287

句型偷吃步　套個單字，想說的都能表達！

sb. suppose (that)... 某人認為⋯。

★ I suppose that he will still make the Thanksgiving dinner on time.
我想他應該來得及吃今天的感恩節晚餐。

★ We supposed that the secretary knew all the details in the plan.
我們認為秘書早就知道詳細的計畫內容。

★ The lawyer supposes that his presence is not entirely **coincidental**.
律師認為他的出席並非只是個巧合。

★ The author supposes that he will still continue writing his unfinished novel series.
那位作家想他還是會繼續寫他那部未完成的連載小說。

★ The biologist supposes that every species is able to create a **caste** system in its society.
那位生物學家覺得每個物種都能創立自己的階級制度。

> **coincidental**
> [ko, ɪnsə`dɛnt]]
> 形 巧合的
> **caste**
> [kæst]
> 名 等級制度

sb. can't wait for sth. to... 某人等不及某事⋯。

★ We can't wait for the Thanksgiving dinner to begin.
我們等不及要開始吃感恩節晚餐了。

★ All **teammates** can't wait for George to come back.
所有隊員都等不及歡迎喬治回歸隊上。

★ Those buyers can't wait for their **purchases** to be delivered.
那些買家等不及想收到他們買的東西。

★ Those people can't wait for the officers to tell them the truth.
那些人等不及想讓警官告訴他們真相。

★ That singer can't wait for her fans to see her latest **music video**.
那位歌手等不及讓她的歌迷看最新的MV。

> **teammate**
> [`tim, met]
> 名 隊友
> **purchase**
> [`pɜtʃəs]
> 名 所購之物
> **music video (MV)**
> 片 音樂錄影帶

Thanksgiving is one of the major holidays of the year.

感恩節是一年之中的主要節日之一。

In the U.S., Thanksgiving is celebrated on the fourth Thursday in November.

在美國，感恩節在十一月的第四個週四慶祝。

The first Thanksgiving was celebrated by the Pilgrims to give thanks to God and Native Americans.

為了對上帝以及印地安人表達感謝，清教徒慶祝了第一個感恩節。

The first Thanksgiving feast lasted for three days, while pilgrims and Native Americans shared their foods together.

第一個感恩節盛宴持續了三天，期間清教徒和美洲原住民共享美食。

It wasn't until the Civil War that Thanksgiving was proclaimed as a national holiday.

直到南北戰爭時，感恩節才被定為國定假日。

Tradition calls for families to gather together and have Thanksgiving dinner.

根據傳統，全家人會團聚、一起享受感恩節晚餐。

Who else is coming for Thanksgiving dinner tonight?

還有誰會來吃今晚的感恩節大餐呢？

I think Thanksgiving is always a wonderful time being with our family, filled with awesome foods and meaningful memories made together.

我覺得感恩節一向是個歡聚的好時光，充滿了美食及許多溫馨的回憶。

What filling did you use in the pie?

你加了什麼餡料進去這個派裡面呢？

My mom makes the most delicious turkey with cranberry sauce in the world.

我媽媽做的蔓越莓醬火雞，是全世界最好吃的。

MP3 ▶ 289

節慶

黑色星期五

Black Friday

單字基本功 掌握關鍵字＝開口第一步

核心聯想

熱血購物 Shopping Therapy

frenzy
[`frɛnzɪ]
名 狂熱

spend
[spɛnd]
動 花費；用盡

squander
[`skwandɚ]
動 浪費；揮霍

buy a lemon
片 花錢買到爛東西

on sale
片 拍賣中

pay for
片 為…付款

pay through the nose
片 盲目購買

window shopping
片 逛街（但無意購買）

掃好貨 Must-have items
進階學習

bargain
[`barɡɪn]
名 特價品 動 討價還價

bustling
[`bʌslɪŋ]
形 忙亂的

coupon
[`kupan]
名 優惠券

discount
[`dɪskaʊnt]
名 折扣

patron
[`petrən]
名 老主顧

cyber sale
片 網路購物

kick off
片 開始

the in-thing
片 正流行的事物

 深度追蹤 Knowing More

　　感恩節隔日就是「黑色星期五」，這天商家會推出各種折扣方案，像是超低價特惠商品（best-buys）來促銷，且凌晨就會開始營業，所以很多為了搶便宜的人會在吃完感恩大餐後，就到店家門前開始排隊。而「黑色星期五」的起源，是因為商店虧損時，帳目上會標赤字（in the red），賺錢時則用黑色墨水表示，而此日商家通常都非常忙碌，所以帳本自然也是黑壓壓一片；同時也有商家以黑色星期五這一名字自嘲，表示當天會忙得要命。

May I remind sb. of/that ...?
我是否能提醒某人…？

★ May I remind you of your maximum credit limit?
我可否提醒你一下你信用卡的最高額度？

★ May I remind you of the meeting at eight a.m. tomorrow?
我是否能提醒你明天早上八點的會議？

★ May I remind the client that the **committee** can make the final decisions?
我能否提醒一下客戶，委員會有權做最後的決定？

★ May I remind the new sales that it is important to communicate with our clients?
可否讓我提醒一下新業務，和客戶溝通很重要？

★ May I remind all employees to finish their jobs based on the **standard procedure**?
可否讓我提醒一下全體員工，須根據標準程序完成工作？

> **committee**
> [kə`mɪtɪ]
> 名 委員會
>
> **standard**
> [`stændəd]
> 形 標準的
>
> **procedure**
> [prə`sidʒə]
> 名 程序

sb. couldn't resist... 某人無法抗拒／忍不住…。

★ Judy couldn't resist buying a lot of jewelries every time there's a sale.
每次有大特價時，茱蒂都忍不住買一堆珠寶首飾。

★ He couldn't resist the **temptations**, so he took the bribes in the end.
他無法抗拒誘惑，所以最後還是收下了賄賂。

★ Marry couldn't resist sharing photos of her cute son to her friends.
瑪莉忍不住向好友分享她兒子的可愛照片。

★ The crowd couldn't resist the **urge** to **applaud**.
群眾忍不住給予熱烈掌聲。

★ Tim couldn't resist peeking through the keyhole.
提姆忍不住一直從鑰匙孔偷看外面。

> **temptation**
> [tɛmp`teʃən]
> 名 誘惑
>
> **urge**
> [ɝdʒ]
> 名 衝動
>
> **applaud**
> [ə`plɔd]
> 動 鼓掌喝采

MP3 ▶ 291

開口必備句 和老外聊開懷，就靠這幾句！

Penny always goes shopping after big exams.
佩妮總是在大考過後逛街購物。

You can get free coupons once you log onto our website.
只要登入我們的網站，就能得到免費的折價券。

Annie's mother is very concerned about the way she squanders money.
安妮的媽媽對於她揮霍金錢的行徑十分憂心。

Whenever my brother sees something he likes, he always pays through the nose for it.
每當我哥看到喜歡的東西，總是不經考慮就買了下去。

We offer free delivery on all purchases over 3,000 dollars.
購物超過三千元可享免運費。

Where is the Men's Department?
男裝部在哪裡？

Where can I get a free catalogue?
我可以在哪裡取得免費的型錄？

Everything with a red tag is 60% off.
有貼紅色標籤的商品全部都打四折。

The cash register is out of order.
收銀機故障了。

Keep an eye on your handbag and belongings, and beware of pickpockets.
請留意您的隨身手提包及財物，並小心扒手。

How would you like to pay? By cash or on credit card?
您要用現金還是信用卡付款？

Keep the receipt in case you want a refund.
記得把收據留著，以免之後想要退貨。

★UNIT★ 旅遊
03 日韓自助行
Trips to Japan & Korea

單字基本功 ▷ 掌握關鍵字 ＝ 開口第一步

核心聯想

日式情懷 Features in Japan

kaiseki [`kaɪˌsɛkɪ] 名 懷石料理	**kimono** [kɪˋmono] 名 和服	**shrine** [ʃraɪn] 名 神社；神龕	**sumo** [`sumo] 名 相撲
inspire [ɪnˋspaɪr] 動 給…靈感	**cherry blossom** 片 櫻花	**hot spring** 片 溫泉	**tour around** 片 四處遊覽

韓國文化特色 Korean cultures

進階學習

bathhouse [`bæθˌhaus] 名 澡堂；公共浴室	**pottery** [`pɑtərɪ] 名 陶器；製陶	**kimchi** [kɪmtʃi] 名 韓國泡菜	**united** [juˋnaɪtɪd] 形 團結的；聯合的
Korean Wave 片 韓流	**rice cake** 片 年糕	**street food** 片 路邊小吃	**ski resort** 片 滑雪場

深度追蹤 🔍

Knowing More

　　在東亞地區，筷子是最普遍的餐具，但各國的筷子形狀不同，也反映出各自的飲食文化，例如在中國，大家常常圍桌用餐，所以筷子長而厚；日本的筷子又短又尖，是因為尖筷較容易剔除魚刺；韓國筷子則以金屬製成、又扁又平，是因為韓國人愛吃烤肉，便發明這種適合吃烤物的金屬筷子。要特別注意的是，日本有許多有關筷子的禁忌，而且每個人有自己專屬的筷子，絕對不能亂用；而用筷子敲打碗邊，有乞丐之意，在中日韓三國都是用餐禁忌。

MP3 ▶ 293

套個單字，想說的都能表達！

A great way to...is to... …是…的好方法。

★ A great way to explore Japan is to visit the shrines.
走訪神社是探索日本的一個好方法。

★ A great way to lose weight is to exercise.
運動是減肥的好方法。

★ A great way to **regain** your confidence is to show your strength.
展現你的長處是重新取回自信心的好方法。

★ A great way to start your business is to find more sponsors first.
先找到更多的贊助者是創辦事業的好方法。

★ A great way to lower the crime rate is to **execute** the law.
實施這個法律是降低犯罪率的好方法。

> **regain**
> [rɪ`gen]
> (動) 取回；收回
>
> **execute**
> [`ɛksɪ.kjut]
> (動) 執行

sth. stop sb. from... 某事使某人無法…。

★ The heavy fog stopped us from seeing a clear view of the mountains.
這場大霧使得我們無法看清楚山上的風景。

★ The **cancer** stops him from having hopes for the future.
得到癌症讓他不再對未來有任何希望。

★ Vaccination will stop people from getting an **influenza**.
接種疫苗可以防止人們感染流行性感冒。

★ Washing your hands can stop you from virus and **bacterial** infections.
洗手可以預防被病毒以及細菌感染。

★ This **repellent** can stop you from being bitten by mosquitoes.
這罐驅蟲劑可以防止被蚊子叮咬。

> **cancer**
> [`kænsɚ]
> (名) 癌症
>
> **influenza**
> [.ɪnflu`ɛnzə]
> (名) 流行性感冒
>
> **bacterial**
> [bæk`tɪrɪəl]
> (形) 細菌的
>
> **repellent**
> [rɪ`pɛlənt]
> (名) 驅蟲劑

開口必備句　和老外聊開懷，就靠這幾句！

Do you know where I can buy a kimono as a souvenir?
你知道在哪可以買到和服當作紀念品嗎？

Dressing up as a geisha is a unique experience for tourists.
打扮成藝妓對遊客來說是個特別的經驗。

Kyoto, the ancient capital of Japan, has an abundance of historic buildings.
京都是日本古都，擁有豐富的歷史古蹟。

The most notable characteristic of garden art in Japan is the Zen garden.
最著名的日本庭園藝術就是融合禪學的庭園風格。

Hikers should carry a bear bell with them at all times in case of a bear attack.
健行者應隨時攜帶熊鈴以防被熊攻擊。

Henry is going to South Korea for the Girls' Generation's concert next month.
亨利下個月要去南韓看少女時代的演唱會。

Ski resorts in South Korea always attract many ski lovers.
南韓的滑雪場總是吸引許多滑雪愛好者。

On a tour to a traditional Korean palace, you will have an opportunity to dress up as an ancient emperor or empress.
參觀傳統韓國皇宮時，你將有機會打扮成古代帝王或王后。

Mandy told me that you went on a tour to Jeju Island last week.
曼蒂跟我說，你上週去濟州島玩了一趟。

You can take the shuttle bus or the airport express to the city.
你可以搭乘接駁巴士或是機場快捷專車到市區。

Which do you prefer, the kimchi hot pot or the miso hot pot?
你喜歡泡菜鍋還是味噌鍋？

MP3 ⊙ 295

UNIT 04 職場

塑造第一印象
First Impression

 單字基本功 掌握關鍵字 = 開口第一步

核心聯想 顯現特質 What's special in you

astute [əˋstjut] 形 精明的	**attentive** [əˋtɛntɪv] 形 體貼的；專心的	**confident** [ˋkɑnfədənt] 形 有自信的	**courteous** [ˋkɜtjəs] 形 有禮貌的
friendly [ˋfrɛndlɪ] 形 友善的	**gracious** [ˋgreʃəs] 形 優雅的；仁慈的	**positive** [ˋpɑzətɪv] 形 樂觀的	**first impression** 片 第一印象

進階學習 個性迥異 Different personalities

characteristic [ˌkærəktəˋrɪstɪk] 名 特徵 形 特有的	**extrovert** [ˋɛkstrovɜt] 名 外向的人	**individual** [ˌɪndəˋvɪdʒuəl] 名 個人 形 個人的	**introvert** [ˋɪntrəˌvɜt] 名 內向的人
personality [ˌpɜsṇˋælətɪ] 名 個性	**perceive** [pɚˋsɪv] 動 察覺；理解	**body language** 片 肢體語言	**under the spotlight** 片 被注意到

深度追蹤 🔍 *Knowing More*

　　很多統計都指出，人們在初次會面的前30秒鐘，給對方留下的印象最為深刻，像是長相、打扮、性別、年齡、表情、姿勢、談吐……等等，都是第一印象的產生關鍵。而國外有項研究也發現，對於人的印象，光外表就佔了93％，這個被稱為「Mehrabian法則」，指的是看到的情報（55％）加上聲音的情報（38％），組合起來的這93％的情報，就決定了對一個人的印象，剩下的7％才是語言情報，例如用字遣詞、說話內容……等等資訊。

套個單字，想說的都能表達！

...no matter... 不論…，…。

★ My manager will try to deal with the difficulties no matter how hard the task is.
不管任務有多難，我的經理還是會試著解決所有難題。

★ The computer keeps **restarting** itself no matter what I do.
不管我怎麼做，電腦還是一直重新開機。

★ I'll take the **matter** to court no matter how much it will cost me.
不管要花多少錢，我都決心告上法庭。

★ All people must stay **calm** no matter what happens.
不管發生什麼事，所有人都必須冷靜下來。

★ He insisted on his **notions** no matter what we said.
不管我們怎麼說，他還是堅持他的想法。

> **restart**
> [rɪ`stɑrt]
> 動 重新啟動
>
> **matter**
> [`mætɚ]
> 名 事情；問題
>
> **calm**
> [kɑm]
> 形 鎮靜的；沈著的
>
> **notion**
> [`noʃən]
> 名 想法；概念

sb. must (not)... 某人一定要 / 絕對不能…。

★ You must make a good impression to your colleagues.
你一定要讓同事們對你有好的第一印象。

★ You must not cross the railway **tracks** if the **barriers** are let down.
平交道柵欄放下時，不得穿越鐵軌。

★ Professor Lin told us that we must turn in the papers this evening.
林教授跟我們說過，今天下午一定要繳報告。

★ We must be aware of the **traps** our competitors set.
我們必須要小心競爭對手設下的陷阱。

★ He must not tell anyone about the project until he completes it.
他在完成計畫之前，不能對任何人透露風聲。

> **track**
> [træk]
> 名 鐵軌
>
> **barrier**
> [`bærɪr]
> 名 障礙物
>
> **trap**
> [træp]
> 名 陷阱

MP3 ▶ 297

開口必備句 和老外聊開懷，就靠這幾句！

Making a great first impression is the key to a successful job interview.
建立良好的第一印象是面試成功的重要關鍵。

When you first meet someone, it only takes a quick glance to evaluate him or her.
當你首次遇見一個人，有時稍瞥一眼就會對其下評斷。

A friendly smile can help create a good first impression.
一抹友善的微笑有助於建立良好的第一印象。

Never judge a book by its cover.
人不可貌相。

Jeff put on his best suit at the dinner tonight, trying to impress his future father-in-law.
傑夫在今天晚餐特意穿上他最好的西裝，想讓他未來的岳父印象深刻。

A good handshake is vital to making a great first impression.
好的握手方式對於建立良好的第一印象很重要。

People will also form their first impression of you based on your hygiene, your clothing and your personality.
人們也會根據你的衛生習慣、穿著和個性建立對你的第一印象。

First impressions are formed on the basis of a person's appearance and communication styles.
外表和溝通風格建立了對一個人的第一印象。

First impressions may sometimes be misleading.
第一印象有時候是錯誤的。

As a famous matchmaker, Mrs. Watson is good at assisting her clients in making great first impressions on each other.
身為有名的媒人，華生太太很擅長協助客戶為彼此留下好印象。

Never underestimate the impact of first impressions.
絕對不要低估第一印象的影響力。

UNIT 05 職場 肩負責任
Taking Full Responsibility

 單字基本功 掌握關鍵字 = 開口第一步

核心聯想 勇於承擔 Shouldering responsibilities

credibility [ˌkrɛdəˋbɪlətɪ] 名 可信性	**enthusiasm** [ɪnˋθjuzɪˌæzəm] 名 熱情	**morale** [məˋræl] 名 倫理	**shoulder** [ˋʃoldɚ] 名 肩膀 動 肩負
ethical [ˋɛθɪkḷ] 形 道德的	**trustworthy** [ˋtrʌstˏwɝɪ] 形 值得信賴的	**help out** 片 替…解圍	**take full responsibility** 片 負起全責

逃避現實 Running away from responsibilities **進階學習**

burden [ˋbɝdṇ] 名 負擔 動 使負重擔	**dilemma** [dəˋlɛmə] 名 進退兩難	**duck** [dʌk] 動 躲避；逃避	**unsettle** [ʌnˋsɛtḷ] 動 使心神不寧
desperate [ˋdɛspərɪt] 形 絕望的	**irresponsible** [ˌɪrɪˋspɑnsəbḷ] 形 不負責任的	**upset** [ʌpˋsɛt] 形 沮喪的	**weigh down** 片 使頹喪

 深度追蹤

Knowing More

　　公司外派員工到國外工作通常包含以下三種方式：(1) 海外派任（expatriate）：公司會替員工辦理當地工作簽證，並在薪資以外提供生活津貼、眷屬津貼、返鄉探親假或探親機票、搬遷補助……等福利。(2) 本地聘用（local hire）：聘任條件等同於當地員工，所以享有與當地員工一樣的福利，不過人事成本較海外派任低。(3) 出差（business trip）：不管是短期或長期出差，都能到另一個城市工作，並依出差長度提供日支費。

MP3 ▶ 299

套個單字，想說的都能表達！

It is worthwhile...　…是很值得的。

★ It's worthwhile to dedicate in my career and to take on the responsibilities.
奉獻於事業並承擔責任，是很值得的。

★ It's worthwhile paying our attention to the matter in **dispute**.
多注意正處於爭議中的話題很值得。

★ It's worthwhile pulling an all-nighter to meet the deadline.
熬夜完成工作以遵守期限是很值得的。

★ It's worthwhile to help the boy **rebuild** his home.
幫助這個男孩重建家園很值得。

★ It's worthwhile taking the trouble to explain a job to new employees.
扛起向新員工說明工作內容的責任很值得。

> **dispute**
> [dɪ`spjut]
> 名 爭論；爭執
> **rebuild**
> [rɪ`bɪld]
> 動 重建；改建

...without any reason.　…毫無理由地…。

★ It was a shock to the team that Matt just took the blame without any reason.
麥特毫無理由就背了黑鍋，他的組員都很驚訝。

★ Jeff's girlfriend left him without any reason.
傑夫的女朋友無緣無故就離開他了。

★ The team leader was criticized and **framed** without any reason.
那位組長無端被批評和栽贓。

★ That **audacious** man searched my apartment without any reason.
那個膽大妄為的男人無緣無故就來搜查我的公寓。

★ The **diligent** technician was **booted out** without any reason.
那個辛勤工作的技術員無緣無故就被開除了。

> **frame**
> [frem]
> 動 陷害
> **audacious**
> [ɔ`deʃəs]
> 形 膽大妄為的
> **diligent**
> [`dɪlədʒənt]
> 形 勤奮的
> **boot out**
> 片 開除

開口必備句 和老外聊開懷，就靠這幾句！

Don't worry. I've got your back.
🔊 別擔心，我挺你。

I'll always stand by you.
🔊 我會永遠支持你。

Hang in there!
🔊 堅持下去！

Let me help you through all your troubles.
🔊 讓我幫你度過所有難關吧。

Cheer up! Things will turn out to be fine.
🔊 開心點！都會沒事的。

A friend in need is a friend indeed.
🔊 患難見真情。

What would you do if your friend were in trouble?
🔊 如果你朋友身陷麻煩，你會怎麼辦？

Larry is glad that he has so many friends to share the load.
🔊 賴瑞很高興有這麼多朋友分攤重擔。

Jessica was really worried about Maria, who just failed math for the second time.
🔊 潔西卡真的很擔心瑪利亞，因為她的數學又被當了。

Helen will never abandon her husband though he is heavily indebted.
🔊 即使丈夫負債累累，海倫也絕對不會拋棄他。

Mrs. Watson always listens to her husband carefully whenever he talks about being depressed over his job.
🔊 每當她丈夫講到工作上沮喪的事時，華生太太總是仔細聆聽。

Maria will do whatever it takes to help out her little sister.
🔊 瑪利亞會做任何事來幫助她妹妹度過難關。

MP3 ▶ 301

★UNIT★
06
職場
溝通方式大不同
Ways Of Communicating

單字基本功 ✎ 掌握關鍵字 ＝ 開口第一步

核心
聯想

理性溝通 Reasoning with people

negotiate
[nɪˋgoʃɪˌet]
動 協商

nonverbal
[ˌnɑnˋvɝbḷ]
形 非言語的

directly
[dəˋrɛktlɪ]
副 直接地

big deal
片 重要大事

get the point cross
片 讓對方理解

reason sth. out
片 找出解決辦法

shake hands
片 握手

stand in one's shoes
片 站在對方角度設想

表達意見 Different viewpoints

進階
學習

bias
[ˋbaɪəs]
名 偏見；偏心

norm
[nɔrm]
名 基準；規範

perspective
[pɚˋspɛktɪv]
名 觀點

stereotype
[ˋstɛrɪəˌtaɪp]
名 刻板印象

value
[ˋvælju]
名 價值 動 重視

objective
[əbˋdʒɛktɪv]
形 客觀的

judgmental
[dʒʌdʒˋmɛntḷ]
形 批判的

false assumption
片 錯誤假設

 深度追蹤🔍

Knowing More

出國旅遊時，可注意以下幾個較特別的打招呼方式：在印度需先雙手合十，點頭說Namaste，並優先向年長者行禮；在日本，鞠躬高度表現出對他人地位尊敬的程度，愈低就表示愈尊敬；在俄國通常會握手招呼，但不能隔著門檻握手，而女性見面時，會從左臉頰開始親吻臉頰三次。除此之外，可別在中東、南美、西非、俄國或希臘比讚的手勢，因為這個手勢對他們來說等於是比中指。各國禮儀方面都有許多差異，所以探訪之前務必事先查清楚喔！

sb. wonder whether...(or not)
某人不知道能否…。

- ★ I wonder whether it's appropriate to send them a present after the meeting or not.
  我不確定在會議之後送他們禮物適不適當。

- ★ Economists wonder whether the economy can ever grow again.
  經濟學家不知道經濟情況是否能再度復甦。

- ★ The **director** wondered whether some of the scenes should be re-shot again.
  導演在想一部分的鏡頭是不是要再重拍一次。

director
[dəˋrɛktə]
名 導演
advocate
[ˋædvəkɪt]
名 律師

- ★ The **advocate** wonders whether there is a reason behind this or not.
  律師思考這件事背後有沒有什麼原因。

- ★ The scholar wonders whether she can develop a resolution.
  那位學者在思考她是否能發展進一步的解答。

The first thing sb. (V) is...   某人首先…的是…。

- ★ The first thing you need to do in cross-cultural communications is to be open-mended.
  跨文化溝通時，你首先需要做的是保持思想開放。

- ★ The first thing the defendant admitted was the crimes he actually did.
  那名被告最先承認的是他實際犯下的罪行。

inconsiderate
[ˌɪnkənˋsɪdərɪt]
形 欠考慮的
constancy
[ˋkɑnstənsɪ]
名 堅定
collective
[kəˋlɛktɪv]
形 集體的

- ★ The first thing she regrets is those **inconsiderate** remarks she made.
  讓她感到遺憾的首先是她的輕率評論。

- ★ The first thing we admire is her courage and **constancy**.
  我們首先敬佩的是她的勇氣和堅定。

- ★ The first thing you can't ignore is **collective** strength.
  你最不能忽視的，首先是團隊的力量。

MP3 ▶ 303

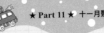

開口必備句　和老外聊開懷，就靠這幾句！

Cross-cultural differences may cause misunderstanding.
文化間的差異可能會引起誤會。

Certain gestures may be offensive in some countries.
在某些國家，有些手勢可能是很無禮的。

Communicating across cultures begins with the basic understanding that one size does not fit all.
跨文化間的溝通，始於了解到一套溝通方式並非適用全世界。

In Taiwan, Sunday is the last day of the week, while it's the first day of the week in Western culture.
在台灣，星期天是一週的最後一天，但在西方文化卻是每週的第一天。

In England, "cheers" means "thank you" and "you are welcome."
在英格蘭，「cheers」的意思是「謝謝你」和「不客氣」。

I am sorry, but I don't really get his joke.
抱歉，但是我真的不懂他的笑點在哪。

What do you mean by that?
你那樣說是什麼意思呢？

Our foreign clients would usually ask us to make our presentation first.
我們的外國客戶通常都會要求我們先進行簡報介紹。

Mr. Watson's heavily accented English is hard to understand.
華生先生的英文腔調很重、很難聽懂。

Chinese people tend to be as circumlocutory as possible to show their politeness while making requests.
中國人在做出請求時，會儘量婉轉以示禮貌。

A smile is always the best way to show your friendliness.
微笑最能表達你的友善。

UNIT 07 職場
工時及薪資
Welfare & Salary

單字基本功 掌握關鍵字 = 開口第一步

核心聯想

平日上班 Going out for work

shift [ʃɪft] 名 輪班時間	**welfare** [`wɛr͵fɛr] 名 福利	**workload** [`wɜk͵lod] 名 工作量	**commute** [kə`mjut] 動 通勤
clock in 片 打卡上班	**clock out** 片 打卡下班	**office worker** 片 上班族	**work hour** 片 工作時間

薪資待遇不佳 Unfair treatments 進階學習

resent [rɪ`zɛnt] 動 憤恨；怨恨	**disgruntled** [dɪs`grʌntḷd] 形 不悅的	**permissible** [pə`mɪsəbḷ] 形 允許的	**be fed up with** 片 受夠了…
file a complaint 片 提出申訴	**minimum wages** 片 最低薪資	**working hours** 片 工作時數	**worth one's salt** 片 稱職的

深度追蹤

Knowing More

　　美國人的工時觀念非常清楚，且一切都依照法律規定，所以當下班時間到了，大家就會準時下班，當然也有人會主動延長工時來賺取更多報酬，或為了獲得薪資、級別的提升而延後下班時間。不過，大家都很重視放鬆身心，所以每當週五就常聽到「TGIF!（Thank Goodness It's Friday）」，很多人也會在晚上開派對來慶祝一週的結束。另外，每當有體育比賽，像是足球賽或籃球賽，就會相約好友，早上就開始一邊烤肉、喝酒，一邊討論比賽。

MP3 ⓘ 305

套個單字，想說的都能表達！

sb. wind up...　　某人最終…。

★ You'll wind up feeling **empty** if you keep focusing only on your career.
如果你只專心於工作，你最終只會感到空虛。

★ He wound up in a hospital because of his careless driving.
他因為開車不注意，結果就進了醫院。

★ My aunt said she wanted to wind up her company and spend her retirement life in Philippine.
我阿姨說她想要關閉公司，然後退休後去菲律賓生活。

★ The President is about to wind up his visit to Somalia.
總統即將要結束探訪索馬利亞的行程了。

★ She will wind up in **bankruptcy** if she keeps spending money without careful thinking.
如果她花錢之前都不先想清楚，她最終一定會破產。

> **empty**
> [`ɛmptɪ]
> 形 空虛的
> **bankruptcy**
> [`bæŋkrəptsɪ]
> 名 破產

sb./sth. end in...　　某人 / 某事以…收場。

★ The manager ended in being sued for his discriminating actions.
那位經理最後因為歧視的行為而被告了。

★ Losing this client will end in a great loss to our company.
失去這名客戶將對我們公司造成很大的損失。

★ That **rebellion** ended in a military **suppression**.
那場叛亂最後被軍事鎮壓。

★ Our discussion ended in **stalemate**.
我們的會談最後陷入僵局。

★ The **summit** meeting ended in a deal-breaker.
高峰會最後以破局收場。

> **rebellion**
> [rɪ`bɛljən]
> 名 叛亂
> **suppression**
> [sə`prɛʃən]
> 名 鎮壓
> **stalemate**
> [`stel‚met]
> 名 僵局
> **summit**
> [`sʌmɪt]
> 形 政府首腦間的

開口必備句

和老外聊開懷，就靠這幾句！

Salaries remain unchanged while the prices of commodities keep going up.
🔊 薪資靜如止水，而物價卻持續飛漲。

Our manager never approves any of our overtime pay sheets.
🔊 我們的經理從不幫我們簽核加班費。

I've been working overtime every night for more than two months.
🔊 我每天加班已經連續超過兩個月了。

The reduction in overtime pay forced many employees to resign in the end.
🔊 刪減加班費的決定最後使許多員工主動辭職。

I'm already fed up with the long hours, so I want to quit.
🔊 我已經受夠超時工作了，所以我想離職。

Are you satisfied with your salary?
🔊 你對你的薪資感到滿意嗎？

Considering the long hours I work, my salary isn't enough.
🔊 我的超長工時和我的薪水根本不成比例。

Mr. Gregg never pays his employees on time.
🔊 桂格先生從來不準時發放薪資。

It is obvious that Mr. Lee is violating the labor laws by asking his workers to work over 12 hours per day.
🔊 李先生要求員工一天工作超過十二個小時，這很明顯違反了勞基法。

Anyone who would like to file a complaint can reach the labor union representative at extension 885.
🔊 任何想申訴的人，都可以撥打分機 885 聯絡工會代表。

A confidential complaint can be made upon request.
🔊 想要匿名申訴的話，都能提出要求。

單字基本功　掌握關鍵字 = 開口第一步

 核心聯想

日常抱怨 Complaining about things

murmur
[`mɝmɚ]
名 動 低語；抱怨

pushover
[`puʃ,ovɚ]
名 易受影響者

complain
[kəm`plen]
動 抱怨；投訴

grumble
[`grʌmbl̩]
動 發牢騷

mumble
[`mʌmbl̩]
動 含糊地說；碎碎念

whine
[hwaɪn]
動 發牢騷

stingy
[`stɪndʒɪ]
形 小氣的

make a fuss
片 大驚小怪

缺德行爲 Being mean to others　進階學習

backstab
[`bæk,stæb]
動 陷害；出賣

betray
[brɪ`tre]
動 背叛；出賣

bully
[`bulɪ]
名 惡霸 動 欺侮

immoral
[ɪ`mɔrəl]
形 不道德的

bite one's head off
片 將某人罵得狗血淋頭

dirty work
片 吃力不討好的事

pull rank on sb.
片 以職位壓人

rat sb. out
片 出賣某人

深度追蹤🔍　　　Knowing More

　　若對服務或產品不滿意時，通常都可以透過電話或是email來進行客訴（file a complaint）。而對處理客訴的客服人員（customer service）來說，只要掌握以下的處理態度，便能夠化危機成轉機，反而讓顧客變成粉絲：(1) 表達歉意，讓顧客感受到想要解決問題的態度；(2) 請顧客說明問題並表達尊重；(3) 展現同理心與傾聽，並試著理解顧客的不安；(4) 確認事情的原委及真實性，同時找出可改善的地方；(5) 提出互相都能接受的解決方案。

 **套個單字，想說的都能表達！**

sb. stand on one's right to... 某人堅持…的權利。

★ All the employees stood on their rights to hold out for better welfare.
所有員工都堅持要有更好的福利。

★ He will stand on his rights to have the case **adjudicated**.
他將堅持他宣告判決的權利。

★ That journalist stands on her right to report the accident **in detail**.
那名記者堅持她有詳細報導的權利。

★ The defendant stands on his right to **appeal** to a higher court.
被告人堅持他上訴的權利。

★ The house owner stood on his right to refuse a search without a **warrant**.
那個屋主堅持他的權利，拒絕無搜索令的搜查。

> **adjudicate**
> [ə`dʒudɪ͵ket]
> ⓥ（法）判決
> **in detail**
> ⓟ 詳細地
> **appeal**
> [ə`pil]
> ⓥ（法）上訴
> **warrant**
> [`wɔrənt]
> ⓝ（法）搜查令

sb. cannot choose but... 某人不得不…。

★ They cannot choose but **undertake** the consequences of their behaviors.
他們除了承擔後果之外，別無選擇。

★ People cannot choose but to move to another city.
人們不得不遷移到別的城市。

★ Her parents cannot choose but let their house **foreclose**.
她的父母別無選擇，只能將屋子法拍。

★ Steve cannot choose but **surrender** to the enemy.
史帝夫最後別無選擇，只好向敵人屈服。

★ He cannot choose but leave the town after graduating from high school.
高中畢業後，他不得不離開這個城鎮。

> **undertake**
> [͵ʌndə`tek]
> ⓥ 承擔
> **foreclose**
> [for`kloz]
> ⓥ（法）失去贖回權
> **surrender**
> [sə`rɛndə]
> ⓥ 投降；放棄

開口必備句 和老外聊開懷，就靠這幾句！

I'm fed up with Stella because she always complains a lot but don't do anything.

🔊 我已經受夠史特拉，她只會埋怨，卻什麼事也不會做。

Erik is such an apple polisher, so no one wants to be friends with him.

🔊 艾力克是個馬屁精，所以沒有人想和他做朋友。

Is there any safe way to complain about your colleagues and your boss?

🔊 有沒有什麼好方法可以私下抱怨同事和老闆？

Sophie keeps nagging everyone, which is really annoying.

🔊 蘇菲一直嘮叨，我們都覺得她很煩。

Constant complaining is so toxic in the workplace that it might erode your relationship with coworkers.

🔊 持續抱怨就像是毒藥一樣，會傷害你和同事間的人際關係。

Ashley always tries to get others to do her work.

🔊 艾希莉總是把自己該負責的工作丟給其他人做。

I cannot stand any sexual harassment in the workplace.

🔊 我完全無法忍受職場性騷擾。

Hazel has been bugging everyone in the office to buy her handmade cookies.

🔊 海瑟一直煩辦公室裡的人、叫大家買她的手作餅乾。

Sean is a real backstabber who loves to speak ill of people behind their backs.

🔊 尚恩常在背後中傷別人，他總愛在人們背後說別人壞話。

Jimmy is a real downer. No one on his team likes to work with him.

🔊 吉米是個掃興鬼，所以他的組員都不喜歡與他共事。

UNIT 09 職場

全球經濟景氣
Global Economy

 單字基本功 ▶ 掌握關鍵字＝開口第一步

核心聯想　經濟相關術語 Economy terms

appreciation [ə͵priʃɪˋeʃən] 名 升值；賞識	devaluation [͵divæljuˋeʃən] 名 貶值	economics [͵ikəˋnɑmɪks] 名 經濟學	growth [groθ] 名 成長
consumer goods 片 消費品	economic recovery 片 經濟復甦	make a comeback 片 東山再起	opportunity cost 片 機會成本

前景堪憂 Bad economic conditions　進階學習

depression [dɪˋprɛʃən] 名 經濟蕭條	downturn [ˋdaʊntɝn] 名（經濟）衰退	inflation [ɪnˋfleʃən] 名 通貨膨脹	recession [rɪˋsɛʃən] 名 衰退
bankrupt [ˋbæŋkrʌpt] 動 使破產 形 破產的	hinge [hɪndʒ] 動 決定於	abnormally [æbˋnɔrməlɪ] 副 反常地	in debt 片 負債

 深度追蹤

Knowing More

　　常常可以看到許多經濟學家，以統計各國的國內生產總值（GDP），來分析、衡量國家的經濟狀況。而根據統計，目前美國的GDP是世界上最高的，中國緊隨其後，日本則居第三位；如果以地域來看，亞洲則處於領先地位，因為東部的經濟重心（中國、日本、韓國）加起來的GDP幾乎與美國一樣多；另外，北美、亞洲、歐洲就占了世界經濟活動的80%以上剩下的20%才是其他國家的占比，足可見富國和窮國之間的鴻溝之深。

MP3 ▶ 311

套個單字，想說的都能表達！

sb. fear that...　某人擔心…。

★ The economists fear that the currency of their country will continue devaluating.
那些經濟學家怕他們國家的貨幣還會再貶值下去。

★ She fears that her brother might drink too much.
她擔心她的弟弟會喝太多酒。

★ The guards fear the prisoner might have escaped from the prison.
警衛都很擔心囚犯已經從監獄逃跑了。

★ The **prosecutor** fears that there isn't sufficient evidence to convict the murderer.
檢察官擔心沒有足夠的罪證能將那個殺人犯定罪。

★ Environmentalists fear that the **exhaust emissions** may **pollute** the **atmospheric** layer.
環境學家們都擔心排放的廢氣會汙染大氣層。

> **prosecutor**
> [`prɑsɪ.kjutə]
> 名 檢察官
>
> **exhaust emission**
> 片 廢氣排放
>
> **pollute**
> [pə`lut]
> 動 汙染
>
> **atmospheric**
> [.ætməs`fɛrɪk]
> 形 大氣的

...only if...　只要…，就會…。

★ Scholars believe that the economy will get better only if the government **implement** the right financial policy.
學者們認為只要政府用對財務政策，經濟就會轉好。

★ The chance will come only if she doesn't give up.
只要她不放棄，機會就會來臨。

★ Kids will be more outstanding only if you compliment them **properly**.
適當地讚美小孩，他們才能更傑出。

★ You'll make progress only if you stay modest.
你要保持謙虛的態度才能進步。

★ Mark **retorts** upon me only if he feels that I misunderstand him.
馬克只要一覺得我誤解他時，就會反駁我。

> **implement**
> [`ɪmplə.mənt]
> 動 執行
>
> **properly**
> [`prɑpəlɪ]
> 副 恰當地
>
> **retort**
> [rɪ`tɔrt]
> 動 反駁；回嘴說

開口必備句　和老外聊開懷，就靠這幾句！

Taiwan's economic growth hinges on the global economic recovery.
台灣的經濟成長與全球經濟復甦息息相關。

The economy has rebounded after the previous downturn.
經濟狀況已於上一次衰退後恢復。

The gradually-dropping unemployment rate is a positive sign.
逐步下降的失業率是一個好的指標。

The stock market is getting better along with the world economy.
股市會跟隨全球經濟狀況一起逐步改善。

It is said that the economic downturn will bottom out in 2017.
據說景氣衰退將於二〇一七年探底。

The booming economy is definitely good news for our country.
經濟的急速發展對我國而言絕對是個好消息。

Due to the European debt crisis and the weak US labor market, many countries have suffered from the economic downturn.
歐債危機與美國勞工市場的疲軟，導致許多國家經濟衰退。

Do you think the new policy can boost the slumping economy?
你認為新政策有助於提振衰退的經濟嗎？

The stock market is still in the red due to the previous slump.
股市仍因前次的經濟蕭條而不振。

Did you suffer any losses during the economic downturn?
經濟衰退時，你是否蒙受任何損失？

Many economic experts believe that the world is experiencing a slow-motion economic crisis.
很多經濟學專家都認為全球正在逐漸走向經濟危機。

Part 12

十二月假期氣氛濃
December Highlights:
Christmas & Career Path

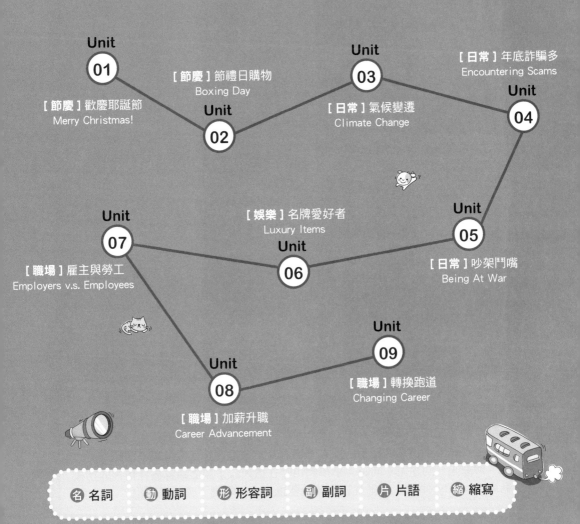

Unit 01
[節慶] 歡慶耶誕節
Merry Christmas!

[節慶] 節禮日購物
Boxing Day

Unit 02

Unit 03
[日常] 氣候變遷
Climate Change

[日常] 年底詐騙多
Encountering Scams

Unit 04

Unit 05
[日常] 吵架鬥嘴
Being At War

[娛樂] 名牌愛好者
Luxury Items

Unit 06

Unit 07
[職場] 雇主與勞工
Employers v.s. Employees

Unit 09
[職場] 轉換跑道
Changing Career

Unit 08
[職場] 加薪升職
Career Advancement

名 名詞　動 動詞　形 形容詞　副 副詞　片 片語　縮 縮寫

UNIT 01

節慶

歡慶耶誕節
Merry Christmas!

單字基本功 ▶ 掌握關鍵字 = 開口第一步

核心聯想
核心聯想　耶誕氛圍 Santa Claus is coming

chimney [`tʃɪmnɪ] 名 煙囪	**jingle** [`dʒɪŋgl̩] 名 叮噹聲	**reindeer** [`ren‚dir] 名 馴鹿	**sleigh** [sle] 名 雪橇　動 駕雪橇
holy [`holɪ] 形 神聖的	**Christmas Eve** 片 耶誕夜	**Christmas tree** 片 耶誕樹	**Santa Claus** 片 耶誕老人

進階學習　耶誕裝飾 Christmas Decorations

angel [`endʒl̩] 名 天使	**candle** [`kændl̩] 名 蠟燭	**carol** [`kærəl] 名 福音歌曲	**Christian** [`krɪstʃən] 名 基督徒
mistletoe [`mɪsl̩‚to] 名 槲寄生	**ornament** [`ɔrnəmənt] 名 裝飾品	**decorate** [`dɛkə‚ret] 動 裝飾；佈置	**stocking stuffer** 片 （放襪子裡面的） 聖誕禮物

深度追蹤 ♪　*Knowing More*

　　每年的十二月二十五日，就是一年一度的聖誕節。每當此時，國外都會放一個禮拜的假，讓大家返鄉與親人同聚；街上也掛滿裝飾燈炮、商店紛紛撥放耶誕歌曲，營造出濃厚的耶誕氣氛。而代表物除了聖誕樹和槲寄生，還有掛在火爐上、塞滿小禮物的襪子，且人們也會互贈禮物，並在聖誕夜準備豐盛的大餐，與家人一同享用。同時，小孩們也會在這天收下象徵耶穌犧牲精神的拐杖糖果（candy cane），並在夜裡等待聖誕老人從煙囪下來贈送禮物。

MP3 ▶ 314

套個單字，想說的都能表達！

sb. spend... in sth./V-ing 某人將(時間)花在某事。

★ I spent the whole day picking Christmas presents for my family.
我花了一整天挑選給家人們的耶誕禮物。

★ The housewife spent her every morning doing her **chores**.
那個家庭主婦花星期六花了一整天做家事。

★ Those hikers spent all day mountaineering in the snow.
那群登山客一整天都在雪地登山。

★ The **publisher** spent lots of money in **compiling** and printing.
出版商花了很多錢匯編和列印。

★ The single mom has spent many years bringing up her child on her own.
那位單親媽媽花了很多年的時間自己把孩子帶大。

chore
[tʃor]
② 家庭雜務
publisher
[`pʌblɪʃə]
② 出版商
compile
[kəm`paɪl]
⑩ 匯編

sb. is looking forward to... 某人很期待…。

★ I am looking forward to unwrapping my Christmas gifts.
我很期待拆我的聖誕禮物。

★ Our manager is looking forward to renewing agreements with customers.
我們經理很期待與客戶續約。

★ The **minister** is looking forward to an economic **boom** in the coming years.
部長很期待接下來幾年的經濟成長。

★ The **citizens** are looking forward to the end of the president's term.
市民們都希望總統任期趕快結束。

★ The fans are looking forward to meeting the **musicians** after the concert.
粉絲們都很期待在音樂會後與那些音樂家見面。

minister
[`mɪnɪstə]
② 部長；神職人員
boom
[bum]
② (商業)繁榮
citizen
[`sɪtəzn]
② 市民；公民
musician
[mju`zɪʃən]
② 音樂家

開口必備句
和老外聊開懷，就靠這幾句！

How are you going to celebrate Christmas?
🔊 你要怎麼慶祝耶誕節呢？

Our family always have a feast to celebrate Christmas.
🔊 我們家總是吃大餐來慶祝耶誕節。

The Christmas season is celebrated differently all around the world.
🔊 世界各地會以不同的方式慶祝耶誕節。

A traditional Christmas dinner features roasted turkey and cranberry sauce.
🔊 傳統耶誕大餐的特色是烤雞和蔓越莓醬。

Emily sent all her friends a Christmas card with some pictures on it.
🔊 艾蜜莉送給朋友們附上照片的耶誕卡片。

It is said that people should kiss under the mistletoe.
🔊 據說人們應該在檞寄生下接吻。

Do you believe in Santa Claus?
🔊 你相信有耶誕老人嗎？

Kids will hang their socks on the fireplace and wait for Santa Claus and his gifts.
🔊 孩子們會把襪子吊在壁爐上，等待耶誕老人和他的禮物。

Rudolph the red-nosed reindeer is Santa Claus's best companion in giving away the gifts.
🔊 馴鹿魯道夫是聖誕老公公最可靠的送禮夥伴。

Ms. Chang gave away candy canes in class last week.
🔊 張老師上週在課堂上發送拐杖糖給她的學生。

The kids can't wait to open their Christmas presents.
🔊 那些小孩等不及想要拆開他們的聖誕禮物。

MP3 ⊙ 316

★UNIT★

節慶

02 節禮日購物
Boxing Day

單字基本功 掌握關鍵字＝開口第一步

核心聯想

起源及傳統 Origin & traditions

nativity [nə`tɪvɪtɪ] 名 耶穌誕生	**pantomime** [`pæntə,maɪm] 名 默劇	**spirit** [`spɪrɪt] 名（宗）聖靈；精神	**perpetuate** [pə`pɛtʃʊ,et] 動 使不朽
venture [`vɛntʃə] 動 冒險	**horse racing** 片 賽馬	**mince pie** 片 碎肉派	**public holiday** 片 國定假日

 節禮日購物 Post-Christmas sales

進階學習

sale [sel] 名 拍賣；廉價出售	**queue** [kju] 名 行列 動 排隊	**discounted** [`dɪskaʊntɪd] 形 打折的	**joyfully** [`dʒɔɪfəlɪ] 副 歡欣地
be known as 片 被認為是	**box up** 片 打包	**price reduction** 片 降價	**wrapping paper** 片 包裝紙

 深度追蹤 Knowing More

　　節禮日（Boxing Day）大多在英國、澳洲和加拿大慶祝，最初源於中世紀的聖誕節，當時的聖誕節隔天，教會人員會打開教堂門口放置的捐款箱，將款項捐給窮人；而十九世紀的英國皇宮貴族，則會將僕人辛勤工作的獎勵用盒子包起來，聖誕節隔日再送給他們。後來，節禮日便逐漸商業化，變成各家商店促銷商品的時間，當天清晨總會看到許多人在店家面前大排長龍。除此之外，人們也會在這天把聖誕裝飾裝箱，留著明年繼續用來布置。

It is hard for sb. to...　對某人來說，…很困難。

★ It's really hard for me to get up at 5 a.m. just to line up for the sales.
對我來說，凌晨五點起床就只為了排隊搶購，真的很困難。

★ It's really hard for him to explain everything in one minute.
要在一分鐘之內解釋所有事情，對他來說真的很困難。

★ It is too hard for the lawyer to prove her **innocence**.
律師很難證明她無罪。

★ It is quite hard for all delegates to accept your **proposition**.
要讓所有代表接都受你的提議有點困難。

★ It was hard for that celebrity to escape from the **cult**'s control.
那個名人經過重重困難才脫離邪教控制。

> **innocence**
> [`ɪnəsn̩s]
> 名 無罪
>
> **proposition**
> [ˌprɑpə`zɪʃən]
> 名 提議
>
> **cult**
> [kʌlt]
> 名 邪教

sb. abstain from...　某人戒除 / 主動放棄…。

★ She finally abstained from shopping impulsively.
她終於戒掉衝動買東西的習慣了。

★ Many people in the support group abstained from drinking alcohol successfully.
很多參加戒酒小組的人都成功戒酒了。

★ **Humanists** abstain from voting on making **abortion** legal.
人道主義者主動放棄墮胎合法化的投票權。

★ Mason just can't abstain from bragging about his great **victory**.
梅森總是無法停止自誇的行為。

★ The patient has to abstain from having food with too much sugar or fat.
那名患者必須戒除吃多糖或多油脂食物的習慣。

> **humanist**
> [`hjumənɪst]
> 名 人道主義者
>
> **abortion**
> [ə`bɔrʃən]
> 名 墮胎
>
> **victory**
> [`vɪktərɪ]
> 名 勝利

MP3 ▶ 318

開口必備句 和老外聊開懷，就靠這幾句！

Boxing Day is celebrated on December 26, the day after Christmas.
十二月二十六日是節禮日，也就是聖誕節的隔天。

Traditionally, December 26 was the day to open the Christmas Box to share with the poor.
傳統上，十二月二十六日是打開聖誕禮物箱和貧者分享的日子。

There will be great sales in shopping centers on Boxing Day.
節禮日當天，購物中心都會祭出特別優惠。

On Boxing Day, most shops have sales with dramatic price reductions.
大部分商店都會在節禮日祭出驚人的降價和折扣。

Do you want to go to Oxford Street with me on Boxing Day for bargains?
節禮日當天，你想和我一起去牛津街搶便宜嗎？

There are always shoulder-to-shoulder crowds in shopping centers on Boxing Day.
節禮日當天，購物中心總是擠滿摩肩擦踵的人潮。

It is always a festive moment when kids open their gift boxes on Boxing Day.
節禮日一向是個歡欣的時刻，因為孩子們終於可以打開他們的禮物了。

As soon as he opened his eyes in the morning, Christ hopped down the stairs to open the gifts.
克里斯一睡醒就跳下樓，去拆他的禮物。

After all the food and drink on Christmas, we all enjoy slouching on the sofa with our family.
在聖誕大餐後，我們喜歡和家人一起窩在沙發上。

Mom always makes delicious mince pies for us.
媽媽總是做好吃的碎肉派給我們吃。

UNIT 03

日常

氣候變遷
Climate Change

 單字基本功　掌握關鍵字＝開口第一步

核心聯想　全球危機 Abnormal climate

adaption
[əˋdæpʃən]
名 適應；適合

deforestation
[ˏdifərəsˋteʃən]
名 砍伐森林

greenhouse
[ˋgrinˏhaʊs]
名 溫室

shifting
[ˋʃɪftɪŋ]
名 變動；改變

acid rain
片 酸雨

climate change
片 氣候異常

global warming
片 全球暖化

retreat of glaciers
片 冰川倒退

環保議題 Problems & solutions　進階學習

disposal
[dɪˋspozl]
名 丟棄物

energy
[ˋɛnədʒɪ]
名 能源；精力

pollution
[pəˋluʃən]
名 汙染

waste
[west]
名 廢料 動 浪費

environmental
[ɪnˏvaɪrənˋmɛntl]
形 環境的

green
[grin]
形 環保的；綠色的

renewable
[rɪˋnjuəbl]
形 可再生的；可恢復的

environmental friendly
片 環保的

深度追蹤　　　　　　Knowing More

　　人們造成的各種汙染，改變了全球氣候以及環境，同時也產生了許多環境問題，例如溫室效應、臭氧層破洞……等等。為提倡愛護環境的觀念，國外也有推行過「碳足跡 carbon footprint」的觀念，這個概念是將每個人在日常生活所產生的溫室氣體（greenhouse gases）數量，以二氧化碳（carbon dioxide）為單位量化，藉以衡量這些活動對環境的影響，例如有些餐廳會將食品製造的碳足跡標在菜單上面，藉此提醒大家要珍惜環境。

MP3 ▶ 320

套個單字，想說的都能表達！

sb. be out of the running for...

某人失去⋯的機會。

★ His team is out of the running for the **execution** of **marine** development.
他的團隊錯失實行海洋發展計畫的機會。

★ He was out of the running for that project.
他失去參加那個企劃的機會了。

★ The engineer is out of the running for the seminar in New York.
那位工程師失去參加紐約研討會的機會。

★ The soldiers have been out of the running for pushing forward.
那些士兵們已經失去往前推進的機會。

★ Our **previous** supervisor was out of the running for a promotion.
我們的前主管失去了升職的機會。

> **execution**
> [ˌɛksɪˋkjuʃən]
> 名 執行
> **marine**
> [məˋrin]
> 形 海生的
> **previous**
> [ˋpriviəs]
> 形 以前的

From one's perspective,...   從某人的觀點來看，⋯。

★ From environmentalists' perspectives, earth won't be able to exist unless human reduce pollutions.
從環境學家的觀點來看，除非人們減少污染，地球將不會存在。

★ From her perspective, a manager should have leadership skills.
她認為一個經理須具備領導特質。

★ From Kate's perspective, we shouldn't step into other's business.
凱特覺得我們都不應該多管別人的閒事。

★ From the **attorney**'s perspective, the defendant should **plead** guilty.
那位律師認為，被告人必須承認有罪。

★ From the boy's perspective, it was his fault not to help out his classmate.
那位男孩覺得沒有伸手幫忙同學是他的錯。

> **attorney**
> [əˋtɜnɪ]
> 名 律師
> **plead**
> [plid]
> 動 （法）承認

開口必備句　和老外聊開懷，就靠這幾句！

Global warming is a complicated and important issue.
全球暖化是個棘手但重要的議題。

The increase in global temperatures causes the rise of the sea level.
地球溫度的增加導致海平面上升。

The oddly high temperature in summer these past several years in Taiwan might be caused by global warming.
台灣近年來夏天的異常高溫可能是全球暖化造成的。

The impact of global warming is far greater than just increasing temperatures.
全球暖化所造成的影響，並非僅止於溫度上升。

Many species have been impacted by rising temperatures.
溫度上升影響了很多動植物。

Extreme weather conditions, such as droughts and heavy rainfall, have happened a lot recently.
極端的氣候狀況，例如乾旱和暴雨，最近頻繁發生。

Carbon dioxide emissions contribute to global warming.
二氧化碳的排放造成了全球暖化。

Sadly, there is no single solution to global warming.
令人難過的是，全球暖化並沒有一個特定的解決方案。

How can we slow down the global warming process?
我們該如何減緩全球暖化的速度？

Car pooling is a way to reduce our CO2 emissions.
汽車共乘是減少二氧化碳排放的一種方法。

There are researchers trying to develop better uses of the renewable energy.
研究者不斷嘗試著發展能更有效利用再生能源的方法。

MP3 ▶ 322

日常

年底詐騙多
Encountering Scams

單字基本功　掌握關鍵字 = 開口第一步

核心聯想

識破詐騙集團 Recognizing scam gangs

scam
[`skæm]
名 動 詐騙

con
[kɑn]
名 動 詐騙

counterfeit
[`kaʊntəˌfɪt]
名 仿製品　形 偽造的

deceit
[dɪ`sit]
名 欺騙；謊言

fraud
[frɔd]
名 詐騙；騙子

criminal
[`krɪmənl̩]
名 罪犯

con artist
片 詐騙高手

set up
片 設局

詐騙手法 Be aware of tricks

進階學習

insecurity
[ˌɪnsɪ`kjʊrətɪ]
名 缺乏安全感

privacy
[`praɪvəsɪ]
名 隱私；私事

spam
[spæm]
名 垃圾郵件

transfer
[`trænsfɝ]
名 轉帳

valuables
[`væljʊəbl̩z]
名 財產

hack
[hæk]
動 用電腦入侵

reconfirm
[ˌrikən`fɝm]
動 再確認

PIN
縮 個人識別號

　深度追蹤

Knowing More

　　為了騙取錢財，詐騙集團不斷想出各種詐騙招數；常見手法其中之一，就是利用網路假冒身分，來騙財或騙色的網路交友詐騙（catfishing）；而網路釣魚（phishing）則是偽裝成官方人士，企圖以email或是即時通訊軟體來竊取密碼或身分認證。另外，因為騙子通常需具備膽量和信心，才能騙取別人的信任，所以騙子的英文常用「con」表示，而「con」一詞為「confidence 自信」的縮寫，可當動詞表示詐騙，也可當名詞表示騙子、騙局。

look out for sth. 小心 / 注意某事。

★ You have to look out for tricks the **scam gangs** use to con people.
你必須小心詐騙集團的詐騙手段。

★ Look out for the **rogue** waves and don't **take** any **chances**.
要小心瘋狗浪，不要冒險。

★ Without looking out for the traffic, he ended up in a hospital.
他因為沒有小心來車，最後就進了醫院。

★ The guards were told to look out for any suspicious behavior.
警衛們被交代一定要注意所有可疑的行為。

★ The patient should look out for the **side effects** of the prescription drugs.
那位病人必須小心藥物的副作用。

> **scam gang**
> 片 詐騙集團
> **rogue**
> [rog]
> 形 危險的
> **take chances**
> 片 冒險
> **side effect**
> 片 副作用

sb. suspect that... 某人懷疑…。

★ She suspected the man trying to talk her into buying diamonds is a fraud.
她懷疑那個一直叫她買鑽石的人是個騙子。

★ Dylan began to suspect that Mandy will leave him.
狄倫開始懷疑曼蒂將會離開他。

★ Our boss suspects that Sam cannot complete the project in time.
我們老闆懷疑山姆無法如期完成專案。

★ The **judge** suspected that the **plaintiff** didn't tell the truth.
法官懷疑原告並沒有說出實情。

★ The police suspect that the **gang is up to** something illegal.
警方懷疑那個幫派正在策畫一些違法的事情。

> **judge**
> [dʒʌdʒ]
> 名 法官
> **plaintiff**
> [`plentɪf]
> 名 原告
> **gang**
> [gæŋ]
> 名 幫派
> **be up to sth.**
> 片 偷偷做某事

MP3 ▶ 324

開口必備句　和老外聊開懷，就靠這幾句！

The man used a fake identity to defraud the bank of thousands of dollars.
一位男子利用偽造證件騙銀行，盜領了好幾萬元。

Some fraudsters pretend to be bank officers, asking you to provide your bank card information.
有些詐騙分子會假扮成銀行人員，並要求你提供提款卡資訊。

Some scammers may even pretend to be judges.
有些詐騙分子甚至會假扮成法官。

The man impersonated as a bank manager to collect account information.
那個男人假扮成銀行經理來蒐集帳戶資訊。

Mrs. Lee was almost defrauded; luckily, her son stopped her from making a big mistake.
李女士差點遭詐騙，所幸她的兒子及時阻止大錯。

Keep your passwords secret in order to avoid frauds.
務必保存好你的密碼以防詐騙。

Never operate an ATM under the instructions of other people.
勿在他人的指示下操作自動提款機。

Phishing refers to emails, text messages and websites made by criminals in an attempt to steal personal information.
網路釣魚是指嫌犯藉由寄發垃圾郵件、簡訊或設計假網頁來竊取個資。

Keep an eye on your credit card, just in case it might be stolen or used to steal money from your account.
謹慎保管你的信用卡，以免遭盜刷，或被盜領存款。

Sasha reported a cybercrime to the police yesterday.
莎夏昨天已向警方報案網路詐欺。

In Taiwan, you can dial 165 to report a fraud.
在台灣，你可以撥打 165 通報詐騙。

UNIT 05

日常 吵架鬥嘴
Being At War

單字基本功 掌握關鍵字 ＝ 開口第一步

核心聯想

激怒他人 Provocative actions

agitate [`ædʒə,tet] 動 激怒；刺激	**irritate** [`irə,tet] 動 惹惱；使疼痛	**provoke** [prə`vok] 動 激怒；激起	**taunt** [tɔnt] 動 奚落；嘲笑
emotional [ɪ`moʃənḷ] 形 情緒激動的	**hysterical** [hɪs`tɛrɪkḷ] 形 歇斯底里的	**drive sb. bananas** 片 使某人發瘋	**piss sb. off** 片 激怒某人

平息怒氣 Trying to solve arguments

進階學習

calm [kɑm] 動 使鎮定 形 鎮靜的	**peacemaker** [`pis,mekɚ] 名 和事佬	**truce** [trus] 名 暫停爭吵；休戰	**mutual** [`mjutʃʊəl] 形 共同的
sympathetic [,sɪmpə`θɛtɪk] 形 有同情心的	**bury the hatchet** 片 和解	**settle the dispute** 片 平息糾紛	**make peace** 片 言歸於好

深度追蹤 *Knowing More*

　　當意見相互衝突時，務必先靜下心來、就事論事！如果一氣之下說出威脅的話，在美國可是會被以「恐怖威脅（Threats of Violence Against Individuals）」的罪名起訴而入獄的；在吵架當中，也常有人以自身生命來威脅對方，如果這樣的情況發生在美國，便會被送進醫院裡、被認定為有自殺傾向而強制住院觀察，還得自掏腰包付醫療費呢。所以在情緒激動時，不妨先平息怒火、傾聽對方意見，同時也要清楚表達想法，以免造成誤會。

MP3 ▶ 326

 套個單字，想說的都能表達！

Don't you think it is no use...?
你不覺得…沒有用嗎？

★ Don't you think it is no use crying over spilt milk?
你不覺得後悔已經無法挽回的事情沒有用嗎？

★ Don't you think it is no use **wailing** about the **defeat**?
你不覺得為了已經輸掉的比賽痛哭沒有用嗎？

★ Don't you think it is no use **blaming** the doctor for the man's death?
你不覺得為了那個男人的死亡責怪醫生沒有用嗎？

★ Don't you think it is no use keeping a **flippant** and rude attitude?
你不覺得採取輕率又無理的態度沒有用嗎？

★ Don't you think it is no use complaining about the noise of jet aircrafts?
你不覺得抱怨噴射機的噪音沒有用嗎？

> **wail**
> [wel]
> (動) 嚎啕大哭；慟哭
>
> **defeat**
> [dɪˋfit]
> (名) 失敗；挫敗
>
> **blame**
> [blem]
> (動) 責備；指責
>
> **flippant**
> [ˋflɪpənt]
> (形) 輕率的

Have sb. ever...?　某人曾經做過…嗎？

★ Have you ever started an argument that you didn't mean to?
你曾經無意引起爭執，但還是和人吵起來了嗎？

★ Have you ever **publicized** a post that you didn't mean to?
你曾經把原本沒有打算公開的文章張貼出去嗎？

★ Has she ever **let the cat out of the bag** without intending to do so?
她曾經不小心洩漏秘密嗎？

★ Has the detective ever tried looking for the evidence for the murder?
那個偵探有試著去找這樁謀殺案的證據嗎？

★ Have you ever **concealed** the truth from others or told any **white lies**?
你曾經對他人隱瞞真相或是說善意的謊言嗎？

> **publicize**
> [ˋpʌblɪͺsaɪz]
> (動) 公布
>
> **let the cat out of the bag**
> (片) 洩漏秘密
>
> **conceal**
> [kənˋsil]
> (動) 隱瞞
>
> **white lie**
> (片) 善意的謊言

I'm sick and tired of her excuses.
我已經受夠她的藉口了。

What can I do to shut him up?
我要怎麼做才能讓他閉嘴？

Jason and David's debate regarding the NBA ended in a heated argument.
傑森和大衛的 NBA 籃球賽辯論以一陣大吵收場。

How do you avoid arguments with your siblings?
你怎麼避免和兄弟姊妹爭吵？

Jason had a fight with a young man, who was very disrespectful to an old man on the MRT.
因為有名男子在捷運上對一位老先生很不尊重，傑森便和他吵了起來。

Some impolite hand gestures may lead to serious fights.
有些不禮貌的手勢，可能會導致嚴重的爭吵。

I am sorry, but I can't agree with you.
我很抱歉，但我不同意你的意見。

Jessica and Amanda haven't talked to each other ever since their fight last week.
潔西卡和亞曼達自從上星期吵架後，彼此就沒再說過話了。

You just really hurt my feelings.
你真的傷了我的心。

I didn't mean to say that. Would you please forgive me?
我不是故意說那些話的，可以請你原諒我嗎？

It's very mean of you to do things like that to your friend.
你很過分，竟然對你最好的朋友做出這種事。

It takes two fools to argue.
爭吵是兩個傻瓜做的事。

MP3 ▶ 328

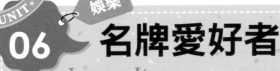

★UNIT★ 娛樂
06

名牌愛好者
Luxury Items

 **單字基本功** 掌握關鍵字 = 開口第一步

核心聯想 有錢人家 Wealthy family

extravagance	**grandeur**	**affluent**	**lavish**
[ɪk`strævəgəns]	[`grændʒɚ]	[`æfluənt]	[`lævɪʃ]
名 奢侈；浪費	名 壯觀；顯赫	形 富裕的	形 奢華的；慷慨的

wealthy	**idle rich**	**in the lap of luxury**	**filthy rich**
[`wɛlθɪ]	片 非常富有的	片 養尊處優的	片 極富有的
形 富有的；豐富的			

昂貴物品 Shopping for luxury goods **進階學習**

brand	**diamond**	**gem**	**jewelry**
[brænd]	[`daɪəmənd]	[dʒɛm]	[`dʒuəlrɪ]
名 品牌	名 鑽石	名 寶石	名 珠寶

luxury	**roadster**	**fancy**	**pure gold**
[`lʌkʃərɪ]	[`rodstɚ]	[`fænsɪ]	片 純金
名 奢侈；奢侈品	名 敞篷車	形 別緻的	

 深度追蹤 *Knowing More*

　　有人買奢侈品是為了炫富，也有人認為名牌才是品質的保障。根據網路調查，名牌的產地就屬義大利最為消費者鍾愛，而消費者在奢侈品類別的偏好則是以鞋類、香水、化妝品和珠寶首飾為主。值得注意的是，為了培養奢侈品管理方面的人才，歐美等地甚至有「奢侈品管理」學位可以攻讀，而法國就是世界上設有最多奢侈品管理課程的國家，讓想要在此方面發展的學生們，學習品牌營銷策略、消費者心理、廣告策略和銷售……等技巧。

句型偷吃步　套個單字，想說的都能表達！

Is it worth...?　…值得嗎？

★ Is it worth the price for those luxuries?
花那麼多錢買奢侈品值得嗎？

★ Is it worth eight hours just to wait in line to buy the limited edition?
花八個小時排隊買限量商品值得嗎？

★ Is it worth **splashing** out on computer **accessories**?
把錢揮霍在電腦週邊產品上值得嗎？

★ Is it worth giving up the opportunity for your family?
為了你家人而放棄這個機會值得嗎？

★ Is it worth paying extra for a **balcony** cabin on a **cruise**?
為了訂郵輪的陽台艙而多花一筆錢，是值得的嗎？

> **splash**
> [splæʃ]
> 動（口）揮霍錢財
>
> **accessory**
> [æk`sɛsərɪ]
> 名 配件
>
> **balcony**
> [`bælkənɪ]
> 名 露台；陽台
>
> **cruise**
> [kruz]
> 名（坐船）旅行

...for the purpose of...　…的目的是…。

★ Some people buy luxuries for the purpose of showing off.
有些人買奢侈品只是為了炫耀。

★ They built an **enclosure** for the purpose of taking **precautions** against **landslides**.
他們為防範土石流而建造圍牆。

★ A stockbroker came this morning for the purpose of assessing the risk of our investment.
股票經紀人今天早上過來評估我們的投資風險。

★ The networks were set up for the purpose of serving the public.
設立網路是為了服務大眾。

★ This auction was held for the purpose of raising funds for the poor.
舉辦這場拍賣主要是為窮人募款。

> **enclosure**
> [ɪn`kloʒɚ]
> 名 圍牆
>
> **precaution**
> [prɪ`kɔʃən]
> 名 預防
>
> **landslide**
> [`lænd,slaɪd]
> 名 坍方

MP3 ▶ 330

開口必備句　和老外聊開懷，就靠這幾句！

Luxury goods are usually associated with affluence, rather than necessity.

奢侈品通常與富裕聯想在一起，而非與必需品。

Some say that possessing luxury goods give them feelings of accomplishment.

有人說，擁有奢侈品讓他們覺得很有成就感。

The diamond is so fabulous that Helen cannot resist taking out her credit card.

那顆鑽石是如此美麗，讓海倫忍不住拿出她的信用卡。

Not everyone can afford a cashmere scarf.

不是每個人都買得起喀什米爾羊毛圍巾。

This Hermes handbag costs her a fortune.

這個愛馬仕手提包花了她很多錢。

The handbag was made by an experienced Italian craftsman.

這個手提包是由一名經驗豐富的義大利工匠製作。

Tourists are limited to the purchase of only two handbags at Louis Vuitton in Paris.

在巴黎的路易威登，每位觀光客只能購買兩個手提包。

Designer brands tend to incorporate new elements into their designs.

設計師都會在他們的設計中融入新的理念。

Cathy's latest jewelry collection is well-received in the market.

凱西最新設計的珠寶在市場上賣得很好。

The car made of fiber glass and titanium costs 2 million dollars.

這輛車以玻璃纖維和鈦打造而成，要價兩百萬元。

The word is that Mercedes Benz will reveal its newest model in summer.

據說賓士將在夏季公布最新車款。

UNIT 07 職場
雇主與勞工
Employers v.s. Employees

單字基本功 ▷ 掌握關鍵字 = 開口第一步

核心聯想　勞資關係 Labor relations

debate
[dɪ`bet]
名 動 爭論；辯論

dispute
[dɪ`spjut]
名 動 爭執

employer
[ɪm`plɔɪə]
名 雇主

union
[`junjən]
名 公會；同盟

labor
[`lebə]
名 勞工 形 勞工的

advocate
[`ædvə‚ket]
動 提倡；支持

working condition
片 工作條件

industrial dispute
片 勞資糾紛

 抗議或協議 Taking actions　進階學習

compromise
[`kɑmprə‚maɪz]
名 動 妥協；和解

lockout
[`lɑk‚aʊt]
名 停工

sit-down
[`sɪt‚daʊn]
名 靜坐抗議

strike
[straɪk]
名 動 罷工

protest
[prə`tɛst]
動 抗議；反對

reconcile
[`rɛkənsaɪl]
動 和解；使和好

bargain over
片 協議

fight against
片 對抗

 深度追蹤　Knowing More

　　在一九九三年，美國曾發生一起空服員罷工事件，因為阿拉斯加航空想調整營運模式，於是把所有的空服員全部解雇，再重新簽訂新契約；但在罷工投票通過以後，空服員竟然還是每天準時上班，直到某一天，空服員才在登機前一刻「間歇性罷工（intermittent strike）」，集體離開登機門去吃早餐，而吃完早餐後又回來繼續上班。最後雙方告上法庭，而聯邦法院判決空服員勝訴，這個判決對美國空服員來說，更是最重要的事件之一。

MP3 ▶ 332

套個單字，想說的都能表達！

...that sb. can hardly believe.

某人無法想像…。

★ The strike casted such a huge impact on the industry that people could hardly believe.
罷工對整個產業造成的影響大到人們都不敢想像。

★ The **plague spread** so **rapidly** that people could hardly believe.
人們幾乎不敢相信瘟疫蔓延的如此迅速。

★ The president fell out of power so fast that all citizens could hardly believe.
人民不敢相信總統這麼快就下台了。

★ The party was like a dream that most guests could hardly believe.
對大部分的客人來說，那場派對就像夢一樣美好。

★ The sales manager set goals so difficult that our team could hardly believe.
業務經理設立了連我們團隊都難以想像的困難目標。

plague
[pleg]
名 瘟疫；鼠疫
spread
[sprɛd]
動 蔓延
rapidly
[`ræpɪdlɪ]
副 迅速地

sb. (V) for sure...   某人確定…。

★ The union couldn't tell for sure whether the government will deal with the **issue** or not.
公會不能確定政府會不會著手處理這項議題。

★ She couldn't tell who that was for sure from a **distance**.
她從遠方看不出那個人是誰。

★ No one knows for sure what happened to his family.
沒有人知道他家人到底出了什麼事。

★ You cannot say for sure whether it will rain tomorrow or not.
你無法判斷出明天到底會不會下雨。

★ He will call for sure since he made us a promise.
既然他都已經答應我們了，他就一定會回電。

issue
[`ɪʃjʊ]
名 問題
distance
[`dɪstəns]
名 距離

 開口必備句　和老外聊開懷，就靠這幾句！

The union is designed to protect the rights of the employees.
工會是維護勞工權益的組織。

I'm in charge of labor relation disputes.
我負責處理勞資間的糾紛。

Employers should provide labor insurance for every employee.
雇主應提供每名雇員勞工保險。

Your employer must take measures to ensure job security.
雇主應為你的工作安全採取措施。

A good employer makes sure his workers earn enough to meet the cost of living.
一個好雇主會確保員工能夠滿足生活需求。

Do you want to file a complaint against your employer?
你想要投訴你的雇主嗎？

Any employer who fails to provide insurance for employees will be fined.
未替勞工投保的雇主將被處以罰鍰。

In the event of a labor dispute, the concerned parties can negotiate by themselves, or follow the jurisdiction channels.
勞資糾紛中，相關人員可彼此協商或訴諸法律。

The failure of negotiations between operators and flight attendants unions led to a lockout.
航空公司與空服員協會雙方談判破裂，而導致了罷工事件。

They organized a sit-in to protest against the unfair treaty signed by the government.
他們策畫了一場靜坐抗議，反對政府簽下的不平等條約。

She was in that protest march last month.
她上個月參加了那場抗議遊行。

MP3 ▶ 334

職場

加薪升職
Career Advancement

單字基本功 掌握關鍵字＝開口第一步

核心聯想

表現亮眼 Outstanding performances

achievement
[ə`tʃivmənt]
名 成就；完成

evaluation
[ɪˏvæljʊ`eʃən]
名 評估；估價

reward
[rɪ`wɔrd]
名 動 獎勵

qualification
[ˏkwɑləfə`keʃən]
名 資格

consult
[kən`sʌlt]
動 請教；商議

further
[`fɝðɚ]
動 促進；助長

outstanding
[aʊt`stændɪŋ]
形 傑出的

sales performance
片 業績

提出加薪升職 Promotion & pay raise

進階學習

advancement
[əd`vænsmənt]
名 晉升；發展

preferment
[prɪ`fɝmənt]
名 晉升

advance
[əd`væns]
動 升職；進步

promote
[prə`mot]
動 晉升；促進

pursue
[pə`su]
動 追求

exalted
[ɪg`zɔltɪd]
形 地位崇高的

proactive
[pro`æktɪv]
形 先採取行動的

pay raise
片 加薪

 深度追蹤 *Knowing More*

　　根據美國勞工部做的調查，3%的加薪幅度儼然成為美國企業的新常態，而在談薪水方面，則須注意以下幾點：(1) 要在合宜的時間，先約好主管再來談「薪事」。(2) 提出對公司的貢獻，來說明為什麼公司要增加你的薪水。(3) 同事之間須避免互相討論薪水。(4) 儘量不在公共場合談論薪水。另外，如果在美國工作的話，也要注意正職的職位通常都是談「年薪」，且每個公司也有自己發薪水的方式，但大多為兩周發一次，或是每月發一次。

...be effective in... …在…上有成效。

★ You have to be effective enough in your work to be qualified for a raise.
工作要有效率，這樣你才有資格來談加薪。

★ This **remedy** has been effective in treating headaches.
這個藥物能有效治療頭痛。

★ Window screens are effective in keeping out mosquitoes.
紗窗能很有效地擋住蚊子。

★ The water-cleaner is effective in **filtering impurities** in the water.
淨水器可以有效過濾水中雜質。

★ The app is effective in providing detailed information of a tourist attraction.
這個應用程式可以提供觀光景點的詳細資訊。

> **effective**
> [ɪ`fɛktɪv]
> 形 有效的
> **remedy**
> [`rɛmədɪ]
> 名 藥物
> **filter**
> [`fɪltə]
> 動 過濾
> **impurity**
> [ɪm`pjʊrətɪ]
> 名 雜質

Seeing that..., ... 由於…，…。

★ Seeing that he really worked hard, the boss decided to promote him.
由於他工作非常認真，老闆便決定讓他升職。

★ Seeing that you insist, I will reconsider the matter.
因為你很堅持，我將重新考慮這個問題。

★ Seeing that a typhoon is coming, they decided to cancel the trip.
因為颱風要來，所以他們決定取消旅遊。

★ Seeing that he lives in **distress**, we **took** the **initiative** to raise **funds**.
由於他非常貧困，我們便為他發起了一個募款活動。

★ Seeing that the manager made a wrong decision, the company is now in debt.
由於經理做出錯誤的決定，導致公司現在負債累累。

> **distress**
> [dɪ`strɛs]
> 名 窮苦；苦惱
> **take initiative**
> 片 倡導；發起
> **fund**
> [fʌnd]
> 名 資金；基金

 和老外聊開懷，就靠這幾句！

Finding the ideal job often takes a lot of research and patience.

找到理想工作之前，通常要花不少時間和耐心

Are there many good job vacancies in your company?

你公司目前有沒有好的職缺呢？

Before bringing up the subject of a raise to your boss, it is best to consider if the department is currently functioning well.

在跟老闆談加薪前，最好先考量你的部門現階段是否運作良好。

As an employee, you sometimes need to ask yourself whether you are worth the price the company pays.

身為員工，你有時該想想自己是否無愧於你領的薪水。

Our company is facing a financial crisis, so you have no grounds to ask for a raise.

我們公司正面臨財務危機，所以你沒有要求加薪的餘地。

This is my old business card. I just got transferred to another department.

這是我之前的名片，我才剛轉調至新部門。

The counselors in the Student Affairs Office provide tips for finding the right job.

學生事務處的輔導老師們會提供尋找合適工作的小訣竅。

I have a bachelor's degree in English Literature, and I am hoping to find a job in which I could make the full use of the language.

我有英語文學的學士文憑，希望做一份能發揮我文學專才的工作。

A high position means more responsibility. Are you sure you're ready for that?

職位愈高，責任就愈重，你確定你準備好了嗎？

Sometimes being promoted doesn't guarantee you a raise.

有時候升官不代表加薪。

09 職場 轉換跑道
Changing Career

 單字基本功 掌握關鍵字＝開口第一步

核心聯想 離職原因 Causes for leaving

abroad [əˋbrɔd] 名 海外 副 在國外	desire [dɪˋzaɪr] 名 動 渴望	downsizing [ˋdaʊnˏsaɪzɪŋ] 名 縮編	obstacle [ˋɑbstəkḷ] 名 障礙物；阻礙
relocate [riˋloket] 動 搬遷；調動	struggle [ˋstrʌgḷ] 動 掙扎；奮鬥	switch departments 片 轉換部門	walk of life 片 行業

期望更好待遇 Looking for a better offer **進階學習**

leadership [ˋlidəʃɪp] 名 領導才能；領導地位	tenure [ˋtɛnjʊr] 名 （教授等的） 終身職位	redirect [ˏridəˋrɛkt] 動 使改方向	flexible [ˋflɛksəbḷ] 形 有彈性的
suitable [ˋsutəbḷ] 形 適宜的	career change 片 更換職業	career planning 片 職涯規劃	crave for 片 渴望獲得

深度追蹤 *Knowing More*

　　美國雜誌《富比士》（Forbes）的其中一位作者麗茲（Liz Ryan）認為每三到五年就換一次工作才是最好的選擇，這樣就不會因為在同一公司工作太久，而限制自己的視野及人際關係；而且換過工作後，也很容易從每份工作中學到新技能，還可以增加適應能力、應付各種人的交際手腕，更能分辨出一個工作環境的優劣；而職場豐富的履歷也是下一個求職階段的利器，幫助你行銷自己。長期又穩定的工作雖好，但多增加不同的經驗也無妨！

MP3 ▶ 338

套個單字，想說的都能表達！

All things considered,...　就各方面看來，…。

★ All things considered, it would be better for him to job-hop to a bigger company.
就各方面看來，跳槽去更大的公司對他來說比較好。

★ All things considered, the retail price is quite reasonable.
就各方面看來，這個價格相當合理。

★ All things considered, the **entrepreneur** has been a great success.
就各方面看來，那位企業家非常成功。

★ All things considered, the future looks **grim** and without hope.
就各方面看來，未來似乎很渺茫、沒有希望。

★ All things considered, the CEO decided to assign that **mission** to him.
就各方面看來，執行長決定把那個任務交給他。

> **entrepreneur**
> [ˌɑntrəprəˈnɜ]
> 名 企業家
>
> **grim**
> [grɪm]
> 形 (口) 糟糕的
>
> **mission**
> [ˈmɪʃən]
> 名 任務

No sooner had sb. ...than...　某人一…就…。

★ No sooner had she realized what she wants than she made a career change.
她一了解什麼才是她想要的，就換了另一份工作。

★ No sooner had I arrived at the station than the train came in.
我一抵達車站，火車就進站了。

★ No sooner had he assigned the tasks than the rescue teams started working.
他一分配好任務，救難隊就開始工作了。

★ No sooner had I bought the **envelopes** than I mailed the **invoice** to the **headquarters**.
我一買到信封，就馬上把發票寄到總公司。

★ No sooner had the ceremony started than everyone in the lobby became silent.
儀式一開始，在大廳的人都馬上安靜下來。

> **envelope**
> [ˈɛnvəˌlop]
> 名 信封；封套
>
> **invoice**
> [ˈɪnvɔɪs]
> 名 發票
>
> **headquarters**
> [ˈhɛdˈkwɔrtɚz]
> 名 總公司

開口必備句 和老外聊開懷，就靠這幾句！

I am thinking about getting a different job.
🔊 我正在考慮換個不同領域的工作。

Many people change their jobs right after getting their annual bonus.
🔊 很多人在領到年終後就換工作了。

Getting a new job takes a lot of effort, but it's also a great opportunity to experience something new.
🔊 找份新工作要花很多精力，但也是個體驗新事物的好機會。

Why do you want to find a new job?
🔊 你為什麼想找新工作？

Kevin decided to try his hand at the real estate business.
🔊 凱文決定到不動產業界試試身手。

Nancy is trying to get a high-paying job that isn't stressful, which is almost a mission impossible.
🔊 南希試著想找份高薪、低壓力的工作，但這幾乎是不可能的任務。

I know a headhunter who's looking for a market analyst like you right now.
🔊 我認識一位人力仲介，她正在找一位像你一樣的市場分析師。

The headhunter is offering a signing bonus of twenty thousand dollars, which is really enticing to me.
🔊 人力仲介提供兩萬元的簽約金，這點很吸引我。

There's no harm in trying out different kinds of jobs when you are still young.
🔊 趁年輕時多試幾份不同的工作也無妨。

Changing jobs in middle age can present challenges, especially for those who don't have specialized skills.
🔊 中年轉職，尤其是對無專業技能的人來說，較具挑戰性。

知識工場
nowledge.

Knowledge is everything！